Crystal Dragon's Kiss

ROYAL DRAGON SHIFTERS OF MOROCCO #2

AVA WARD

A RED LETTER HOTEL PARANORMAL ROMANCE

COPYRIGHT

First Print Edition, 2019
ISBN 978-1-073877-97-3

Edited By: Jean Lowe Carlson.
Proofread By: Jean Lowe Carlson and Matt Carlson.
Cover Design: Copyright 2019 by Damonza. All Rights Reserved.
Chapter Graphics: FreeTiles http://www.dafont.com/ Free Commercial Use.

ACKNOWLEDGEMENTS

To everyone who made this second book possible, you rock! Special thanks to Lela and Josh, Louie and Brenda, Sam and Ben, Marc and Claire, Michelle and Carrie for supporting this series. Thanks to Amber for her continued encouragement, and to Dave S. for helping me celebrate my successes. Thanks to my family Wendy, Dave, and Stephany for having my back.

Special shout-out to my Beta Readers and Launch Team – Joy, Linda, April, Tanya, Jules, Georganne, Carrie, Fiona, Nikhil, Michelle, Kimmy, Penelope, Queen, Eileen, Marco, Jessica, Erin, Rosemarie, Christiane, Alfreda, Sierra, Joel, Jean, Brittany, Claire, Susanne, Kona, Ruth, Stephanie, Katie, Lynda, Melissa, Terry, Jeanette, Dottie, Raquel, Mike, Bill, Susan, Wendy, Melissa, Kim, Amy, Cori, Bobby, Alison, Angie, Kam, Cyndi, Daniel, Elizabeth, Terri, Robin, Felicia, Christine, Kahlia, Victoria, Julie, Susan, Juan, Hannelore, Jen, Bobbi, Tina, Jody, Shannon, Marlys, Sandra, Tara, Kathy, Heather, Jewell, Deborah, Sue, Catherine, Liz – you are amazing!

And as always, a tremendous thanks to my husband Matt. You are the best, baby!

OTHER WORKS BY AVA WARD

RED LETTER HOTEL PARANORMAL ROMANCE

Royal Dragon Shifters of Morocco
Royal Dragon Bind
Crystal Dragon's Kiss
Sea Dragon's Command

SHORT FICTION

The Man in White
The Grasses of Hazma-Din

ABOUT CRYSTAL DRAGON'S KISS

She's the strongest Dragon of the century. But can she master her power before someone else traps her with it?

Layla Price is a Royal Dragon Bind, a rare and dangerous type of Dragon-shifter. Able to bind other Dragons to her will, Layla's power calls only the strongest mates.

But after nearly killing her ex-boyfriend in Seattle with her magic, she's got a target on her back. As a dark force begins to hunt her, Layla finds herself fighting alone – her Royal Dragon lover, the renegade billionaire Adrian Rhakvir, absent on mysterious business.

And when her power attracts new protectors – including her hot Crystal Dragon boss at the Red Letter Hotel Paris – Layla must make a choice.

Can she wait for Adrian to return?

Or will she take a new lover to fight at her side?

AUTHOR'S NOTE

Welcome to the passionate world of the Royal Dragon Shifters of Morocco!

This series is a *billionaire reverse harem dragon-shifter romance*, involving a strong, intelligent heroine who attracts multiple sexy bad-boy billionaire dragon lovers over the course of the series.

The world is racy, opulent, and sensual, with intense action sequences, political intrigue, and dangerous enemies. The themes are uplifting with HFN endings and for the best experience, the books should be read in sequence.

Thanks for joining the Royal Dragons at the Red Letter Hotel! *Are you ready for the heat?*

CHAPTER 1 – PROBLEMS

Dusk Arlohaim, Head Concierge at the Red Letter Hotel Paris, slammed closed an enormous ledger just as a flash of lightning and thunder lit the grey afternoon. Standing at a computer monitor behind the curved mahogany Concierge desk, Layla Price startled from fixing the week's activity schedule. The vaulted French Baroque hall of the Palace of Versailles echoed with the peal and Dusk's vigorous movement, smoothed by a rush of water cascading down a gilded mer-woman fountain nearby. Crystal chandeliers were lit bright against the dark afternoon, yellow leaves swirling in a brisk wind beyond the high windows as the sky roiled with an impending thunderstorm.

October had arrived in the Twilight Realm, with storms not unlike Layla's former home of Seattle. Wearing a cream cocktail dress with burgundy lace shoulders that hugged her tall hourglass curves, Layla's sable curls were pulled up in a chignon for work, her silver Moroccan hamsa-cuff on her left wrist – like it had been ever since that last fateful day in Seattle two months ago.

The day she'd nearly killed her ex-boyfriend with her newly opened Dragon powers and had to leave her old home behind.

Lifting her gaze to a mahogany grandfather clock down the hall carved with phoenix, Layla blinked away exhaustion. The Red Letter Hotel Paris was making final preparations for the Samhain Masquerade on Halloween – now only ten days away. Groundskeepers in beige and Guardsmen in crimson 1800's uniforms were decking marble pillars and vaulted alcoves with autumnal decorations. Cocktail hour was in full swing, copper bars surrounded by potted greenery and silk chaises absolutely stuffed with human and Twilight Realm patrons dressed to the nines. The Hotel was packed with guests, and Dusk had Layla working double shifts as patrons flocked in from all over Europe to attend the carnally decadent celebrations.

"Alright, that's it for the day, Layla. Time to pack it up."

Turning with a flash of iridescence in his artfully sculpted black hair, Dusk's sapphire eyes pierced Layla as he leaned his tall soccer-player's frame against the inner arc of the desk, finally relaxing his do-it-all vigilance as Head Concierge. Dressed in a light grey Italian suit with a crimson silk tie and pocket square, Dusk's impeccable ensemble highlighted his tanned yet slightly grey-blue skin, straight dark brows, and full lips. Midnight iridescent dragon-scale ridges cascaded from his temples, outer cheekbones, and over the backs of his hands. Devilishly handsome and unfailingly unique, Layla's boss was always on-point even well past shift's end.

It made Layla perk to realize he was calling a quit two hours early.

"It's only four p.m." Layla spoke, pushing her computer screen away on its swivel-arm. "Our shift lasts another two hours. Plus the six-to-midnight rotation you've got me on until Samhain."

"We're changing shifts early. You and I are off for the night, even though there's still a lot to do. We've got a party to attend." Dusk spoke in his usual brisk manner, though he gave a grin as he hefted his enormous gilded ledger of Assignations – private trysts with the sought-after Courtiers and Courtesans of the Hotel – and slid it into a safe below the desk. As he waved his hand over the steel safe, Layla watched a complex clockwork mechanism seal the vault. And then the safe wavered like a mirage, disappearing into a space that looked like an empty cubby. "I've summoned the evening shift to take over early so we can get ready."

"We?" Layla arched a dark eyebrow, giving Dusk a smile from her red lips. Elegant makeup was required in Concierge Services, and she had darkened her eyes to make her jade-green irises pop today, the crimson lipstick perfect with her dress.

"You, me, and Rikyava." Dusk grinned, his witty summer-blue eyes full of trouble, his normal mode when he was off-duty. Dusk had two modes: problem-solver by day with the Hotel's exorbitantly wealthy and influential clients, and troublemaker by night when he could do as he pleased with his off-hours. Layla had found she quite liked both modes, and Dusk was quickly becoming a friend, though he was a tough mentor behind the desk.

"We've got Dragons staying in the Hotel until Samhain," Dusk continued briskly. "There's a welcome party this evening and we, as members of Dragon clans who represent the Hotel, are expected to attend."

"A Dragon party?" Layla's brows rose. Though she'd been working at the Hotel nearly two months, she'd met no other Dragon Shifters yet besides the ones she worked with. New to the knowledge that she was a Desert Dragon out of Morocco, Layla was still adjusting to the powers that had awakened in her as a Royal Dragon Bind, a rare and tempestuous sub-Lineage of Dragon Shifter. Dusk and her friend Rikyava Andersen, Head of the Hotel Guard, were illuminating her on what being a Dragon meant – but still, Layla was curious about their kind.

A desert heat scented with orange peels and bourbon rose from Layla as eagerness moved inside her at the prospect of meeting other Dragons. Dusk gave a smile as he smelled it, picking up on her anticipation, his blue eyes bright as he chuckled.

"I see that smile, Layla. I felt your magic move, too. Which is why we're quitting early – so I can get you prepped for tonight."

Dusk was about to say more when a drop-dead gorgeous guy strolled up to the curved mahogany desk. Tall and tanned with unruly ash blond hair and a short blond beard, his vivid jade-green eyes were ringed with dark violet. Wearing a chocolate motorcycle jacket with white rabbit-fur lapels and crossover flaps, jeans hugged his thighs with motorcycle boots, making him look like a WWII-bombardier meets Roman conqueror. Flashing a fifty-megawatt smile, he leaned one elbow on the desk. A dragon-ring of malachite and jade set in platinum coiled around a massive emerald on his left index finger, catching the light.

"Dusk!" The man hailed Layla's boss in a laughing tenor. "Working hard or slacking off?"

"Adam!" Dusk gave a laugh, rounding the desk and clapping the sexy bombardier in an hearty embrace. There was much slapping of backs, the tall fellow gripping Dusk behind the neck and shaking him. Dusk was nearly six feet, but his friend stood a good four inches taller, with sexy muscle under his modern bomber-gear.

The newcomer's vivid jade eyes strayed to Layla and he gave a whistle, slinging his arm around Dusk's shoulders. "Wow! I like the wares Concierge is sporting these days! Well done!"

"*Excuse* me?" Layla crossed her arms, giving Bombardier Guy a chilly stare.

Dusk cleared his throat with a small grin at Layla's sass, clapping his friend on the back again before returning behind the desk. He beckoned to Layla as Adam settled into an artful slouch at the desk, grinning like a Roman brigand who'd just stormed all of Gaul.

"Adam Rhakvir, Clan Second of the Moroccan Desert Dragons, please meet Layla Price, Concierge of the Hotel and Royal Dragon Bind, also of your clan."

"Well, well. The Royal Dragon Bind. No one said she'd be the

Madonna of my dreams!"

Adam's gaze was penetrating and deviant as he gave Layla an obvious up-and-down. She was about to sass him like she would any out-of-line asshat, when power suddenly surged around her. She'd been one breath from tearing Adam Rhakvir a new one, when that dark, hot look suddenly pummeled her with a drowning scent of orchards and honey, like apple blossoms in a spring wind. She'd felt other Twilight Lineages test her with magic before, but this was something far deeper. As it drove home like a spear inside her body, making the vicious beast deep within Layla's veins roar with a carnal delight, Layla knew what it was.

Dragon power.

Royal Dragon power.

Cloying and heady, Adam's sudden rush of power devoured Layla, and she felt her own Dragon-magic roar – surging up with a hot passion like molten gold inside her body. Layla's magic was usually dormant beneath her Moroccan wrist-cuff with its bone hamsa and teardrop coral, but now it was like a searing sand-funnel as her inner Dragon surged up to meet Adam's.

A spiced orange-bourbon scent exploded in the air, as curls of etheric golden flame sparked around Layla. A small sound escaped her lips as she rocked forward. Bracing a hand on the desk, she struggled against the roaring twist of passion consuming her. Gasping, she shuddered with ecstasy, waves of heat pouring through her like a summer mirage. She didn't have control over her magics yet and couldn't put her surging heat away, nor stop his. The Dragon that lived inside her roared – wanting this man with a passion unlike any she'd felt since she and her Royal Dragon Adrian Rhakvir had bonded in Seattle. Like barbed coils slid out from her body, and answering ones roared out from his, Layla felt herself and Adam twining closer into a

10

carnal, delicious dance.

Pulling towards each other – into a hot and devastating mystical embrace.

"Stop it, whatever you're doing!" Layla hissed through clenched teeth, fear rushing through her along with heat.

"Easy, Adam." Dusk looked between them with a warning scowl, his sapphire gaze pinning his friend. "Leave off. Layla doesn't have enough control of her powers to tell you to fuck off, magically speaking. She can with other Lineages, but not with Dragons just yet."

"What if I don't want to fuck off?" Adam leaned in towards Layla at the desk with a terribly alluring smile. Pulled in by the strength of whatever was happening, his lips were mere inches from Layla's now, his jade eyes darkened to a deep hunter-green as he watched her with a desirous intensity. "What if I like lighting your magics up like Yuletide, Ms. Price?"

"Can it, asshole." Layla growled. But though her words were strong, she was breathing hard as she tried to haul herself back from his so-close lips, her hands white as she gripped the desk. The screaming rise in energy was starting to turn heads all through the busy hall. Layla tried stuffing her wild magic back down, channeling all that heat into her left wrist beneath her Moroccan talisman – but it wouldn't go. Swaying, her heart rioting, she began to panic – not just because Adam had an energy she couldn't escape, but because Dusk had told her in no uncertain terms that if she couldn't control her magic at the desk, she'd get more than a stern talking-to.

She'd get suspended from her job.

"That's enough, Adam." Stepping in front of Layla and moving her behind himself, Dusk took a protective stance, squaring off to Adam. With his chin lowered and a deep basso growl, Dusk suddenly slammed up a magical barrier between Layla and her Clan's Second.

Layla staggered as her connection to Adam snapped with a searing recoil, making her stumble into Dusk, her hands gripping his expensive suit. But Dusk's fit frame was firm as stone. Layla could feel his enormous power as a Crystal Dragon thrown up like a shield spiked with crystal shards all along the Concierge desk – keeping whatever Adam was doing from touching her.

"Don't make me ban you from the Hotel, Adam." Dusk's voice was all growl now, in a way he reserved for only the worst-behaved guests. Rumbling with power, his voice made the polished marble floor shudder beneath Layla's feet. "Fuck with my employees and get yourself banned for life, I don't care how many years we grew up together. Got it?"

"Whoa! I was just teasing, Dusk! Easy." Adam held up both hands, a rakish smile on his chiseled face. But the clever twist of his lips beneath his short blond beard said he wasn't sorry at all. He'd meant to spark Layla's magics and make her writhe in her Dragon's heat. His jade-green eyes were still a deep hunter green, pinning Layla with sexual delight even though she was mostly behind Dusk.

"That was a lot more than teasing." Dusk held his stern posture, his magics shuddering the floor like he was about to fight. Layla could feel his power humming all around her now – a lower-than-sound vibration like the first tremor before a big earthquake. "That was a mate-taste. Mess with Layla again while you're here and get the boot. Got it?"

"I got it, I got it." Adam finally looked chagrined that his scheme had been found out – though Layla had no clue what a mate-taste was. But apology was far from Adam's cunning eyes as he leaned upon the desk again. "So can I hire her for an Assignation?"

"No." Dusk's voice was firm. "Apologize. Now."

"But she's so sexy when she's angry." Adam grinned at Layla

now, renegade and not even close to giving her an apology. "I want to know what all that passion is like in my bed."

"In your dreams, pal." Layla snarled, stepping out from behind Dusk with her arms crossed. She was still behind whatever wall Dusk had erected, and was finally able to cram her own magic back beneath her Moroccan cuff. It took some doing, her skin searing like she had stuck her wrist over a broiler, but at least she wasn't reeling from Adam's power anymore – just furiously pissed.

Which had its own scent, rippling up from Layla's skin like oranges burned with a blowtorch.

"Layla." Dusk murmured without turning. "Master your emotions, please. A Concierge must have poise at all times. Even when assholes invade your magical privacy."

It was a reprimand but a gentle one, and Layla realized Dusk was right; she needed to learn control of her magics. The first level was mastering her emotions, since her rage fed her magical heat like a searing bonfire. With a deep in-breath, Layla eased back on her fury, though it was difficult still staring at Adam's rakish, unapologetic face. Finally, the air around her ceased to smell charred and the waves of heat sluicing off her eased away.

Her veins still simmered, but at least her rage wasn't affecting the Hotel anymore.

"I was wondering what a Royal Dragon Bind would taste like. It's positively intriguing." Adam gave a roguish grin.

"You've had your taste, now fuck off." Layla growled, holding back another lash of fury. But underneath that fury was sex, her inner Dragon writhing with coils and fangs to claw into Adam and taste that apple-honey scent again. Staring into those witty, renegade eyes, Layla felt her beast try to surge to him – feeling the vague sensation of Adam doing the same on the other side of Dusk's crystal wall. She saw a

13

shimmer explode between their magics as they collided upon the invisible barrier, before the ripple of light eased away.

Dusk turned, frowning at Layla. Reproach was in his eyes, but also concern – as if whatever was happening between her and Adam was cause for worry. He cleared his throat. "Adam, did you have actual business at the desk?"

"I just came to give you a little hell, cousin, since it's been so long." Adam was still staring at Layla, though she could feel he'd put his magics away now upon the other side of Dusk's barrier. Layla blinked at the word *cousin*, her gaze moving between the two men.

But Dusk didn't flinch, only gave Adam a tight smile. "We can catch up later at the party. Until then, please keep my ultimatum in mind. And even then. Test my patience in my domain, Adam, and you'll find it won't go well. And I believe you still owe Layla an apology."

"Fine! Fine. I apologize. Happy?" Adam chuckled then slapped the desk with his palm, flashing a brilliant smile, still far from apologetic. "You're a hard diamond to crack, Dusk. Good to know some things haven't changed. I do want to schedule a few Assignations, but I'll do that tomorrow. Give Adrian my best if you see him. Layla. Exquisite to meet the Royal Dragon Bind."

"Not returned, I'm sure." Layla sassed with narrowed eyes, still pissed.

Adam Rhakvir laughed in his smooth tenor voice, then pinned her with his conqueror's gaze. "I'll see you tonight." With one last slap of the desk he was gone, rounding the stairs and taking them two at a time up to the second level.

"Who the fuck was that? And *cousin?*" Layla had her magics under control now, though she was still hot with fury and deeper things. She felt Dusk's barrier dissipate all along the Concierge desk like water pouring down a crystal wall as he gave a wry smile, his summer-blue eyes apologetic.

"That's Adam Rhakvir. He's your clan's Second, but he's also Adrian's cousin, twice removed and born into the Italian family rather than the Moroccan. Since I'm adopted into the Rhakvir family, Adam's my *cousin* also, though we're not related. Although, it seems your magic has a taste for very strong, very bad boys, Layla Price."

"What do you mean?" Layla asked, feeling a tingle where her Dragon roiled, still wanting to taste Adam's orchard-sweet scent.

"Adam's not just Adrian's cousin, he's also a Royal Dragon like Adrian." Dusk lifted a dark eyebrow. "He's Second in your clan rather than First, because Adrian's stronger than he is. But next to Adrian, Adam is one of the strongest Dragons in all of Europe."

"That Roman *brigand* is a Royal Dragon?" Layla's arms uncrossed as she gave an exasperated sigh. But she'd already known. The moment she'd tasted his magic, she'd known. "Fuck my life. Why does my magic have to leap to assholes like that? As if Adrian wasn't bad enough."

But before Dusk could answer, two members of Concierge Services arrived for the evening shift. Jenna Ostlheim was a Furie from Oslo, and beamed at Layla as she rounded the desk with her willowy blonde loveliness and utterly black eyes. Red tattooing extended from the sides of her eyes, curving up beneath her platinum hair and racing down her neck over her collarbones beneath her beige dress. Her partner was Lars Kurs, tall and lithe like a skiing champion and tattooed nearly as much as she was. The duo were stunning; their tattooing a Furie's badge of battle-prowess, and both grinned at Layla as they arrived.

"Off to the Dragon party?" Lars rumbled in his pleasant baritone, effortlessly genial.

"I hear it's going to be a *rager*." Jenna laughed at her joke – that Dragons had tempers. Though Furies had tempers also, and had become famous for it in human legend. Living in the Twilight Realm, Layla had found a lot of truths humans had picked up about the Twilight Lineages they called fae and shape-shifters, gods and demigods. All of them came from the Twilight Realm – from Furies and Valkyries, to Phoenixes and Satyrs and all manner of celestial or viciously demonic creatures.

Including Dragons – shape-shifting humans who could actually take the form of those powerful, mythical beasts.

"Does everyone know about this party except me?" Layla lifted an eyebrow at Dusk.

He chuckled, then beckoned. "I'll fill you in as we get ready. Jenna; Lars – you have the helm. Shift change in the morning will be Kiva and Bhern."

Jenna and Lars nodded like twinsies, and then Layla and Dusk were moving out from behind the desk and up the crimson-carpeted French Baroque grand staircase to the second level. Layla frowned as they ascended the enormous curved double-staircase, glancing to Dusk as they passed a set of cream silk banners with the house emblem – the crimson 'R' in a stylized script inside a golden crown.

"I thought you and I are on the desk Saturdays?"

"I switched up the rotation tomorrow also," Dusk gave Layla a knowing glance. "You'll want to sleep in after a Dragon party."

"That much fun?" Layla grinned as they reached the landing.

"To say it may be a rager is probably an understatement." Dusk eyeballed her, though his smooth lips held a dark humor. "Adam's tasting of you is only the start, Layla. Everyone wants to meet the Royal Dragon Bind. And Adrian and Adam won't be the only Royal Dragons in the house."

"Shit." Layla glanced at Dusk as her stomach sank. "What am I in for tonight, Dusk?"

"Far more than you know." But Dusk's smile was kind as he extended his arm like a gentleman to escort her down the hall. "Come on. Let's get you ready to meet some Dragons."

CHAPTER 2 – SOLUTIONS

Crystal chandeliers stretched in either direction as Layla and Dusk moved up the stairs, ballrooms and guest suites branching off long marble halls gilded with mythical beasts. Reaching the third level where staff apartments were, the Hotel's opulence was unmarred by the autumnal delights consuming the halls below. Though decadent with French Baroque details, the Twilight Realm had differences from the human world; a near-realm where events in one world could influence the other, and had in the case of the Palace of Versailles.

A Crystal Dragon King named Lorenz DuVir had originally conceived the Palace. His build in the Twilight Realm had influenced the dreams of King Louis XIV of France through a resonance between the Realms. And though King DuVir lost this original palace during a blood-feud in 1690 to the Czech Crystal Dragons, which was then sold to the Red Letter Hotel, this structure retained the true designer's lust for decadence.

Enormous blue and white Ming vases dripped with lace-hair ferns; ornate gilded chaises decorated every vaulted alcove. Beneath atriums of stained glass, Layla looked up to see a starry night sky made from glass, then a vivid sunset over a Persian garden decorated with peacocks and birds of paradise. Frescoes surrounded her of fae out for fox-hunts, lounging in hot-pools, and engaged in an orgy in a colonnaded Greek temple – King DuVir's famed appetites reflected in glass and gilding.

Reaching Layla's apartment, she touched one handle of the gilded double-doors and pushed in. Decorated in French Baroque style, Layla's apartment featured dragons of her Lineage snarling from every picture-frame and rug – even a massive winged dragon roaring above the stone fireplace. Kicking off her heels and inviting Dusk to her small gilded breakfast table, Layla poured two bourbons from a collection of crystal decanters. Passing one tumbler to Dusk, they clinked and drank, as they occasionally did after shift these past few weeks.

Stepping to her phone on a side-table, Layla checked for texts. Seeing one from her ex-boyfriend Luke Murphy, she smiled. Two months ago, Luke had almost died from an accident Layla caused when her Dragon-magic had suddenly attacked him. Now he knew about the Twilight Realm and about Layla being a Dragon. He'd told the rest of Layla's housemates in Seattle, and now all of them texted constantly, wanting to know how her strange new life was going.

They'd signed a non-disclosure agreement, to not blab about the Twilight Realm or the Hotel, and Layla had received special permission to use a magically-secure cell phone from Concierge Services to call them once a week. Though her life had changed, her friends in Seattle weren't about to let her go – and she wasn't about to let them go, either.

Layla heard Dusk clear his throat and she looked up, seeing him watch her with a subtle gleam in his summer-blue eyes. "Don't you want to hear about the Dragon party, Layla?"

"Sorry." She put the phone back on the charging station. "I just like checking what my housemates have written when I get off work."

"Your friends in Seattle really miss you, don't they?" Dusk's smile was sincere; kind.

"I miss them, too." Layla sank into one of the cobalt and gold brocaded chairs at her breakfast table. Dusk pulled another out and angled it so they sat facing each other.

"And how is Luke?" Dusk asked as he took up his bourbon and

sipped. Dusk had stabilized Luke back in September when Layla's Dragon-magic had nearly killed Luke from judging him an inferior mate. Layla hadn't been wearing her hamsa-cuff to control her magics and Luke had paid the price. Dusk's fast, selfless actions had kept Luke alive long enough for the paramedics to arrive. It was Dusk's credo to solve problems for people and earn their friendship, and he'd more than earned Layla's friendship that night.

"Better," Layla nodded, setting her bourbon on the table. "Luke's made a full recovery from his injuries. He just has to be careful for a while. Not hard for him: he's a health-nut. He's already on six different supplements to repair the damage my magic did."

"Good." Dusk chuckled, then lifted a dark eyebrow at Layla, a wave of oilslick iridescence passing through his artfully-sculpted hair. "I might just have left some healing vibrations inside his body when I helped stabilize him. He should make a fast recovery."

"He has actually," Layla smiled, grateful for Dusk's strange vibrational abilities as a Crystal Dragon. "He's healing five times faster than the doctors expected. He's already back in Crossfit; has been for weeks. You did a wonder for him, Dusk. I don't know how I'll ever repay you."

"Just buy me a bottle of good bourbon. This is excellent stuff, whatever you have in here." Dusk grinned as he raised his glass and sipped again.

"Ex-bartender's secret," Layla grinned back. "What's in my decanters is between me and Rake André – he gets it for me in New Orleans when he's out shopping for unique mixers. And don't you dare try to wrangle the name out of him."

"Well then, keep your secrets!" Dusk lifted a dark eyebrow as he mimicked Frodo Baggins from the Lords of the Rings movies, then gave a smooth chuckle. "But I'll wrangle the name of this bourbon out of you eventually, Layla Price. You know I will."

He saluted with a laugh and they both drank again, settling into an easy familiarity. Layla smiled as she watched Dusk, realizing that somewhere in the past months he'd gone from being a pain in the ass to being a friend. He'd defended her today and had helped her deal with countless troublesome magical guests in Concierge Services. Not to mention stopping her from nearly killing Luke. That had been Layla's first lesson in her otherness; that she wasn't human and couldn't pretend anymore, not when lives were at stake. Fortunately, friends like Dusk had eased her transition into this new world of magic, and she was grateful.

Seeing her watch him as he sipped, Dusk cocked his head, smiling with a winsome delight in his summer-blue eyes. "Layla Price. I do believe you're ogling your boss."

"I was just thinking I'm glad we've become friends." Layla smiled, sipping her bourbon. "You really helped me out with that asshat cousin of yours. I appreciate it. I've been able to weather a lot of magical testing in the past months, but that was *really* something else."

"Ah." Dusk blinked, then set his glass down with a precise movement to the polished table. A frown knit his dark brows and a wave of midnight color flowed through his sculpted hair before he smiled back, genuine. "I'm glad, too. And Adam really isn't that much of an asshat, Layla. He's a rogue, but he's usually far more level-headed than today. Your magic has an affinity for Royal Dragons – which makes it hard to control around them. And I also believe, makes their magic hard to control around you. Anyone whom our magics seriously resonate with will cause a reaction like that. It's like two tuning forks entraining – *harmonic resonance.* If it's very strong, it produces a ridiculous natural attraction. We call that a *mate-taste,* especially if it's allowed to be fully unleashed."

21

"So that's what Adam did when he pushed his magic on me today?" Layla frowned.

"Adam didn't push his magic on you, Layla," Dusk eyeballed her, "he just didn't hold back when he felt his magic resonate with yours. It was rude, tremendously so, and in my opinion, he still owes you a far better apology than he gave you. Unleashing your magic on someone else when you feel a resonance like that is like the magical equivalent of rubbing your genitals all over them. Bad Dragon."

Layla laughed so suddenly that she snorted bourbon up her nose. She spent the next few moments laughing and coughing while Dusk grinned wickedly. As Layla recovered, her thoughts returned to Adam. Her wrist gave a searing throb and she glanced down to the six-inch silver cuff on her left forearm. An antique Moroccan Berber design with a hamsa-hand inlaid in bone, inset with a blood-red coral teardrop and surrounded by ornate canary, cerulean, and scarlet enamel, her talisman controlled her magics – but for whatever reason, had failed to control her magical desires today around another Royal Dragon.

Layla relied on the cuff to keep herself sane and others safe around her. The cuff controlled ninety percent of her sudden magical flushes. But she'd been so busy these past weeks that she'd not had time to study control with Dusk or Rikyava yet. And the Royal Dragon who had clapped this thing on her wrist to begin with, Adrian Rhakvir, had been traveling these past months – unavailable even by phone to answer her questions or train her.

It seemed an oversight now. Layla's untrained magic had been more than palpable today, and she could still feel her rage like a throb in her inner wrist, the place where the cuff collected her intense emotions. It was still burning from the resonance she'd had with Adam, and that didn't seem like a good thing.

"What just happened at the desk with Adam – that harmonic

resonance thing." Layla glanced up at Dusk. "Is that going to happen with all the Royal Dragons I'll meet tonight?"

"That's a deep question, Layla," Dusk lifted an eyebrow, his smooth blue-grey lips smiling at the corners. "One that requires dinner. Good thing I ordered some. Oh, and I got you a new gown for tonight. You had a distinct problem of having nothing stunning enough in your wardrobe for your first Dragon party."

Dusk clapped his hands, and as if they had been on-call in the hallway, a stream of Catering staff in impeccable black and white uniforms came rushing in, whisking to the table. Wilting five-day-old peonies were replaced by a new bouquet of lilacs in a gilded vase. Crystal decanters were moved to the side-bar, linens whipped away to a new setting of white china with gilded rims and sleek cream napkins. A bottle of chardonnay was poured as silver platters of shrimp in a butter sauce, asparagus fettuccine, and a crisp green salad arrived. Layla's plate was served before the staff whisked out, rolling their trolleys with them. Glancing over to her enormous walk-in closet, Layla saw two new crystal clothing-cases hanging from the open doors – one containing a men's suit and one holding a fabulous silk evening gown in bloody crimson.

"Well done, Maestro!" Layla laughed as she clapped her hands at Dusk's orchestrations. As Head Concierge, Dusk was always arranging ostentatious displays, and his planning of this moment showed. Even from here, Layla could tell the sleek silk dress inside the case was stunning – far more ornate than anything Head Clothier Amalia DuFane had provided her with yet. The entire evening was a problem Layla hadn't known she'd had, and everything about what Dusk had done communicated the opulence of the Red Letter Hotel Paris.

And Dusk Arlohaim's personal impeccability.

A sudden gratefulness filled Layla and she leaned over, pressing a kiss to Dusk's cheek as he settled his napkin in his lap. The ridges of midnight dragon-scales on his outer cheekbone flashed, and she felt him startle as he turned toward her. A very pleased, very male smile lifted his grey-blue lips, making his handsome face utterly delightful. A lower-than-sound vibration thrummed through the floor – sending a deep, erotic tingle up through Layla's seat.

"What was that for?" Dusk rumbled sexily.

"You solved my problem. One I didn't even know I had." Though Layla's words were glib, she felt a hot cord simmer between them now as Dusk's magics continued to vibrate – making her flush as a spiced orange-peel bourbon scent rose from her skin. She had meant her statement to be teasing but it came out sexy, as she couldn't quite catch her breath from the pleasure of Dusk's magic.

Dusk chuckled, watching her with eyes darkened to a clear sapphire as his lips parted to inhale Layla's scent. A dark carnality took him as he set down his wine, his skin scenting of his magics now like river-water pouring through a dark cavern – flowing around Layla.

"I will always solve your problems, Layla. Even if you don't know what they are just yet."

"What problem do I have now?" Layla sassed, settling back in her chair and reaching for her wine. She sipped to distract herself, though there was no distracting her body from Dusk's teasing, rolling pleasures.

"The problem that your Dragon is hunting Royal mates," Dusk chuckled with his devilish smile. "Because Adrian was an idiot to leave you alone for two months after he bound you."

Layla blinked, setting down her wineglass. Though Dusk's words were teasing, the look he gave her was not. Brimming with dark heat, that look was very male and not at all the man who ordered Layla around all day. This was not the daytime Head Concierge she faced now, this was the debonair rogue who came out nightly in Dusk's off-hours. This was the Dusk who had so many secret trysts and sexual partners it was a hotly debated mystery among the staff as to just how many people he slept with – weekly.

This was the Dusk that Layla had felt the moment their eyes locked during her Hotel entrance interview two months ago. But in all their weeks working together, Dusk had not used his magics on her since their strangely hot and contentious attraction that first day. But now as their gazes connected, another roll of pleasure rumbled through Layla from his simmering presence – and it was all she could do to not shiver as ecstasy thrilled her. A hot pleasure blossomed in her and Layla felt her Dragon rise in a flood of need and heat – just like it had done with Adam. It flushed her, her body rocking from the enormity of that power.

Gritting her teeth, Layla gripped the table even as her head fell back and her eyelids fluttered. "What the hell is going on?"

With a deep inhalation, Dusk ceased his rumblings, though he had to close his eyes like it had taken effort. When he opened his eyes again, they were still sapphire-deep.

"Layla. Adrian may have tricked you into being bound to him by your talisman two months ago," Dusk nodded to the Moroccan cuff, "but in true Royal Dragon Bind style, your *unsatisfied* beast is hunting more lovers than just him these past months. Believe me, I've felt it at the Concierge desk – and not just with Adam. Rake André has mentioned it also; that your energy is ranging out to him during yoga class. Your magic is on the hunt. And the interesting thing is that it's hunting not just Royal Dragons, but also Royals of other Twilight Lineages, like Rake."

"Shit. Are you saying my Dragon wants me to take a lover? And that if Adrian's not available, anyone will do?" Layla breathed hard as the realization hit home. Now that Dusk's rumblings had subsided, she was able to release her death-grip on the table and reach shakily for her wine – though the dark sensations inside her weren't gone.

"Anyone *powerful* will do." Dusk's gaze was level, a deep carefulness in his eyes. "Rikyava and I talked about it and she says you've not taken any lovers at the Hotel yet. Why not?"

"I'm perfectly happy being single right now." Layla sipped her wine, covering a hot whip of ire that raised a citrus scorch around her as her cheeks flared from embarrassment. She and Dusk talked about sexual appetites of Hotel guests daily, but it was different discussing her own private life with him. She was used to talking about everything from BDSM Assignations to arranging orgies out in the gardens, but now they were getting personal – and that was too personal for Layla.

"You're lying." Dusk gave her a knowing look. "Your Dragon is roaring inside you, Layla. It's not just your scent that gives you away; your vibrations do, too. You're roaring for a mate –even a casual one."

"Well, if Adrian had tried a little harder to stick around, I wouldn't be hunting!" Layla growled, feeling put-out and drinking deep of her wine. Her magic had turned with her emotions as she thought about Adrian, from a hot orange scent of passion to a scorched, bitter-citrus rage like molten lava. "I mean, I've not seen hide nor hair of him for five weeks. He disappeared yet again after we came back from Seattle. He didn't even stay the night, Dusk! And now – no phone calls, not even a damn email. Adrian's disappearing act after we made such a connection is *really* not helping anything."

"Maybe." Dusk lifted an eyebrow as he swirled his wineglass.

"What's that supposed to mean?" Layla crossed her arms, anger searing through her.

"It means," Dusk gave her a patient look as a wave of sapphire flowed through his dark hair and scaled ridges, "that you are a Royal

Dragon Bind, Layla. Like your mother Mimi Zakir, your magic will likely hunt a variety of lovers. Mimi had lovers all around the world. Adrian's mother Juliette was her primary mate but they were by no means exclusive."

"So what, like mother like daughter?" Layla sassed viciously.

"Dragons are adventurous creatures, Layla," Dusk sighed, watching her intently. "Exclusivity is rare with us. You've been trained to value monogamy by the human world, but what I feel from your beast – and what Rake and Rikyava noticed also – is that you need more than the attention Adrian is giving you. Adam tried to exploit it today and I shut him down, but it doesn't make what your beast is doing any less true. You're trying to be loyal to Adrian. I get that, and it's admirable. But your Dragon doesn't play by human-world rules."

"Bullshit." Layla took a deep drink of her wine and set it down decisively. But she couldn't control the roaring energy that surged up inside her as Dusk gave another lower-than-sound rumble, thundering deliciously up Layla's ankles into her thighs. She rocked, gripping the table as pleasure surged through her – only the smallest bit of it from Dusk's magic. The rest was entirely her own Dragon slithering inside her sinews and erotic places with a roaring intensity.

An intensity that wasn't about to be denied.

"You're hunting, Layla." Dusk spoke, watching her as he swirled his wine. "Even though Adrian bound you, your Dragon isn't content being bound by his on-and-off attentions. The harder you deny it, the harder the creature within you will roar, until you give in. Choose a mate, Layla, someone in addition to Adrian to tide you over while he's away – or have one get chosen for you. And probably not in a way you'd like."

As Layla's Dragon rose inside her with a slide of scales and muscled talons, she realized Dusk was right. She did have a problem; a problem that hadn't been solved by Adrian binding her newly-awakened magics. A problem that didn't care if Adrian was far away or if Layla felt exclusive to him. A problem that she could feel as her body responded to Dusk just like it had Adam with a slow, rolling pulse that had nothing to do with rageful desert winds – and everything to do with dark, pleasurable lust.

Dusk was right – she did have a problem.

And her Dragon wanted someone to solve it soon.

CHAPTER 3 – HUNTING

At last, Layla was able to achieve some control over her magic. With a deep inhalation, she folded up all that hot, pleasurable energy, stuffing it back beneath her wrist and the hamsa-cuff. The burn in her tendons was excruciating but worth it. She had control over her body again, not letting her lust drive the bus. And though Dusk's quiet presence was still arousing beside her, she didn't want to just ride him straight to bed anymore.

With a steady out-breath, she gave him an eyeball and took up her wine. "Bad Dragon. Using your magic on me."

"I'm sorry. Truly." But Dusk's brisk smile was hard as he began tucking into his salad. "But my observations stand, Layla. Your Dragon is doing the magical equivalent of spraying like a cat – though it's only attracting the most powerful Royals. Did you know you've had over thirty requests for Assignations? All from Firsts or Seconds or Thirds of prominent clans – powerful Royals in their own Lineages."

"*Assignation* requests?" Layla gaped at him, pausing with her fork in hand as she dug into some pasta. "But I'm not a Courtesan!"

"Tell that to your Dragon." Dusk eyeballed her with a level frankness, the same look he gave her when impressing a lesson at the desk. "Adam isn't the only one I've had to turn down. People have been confused by your magic, assuming that you're a dual-position at the Hotel like Rake André – a Concierge by day and a Courtesan by night. Even the Madame approached me last week after you got seven requests in one day, asking me if we shouldn't be training you as a

Courtesan."

"But I don't want to be a Courtesan!" Layla protested, horrified. Even though Courtesans and Courtiers made egregiously good money and had the highest standing at the Hotel, other than the Department Heads and the Madame, selling her body for money was not something Layla was into. It had been a sticking point with her when Adrian was trying to get her to come work for the Hotel, and only when she found out she'd be working in Concierge Services had that point smoothed.

"Then you need to get a handle on your magic. Before the Madame makes a decision for you, as to what department you belong in." Dusk's gaze was level, no teasing in his frank sapphire stare. "That cuff on your wrist does a lot to contain your eros, but people are feeling your Dragon's passions. I truly would recommend you think about taking a lover. Someone you find interesting, who you'd like to have a little fun with while Adrian isn't around. Believe me, Adrian would understand, even if he doesn't like it."

"You talked to him about this, didn't you?" Layla shook her head. "Fucking Christ."

"You need to bleed off your tension in order to do your job here. Adrian understands that." Dusk's gaze was unapologetic. "I almost told him to cancel the Dragon party tonight because I wasn't sure you'd be able to go with your magic flaring like it is. But this problem could be an advantage if your beast is intrigued by someone in your Lineage, like Adam. If it likes a few other Dragons present tonight, you might be able to form some strong alliances."

"Alliances. You mean fuck-buddies." Layla lifted an eyebrow at Dusk, feeling furious. She covered her fury by digging into her meal. The shrimp was incredible; the butter sauce divine, even though they did nothing to cool the rage that flashed through her. Scorch rose in the air, making the shrimp taste burnt. Layla reached for her wine but

Dusk's hand whipped out, settling to hers before she could drink heavily. A soothing energy rippled from him like cool water running through deep caverns as iridescence flowed through the ridged scales on the backs of his hands. It eased Layla's rage and she took a breath, regaining control as he watched her.

"Don't discount alliances forged in the bedroom. They can last a lifetime." Dusk's frank stare held no proposition, but he held her gaze with his deepest intensity. "There will be some *very* strong Royal Dragons in attendance at the party tonight. Adrian's not the only one with power in our clans, and he may not be the only person you can recruit to watch your back."

"So you want me to make a grand entrance and turn heads so I can attract sex partners and form alliances in the Dragon clans. Hence the dress." Layla glanced at the closet, to the red silk gown hanging in its crystal case. The rich crimson color was the exact color of spilled blood and just the sight of it set Layla's veins boiling.

The color red had always attracted her, but now an overwhelming urge bit into her, making her want to rush over there and rub her skin all over that bloody color – to bathe in its vividness like she'd just sliced someone's throat open. She could practically smell an iron tang in her nostrils as her Dragon gave an eager stir, flexing talons that Layla could actually feel raking her insides. It was both painful and erotic, and she shuddered as she lifted her hand for her wineglass.

"That's exactly the impression we want you to make tonight." Dusk gave her a deep look as he let her hand go, his blue eyes level. "Don't be pissed with me, Layla. I'm merely telling you to your face what everyone has been saying behind your back. You can fight what your Dragon wants, but it won't go well, believe me. As for the gown – well every hot woman needs a hot red dress. It just makes sense."

Layla felt herself flush. Dusk was teasing, but there was

something simmering between them still. She could feel the cord of their magics licking at each other – and yet, Dusk seemed to be encouraging her to take a lover other than himself. "So I'm supposed to fuck Adam, is that it? Or you?"

"I have plenty of lovers, Layla." Dusk's glance was level as he leaned back in his chair. "Yes, you and I have a connection; I feel it too, ever since we met. But I'm your boss. Though it would be fun to roll in bed and feel your desert wind pouring over me, I have responsibilities. To train you and make sure you succeed in the tense political situations our world will probably dump you in sooner rather than later. Besides, Adrian would hate me if I slept with you. More than he already does."

"He hates you?" Layla's brows rose.

"It's a brotherly rivalry." Dusk gave a tight smile, reaching for his bourbon rather than his wine. Layla felt him shut that conversation down, the topic of Adrian almost always a sore point.

"So how many lovers do you have?" Layla changed topics, curious about Dusk. Just like they'd never really spoken about Layla's personal life, they'd also never really spoken about Dusk's. It was becoming normal for Layla to see sex out in the open and discuss all kinds of kinks. Yet, though the staff at the Red Letter Hotel Paris were frank, most of them were tight-lipped about who they were or weren't doing.

Dusk was no exception, having never made a single casual comment about the people he slept with. Everything Layla had heard about him was rumor and hearsay – some of it ferociously scandalous. Layla wondered about it now, since he had just suggested in no uncertain terms that she would be better off having another lover.

Or several.

Dusk's gaze simmered now, a teasingly dark smile curling his full lips as he set his bourbon down. "I have as many lovers as I need,

Layla. Why do you ask?"

"Come on." Layla pressed, a smile creeping around the edges of her lips as the mood lightened. She needed something to distract her from her own botched love life. "How many?"

"How many lovers do you think I have?" Dusk chuckled back as he finished his shrimp, eyeballing her with a roguish grin. Reaching out, he scooted Layla's plate toward her with a pointed nod at her meal. Layla took Dusk's insinuation and began eating again, knowing that a full belly would help keep her magics under control tonight, while being drunk on an empty stomach would only worsen things. The shrimp tasted fine again, now that she wasn't flooding scorch into the air.

"Seven." Layla answered. It was an outrageous number, but seemed accurate.

"Try twice that." Dusk chuckled, wiping his mouth with his linen napkin. "The ones I see regularly, at least."

"Are you serious?!" Layla couldn't help it; she laughed as amazement flooded her. "Who?"

"A gentleman never tells." Dusk gave a cheeky wink, pouring them both more wine. Swirling his glass, his sapphire eyes positively glowed as Layla sat back, shaking her head.

"You're shitting me."

"I shit you not. Crystal Dragons have tremendous appetites for all the finest things. Sex is no exception. The Crystal Dragon King Lorenz DuVir who built this palace was not the biggest lecher of his era, believe it or not."

"You mean it was you?" Layla sassed with a grin.

"Come on. That was the 1600's – I wasn't born yet." Dusk grinned back over the rim of his wine glass, darkly sexy. "But there are a few rumors that I was the most lecherous lover of the Victorian age.

At least, here in France."

"You are so seriously pulling my leg right now!" Layla laughed.

"I'm not." Dusk swirled his wine, something deviant and delightful in his summer-blue gaze. "I am a lecherous playboy, and that's the way I like it."

"Who are your lovers? I want names or I won't believe you."

"Alright. I'll give you the most obvious." Dusk sat back, grinning. "Etienne Voulouer, though she and I aren't primary lovers. She's a hellcat in bed – literally. She was Head Courtesan here in her time and she's lost none of her skills, believe me."

"The Madame?" Layla blinked, astonished. "I thought she was with Reginald."

"She is." Dusk nodded. "Sort of. But Reginald's primary lover is Sylvania."

"So the Head Courtier and Head Courtesan are together?" Layla pondered that; it made a strange amount of sense. The Head Courtier and North Sea Siren Reginald Durant was as intense and austere as the Head Courtesan and Silver Passion Sylvania Eroganis was beautiful and generous. Somehow, it made sense that the one person who could win any heart was with the one person who could chill them all.

"They are an oddly perfect match." Dusk nodded, as if reading Layla's thoughts.

"Who else are you with?"

"Amalia DuFane." Dusk gave rakish lift of one eyebrow and a sly grin.

"The Head Clothier!" Layla laughed. "No wonder she always dresses you so well!"

"I do get the finest suits in the entire Hotel." Dusk chuckled, immensely pleased with himself. "And Amalia doesn't mind my antics. She's a busy little bee herself. Has at least ten lovers that I know of, and she's not even a Dragon."

"Who else?" Layla laughed. "Give me one more name and I'll believe you."

"Rikyava, actually." Dusk gave a lecherous smile. "I'm one of her three regular partners. But she's going to deny it up one side and down the other, so that's not one you can confirm."

"No!" Layla grinned wide. "Were you – when you sent her over to my apartments to share chocolates and chat a few months back? Had you two been together that night?"

"We'd just finished." Dusk's gaze was merciless, teasing and delightful. "She didn't have time to get dressed in her Guardsman gear before I insisted she go check on you. Rikyava hates me but whenever she wants a good, uncomplicated romp, she comes to my bed. She likes to take her fury out on me, and I really don't mind."

"You devil!" Layla grinned, swirling her wine. Somehow she knew it was true, even though she also knew her Swedish Blood Dragon friend and Head of the Hotel Guard Rikyava Andersen would deny it to hell and back.

Raising her glass, Layla saluted Dusk and he saluted back. Layla was starting to believe the rumors of him being a ridiculous playboy. He was just like that; full of energy. Sometimes he felt like a live wire when he stood next to Layla at the Concierge desk, as if an electrical sub-station was held inside that tightly wired soccer-player's frame. It seemed strange that Dusk was close with Adam, a man Layla had judged badly. But then again, Dusk hadn't made the best impression when he and Layla had first met, either.

"So do you solve people's problems in bed?" Layla laughed, shaking her head.

"As often as I can." Dusk grinned back, then sobered, downing the last of his wine. "But if you're finished, we really should get dressed and discuss the party tonight. Adam isn't likely to be the only Dragon who will test you this evening, and I'd like to prepare you for what you may face. Shall we?" He gestured toward the walk-in closet.

"Sure." Layla pushed away from the table. Moving to the doors of her gargantuan closet, she stood back as Dusk unlocked one crystal garment-case and took out his suit. Exquisite, Dusk's suit for the evening was the slim modern Italian look he favored, the sleek charcoal weave of the jacket holding a shine that caught the light. The pants were similar, a midnight-blue pocket square and luminous sapphire tie to match. Inside the jacket's lapels, sapphire piping and a sapphire fleur-de-lis silk lining showed. The ensemble came with a smaller crystal case and as Dusk opened it, Layla saw a platinum and sapphire cufflink set with diamonds, plus a matching men's Rolex.

"Holy hell, Batman." Layla whistled as she reached out to touch the cufflinks.

"Wait till you see your gown." Dusk glanced at her with a sly grin. "Amalia outdid herself this time."

"Your design or hers?" Layla asked as Dusk reached out to unlatch the crystal case containing her evening gown. "And brainstormed in the bedroom or out of it?"

"A bit of both. On both counts." Dusk grinned.

He finished undoing the latches and the case came undone with a spill of crimson silk draping over the carpet in long, sleek folds. Dark like blood but with a shine that threw the light, the gown was a mermaid cut, a long train cascading from the back. Bias-cut so the silk smoothed down in sleek folds, the waist was a corset, the strapless bodice entirely beaded with rubies, garnets, fire-opals, and diamonds. The unholy wealth of gems swirled like a mirage, the dangerous opulence arresting Layla as she watched the pattern shift like a desert wind through blistering sands. Dusk opened a jewelry-case next, displaying a ruby and diamond tennis-bracelet to match, plus earrings.

"Holy fuck." Layla stared at it all, dumbfounded.

"Like it?" Dusk smiled gently, something careful in his eyes.

"Adrian's not the only man who can pick a gown, apparently."

The careful look in Dusk's eyes cleared, replaced by pleasure. "Amalia gets the credit. It's her magics that make the gems and fabrics dance, I just picked out the color. Shall we?"

"I guess so." But staring at that hot red gown, knowing she would be wearing hundreds of thousands of dollars in gems tonight, Layla paused. She reached out, her fingers fidgeting with the sleek silk, wondering if she should attract that much attention or if it would be better to wear something more plain to the party.

Or maybe not go at all.

"What's wrong?" Dusk spoke as if he could read her mind, though Layla knew he was only reading her emotional vibrations.

"Do I want to call this much attention to myself?" Layla asked, watching the diamonds shift upon the dress' corset like a desert mirage. Dusk reached out, smoothing his strong fingers over hers and clasping her hand. As she glanced over, a lower-than-sound vibration eased through her. It was Dusk's calming vibration and didn't raise Layla's Dragon except for a soothing stretch, like stroking a hand down a cat's back. His sapphire eyes were kind as he gazed at her, a mysterious smile upon his smooth lips.

"The world needs to see who you are, Layla. You are a Royal Dragon Bind. Once mature, your magic will rival Royals of any Lineage in the Twilight Realm. You'll be considered Adrian's equal in the Moroccan clan – or his rival. Everyone wants to meet you. Because you will be a power to be reckoned with someday. I know it. And so do they."

Gazing at Dusk and hearing how the Dragon clans viewed her,

Layla realized she still didn't know anything about this world, not really. She'd learned how to navigate tricky international politics in grad school, but that was for humans – the politics of Dragons was entirely different. A spike of icy trepidation drove deep inside Layla, a dark worry with the sensation of a black pit beneath it, and she shivered.

"I'm not ready for this, Dusk."

Dusk's gaze softened. Lifting his fingers, he stroked Layla's cheek with his knuckles, his touch smooth even though Layla could feel the scaled ridges on the backs of his fingers. "Just be yourself. Some Dragons will want to curry favor with you tonight; others will want to test you like Adam did. I'll be by your side the entire time, to buffer anything that gets out of hand. You don't have to worry about controlling your magics at the party – we'll be far enough from the rest of the Hotel that it won't matter. And once we see how the clans respond to you, I'll be able to advise you on next steps. Breathe, Layla. I am on your side in this venture; not Adrian's, not Adam's, not any of the clans."

"But I thought you were representing the Hotel and your own clan tonight?"

"I will be. But *you're* my priority." Dusk's gaze was serious as he lifted her hand and kissed it. His lips were smooth and his gesture made Layla's heart clench. As if Dusk knew what she needed to help her through this, his sexual nature was just gone, replaced by a smooth, supportive presence. "Come on. Let's get dressed. Quit fretting and get your sexy ass into that hot red gown so I can see it."

"You just want to see me naked."

Layla couldn't stop her flirting; it just came out. Her Dragon enjoyed Dusk's touch and it was like its thoughts had suddenly hijacked her mouth. Dusk laughed. A bright sound, it was a very good laugh, rumbling with masculine basso. Still holding Layla's hand, he stepped close – growling down with a hot, sexual thrum and making a ripple of pleasure cascade through her.

"Get in that closet, wench," he growled, his sapphire eyes dark with glee. "Or I swear I'll tear your clothes off and stuff you into that gown myself."

Though he teased, something suddenly unleashed inside Layla at Dusk's growling vibration and sexy, forceful words. A roaring energy snapped between them, so hot and fast it left Layla breathless. Like her Dragon had dug fangs into Dusk and his did the same to her, heat tightened between them in a hard rush – far harder than with Adam.

Dusk's breath caught; his sapphire eyes blazed as he stumbled to that sudden pull, falling forwards. His arms closed around Layla, his strong hands searing her waist as he gripped her hard, as if he was going to scoop her up and carry her to the bed or simply slam her to the wall and fuck her.

But even as he seized her, Layla felt a hard pulse of pure willpower hit her. Dusk's power hammered her, thrusting her roughly back upon the closet doors and out of his hands. Though it had been meant to push her away, the rough energy scorched her with desire; both his and hers. Layla felt a spike in her adrenaline at the sexual forcefulness, and a responding spike in her Dragon's eagerness.

A hot prelude for everything that simmered between them, as yet unexplored.

"Shit." Dusk cursed softly, his breath heaving as his wide eyes devoured her. Layla trembled as his gaze raked her, drinking in every curve of her body. His power had pushed her just out of reach, and she watched Dusk fight himself to make contact with her again. Reaching out, his fingertips nearly touched her cheek, but then he set his jaw and forced his hand past – taking his suit down from the door behind her instead. Waves of midnight light flowed through his scaled ridges and dark hair as he breathed hard, but more controlled now. Giving her a complex glance full of heat, he turned towards her bathroom.

Layla felt him go like a shudder of earthquakes, and realized she hadn't been breathing until Dusk shut the bathroom door solidly behind himself. But as Layla turned to the closet, she could still feel their twined energy. Thrumming like a cord, it roared with a power not to be denied, sending shudders of heat deep into her body. As if Layla's Dragon had already chosen the new mate it wanted; the vibration it liked most from everything it had tasted so far except Adrian.

The vibration of her boss – and the adopted brother of the man she was bound to.

CHAPTER 4 – PASSIONS

Dressed in her crimson gown with her new jewelry, accompanied by strappy silk high-heels, Layla exited the walk-in closet and moved to the bathroom door. The sexual tension between her and Dusk had cleared from a roar to a simmer, and she was almost relieved to find it was still low the closer she approached the bathroom. Not expecting that he would take a longer time dressing than she had, Layla knocked on the gilded bathroom door.

"Dusk? I need to do my makeup and hair."

Through the door, she heard Dusk shift. "Sure. Come in."

Layla opened the door to find he wasn't even dressed yet, his suit hanging from a wrought-iron bathroom shelf. He sat crosslegged on a blue silk ottoman near the clawfoot tub, his wrists relaxed over his knees as he took deep, slow breaths. Shirtless and barefoot, he wore only the trousers from his new ensemble, and took a deep inhalation as Layla opened the door, glancing up with vibrant blue eyes as she entered.

"Oh! Sorry." Layla mumbled, feeling like she had interrupted something private.

"Come in. I was just meditating. You can do your makeup and hair while I dress."

With a lithe movement, Dusk rose from the ottoman and Layla was confronted by the sight of him shirtless. Slender with cut shoulders and strong legs, he was ripped like an Olympic soccer-player. The skin of his torso was a dusky tan, the midnight oilslick color on his outer arms, shoulders, and sides. As he turned to retrieve his shirt, Layla watched how the scaled ridges at his temples continued down the back of his neck, then spread over his shoulder-blades and down his muscular back in a sexy v-shape. From the backs of his hands, those ridges continued up his outer arms, connecting behind his shoulders. As he pulled on his shirt, Layla saw the ridges curled in over his hipbones to his low abdomen – diving beneath his slacks toward his groin, which bulged appealingly in his slim-cut trousers.

Dusk glanced up, meeting her gaze as he finished pulling on his shirt with unabashed grace. Heat simmered there and Layla felt passion flare between them again, though she also felt impeccable control surrounding Dusk now. He'd erected an invisible wall of crystal between them like he'd placed between her and Adam earlier – a solid, cool presence in the air. It had a clarity to it, like the shine of his sapphire eyes. His barrier helped calm her arousal, and Layla found she was grateful for it as he buttoned up his shirt.

Though she couldn't help but watch that silky-smooth, rippling abdomen disappear.

"You're ogling me again," Dusk rumbled gently, though it was a mild teasing from behind his crystal barrier.

"Can I help it if you're built like a Greek god?" Layla sassed as she attempted to raise her eyes to his face. That angled jawline, those piercing blue eyes; those high cheekbones accentuated by his dark, straight brows and the beautiful ruggedness of his scaled ridges. He slowed his buttoning, letting her watch. Heat simmered in his eyes, though his wall of power remained firmly in place. Even so, a wash of iridescence rippled through his ridges, making the artful waves of his black hair shine. Layla's lips fell open and she hitched a breath, willing her mind to function.

"Egyptian god." Dusk chuckled, watching her admire him.

42

"What?" Layla blinked at him, stupid for a moment.

"I'm built like an Egyptian god, not Greek." He winked at her. "Leaner. And taller. And a bit more tan. Egyptian Crystal Dragon. You know."

Layla blinked, her face blossoming into a smile. It was true. He did look far more Egyptian than Greek. "Touché. So tell me about this party you planned tonight, sexy Anubis."

"Sexy Anubis?" He grinned wider as he finished his buttons, playfulness glinting in his sapphire eyes. "I like that one."

"Good." Mastering her ardor at last, Layla moved into the bathroom and Dusk stepped aside, allowing her passage to her gilded mirror and makeup table. Layla sat upon her cobalt silk ottoman and set to, picking through her sable curls with a comb and misting them with setting-spray. "So tell me about the party."

"Adrian planned it, actually, not me." Dusk gave her a smile, then turned and began tucking his shirt into his slacks. "The party serves two purposes. The first is to introduce you to some important Dragon clan Firsts and Seconds."

"Adrian's allies?"

"Mostly." Dusk nodded, finished with his shirt and beginning with his tie. "As an unknown newcomer among the clans, you'll be the spice of the night. Expect to be approached, courted, teased – Dragons are frank. Some of them make my teasing look like a nun at prayers. Keep a level head, but by all means use your wit; Dragons love banter. Except the ones who are easily offended, and those you'll notice right off."

"Got it." After working two months in Concierge Services, Layla had a good sense of the Twilight Realm Lineages who loved banter and those who didn't. "What else?"

"Watch the room; expect some drama. Just because the clans here tonight are generally friendly doesn't mean all the individual members are. Dragons are constantly vying for position, and sometimes it can get public." Dusk watched her in the mirror as he did his tie in an impeccable Double Windsor, his fingers deft as he wound the knot.

"And the second reason for this party?" Layla prompted, twisting her curls up at the side of her neck and setting them with her mother Mimi's diamond hair-pins.

"The second reason we're gathering, and that these particular clans are staying until the Samhain Masquerade, is for Adrian to take the temperature of his alliances."

"How come?" Layla paused with her hair, watching Dusk in the mirror.

"All his life, but especially in the last thirty years, Adrian's cultivated powerful allies from the Dragon clans across Europe. Many of them will be present, plus a few of his strongest officers from Morocco. But just because they're allies at the moment doesn't mean they'll stay that way."

"They might shift alliances." Layla frowned, realizing that Dragon clans sounded not so much like European royalty but like powerful American mobsters.

"It's possible." Dusk glanced at her in the mirror. "At a hundred and fifty years, Adrian's still quite young for a Dragon, but his power is growing. Because of his abilities and also his shrewd investments, Adrian's got rivals even among his allies. But there are those who would follow him if—" Dusk cut off suddenly, a frown coming over his features.

"If?" Layla glanced at him in the mirror, pausing with her golden eyeshadow.

"If we ever needed to rally." Dusk responded, taking up his elegant jacket and slinging it on, the sapphire piping and fleur-de-lis satin flashing in the makeup-lights. The jacket fit his sculpted shoulders like a dream, hugging his slim waist in a way that made Layla want to faint as he buttoned it then stepped forward, adjusting his tie in the mirror.

"Rally?" Layla watched Dusk, realizing he was holding something important back from her. It was one of the first times he hadn't been straight with her and Layla frowned, wondering what he was trying to protect her from. "Rally for what?"

Dusk glanced at her sidelong in the mirror as he finished adjusting his tie. "I'm not at liberty to say, Layla. It's something you'll have to ask Adrian about."

"If he ever comes back." Layla grumped, leaning forward to apply her mascara, realizing that whatever Dusk was holding back was at Adrian's request. More of Adrian's Royal Dragon secrets that he guarded as close as Smaug's treasure. "Where in the world is Carmen Sandiego, anyway?"

"Adrian's back, actually." Dusk gave Layla a careful gaze in the mirror. "He arrived last night. You'll see him at the soirée."

Layla stared at Dusk, setting her mascara down. Heat swirled inside her, scalding her veins; she was far past furious that she had to find out from Dusk that Adrian was back at the Hotel. Her Dragon snarled inside her, adding to the scorching sensation that made the air smell like oranges burned in a blowtorch as a halo of heat simmered through the room.

"Adrian was here at the Hotel today and didn't even stop by the Concierge desk to say hello? It's not fucking rocket science where I am from six to six everyday. Jesus."

"Easy, mad drakaina." Dusk gave a wry smile, rifling a hand through his artful black waves. His hair rippled through deep colors as he did it, from midnight-blue to a brighter cobalt, then a flash of gold

45

before he lowered his hand. Dusk's midnight ridges and hair rippled with color when he was feeling intense emotions, and it showed in his irritation with Adrian. "Adrian's not used to reporting his whereabouts to anyone. I don't know why I'm defending his idiot ass right now, but there it is. The two of you may have a bond because of your talisman, but that doesn't mean he understands relationships."

"Apparently." Layla still felt pissed as she started on her crimson lipstick. The halo of heat around her dissipated, but it was still pouring through her veins and Layla didn't bother stifling it beneath the hamsa-cuff. It gave her cheeks and chest a hot flush in the mirror like she'd been fucking or fighting, and Layla found she rather enjoyed the sensation of letting herself be as angry as she wanted to be at Adrian Rhakvir. Dusk paused, watching her in the mirror – almost hauntingly still as she glanced at him and capped her lipstick. "What?"

"You know Adrian's been celibate since he met you."

"I didn't know." Layla blinked, setting down her lipstick. Her anger cooled suddenly to puzzlement. She could practically feel the Dragon inside her veins ask *why in blazes would he do that?* Though it would have been a normal response to dating someone in the human world.

"It's not like him." Dusk spoke again, frowning. "Adrian usually has two or three casual partners at any given time, but that all stopped when he met you. As you've probably guessed, he has trouble… committing. Ever since—" But Dusk cut off again abruptly, rifling a hand through his hair and producing a sleek shine of cobalt. He gave a deep growl as if frustrated before continuing. "His better relationships usually blow up in his face because of his clandestine ways. But he's different with you. I can see him trying to do something right, even if he still manages to get it all wrong. I don't know what that means, but it's worth noting."

Layla touched her bottle of hair-spritz, smoothing her thumb over the label. Conflicting emotions rose in her, a hot-and-cold sensation of both fury and doubt. "This bond he made with me through the hamsa-cuff... I feel it all the time, Dusk. I forget it while I'm working, but it's like there's a part of me that would leap to see him again, no matter how awful he's been. I hate that. And I hate him, too, for doing this to me. For binding me into a relationship before I had a chance to choose."

"I know."

Dusk's words were soft behind her. Layla looked up to see his face in the mirror. As if her torpid conflict over Adrian was a sickness that could be caught, sadness etched Dusk's handsome face, a pained expression in his eyes. He moved forward, then stopped. Then moved again, coming to stand behind her with his hands resting on her shoulders. They watched each other in the mirror and for some reason, Layla felt compelled to reach up and touch his fingers. Gently, their fingertips twined together. Something in Dusk's eyes eased, a slow tenderness passing between them as they touched.

"I cannot apologize enough for what Adrian did to you," Dusk breathed at last. "If I had known the full truth of what that cuff would do, binding you to him this way—"

"You don't have to apologize for Adrian."

"I do." Something conflicted etched Dusk's features again.

"You're his brother, not his keeper, Dusk." Layla spoke directly, watching him in the mirror. "Adrian chose to do what he did. He chose to use the Hamsa Bind talisman to bind me to him the moment my magic awakened – without my knowledge or consent. None of that was your fault."

Dusk opened his mouth as if to argue, then shut it. He watched her a moment longer in the mirror, then leaned down and pressed a soft kiss to her neck. Layla stilled, a thrill passing through her. Dusk had used none of his rumblings, but his lips were smooth like satin as they touched her neck, his breath hot as he paused, then pulled away. His hands slid from her shoulders and Layla turned, watching him as he stepped away.

He wouldn't meet her eyes. Moving back to dressing, Dusk took out his crystal case of men's jewelry and set it upon the makeup table, removing his platinum watch. Brows furrowing at his strange mood, Layla turned back to the mirror. She watched him as she put the last touches on her hair, adding a spritz that would give her curls shine, but Dusk's silent mood held.

"So. Anything else about the clans?" Layla prompted, to break him from his reverie.

"Right." Dusk had finished donning his watch and was now struggling with the cufflinks in a frustrated way that was uncharacteristic for him. Layla's lips quirked. She turned on the ottoman and took the cufflink from his fingertips, doing it for him. He held still, watching her with amusement curling his lips, a flash of diamond-light brightening his sapphire eyes at last. "I can do that, you know. I'm not a complete imbecile."

"You were getting nowhere fast. Hold still." Layla admonished.

"Yes, Matron." He grinned, winsomeness brightening his eyes again as Layla finished the first cufflink and started on the other. "You just want an excuse to touch me."

Layla realized with a flush of heat that he was right. His hands had been so gentle and strong upon her shoulders; his lips so smooth at her neck that some part of Layla did want an excuse to touch him again. That thought made her Dragon roil and Layla heated with a combination of attraction, embarrassment, and anger that she'd been found out. Fumbling the second platinum and sapphire link, she nearly dropped it.

"You're as bad at this as I am. And you smell like burning oranges again. Are you secretly harboring a dark desire for your boss, Layla Price?" Dusk grinned, back to being rakish and sexy as hell, though Layla knew it was a cover-up. He was as attracted to her as she was to him, but Dusk used his blithe innuendo to gloss over his strange mood and that hot energy that had exploded between them earlier – still simmering like a braided coil between their bodies.

"Enough, you." Layla sassed to cover her own attraction as she affixed the cufflink, adjusting his French cuff into place. "There. Now tell me what else I can expect at the party."

"Not before you slide out of that hot red dress and get down and dirty with me on the bathroom floor." Dusk's eyes positively sparkled with rapier humor.

"In your dreams, pal." Layla gave him an eyebrow, though she was smiling in truth now.

"Alright! You win this round. Can't say I won't try for a round two, though."

Dusk gave a beaming grin, extending his arms and adjusting the French cuffs to the perfect length under his jacket. Layla rose, feeling like she and Dusk were back on familiar ground though tension still simmered between them – plus the strange sensation of whatever he wasn't telling her. Dusk gestured for her to exit the bathroom ahead of him and Layla did. She noted his gaze following her, though – sliding up her body, drinking in her every curve in the sleek crimson gown. Pleased, Layla sashayed away so he could get a good rear-view. Moving to the closet, she fetched a short crimson cape of feathers that went with her gown – and saw Dusk's stare, his sapphire eyes so hot they could have erupted the Ring of Fire all around the Pacific.

"You are one hell of a woman, Layla Price," he spoke, a dark smile curling the edges of his lips. "Damn you. I never should have chosen crimson. I'll be battling Dragon-lords back from that exceptionally firm ass of yours all night."

Layla grinned; she couldn't help it. She loved Dusk's frankness, his beautiful blue-grey lips that spilled such lurid innuendo. His burning sapphire eyes watched her every move as she slung on the cape, tying it about her shoulders with the crimson ribbons. She loved how she could see the hard length of him pressed against his slim trousers – and the way a rumbling vibration suddenly slipped past his solid barrier. It rocked Layla and her lips fell open, her breath fast as they stared at each other from across the room.

"Your magic's leaking," Layla breathed, shaken.

"Damn straight." Dusk growled, as shakily as she. Pursing his lips, he blew out a slow breath, wrestling control over his magics again. Layla felt the vibration in the air cease as he solidified that crystal barrier between them; so hard she could actually see glints of refracted light shimmer in the air. Moving to the side-bar, Dusk poured two new tumblers of bourbon, extending one. Layla glided forward to accept it, her silk train slithering over the carpet. They clinked glasses and drank, Dusk downing his in one fell swoop.

Layla's eyebrows rose. "Careful there, honcho. Save some for later, or I'll be carrying you home from the party."

"I'm going to need it; all night, probably. And you'd be surprised at how much a Crystal Dragon can drink." Dusk gave her a dark smile then set the tumbler aside, his gaze becoming serious again. "Layla. Before we go—"

"Yes?" Layla paused with her bourbon.

Dusk opened his lips, frowned, then spoke. "You're going to see Adrian tonight, but please, no touching him. I know you'll feel compelled to because of the Bind, even if you're pissed at him."

50

"What makes you say that?" Layla swirled her bourbon, scowling as a hot whip of her scorched-orange scent rose around her again. Making nice with Adrian was the last thing she wanted to do tonight, no matter how magically bonded to him she felt.

"Your vibrations don't lie." Dusk gave her a small smile, sad. "I know you'll want to go to him when you see him... but we can't have your Bind flaring all over the clans tonight. Some Dragons would adore it and try to scoop you up and fuck you in the pantry. Others would be *extremely* offended at the magical bleed-off. Plus, Adrian displaying a bond that strong with the only known Royal Dragon Bind in the world would raise far too much interest in you as a game-piece for others to meddle with. As much as you may feel compelled to go to him tonight... *decorum* with Adrian is the name of the game this evening. With everyone else, let your magic do as it will. But with him – please be careful."

Something in Dusk's manner was so somber, so deeply warning that Layla realized he was worried about the evening. She had seen him protective, and had seen him act with no-nonsense in an emergency, but this was beyond all that. Something about this party, about meeting the Dragon clans was dangerous for her, but Dusk wouldn't tell her why.

Or couldn't – one of Adrian's secrets he had to hold close to his chest.

"Are you afraid for me tonight?" She murmured, lowering her bourbon.

"Yes." Dusk's soft response held everything Layla suspected. And for the first time in this new world of magic and monsters, other than when her Dragon had attacked Luke, Layla felt truly afraid. She tried to not let it show as a slither of ice tightened her gut, chilling her core and making her feel like a black void opened deep within her. Raising her glass, Layla downed the rest of her bourbon, then set it decisively upon

51

the side-bar.

"Well. Even if the stakes are high, I don't think it'll be too hard to ignore Adrian tonight. He let me stew in our Bind for two months; he can deal with me doing the same to him for a night. I'm fine giving him my best cold shoulder. Let the bastard Royal Dragon have a taste of his own bitter fruit tonight and see how he likes it." Reaching out, she set her hand to Dusk's arm so he could escort her. "Let's go."

"As you like." Dusk smiled, lifting his arm into an escorting position.

But as he set his hand atop hers, clasping her fingers to his sleeve, another hard pulse of energy suddenly shot between them. Layla rocked where she stood, a small gasp leaving her, and Dusk shuddered hard as if their connection had done the same to him. Layla suddenly couldn't get enough air as her heart pounded and her Dragon screamed for sex or fighting or some wickedly powerful combination of both.

Dusk's fingers gripped hers and his lips parted. For a moment, she saw something rash consume his bright eyes; felt the crystal wall between them shudder and spiderweb with cracks. But he closed his eyes. Drawing his energy back, Dusk slammed up the crystal barrier between them so strongly that Layla saw a flash of light burst in the air. Though his hand was warm, Layla could feel that crystal wall like a second skin between them now – cool and impeccable. When his eyes opened again, his gaze met hers, and Layla saw struggle there. As much as he kept his barrier firm against her, he also wanted to drop it.

Drop it completely – and let fate do what it would.

"Let's get to the party." Dusk gave a wry smile, though his eyes said something else.

"Let's go get hammered, you mean." Layla smiled wryly back. "And see if we can drink away our problems with bourbon and maybe some tequila."

"You don't want to see me drunk on tequila." Dusk's lips quirked, humor lighting his face despite everything. "I do strange things. It really is the devil's drink."

"Maybe I want to see that." Layla grinned, enjoying their camaraderie once more; trying to forget the sexual tension racing between them.

"Maybe I'll let you see it sometime. If you behave, hot little drakaina."

"Hot *little* drakaina?" Layla lifted an eyebrow with a grin. "I'm as tall as you are. In my shiny new heels."

"Touché. But if you let me drink tequila, I'll most likely steal those heels. And end up wearing them. Probably dancing in them, too."

"My own Dusk Arlohaim drag show? I need to see that. Tequila shots, here we come." Layla laughed.

"You are going to be the death of me, woman. Fine. Tequila shots, here we come." With a rolling laugh, Dusk turned, escorting Layla out the door and into the hall. And though Layla laughed with him, enjoying their banter once more as she felt the air clear at last, she could still feel a deep, simmering tension between them.

It was not gone. And no amount of tequila was going to banish it.

CHAPTER 5 – EVENING

The soirée for the Dragon Shifter clans was not in the Palace of Versailles but in one of the out-buildings in the sprawling gardens. Escorted on Dusk's arm over the flagstone paths, Layla breathed deep of the night air as crimson and gold from the setting sun painted the heavy thunderclouds above. Topiaries and hedge-mazes were lined by roses still blooming unnaturally late in the Twilight Realm, their intoxicating scent swirled up by the brisk wind. Fountains burbled as thunder rumbled overhead, fae-lights swirling atop pedestals like fireflies as lightning flashed in the clouds.

But though the wind shook golden leaves down from the trees, the weather held as Dusk led Layla through the manicured gardens. Taking a path between fountains leaping with lions and gryphons, the private nooks teemed with guests reveling in the electrified evening. Hotel Guard in crimson held watchful expressions, bristling with rapiers and daggers as they guarded the paths and trysts all around. A pair of Guards nodded deferentially to the Head Concierge as he passed with Layla. Dusk nodded back as they walked past a row of lilac trees blossoming out of season by magic, even though their leaves were shriveled and dead.

Lilac were Layla's favorite flower and she paused as they passed. Dusk sensed it and graciously turned toward one towering tree. Reaching up, he snagged a branch down so Layla could inhale. She did, reveling in the heady fragrance. When she pulled back, Dusk was smiling at her wistfully, his crystalline wall still firmly in place between them.

"What?" Layla asked as a heavy roll of thunder rippled through the bruised sky.

"I can see why he bound you." Dusk spoke, mysterious and sad. "Adrian. When he had the chance in that art gallery back in Seattle."

"Why?" His statement was not what Layla had expected, and she frowned. It said a lot about what had been on his mind these last silent minutes since they'd left her apartment. The tension between Dusk and Layla from earlier simmered like the clouds overhead, and Dusk smiled wryly as another roll of thunder consumed the night. His gaze was deep as he reached out, brushing back a curl that had escaped Layla's chignon and tucking it gently behind her ear.

"Adrian may act like an asshole, but he's been struck by you, Layla," Dusk spoke quietly, "in a way no other woman has ever affected him. He hasn't cooperated easily with me on anything for years, but since Seattle… you haven't seen the meetings our Hotel leadership have had these past weeks. Adrian's phoned in, and he's been positively civil with me – not his usual. You've had an effect on him, even though you may not see it."

Layla paused, unsure how to respond. She heard Dusk talking about Adrian, but the gravitas with which he gazed at her said something vastly different. This was a side of Dusk that Layla had glimpsed before; the side of him that was neither playboy nor do-it-all Head Concierge. There was something deep inside Dusk, something he didn't show casually but which Layla had sensed ever since they met. Like the grounded clarity of an actual crystal growing in an underground cavern, Dusk was rooted in reality and also honest about himself. Layla saw it now as he spoke of Adrian with his own emotions shining in his sapphire eyes – and refracting through his dark hair in a gentle wave of light.

"Dusk, I—" Layla breathed, not sure what to do with this new side of him.

"Just say you're welcome." He spoke softly, a wry smile lifting his lips though his eyes filled with tender humor.

"You're welcome?" Layla spoke at last, still undone by the mood between them.

Dusk laughed. It was musical and sweet, his lovely baritone ringing out in the settling dark. Layla felt deep vibrations in it despite his crystal barrier; all around them, couples cried out in the darkening night as if pushed to ecstasy by it. Layla blushed as those vibrations found her, the searing passion of her own magic rising with the briskness of the impending storm. But as before, her wind hit Dusk's solid wall of crystalline energy and was turned aside.

"Come on." Dusk offered his arm again. Meandering through a garden of streams and stepping-stones lush with waterlilies, he said nothing for a long moment. Layla felt his mood shift as he drew a deep breath, mastering his energy so she felt nothing through his crystalline barrier any longer. As they angled past a row of sphinx statues, he finally spoke again.

"So I should prep you for the drama we're about to encounter. I mentioned a bit about it, but there's never really an end to how much one can prep for Dragon gatherings."

"Drama? You mean pissing matches." Layla lifted an eyebrow at him, knowing they were back to learning mode. Dusk wasn't going to speak with her directly about what he was feeling, and Layla didn't quite know what she was feeling for him, so she didn't push.

"Pissing matches. Completely." Dusk gave her a knowing smile as they walked. "Dragons are territorial and vie for power with games, backstabbing, and the sudden forming and un-forming of alliances – along with demonstrations of wit and strength. A majestic yet temperamental Lineage, we tend to make grand plans and just as spectacularly burn them down because of hot-headedness."

"Sounds like someone we both know," Layla grinned, trying to make light of the situation.

"You, me, or Adrian?" Dusk laughed, his masculine laugh robust in the night.

"Adrian." Layla spoke decisively, still trying to keep it light. Dusk's mood was easing, though conflict still lingered in him. Layla brightened to see him relaxing though, realizing how much it had hurt her to see Dusk so deeply sad.

A wind picked up, chill with impending rain, and Layla cuddled closer to Dusk's side. He glanced over as if pleased, changing his escorting position so he wrapped one arm around her waist, pulling her close. He was warm and smelled like rivers rushing through underground caverns, and Layla enjoyed snuggling close to his firm, lean body. It seemed right somehow, and they walked a moment in silence before Dusk spoke again.

"Adrian is representative of his breed," Dusk continued. "Each Dragon Lineage has their own temperament. As a Desert Dragon, you're familiar with your hot passion and tendency to get furious. Though it's because of that passion that Desert Dragons are exceptionally loving and family-oriented – though they tend to be territorial with mates." That last was said with a hint of Dusk's earlier mood, and Layla wasn't stupid. She caught the subtext – that Adrian was already possessive of her, even though they hadn't even slept together yet.

"And your Lineage? Crystal Dragons? Will any of your kind be here tonight?" Layla continued, trying to keep the conversation going.

"I'll represent the Crystal Dragons alone tonight," Dusk scowled as they walked, the topic apparently not easing his mind. "There aren't any left in France since King Markus Ambrose of the Czech Crystal Dragons battled King Lorenz DuVir in their blood-feud back in the 1600's and won this very palace. Markus is still King of my Lineage, and he doesn't need wealth or new allies; he owns a generous amount of the precious gem mines in both the human and Twilight Realm, and can buy all the power he wants. That's why he sold this palace off to the Hotel; he didn't need it. And he doesn't need Adrian's friendship. Adrian invited King Markus's retinue here tonight – the Austrian and Czech Crystal Dragon clans – but they've not responded."

"So King Markus thinks he's better than Adrian." Layla mused.

"He knows he is." Dusk glanced at her sidelong. "King Markus is a fantastic beast, Layla, and if you ever have a chance to meet him, tread carefully. He's a slick, debonair bastard, and a fucking brute in a fight. He's got the Austrian and Czech clans wrapped around his smallest talon. We know he's watching both Adrian and I carefully – though we don't precisely know to what end."

"Why is the King of the Crystal Dragons watching you?" Layla asked as they rounded a wall of topiaries.

"I'm Clan First of the Crystal Dragons of Egypt, Layla." Dusk gave her a frank glance as thunder rippled above, the sky swaddled in a heavy darkness now. "Though it's by default, since I'm the only one left since my clan and the Tunisian clan killed each other off. There's another Crystal clan in Saudi Arabia, but they're generally not involved with Afro-European politics."

Dusk fell into a brooding silence and Layla could only imagine what he was feeling. She'd heard about how he'd been found as child by Adrian's father, wandering the Sahara and causing earthquakes after the battle that had killed his entire clan. Layla could only imagine what that battle had looked like – and what it had done to a six-year-old boy left orphaned after the carnage.

"Is King Markus your enemy?" Layla asked.

"Not yet." Dusk nodded at a side-path past a row of glowing orbs and they angled to it. "I don't think he considers me powerful enough of a rival just yet."

"So how powerful is he?"

"You know that every Twilight Lineage has a dominant," Dusk spoke, glancing at Layla. "Someone at the pinnacle of the Lineage who is called King or Queen. It's separate from having Royal magic, though dominants are often also Royals. Among Dragons, someone who carries the title King or Queen has either been appointed by a vote of Clan Firsts, or fought their way to the top of the pecking-order through dominance battles."

"Let me guess. King Markus Ambrose was definitely not voted in." Layla spoke, wondering what kind of person he was to have battled his way to the top of his entire Lineage.

"Markus rules well, but I don't think anyone would vote someone like him into a dominant spot. He has a cruel streak, and doesn't hesitate to use it." As Dusk spoke, a wash of iridescence flowed through his dark hair. He wasn't saying more, and Layla wondered what his tense silence held. Clearly, Dusk had a past with King Markus Ambrose, and Layla wondered how bad it was. Or what King Markus might have done when Dusk's entire clan had died – to put Dusk in his place and ensure loyalty as a new Clan First.

"Who else will be present?" Layla spoke, changing the topic away from bad memories.

"Blood Dragons," Dusk gave a lighter smile as he angled them down a side-path, orbs brightening as a flicker of lightning flashed above. "The Swedish clan is here with their King – Huttr Erdhelm, Rikyava's uncle – and the Danish clan is supposed to show from Copenhagen. The Danes were supposed to confirm their arrival in

Paris, but of course they haven't. Try asking Danish Blood Dragons to do anything by the book and get that book thrown back at you on fire, along with a severed head. But they love parties, especially any they can crash unexpectedly, so I'm assuming they'll be here."

"That paints a good picture." Layla laughed, enjoying Dusk's wit. Even though he was in a strange mood, he was also trying his best to be lighthearted. Suddenly, Layla understood what his multitude of lovers saw in him. Dusk was witty, debonair, charming – and deeply thoughtful. Layla cuddled closer to him, enjoying his steady warmth in the stormy night. He glanced down at her, a subtle smile curling his lips as his tension eased. Layla could smell cool rivers as she glanced at him. He gave her a sidelong smile, pleasure in his eyes that she had cuddled close.

"What else would you like to know before we arrive?" He murmured.

"What other clans will be there?"

"We'll have a delegation of Ice Dragons from St. Petersburg," Dusk continued as they took a flagstone path through a manicured forest that abutted the topiary gardens. Cedars, leafless elms, and oaks towered above as they followed a path of firefly pedestals. "Ice Dragons are as showy as Desert Dragons. And they *love* seduction and manipulation nearly as much as they love vodka – you've been warned."

"Noted." Layla nodded with a small smile as they continued onward. "Who else?"

"The Storm Dragons of France will be here tonight. The Storm Dragon Queen has a clan-estate at Chambord, and she'll be here tonight with a portion of her retinue."

"Let me guess, she lives at Château de Chambord," Layla snorted with a wry smile. "Except in the Twilight Realm."

"Queen Justine Toulet is aligned with Adrian," Dusk nodded, confirming her statement, "though she's old, and a few of the younger drakes are trying to challenge her, so we'll see about the future. Storm Dragons are robust and tend to be elegant and level-headed – until you piss them off. I'd recommend not doing that. Be frank with them and pleasant, but no shenanigans – not like you can pull with Blood Dragons."

"Got it. Who else?"

"Our Head Courtier Reginald Durant will be there," Dusk's brow furrowed and another branch of lightning flashed far above the manicured forest, as if outlining his tension. "Representing the North Sea Sirens."

Layla's brows knit as she glanced at Dusk. "Rikyava told me Reginald was a Siren months ago, but she didn't elaborate on what that is. Aren't Sirens like mermaids?"

"Not at all." Dusk corrected with a wry smile. "Sirens are an ancient offshoot of the Dragon Lineage. Though they hate to be reminded of it, *Chiari drachans-sirenni* are just as Dragon as you and I. They're sea-Dragons. Closely related to Leviathans, which are an offshoot of the Siren Lineage, but different enough that Leviathans are not considered within the Dragon genus. Leviathans don't have a human form. Sirens do."

"So the Head Courtier really is a Dragon." As if she had called up Reginald Durant's power, the Head Courtier's oceanic feel came back to Layla suddenly. Seagulls called in her ears along with cold northern oceans, and in her mind's eye his ice-pale eyes rose, piercing her to the quick. She shivered as a brisk wind shook the trees, and Dusk snugged her closer to his warm body. "I take it Sirens have very little sense of humor. Or at least Reginald."

"They're one of the Dragon Lineages you do not want to tease, yes." Dusk nodded soberly as they continued past the pond. "They're quite strong, very large when they change into their beast, and have mesmer abilities to boot. Thankfully, only Reginald will be there tonight, and he knows how to control his darker nature. Somewhat."

"Who else?" Layla asked, musing on that.

"The only other clan present will be the Phoenix of Italy and Spain." Dusk glanced over, his gaze eloquent. "Phoenix love harmony, but of all the Dragons, they are the quickest to fight when attacked. Their King, Falliro Arini, is an amazingly steady man despite his many centuries of stunning battle-prowess. Though he's hard to get to know."

"But I thought Phoenixes were birds?"

"Phoenix are not birds, but an ancient and powerful race of feathered Dragons, another offshoot like Sirens," Dusk spoke levelly, an edge of warning in his voice. "They do regenerate upon death if they so choose, and have *very* long memories. Not a Lineage to make enemies of – for yourself, or for Adrian."

"Noted." Layla was about to ask another question when their destination suddenly loomed from a clearing in the trees. Near a border of hedges and firefly pedestals, a gargantuan building rose through the night. Made of crystal, vaulted domes led to twisting spires lit from inside by swirling fae-lights. Like a French Gothic cathedral, the vaults were rose quartz, pinnacles of purple amethyst blending into the storm-dark sky. Bright yellow citrine created arched ingresses, moss-green aventurine creating a glassy ingress like walking on a summer river.

As they approached, Layla saw vines of trumpet-flowers like morning glory twining up every column inside. The Dragon party was in full swing, hundreds of men and women in elegant evening dress meandering with drinks within. A chamber ensemble played on a gilded dais as Catering staff in black and white freshened drinks, working the party with golden platters of hors d'oeuvres. Elegantly-dressed people gathered at the doors, being announced by a Herald. But as Dusk and Layla stepped up near the vaulted crystal doors, Dusk moved her aside.

"Are you ready for this?"

"I don't know, am I?" Layla quipped, marveling at the scene. Even after working at the Hotel for nearly two months, its opulence never ceased to surprise her.

"Don't sass, Layla, I'm serious." Dusk gave a smile, though his gaze was level. "Have you considered how you want to position yourself among the Dragon clans? Before we go in there?"

Layla inhaled, turning to him. "I really don't know. This is all so foreign. I mean, if Adrian had prepped me more, I might have an idea of where to start, but as it is…"

Dusk gave a kind smile. Reaching out, he smoothed one of Layla's sable curls back with tender fingers. "I'm sorry I didn't give you more information about all of this. I thought we'd have months to get you up to speed on Dragon society, so I focused on getting you comfortable in Concierge Services first. Adrian sprung this on me just a few days ago, and I've been too busy with the Samhain Masquerade preparations to address any of this properly. I owe you a deep apology, not getting you ready to face this, Layla."

"It's not you who should be apologizing," Layla spoke, watching Dusk's sapphire-bright eyes and feeling his sincerity.

"Still." He gave a wry smile. "Watch me for cues tonight on etiquette. And don't worry. I will be a barnacle on your ass all night, so you don't have to fret about being alone with anyone."

"Except with you." Layla felt a slow, flirtatious smile lift her lips. "Right now."

"I don't count."

Though his words were dismissive, Dusk's eyes darkened to a simmering midnight blue that Layla wanted to drown in suddenly.

Passion as deep as nighttime caverns moved through those eyes, before he lifted Layla's hand to his lips and pressed her fingers with a kiss. It didn't have any of his rumblings in it, as his crystal wall was still up between them. But watching those eyes, feeling their devouring darkness, Layla almost wished he'd cast his wall down.

Her beast stirred inside her with a deep roil of heat and Layla shivered, though not from the wind as Dusk set her hand to his arm. Moving forward, he escorted Layla through the throng at the vaulted doors.

And into the Dragon party.

CHAPTER 6 – SOIREE

Dusk was conspicuous at the Red Letter Hotel Paris; Dragons all around bowed to the Head Concierge or sank into elegant curtsies as he and Layla approached the doors to the crystal cathedral. Impeccable, he gave nods and a friendly smile, but walked Layla on through the masses without pause. In her sleek crimson silk with its elegant train and bodice of diamonds and rubies, Layla got stares and whispers. Eyes followed her, astounded, curious, or appraising. But Dusk walked her through it all, stepping beneath the citrine arches and nodding at the Herald just inside by the rose quartz columns, who raised his crowd-piercing tenor to announce them.

"Dusk Arlohaim, Clan First of the Crystal Dragons of Egypt and Head Concierge of the Red Letter Hotel Paris! With Layla Price of the Desert Dragons of Morocco and the Mediterranean, Concierge of the Red Letter Hotel Paris!"

Talked ceased in the vaulted crystal foyer as everyone turned to stare. The party was in full swing, the soaring hall holding at least two hundred people. As had happened outside, many of the Dragons in attendance sank into graceful bows or curtsies for Dusk, but Layla got more whispers and evaluating glances – and more than a few people saying *Dragon Bind*.

Dusk ignored it all, though he smiled at a number of people and clasped hands in a friendly manner as he led Layla through the rose quartz foyer over to a refreshments table. The throng parted like minnows to a shark, as if many of the other Dragons were strangely afraid of the debonair Crystal Dragon with the Royal Dragon Bind on his arm.

But Dusk was effortlessly gracious as he spoke more pleasantries to Dragons he knew, laughing and witty. At the drinks table, he selected a glass of white wine and scented it, handing it to Layla with a quick wink. She sipped, enjoying a mellow chardonnay of just the kind she liked. Dusk took one up also, then nodded to a group talking near a rose quartz column twined with white trumpet-blossoms.

All eyes pinned Layla as Dusk escorted her over, though this group gave the Head Concierge affable hails of welcome rather than bows. It was clear these Dragons were actually friends of Dusk's, and Layla was relieved to see her friend the Head of the Hotel Guard Rikyava Andersen standing among them. Dressed in a ravishing lavender gown studded with diamonds that flowed down her fit curves, Rikyava's Scandinavian-blonde hair was done back in ornate braids, cascading down her back in a fiercely elegant Viking style. Raindrop jewelry of diamonds and amethyst dripped over her collarbones, her pure lavender eyes smudged and arresting as she flowed forward – giving Layla a hug but pursing her rouged lips in an irritated fashion at Dusk.

"Layla! Finally! I thought maybe Dusk had locked you in your closet rather than bring you to the party tonight." Rikyava spoke in her usual no-bullshit Guardswoman manner. She wore no rapier or knives tonight, though her draping gown most likely hid a thigh-sheath or two. Layla blushed at her friend's statement, the thought of being locked in a closet with Dusk intimately appealing this evening. But Rikyava missed it, continuing, "I was just telling my Swedish Blood Dragon clan about you. Come here, meet my uncle and cousins from Stockholm."

"Let Layla breathe, Rikyava, for heaven's sake." Dusk chuckled, sipping his wine with a grin – though his gaze flicked to Layla with distinct pleasure, and she knew he had not missed the change in her vibration at Rikyava's offhand comment about the closet.

"Shut up, you! You don't get to talk – you made our girl late." Layla felt Rikyava's ash-hot Blood Dragon energy slap out at Dusk, and Layla laughed internally. She was aware now of why the two were constantly at odds yet worked so well together at the Hotel; lovers who would never admit it, at least not on Rikyava's end. Stepping to Layla's side, Rikyava settled her arm around Layla's waist, pulling her away from Dusk and turning Layla to meet an enormous man who grinned as if he'd just watched a sporting match between Dusk and his niece.

"Layla Price, may I introduce my uncle, King Huttr Erdhelm of the Blood Dragons of Sweden."

The enormous Blood Dragon King's red-gold eyes glowed with humor as Layla stood, debating how formal to be with him. She couldn't curtsey with Rikyava's arm threaded around her; plus, the atmosphere in this group was casual. As white-blond as Rikyava, King Huttr's enormous mane was braided back from his blocky skull and shaved on the sides with dragons like he'd stepped right off a medieval Viking raiding ship. The Blood Dragon King was enormously fit, wearing an expensive tuxedo over his massively-built chest and shoulders. Chains of gold cascaded between his lapels with pins of archaic valor clipped to his breast. A white polar bear pelt was slung about his shoulders, his blond beard braided. Grinning with impeccably white teeth, he seized Layla's hand in a crushing grip, lifting it to his lips.

"Well! The Royal Dragon Bind! I feel a wrath of fire in you, desert mistress. Pour those charms through old Huttr, and we'll see who winds up on top in the sweaty sheets. Ha!"

"Not tonight, Huttr." With a wry smile, Dusk plucked Layla's hand from the big Blood Dragon King – who gave a genial laugh, obviously not offended. His laugh was infectious and Layla grinned, liking King Huttr immediately. Pleasure and a lust for life beamed from the big King's every sinew. He was very much like Rikyava – all direct bravado, teasing fun, and no bullshit.

"Dearest King. So excellent to meet family of Rikyava's." Layla gave a deferential nod, bending her head and lowering her eyes for a three-count. As a King, Huttr outranked her, but as an employee of the Hotel with Royal magic, Layla had high standing. When she lifted her head, he was grinning, his eyes brightened to an impossibly glorious battle-blood red, though Layla felt no power cresting off of him. The big Blood Dragon King obviously had impeccable control of his magic, and Layla felt nothing but an infectious levity with the scent of peat whiskey coming from him – though that could have been the whiskey glass he held in his hand.

"My, my!" Huttr chuckled, saluting Dusk with his glass. "I envy you, Milord Arlohaim, getting to taste her tonight. I'm sure I could do you one better – though my niece tells me you have ample skill in the bedroom."

"I do my best." Dusk gave Huttr a rakish wink and the man laughed uproariously. Rikyava scowled, however, a surge of scorch-hot battle winds swirling up around her.

"Uncle! What I told you was *private*." Rikyava growled.

"Nothing is private with me, sweet niece," King Huttr chuckled as he sipped his whiskey, "especially not matters of the bedchamber. The advice I gave you still stands on how to wrangle your men." Huttr gave a big grin, teasing his niece as he gave Dusk a wink. Rikyava scowled and opened her mouth to retort, but Huttr boomed, "Dragon Bind, come! You must meet my sons; my eldest Halfdir, and my youngest Rhennic. Perhaps one of them will be more to your taste than a Crystal cad with so many womenfolk he doesn't know what to do with them all!"

King Huttr beckoned to the outstandingly handsome men beside him. Huttr's sons were more slender than their father, though still towering in stature, both of them in their early thirties with Viking-blond hair and lavender eyes. Halfdir sported a short mohawk shaven with dragons like his father, a shaggy white wolf pelt chained over his tux's shoulders. Rhennic was the more modern, with gladiator-short hair and a neatly trimmed beard, wearing an elegant charcoal suit with a blood-red ruby pinned through his black tie. Huttr's sons gave Layla appreciative smiles, though Halfdir's was grinningly bold and Rhennic's more sexily subtle.

They took turns kissing her hand, though when his turn came, Rhennic turned Layla's hand over and kissed the inside of her wrist. It sent shivers through Layla with a wash of heat. And though Rhennic's touch held an attraction similar to what she'd felt with Adam, the tendrils of his energy easing into her from his kiss were elegantly subtle. Rhennic was mate-tasting her, she realized, but he was being appropriate about it in public. A scent of lavender and heather filled Layla's nostrils and as her inner beast rose, a responding orange spice scent wafted up around Layla. Rhennic Erdhelm gave her a subtle smile that said he knew exactly what he'd just done – though again, it had been done with far more decorum than Adam Rhakvir.

"Desert beauty," Rhennic murmured in a melodious baritone. "Forgive my father's coarse ways. He really has no clue how to treat women."

"So I've seen." Layla sassed with a lift of her eyebrow, shaken by Rhennic's mate-taste but trying to be casual about it. "And I suppose you do?"

King Huttr exploded into laughter as Rhennic's smile startled into a grin. It was a good look, far more playful than he'd been earlier. It showed his relationship to his family, though it was clear Rhennic was the most sly and careful of the Erdhelm Blood Dragons. He straightened with a chuckle, giving Layla's wrist a small squeeze that caught her breath before he let her go – as his father boomed more laughter, turning to Dusk.

"Well! I've got ten thousand riding on the Dragon Bind, Arlohaim. I think she'll make waves in our community. That is, if Justine thinks she's worthy, of course. That bitch has been giving me hell, telling me we—"

But he got no further as an immensely elegant older woman in a midnight blue ballgown covered with sapphires and onyx stepped up. Mature but exquisitely regal like Meryl Streep, the woman was fiercely beautiful. Her silver hair was brushed up in an elegant twist through an onyx and sapphire tiara, her fine-boned body supercharged with calm intensity. The same intensity shone in midnight blue eyes, which seemed to flash with storms beneath the chandeliers. Enormous amounts of nerve-tingling electricity surged off her thin frame, as if she couldn't help the intensity of her Dragon-magics. Layla shivered hard, feeling it crackle over her skin – every nerve in her body coming alight like she stood next to a power plant.

"Queen Justine Toulet. Thank you for gracing our Hotel with your esteemed presence." Dusk bowed low with a hand over his breast, a gesture he'd not made with anyone else. Touching a hand to his shoulder, Queen Justine indicated for him to straighten and Layla saw Dusk shiver as the Queen's spine-electrifying magic poured over him.

"Dusk Arlohaim," Queen Justine murmured in a melodious alto with a thick French accent as she air-kissed his cheeks, her stormy blue eyes shining. "So good to see you. The honor is mine, for you have thrown such a *lovely* party. They say the party is Adrian's, but I know the quality of Arlohaim handicraft. A shining example of what every

Hotel should be."

"You are too kind, my Queen." Pleasure glowed in Dusk's eyes as he took up the woman's thin hand and gave it a light kiss. Though her skin was delicately aged, that hand was far from frail. As if the Dragon inside Queen Justine was just underneath her flesh, those long, thin fingers looked like vicious talons – ready to rip forth at any moment and wreak ruin.

"Indeed," Queen Justine spoke back, electricity searing about her person as her dark blue eyes flashed with a spear of lightning. Layla blinked, thinking it had been a trick of the light, when the Storm Dragon Queen pinned Layla with her gaze and it happened again. Layla felt a spark of lightning bite over her skin, as if the Queen had somehow read her entire energy in a glance, like taking a flash-photograph. It was unnerving in the extreme and Layla shuddered, though the Storm Queen merely smiled.

"Queen Justine," King Huttr seized the woman's hand, pressing it with a fierce kiss that was rather uncouth, though the elderly lady weathered it well. "Excellent to see you."

"King Huttr." She leaned in, air-kissing him on both cheeks with elegant grace. "I hear you are bad-mouthing me again?"

"Dearest Queen—" he blustered, a scorching heat rising around him with a strong scent of peat. But Queen Justine held up a hand, stalling him instantly, her posture regal.

"Peace, Huttr. I know we have our differences. You and I will speak anon." Those fierce, storm-raging eyes returned to Layla, looking her deftly up and down as they flashed again. Layla shivered violently, feeling the Queen's intense magic coursing through her. "So, this is Mimi Zakir's daughter. Like mother, like child. You look just like Mimi in her heyday, young Layla. A compliment, by all counts. Mimi Zakir was a great light in our community; she came to sing at my palace many a long night."

"Thank you, Queen of Storms. In my deepest heart, I hope to live up to my mother's example."

It was still strange to Layla, thinking of Mimi as her mother rather than her grandmother. And from Queen Justine's words, Layla wondered if the Storm Dragon Queen had been one of her mother's lovers. But now was not the time to ask and Layla paid her respects, sinking into a deep curtsey. She didn't have to; a kiss to Justine's hand would have sufficed. But with the woman's overwhelming presence surging over her like a live power line, like hell was Layla going to reach out and touch that.

Queen Justine laughed, florid and lovely. Reaching out, she set her fingertips beneath Layla's chin, ostensibly to raise her up. But as her fingers touched Layla's skin, electric currents flooded Layla, shuddering her in a disastrous wave. Her knees weakened and Dusk surged in to catch her from sinking to the floor as she found herself zapped by the Storm Queen's energy.

Layla's desert heat whirled at the Queen's touch, swirling in a rush that Layla couldn't control. Even with her hamsa-cuff, she was powerless – sinking beneath Queen Justine's energy in a searing wave as orange-citrus scent flooded up all around her. Layla heaved hard breaths, stunned and shivering as Dusk held her, the Storm Queen's touch slipping away. Like she'd just stuck her finger in a light socket, Layla's whole body hummed with a sensation that was just this side of pain as Justine's searing lightning-dark eyes moved from her to Dusk.

"Take care of her, young Dusk," The Storm Queen spoke, pinning Dusk with her intense gaze. "I scent her fate upon the winds; she will need your support, soon. For twin sand-funnels need a grounding agent, and crystal will do better than most. Heed me. Keep the Dragon Bind close and all may yet be well."

"Yes, my Queen." Dusk managed a bow, even though he was still holding Layla up from sinking to the floor. But Layla saw his deep frown at the Storm Queen's enigmatic words. In a way it sounded like prophecy, and in a way it just sounded like advice – but whatever Queen Justine had read in Layla's energy had given her insight into Layla's predicament as a Royal Dragon Bind.

But she said no more, only giving a mysterious smile and moving over to a group of people with roiling dark blue eyes nearly as impressive as hers – Storm Dragons. Layla was left breathless, shuddering as Dusk's steady arm kept her from falling to the floor. Swallowing hard, she could still feel Justine's energy rioting through her like a hurricane. Glancing to Rikyava, Layla saw even her fierce Blood Dragon friend seemed shaken by Queen Justine's presence, swigging back her entire flute of champagne.

As Justine left, a group of handsomely Russian men and women approached, exchanging laughs and handshakes with King Huttr's folk. Layla was finally able to stand, though Dusk gave her a look before turning to clasp hands with a lean man with ash-blond hair, dark brows, and exquisitely Russian high cheekbones.

Excusing herself before she could be introduced, Layla went to hide behind some potted palms near the drinks table. Leaning back against a crystal column, electrified currents still swirled through her. Breathing slowly, she felt a soothing vibration ripple the air and opened her eyes to see Dusk before her, his summer-blue eyes deep with concern.

"Are you alright?" Dusk's voice was low as he watched her.

"Queen Justine…" Layla shook her head, reaching up to massage her temples. "I feel like she just poured herself inside me. Whirling around inside my head, my body, my magic. Even the hamsa-cuff couldn't control it."

"Justine's not like other Storm Dragons." Dusk's sapphire gaze was knowing as he stepped close. "Like I can, she uses her energy to read people. It's nearly impossible to block, and she's ruled the Storm Dragons for over a thousand years because of the insights she gleans from rolling her power through other people's magic. Here."

Brushing his fingers over Layla's collarbones, Dusk lowered his invisible crystal shield enough to pour a soothing vibration into her. She shuddered, feeling his energy ground her as if he rooted her in the deepest caverns of the earth. Her fugue cleared and she exhaled with relief. As he stowed his energy back behind his crystal shield, Layla found herself grateful for Dusk's fingertips still stroking her. It was comforting – and he didn't draw his fingers away, as if he enjoyed the contact also.

"Thanks," she breathed.

"Don't mention it," he murmured, his gaze complex like it had been on their walk earlier. He moved as if he was about to let her go – when that tight coil of power suddenly caught them again. Layla inhaled, feeling that strong tension haul them closer, as if their Dragons couldn't stand to be apart even by a few inches.

Dusk's lips fell open as his eyes darkened to a deep sapphire, something intensely bright in them like diamonds. Slipping a hand around Layla's waist, he drew her close. Stroking her collarbones, he traced his fingertips with his eyes – and somehow, it drove their coiling magic deeper inside Layla. She shuddered at his touch, finding herself yielding to him, her heart racing. He wasn't using his magic, but it was as if his very touch was stirring her, moving emotions deep within her body. Her Dragon turned over inside her veins with a slow, delicious movement, like warm gold. Dusk's gaze was complicated as his eyes found hers again. He inhaled to speak – when they were suddenly interrupted by a jovial chuckle.

74

"Making out in the greenery, cousin? I thought you had a bit more class than that. Ms. Price does, that's for certain."

They turned and Layla saw the last person she wanted to be confronted with right now. Adam Rhakvir stood behind them, a roguish smile upon his golden-bearded face. He'd traded out his bombardier look for a classy tan and creme pinstriped vest and slacks, shirtsleeves rolled to his elbows with russet Oxfords. A jade pocket square complemented his irises, his collar undone to the third button. His emerald dragon-ring flashed as he raised a Tom Collins to his lips and sipped. Lecherous like a Roman soldier at a brothel, Adam swirled his drink as he grinned at Layla.

"Dragon Bind."

"Asshole." Layla resisted crossing her arms to show her displeasure. Her dress was really too classy for her to act like an irate tween in it.

"Adam!" Dusk turned, clapping Adam's shoulder with an affable smile, his previous mood banished at his cousin's arrival, along with his tension with Layla. "Thanks for not accosting Layla with your magics tonight. She's already had enough from the Storm Queen."

"Justine got to her, huh? Figures. When there's power in a room, that woman can't resist a big old taste." Adam set his drink aside upon a tall table, glancing from Dusk to Layla.

"You should talk," Layla soured at Adam, setting her jaw and feeling a hot whip of rage surface. "You accosting me earlier wasn't too far off from what Justine did just now."

"Actually…" Adam's gaze sobered, darkening to a deep hunter-green as it rested upon Layla. "I came over to offer you a formal apology for my behavior earlier."

"Oh, really?" Layla sassed him, narrowing her eyes.

"Really." Adam Rhakvir spoke calmly, not rakish at all now but serious. It seemed he had his cousin Adrian's ability to change emotions on a dime and it made Layla perk, watching him.

Gone was his teasing flyboy demeanor, replaced by something far more sober. And before Layla knew what was happening, Adam had descended to one knee before her. Reaching inside the inner left pocket of his vest, he liberated a small silver knife etched with archaic sigils from a silver sheath. Layla startled, but before she could do anything, Adam had slashed a red line on his left upper chest, over his heart. Layla gaped as Adam reached out, claiming her hand and folding the hilt of the bloodied knife in her fingers. Looking up, his eyes were a searing hunter-green, their ring of violet entirely lost to that dark, sensual color as he regarded her with a scalding intensity.

"Ms. Layla Price. I deeply apologize for my actions at the Concierge desk earlier. It was rash of me to mate-taste you that strongly without your consent. But seeing Adrian's prize, I fear my emotions ran away with me. Consummating a Royal Dragon Bind to oneself is a rare thing, and I admit, today was one of my baser moments, feeling my Dragon roar with jealousy. My cousin is a lucky man. And you, Ms. Price, are stunning."

Layla found herself dumbstruck, staring at Adam open-mouthed. Without rising, he gave her fingers a gentle squeeze then let go, leaving the bloodied knife clasped in her hand. She frowned, unsure what to do. Dusk had never prepped her for a formal Dragon-apology, and Layla had a feeling this was over-the-top even for most occasions.

Adam, it seemed, didn't do anything by halves, and his archaic gesture put Layla up on a pedestal like a Queen.

A position she so did not want.

CHAPTER 7 – ROYALS

Adam Rhakvir waited on one knee before Layla in the crystal hall, the slash on his upper left chest trickling blood. People were staring, a growing circle gathering around Adam, Dusk, and Layla – the Blood Dragons, the Storm Queen with her retinue, the Russians, and others. All eyes were on Layla and the bloodied knife in her hand, watching the interaction with a rising intensity. Through the pounding of her blood, Layla noted the orchestra had ceased playing. Talk had silenced; the entire hall seemed to breathe with a slow-roaring energy as Dragons craned their necks to see what was happening by the drinks table.

"Dusk? Some help?" Layla hissed, knowing that Adam's display was far more than she had previously thought. The Storm Queen's gaze flashed upon her with a slight smile, while King Huttr scowled, his frown intense as he glanced between Adam and Layla – though his son Rhennic seemed calm, his violet gaze thoughtful.

"Adam has offered you his life, Layla, for his slight against you earlier today." Dusk's voice was calm beside her, but Layla could feel his magic hammering hard behind his crystal barrier – he was as unnerved as she at this sudden situation, though he was expert at keeping his cool. "You can take it now, by slashing the knife in your hand across his throat, and he won't fight. Or you can forgive him, by licking his blood from the knife and keeping the blade as a gift."

"Is this usual for a Dragon apology?" Layla hissed back softly.

"No. It's a very old gesture, and rarely used." Something in Dusk's voice was odd, but Layla didn't want to take her eyes off Adam with everyone staring. "I'd recommend sparing his life. He's your Clan Second, and Adrian's right-hand officer. Not to mention Adrian's cousin."

"And yours."

"And mine." Dusk fell silent, though he stayed near Layla with a supportive hand resting at the small of her back. He wasn't pouring his soothing charms through her though, letting her make the decision unswayed.

Adam's blond brows were knitted now as he remained kneeling before her, his gaze careful as if he were worried she actually might kill him, she had paused so long. Layla's Dragon was strangely quiet inside her, watching him. But killing people wasn't Layla's style. Other Dragons could enjoy dominance and bloodshed, but even if her Lineage was vicious, Layla wasn't going to play ball that way.

Even if Adam had forced her into a public acceptance of his antics earlier.

Pinning Adam with her eyes and making him feel how royally pissed off she was at being manipulated this way, Layla raised the silver knife to her lips. Dragon blood was remarkably free of disease; she wasn't going to catch anything. But the iron scent of Adam's offering mixed with his heady apple orchard fragrance made Layla pause. She'd never tasted anyone's blood before, but her Dragon uncoiled inside her, raising its head eagerly toward the blade. In a hot wave, it took control of Layla's lips, making her open her mouth and gently draw the blade through, licking Adam's blood from the silver with the tip of her tongue.

It was divine. Layla paused deeply as she tasted him – as if she could taste all of him in that one scintillating line of crimson. Dusk's hand was the only thing steadying her from sinking to the floor and trying to crawl to Adam, to rip into him with talons and fangs as she shuddered, her head falling back. A sweet orange and bourbon scent flooded from her and Dragons came alert all around, some drawn closer by her seething scent, some moving back with wide eyes. Layla barely registered that Dusk now gripped her by both arms, holding her back from Adam.

And that she was fighting him, trying to get to the Royal Dragon still kneeling on the floor.

Adam watched her with an answering heat shining in his hunter-green eyes – an unmistakeable look. As if he had planned this; as if he had planned all this just to get Layla to taste one drop of his apple-sweet blood. To make her want him; to make her fight to get to him. But he was holding onto his own magic as furiously as Dusk, remaining motionless in his kneeling position before her. He wouldn't go to her; he wanted her to come to him. Seeing that knowledge in his eyes, Layla gathered herself at last. Staring down at Adam, she seethed with heat that had nothing to do with passion, furious at the depth of his games.

"Adrian doesn't own me; we haven't consummated anything." She spoke down to Adam coldly, rage flooding her. "And if you think you'll have a try, you are sadly mistaken, bucko. No matter what your blood tastes like."

Adam Rhakvir's green eyes went wide as he laughed in astonishment at Layla's response. It was a strong laugh, ending in a sexy chuckle. He didn't seem perturbed that Layla was boiling mad at him, and didn't seem to care how deeply he'd manipulated her – only that it had nearly gotten him everything he wanted. Layla was still fuming as they locked gazes, and at last Adam showed a little contrition. Setting a hand over his heart, his skin already ceased bleeding since his cut hadn't been all that deep, he gave a low bow, lowering his gaze like he meant it.

"Forgive me. I have a flare for the dramatic, as do most Dragons."

He murmured, rising and giving Layla a softer, more genuine smile at last. "I can see you don't appreciate it. But I like your spirit, Layla Price. And if Adrian hasn't consummated anything with you yet, he's a fool. I have a feeling that binding you will be *quite* a lot more than my cousin bargained for."

"Layla's not one to piss off lightly, Adam. Fuck with her at your own risk." Dusk gave Layla a look as he released her and stepped to her side. Tension had eased around them now and Layla saw smiles all around. A polite ripple of clapping passed through the crowd at what had just happened, and Layla had a feeling it had been a good show. People returned to milling, though a number of eyes remained on her – especially the Storm Queen's.

"Laugh it up, boys." Layla gestured at both Dusk and Adam with the bloodied knife, though she was less pissed now that the show was over almost as suddenly as it had begun. It had been a manipulation, but it seemed Adam's little event had evened the score between himself and Layla as far as the clans were concerned. An extreme offering, it had somehow put her in a higher social position than him, at least for now. But having no idea what to do with the silver knife, she lifted an eyebrow at Adrian's renegade cousin.

"If you want me to keep this blade, jackass, then hand that sheath over."

"*As you wish.*" With a cheeky grin, Adam handed over the silver sheath. She scowled at his intentional quoting of the *Princess Bride* – so not cool right now. Looking daggers at Adam, Layla slid the knife in the sheath, then tucked it down her cleavage. The blade still had blood on it, but she'd wash that off later. Glancing between them, Layla realized that both Adam and Dusk were grinning like brigand brothers.

"You two are just a couple of peas in a pod, aren't you?" Layla grumped.

"Don't be pissed, Layla," Dusk spoke calmly, his gaze level with her though he was unable to stifle his smile. "Adam's offering right now gave you a lot of clout with the clans. It was a dumb idea, but also kind of genius – I wish I had thought of it, actually. He's shown them that you hold higher standing than he does, which is saying something as a Clan Second. It automatically bumps you up to the level of a Second or almost a First, even though you've fought no dominance battles. Adam essentially provided you with one, right now, in public. And you won." Dusk glanced to Adam, who was now grinning at his cousin with reckless pleasure.

"What can I say? I have good ideas now and again." Adam retrieved his drink from the side-table and had a sip, grinning at Layla.

"And pulling me with your magic to get me to crawl to you like an animal?" Layla did cross her arms over her chest now, giving him a severe eyeball.

"A man can but try." He chuckled darkly. "In any case, you resisted just fine, even without Dusk's help. He could have stopped it. His magic is stronger than mine, you know. *That* one was constantly encasing me in crystal cocoons I couldn't get out of when we were kids."

"Until aunt Rachida blasted you out of them, then tanned my backside." Dusk chuckled, glancing at Adam as he sipped his wine. He turned to Layla. "Adam, Adrian, and I were all raised together. Adam's the youngest, I'm in the middle, Adrian's the oldest. Adam's adopted like I am, by Adrian's great-aunt Rachida Rhakvir when his parents were killed at their home in Florence."

"I'm sorry to hear that," Layla blinked, wondering if any of the Dragons in her clan had normal pasts. She was betting not. She was learning that Dragons were tempestuous creatures and held intense grudges. And that Dusk's adoption into Adrian's clan had actually been a rare thing.

"Don't be sorry. It's ancient history. But I appreciate the sentiment." Adam's eyes were serious now, a dark hunter-green with very little violet. "My parents were cursed; a Romeo and Juliet situation. My mother was from the Italian Desert Dragon clan, my father was a Blood Dragon from Copenhagen. The Danish Blood Dragons and the Italian Desert Dragons have been at each other's throats a long time. My father was actually sent as an assassin to kill my mother, but he fell in love with her instead and they had me. When the Copenhagen clan decided to finish the job a few years later, the hit included him, and me."

"The Copenhagen Blood Dragons tried to assassinate you?" Layla sipped her drink, her fury cooling as she listened to the tale.

"When I was a child." Adam smiled wryly. "I was supposed to die the day they busted into our fortress. But I shape-shifted for the first time out of terror – into a dog! I was so little and so scared they missed me, hiding under the bed. Rachida was the one who figured it out when she came to assess the carnage. She lured me out with bacon. It took me a full month for me to figure out I could change back to human. She took me back to Morocco and the rest is history. I was raised with this asshole, and with Adrian."

Adam jostled Dusk and grinned. Layla felt terrible hearing of Adam's past, though it was fascinating. With his tall, striking blond looks and amazing green-violet eyes, she believed that he was a Danish-Italian Dragon mix – a very handsome combination.

"Are there many Dragons of mixed Lineage?" She asked, sipping her wine.

"Not so many," Adam answered with a small smile. "Clan feuds are rampant. Something Adrian wants to rectify, and I support him in that."

"You're his Second, and also a Royal?" Layla asked, cocking her head. "Why does Adrian lead the Mediterranean clan and not you?"

"I can't shape-shift into much more than dogs, can I?" Adam snorted with a self-deprecating grin, but there was truth in the subtle pain behind his eyes. "Adrian's not filled you in on our clan history, has he?"

"Not so much."

"Would you like to hear it?" Adam's gaze sobered, his eyes searching Layla's. "I'd love to answer any questions you have, Layla. Perhaps we could have dinner tomorrow night. You could ask me any question you have concerning Desert Dragons, and I'll fill you in."

"Not like a date." Layla lifted an eyebrow, suddenly wondering if all this was just an elaborate ruse for him to try and get her in the sack. But Adam laughed, and still there was no trace of his heated magics. In fact, his pleasant apple-blossom scent issued from him only subtly now, like picking fruit on a sunny day.

"No, not a date, just time for you to pick my brain about our clan. I won't try anything like I did today, I swear it."

Layla looked to Dusk, who gave her a reassuring smile. "If Adam says he won't try anything, he won't. Because he knows what I'll do to him."

"I do." Adam chuckled, finishing his drink and setting it aside on a tall table. "Dusk can still beat me senseless in a fight. He's stronger than he seems, Layla; don't let his affable nature fool you. He's a Royal. He just can't shape-shift for shit."

"You're a Royal? Why did you never tell me that?" Layla eyed Dusk. Clearly, he wasn't very forthcoming about what he could and couldn't do – nor where he stood in his Crystal Dragon Lineage, which Layla was finally understanding was actually quite far up. So much about the evening suddenly made sense. Their sudden, hard attraction up in her apartment earlier. The reaction of the crowd at their arrival to the party; they way people had bowed to Dusk with such reverence. It wasn't just because he was the Hotel's Head Concierge.

It was because he had power – and somehow, everyone knew it.

There was a great, big hole in Layla's knowledge of him, she realized suddenly. And she was understanding a helluva lot more about Dusk now as she stared at him. Dusk watched her back, and Layla saw iridescence flash through his hair as his cheeks flushed. His sapphire eyes were desperate; whatever secrets he held in addition to having Royal magic, Layla was fairly sure he'd rather not have her know about it.

"Way to be a wingman, Adam." Dusk spoke, though his eyes remained on Layla.

Adam gave a laugh, clapping Dusk on the shoulder. "Sorry cousin, but you really should embrace that Royal power of yours someday. No matter who's watching. Excuse me, I see my mother giving me the eyeball."

Adam moved off, hailing someone that Layla couldn't see through the throng. Layla faced Dusk, about to ask him what Adam meant, when an elegantly tall man suddenly stepped over to them, and Layla realized it was the same bird-man who had smiled at her in the Hotel the first day she'd arrived.

At least eight feet tall, the bird-man was entirely naked, yet covered in iridescent cobalt down, sleek and glossy. Chained across his lean shoulders, a multi-hued robe of long, curling blue feathers with a high collar cascaded down his exquisitely lean frame, trailing behind him. His long, slender arms were hidden within the sleeves of the robe, but the front was left wide open and baring his unique nakedness, scintillating golden beadwork edging the robe's long lapels. Raising a sky-blue crest of feathers, the bird-man's lips twisted into a smile as he approached, his golden eyes piercing Layla with extreme cunning. In her mind, she heard the call of a thousand birds, and Dusk gave a gracious bow of deference as the man arrived.

"King Falliro Arini of the Phoenix of Italy and Spain," Dusk spoke, deeply reverent but also with a pleased smile as he straightened. "Well met."

"Dusk Arlohaim, First of the Crystal Dragons of Egypt. Well-met, indeed." The man nodded his head elegantly, speaking in a melodious, low voice before his gaze pierced Layla. "That was an impressive display earlier, dear heart."

"King Falliro." Dusk cleared his throat as he turned to Layla with an elegant gesture. "May I present Ms. Layla Price, Royal Dragon Bind of the Desert Dragons of Morocco and the Mediterranean."

"Astonishing, truly." The feathered man bowed low to Layla before she could do so to him, and she blinked, realizing the honor he did her. Making no move to touch her, King Falliro Arini straightened, his golden eyes piercing her to her core; weighing her with exceptional cunning. She had a feeling of centuries from him, as if he was actually the most ancient person in the hall tonight, even including the Storm Queen. As she watched him he gave a subtle smile, his golden eyes piercing but also calm. "When I saw you before in the Hotel's hall on the day of your arrival, Ms. Price, I felt your call like a Siren in my mind. And now that I face you again, I feel it no less. The power to call a King to do your bidding… it is no small thing, Dragon Bind."

"I'm sorry?" Layla found herself stymied, having not known her magic had reached out to King Arini when she'd seen him before in the Hotel. It was a problem, she realized, that she didn't know when her Dragon was reaching out. Layla shifted, uncomfortable, and the Phoenix King saw it. He gave a genial laugh, his bright eyes flashing humor.

"No apology is necessary," he murmured in his low birdsong voice. "Like us all, you will learn your power eventually. Until then, know that you have an invitation among the Phoenix – to come to my Aviary in Manarola, Italy and visit with me personally. I would love to learn of your human life. It is not every day that we encounter a Dragon raised without magic. I find it… intriguing. Be well, Ms. Price, enjoy the party. And consider my offer. Should you wish to accept, merely bring this with you to Manarola, and you will be guided to me."

Plucking a downy cobalt feather from over his heart, the Phoenix King placed it in Layla's palm. His hands were warm as he curled his long, black-taloned fingers around hers, closing her hand upon his gift. With that, he departed, giving a genteel nod to Dusk. Layla found herself confused, having no clue what the interaction had meant.

"What was that?" She turned to Dusk.

Dusk frowned, a strange look upon his face as he watched King Arini go, then stared at the downy feather in her palm. "You just received a personal invitation from King Falliro Arini to visit his Aviary in Manarola."

"So?"

"So," Dusk turned to her with astonishment in his gaze. "King Falliro is exceptionally private, Layla. Few outsiders get an invitation to his personal Aviary, his fortress stronghold and the central hub of the Phoenix. I'd keep that feather safe if I were you. It is a rare gift. Not one that even Adrian's been offered, and he and King Falliro are close allies."

Glancing at her palm, Layla gazed at the cobalt feather. Other than an exceptional softness and a luminous, iridescent color, it seemed normal. But she tucked it in the cleavage of her gown, in with the silver knife for safekeeping. Dusk opened his mouth to say more, when suddenly a name was announced by the doors.

The one name Layla had been hoping to hear all night – and dreading.

"Adrian Rhakvir, Clan First of the Desert Dragons of Morocco and the Mediterranean, and Head of the Red Letter Hotel Paris!"

Adrian had been announced with no escort. Heat flooding her, Layla could already smell his cinnamon-jasmine scent as it eased through the hall. Stepping past a column, Adrian was glorious in a black smoking-jacket with midnight-blue silk lapels and cuffs. The silk gleamed as he entered the hall, his shirt collar undone with no tie – his stunning aqua eyes on fire with gold as they met Layla's.

One taste of him; one glance was all it took. Layla's Dragon roared in a surge of passion, spilling up through her body and hammering straight to Adrian. Moving forward with his hands in his pockets, Adrian was effortless grace and strength, his high cheekbones and short black hair complementing his lean frame, striking jaw, and bare collarbones. Across the distance, their magics careened to each other after being so long denied, searing like wind and sand as they twisted into a fiery coil. Layla felt something enormous ripple over her skin with a rake of talons and fangs as her magic twined deep into Adrian's, and his into hers. Like Adrian's Dragon coiled around her, Layla felt muscled heat slide over her skin, roping her and squeezing hard in their searing connection.

Devouring her to her core.

People backed away until an empty path connected Layla to Adrian. She could barely breathe; their magic was so thick as he approached. Thick like searing molasses, thick like a boa constrictor of heat and power coiling all around her. Burning her up though only a cinnamon-jasmine wind swirled around her. Curls of golden flame burst around Layla in a rippling wave, and she felt bare beneath Adrian's devastating aqua-gold gaze, like she was naked in the hall, wearing only his scales sliding over her skin.

Devouring her from head to heels – even though she was only being devoured by his eyes.

Moving close, Adrian did not touch her but placed himself a mere breath away. Layla was annihilated by his scent and the pounding of her heart as he leaned in, nuzzling his nose in her hair in a gesture both sweet and intimately possessive.

"You look beautiful in crimson," he breathed.

"Thank you," Layla breathed back, not trusting herself to say more as she trembled with molten energy. Roaring between them, their combined heat and fire was almost catastrophic, and exquisitely pleasurable. Curls of etheric golden fire flared in the air around her as Layla felt that intense muscled sensation again; like her Dragon and Adrian's were coiling through each other, winding into each other.

Mating magically – though their flesh had still been denied that same consummation.

As her heart hammered, Layla felt Adrian catch his breath by her neck. She felt him pause as that scalding sensation between their bodies intensified, twisting into a coil of searing desert heat and golden fire. And then with a sigh, Adrian fell into it; drawn by the power that bound them. Nuzzling his nose beneath her hair, he brushed his warm lips over her neck, pressing a soft kiss to her skin.

Making passion riot through Layla like a continent on fire, as her world burst into golden flame.

CHAPTER 8 – RISE

Layla's head whirled, her entire body alight with pain as she felt herself being whisked out of the hall in strong arms. Cries surrounded her, a hubbub as she was carried out of the party fast and into the blustery night. Something had happened, but she couldn't remember it. Inside her, her beast roared and roiled, insane. Cinnamon-jasmine wafted upon the air and her Dragon focused – rushing toward it again in a wave of blistering pain.

Layla screamed as her body arched, every limb roaring with fire as a rush of talons and burning scales tried to escape her flesh again. The pain was pure agony, like someone had poured molten gold through every vein and sinew. Vaguely, she felt herself laid upon a cold stone bench as her magics careened through her. Rain pattered her; heavy drops cooling her enough that her eyelashes fluttered and she saw Dusk's face.

"Layla! Layla, can you hear me?"

Cupping her neck in his hands, Dusk poured a bolstering vibration through her body like a sluice of clear water, augmenting the cooling sensation of the rain. But Layla couldn't answer him. Pain devoured her, consumed her from the inside out. She smelled jasmine, like the night had been washed with it as someone moved quickly to her side. Layla screamed as that scent triggered her; her Dragon suddenly clawing at her insides again, skewering her with its talons.

Fighting to get to Adrian.

Fighting to get out.

"Get back, Adrian! Can't you feel her Dragon's trying to rise to yours?!" She felt Dusk shove Adrian away, slamming up his crystal barrier between Adrian and Layla.

"Layla!" Adrian's growl was passionate with rage and hunger as she felt him surge toward her again, hammering his desert-wind energy against Dusk's barrier. At Adrian's surge, another seizure ripped through Layla and she screamed, every nerve alight with burning wind. Her eyelashes fluttered, her eyes rolling back. Coils roiled within her; fangs tore at her insides. Her body spasmed as her Dragon surged with muscled intent – trying to break through the confines of her body to reach Adrian, even as Dusk poured his soothing currents into her.

Layla felt her Dragon fight Dusk, swiping at the flow of crystalline water he poured through her. But he was relentless, and at last the beast inside her was swamped by it, though she continued to roil, hot coils with barbs turning over inside Layla's flesh. Layla felt her mind return as she gasped gratefully, tears squeezing from between her eyelids.

"Dusk!" She gasped, trembling. Her Dragon was still fighting Dusk's but losing, their battle too great to be controlled by the hamsa cuff at her wrist.

"I'm here. Shh, easy…" Dusk soothed, redoubling his efforts until Layla felt like a crystalline waterfall poured through her veins. Her Dragon gave up the fight at last, and Layla was able to gasp another breath, though it came out in sobs. The pain was still scorching, like a burn over every part of her skin and blistering deep inside her. As if someone had taken her nerves and set them on fire, her head reeled, her stomach clenched in knots so hard she thought she would vomit.

"What's happening?" She gasped.

"Your Dragon rose to Adrian's call," Dusk spoke softly, still pouring his wellspring-deep vibrations through her body. "It tried to shift you just now, a few times. I had to stop it. The Hotel doesn't allow new Dragons to shift on-site. Not in public at least…"

"What?" Layla didn't understand, only aware of the pain Dusk was gradually pushing back with his abilities.

"Layla, I'm so sorry." Adrian stood beside the stone bench, and had finally ceased throwing his energy at Dusk's barrier. He now stared at Layla as if he could finally see the agony she was in – the agony his kiss had caused her. He had control of himself, though Layla noticed Adam standing behind him, restraining Adrian by the arms from either touching Dusk's barrier or Layla. She could see Adrian's beautiful aqua-gold eyes; agony suffused him as his own Dragon still roiled inside, desperate to reach her. "I didn't know our beasts would react like this—"

"Bullshit!" Dusk growled at Adrian, still pouring his river-water through Layla. "You walked away from her, Adrian! After binding her Dragon to yours by magics that haven't been used in *centuries*! How *dare* you walk in here and pretend to care? You almost perpetrated her first shift – on Hotel grounds! You know what the Board would do to her if she shifted here, not to mention what the High Court would do to you both if they found out a Magna Dicta protector caused the first shift of his protectee in public! If I hadn't been here to stop it, her death would be on you, you fucking dick. Goddammit!"

Dusk's tirade fizzled out as he continued working on Layla. The next voice she heard was Adam's, an apple orchard smell rising around her in the night. "Adrian. Come on. Give them some space, cuz. Let Dusk do his thing."

Layla was more aware of her surroundings now as her body pulled back from excruciating agony to merely throbbing nightmare. She was in a secluded bower of willows behind the cathedral. Dusk sat on the bench with her, still pouring his cooling energy through her as rain pattered down, lightning flickering in the storm-clouds far above with low rolls of thunder. Adrian's swirling desert-heat was tortured beside her, regal and devastated though still held away by Dusk's barrier. Adam stood by Adrian, all the violet gone from his hunter-green eyes, his energy high like drinking hot cider under an October moon. Rikyava stood behind them, her violet eyes flinty as she murmured to a knot of Guards, ordering them to keep a perimeter.

Able to breathe at last, Layla finally pushed to sitting with Dusk's hand at her back to help her up. Her head reeled and she clutched his arm, a wave of nausea passing through her as she bit back bile. "Holy hell, Batman!"

"Layla, I'm so sorry. I truly didn't know my Dragon would try to raise yours." Adrian reached out as if to touch her, but Dusk slapped his hand away and Adam pulled Adrian back again in a firm grip. Adrian glared at them both, but his hand dropped rather than try to touch Layla again. His brows knit, Adrian watched her with a terrible darkness as the rain came down, his blue-green eyes intense.

"So… what…?" Layla spoke again, trying to get a grip on what had just happened. "I almost shifted into my Dragon? For real?"

"About five times. It's a miracle you didn't, really." Dusk spoke gravely as he moved one hand to Layla's upper chest, the other over her spine as she sat on the stone bench. Rain pattered down around them, fat wet drops that helped ease Layla's heat. She leaned back on Dusk's thighs, drinking in his cool vibrations as he stood behind her. Strong like the caverns of the earth, Dusk shifted his hands so one cupped her forehead, Layla's head falling back – exhausted now that the pain was rolling away.

"Why does it hurt so much?" Layla breathed, feeling exhausted to her bones.

"When we shift, our magic tries to spill out through our flesh to change us into our beast." It was Adam who answered her, his voice level as he watched her with a curious glint in his forest-green eyes. "Your Dragon literally re-made every molecule in your body, preparing for the shift. Neurotransmitters, blood chemistry, structural proteins. The change is painful, but when it's forced to halt, it's quadruply so. Dusk forced your shift to stop five times, and he's literally washing those chemicals out of your body with his vibrations right now. Be glad he's here. It's a unique talent of Crystal Dragon Royals that they can not only halt a shift, but also purify the body afterwards. Your sweat's gonna smell like hell for a few days, though. Expect fevers as you clear everything out."

"Could I have died from the shift?" Though her spine screamed in protestation, Layla gazed up at Dusk.

"No. But the Hotel Board of Owners would have killed you." Dusk's voice was an accusatory growl in the night – and he wasn't accusing Layla. "A public first shift for a Dragon is unlawful on Hotel grounds. Other shapeshifter Lineages like werewolves can shift for the first time and be contained by our Guard. Sometimes they get banned from the Hotel, but only until they have their magic under control. Dragons can't be contained when they have their first shift, Layla. The human mind is gone, replaced by the beast. As the largest and most powerful of the shape-shifting predators, we often do a lot of damage the first time we become our beast. Even if people don't die, it's Hotel policy to seize the person who shifted and *euthanize* them."

"Euthanize?" Layla's breath caught, grateful that Dusk had just saved her life. And probably a lot of lives if what he said was true about Dragons going ballistic the first time they changed.

Adrian had knelt next to Layla as Dusk spoke, his beautiful eyes obliterated. "Layla. I can't apologize enough for what just happened. Dragons aren't generally able to shift for years after their magic opens.

93

I had no idea you'd be capable of it so soon—"

"Our Bind sparked it?" Layla asked, opening her eyes and peering at him.

Adrian nodded, his gaze devastated. "The Bind I placed upon you through the hamsa-cuff sparked it when I kissed you. I'm so sorry."

"That's what you get for playing with ancient magics you don't understand, Adrian." Dusk's voice was murderous as he set a hand gently to Layla's throat, his other hand sliding down her back beneath her gown. It wasn't erotic, merely soothing as he poured his cleansing vibrations through the glass-ground pain in her spine. "You're playing with Layla's life, dickhead."

"Easy, Dusk, come on. No one got hurt." Adam's voice was mild beside Adrian.

"Only because I was standing *right* next to Layla when fuckboy here kissed her. And we were inside the crystal cathedral." Dusk growled back, his sapphire gaze piercing upon Adrian as rain cascaded down his face. He didn't palm it away, keeping his hands on Layla.

"I already told you I'm sorry! What do you want from me, Dusk?!" Adrian raked a hand through his wet hair, rising with a searing wind as he squared off with Dusk in the driving rain. Dusk merely stared at him with a dark gaze, his hands not leaving Layla. Layla felt Adrian's energy riot up ten notches until the willows whipped with his power in the rain. Adrian's power hammered Dusk's barrier, and Layla felt a strain in Dusk's energies as he gave a low, thundering growl back. The bench shuddered, the ground around the bower heaved with an earthquake as Dusk's ministrations through Layla paused – all that energy thrust now at Adrian.

"Adrian! Dusk! That's enough!" Rikyava's voice was a harsh bark as she stepped between the two men with her hands gripped into talons, a brimstone battle energy rising from her as her eyes burned a bloody crimson in the darkness and rain. Layla blinked to see that Rikyava actually *had* manifested talons – enormous black-tipped crimson talons like knives. She wore no rapier with her ballgown, but Layla felt how cruel those appendages were. A hot iron scent whipped through the bower as Rikyava flexed those hands – one at Dusk, the other at Adrian.

"Whoa, kids!" Adam's energy suffused the bower with apple-sweet vapors, spreading out in an arc between Adrian's viciousness and the last of Dusk's barrier, blocking Dusk and Layla from Adrian's fury and Rikyava's. "Let's give the magic a break and settle this like people, huh?"

With a growl, Adrian held up his hands in submission, though his gaze still simmered a vibrant gold in the night. His wind ceased to whip, and Layla felt Adam's smooth energy pull back also. Dusk's rumblings were the only power still heaving through the bower, and Rikyava gave Dusk an eyeball until his shuddering quake ceased. Though the Guardswoman remained ready in her sodden evening gown – her hands cruelly taloned – as the tense energy between the two brothers finally settled.

Exhaustion swamped Layla suddenly. As if all the tension in the air had sapped energy from every part of her, a deep urge to sleep devoured her. She wanted nothing more than to curl up in a warm little nest somewhere and let oblivion take her. Turning, she cuddled back into Dusk and he sat, wrapping her in his arms with his smooth lips at her temple. Cradling her in the rain, he resumed pouring his clear vibrations through her aching bones as she cuddled further into him, breathing deep of his clear scent.

Staring down at her, watching her cuddle into Dusk and practically fall asleep in the rain, the fight went out of Adrian. As if he could feel Layla's exhaustion, he sank to one knee on the sodden flagstones, reaching out, his eyes bled from molten gold back to a deep Mediterranean aqua. His handsome face was so beautiful in the rain, his eyes so vibrant, that the sight of him made Layla's heart hurt. Their fingers touched and though heat stirred in Layla, it wasn't the same energy as before. As if Adrian was controlling his own passions with exquisite care or she was simply too exhausted, Layla barely felt her Dragon stir to his touch now.

"Layla, I'm so sorry." Adrian cradled her hand, annihilation in his eyes.

"Where were you these past weeks?" Layla breathed, hating him and loving him at the same time. She hated that he had this effect upon her. But she loved his simmering energy caressing her like a breath of wind and fire in the rain.

"I had business that couldn't wait." He murmured, aching with tenderness in his aqua eyes. "If I could have stayed these past weeks, I would have. Please believe me…"

"Are you ever going to stick around, Adrian?" Layla spoke softly, angry tears stinging her eyes now. They shed down her cheeks as she blinked, too exhausted to hold them in. She didn't care. As if all the spitfire had been ripped out of her, she just felt tired. Tired of loving Adrian Rhakvir and getting nothing in return.

Something dark opened up deep inside Layla with that thought, like a black pit. She closed her eyes, turning her face into Dusk's warm shoulder.

"Layla, please…" Adrian reached out, caressing her cheek.

"Just…don't. Don't touch me. Don't talk to me. Just go away."

Layla kept her eyes closed so she wouldn't see him, wouldn't break to his beautiful devastation. Adrian did as she asked, pulling his warm touch from her skin and leaving her bereft. A hard breath rasped Layla's throat as her Dragon screamed inside her – because they both knew Adrian was supposed to be theirs. Layla could feel their Bind like a golden rope, twining through the coils of her Dragon, looped around her limbs and neck; a pleasure that should have been blissful and made them whole.

But it hadn't – because Adrian kept walking away from it.

A chill sensation swept Layla, leaving her cold in the rain as her heart darkened.

"We need to get her back to her room, she's too chilly."

Dusk was scooping Layla up in his arms. She didn't resist, too tired and heartbroken. Cradled close to his strong body, Layla felt herself whisked back along the path through the sodden night, leaving the others behind. Turning her face into Dusk's shoulder, she felt like it was only moments until she was back inside her apartment, though in some ways it felt like years.

Chills had set in, and Layla shivered as Dusk helped her undress from her sodden gown without a single quip of innuendo. Swaddling her in her royal blue silk robe, he tucked her into bed then slid in next to her, cradling her close to his body – soothing her with heat and kindness.

Layla was grateful Dusk was the only one with her tonight. She let her tears fall quietly as he lay with her, cradling her back into his body with a hand on her chest and one wrapped around her middle, pouring his soothing vibrations through her in the endless night.

CHAPTER 9 – PHOENIX

Layla woke to grey, heavy clouds beyond the windows of her apartment. Dusk wasn't with her anymore, but Rikyava sat in a chair at her bedside, the Blood Dragon back in her regular crimson Guard attire. Her 1800's uniform bristled with daggers in her weapons harness, a rapier at her hip as she sat with one black boot crossed over her knee. A fire blazed in the hearth and someone had found Layla's dappled stuffed horse she'd kept since childhood and tucked it under her arm while she was out – probably Dusk. Layla cuddled it, feeling disoriented like she'd been having fever-dreams, though she couldn't remember them.

Rikyava stirred, gazing at the bed. A smile lit her violet eyes as she sat forward, reaching out to pour a glass of water from a copper pitcher upon the bedstand. "Hey, girl. Good to see you finally came out of it."

"Came out of what?" Layla's eyes were gluey as she pushed to sitting and accepted the glass. Drinking gratefully, her parched mouth was relieved as she finished and set the glass aside. "I remember having a fever."

"Fevers are part of shift-stasis," Rikyava spoke with her Guardswoman no-nonsense, giving Layla the lowdown. "Anytime we shift into our Dragon and shift back, we need down time while the body re-adjusts to being human again. It's like if you get wounded and have to rest while your body grows new tissue. Technically, you didn't shift three nights ago at the Dragon party, but your body went through a similar kind of hell."

"Wait… *three* nights ago?" Layla blinked, staring at her friend. "I've been out for three whole days?"

"Wakey, wakey, Sleeping Beauty," Rikyava teased. "But sleeping a lot during shift-stasis does keep us Dragons lookin' hot and young through the centuries, so you got that going for you now."

"Shit. But I was supposed to be on the Concierge desk yesterday!" Layla protested.

"Don't fret. Dusk changed the schedule. You're off for three more days. Your body's going to feel like hell for a while, even with everything he did to help. There's some chicken soup on the table, you want?"

"Yeah, I'm pretty hungry actually." Layla realized, as her stomach rumbled for food.

"Coming right up." Rikyava motioned for Layla to stay in bed as she rose, striding to the breakfast table and ladling out a bowl of soup from a ceramic crock. Putting it on a silver tray with a bowl of oyster crackers, she returned, setting the tray on the duvet over Layla's knees.

"Want me to feed you, sweetie?" Rikyava teased in a motherly voice.

"As if." Layla grinned then took up the spoon, scattering a handful of oyster crackers in the soup. The chicken soup was rich and hearty, thick with flavorful oils and vegetables. It immediately lifted her spirits, ease flowing through her tired muscles as she ate. "What's in this soup? Crack?" She joked lightly, feeling better.

Rikyava gave a laugh as she went to the table and poured two coffees from a French press, then mixed in cream and returned, handing one to Layla. Layla took the mug and sipped gratefully as Rikyava spoke, her fatigue rolling back more.

"Nah, my friend Justin in Catering just worked his usual wonders.

99

But when I was having him bring everything up, Rake André waylaid us in the hall. He breathed a little of his magic in the soup. Says they've missed you at yoga, and to heal up fast. I think he's got a crush on you, Layla Price."

Layla smiled, recognizing the yoga instructor and Head Bartender Rake André's signature calming energy in the vapors of the soup now. As if the power of the *Om* could be made manifest as scent and taste, Rake's magic was able to charm any food or drink. Layla felt his soothing, uplifting sensations pour through her with every bite, and a feeling of gratefulness swamped her.

"Rake's really thoughtful."

"He is." Rikyava smiled, stretching her boots out and leaning back on her elbows upon the bed. "You've had other visitors. Dusk's been in and out, checking on you. The Madame stopped by last night and also Reginald, to see how you were. Sylvania's been busy with Assignations, but says she'll say hi today."

A tender feeling moved through Layla, that so many people had been worried about her. "Wow. I never thought I'd be so missed."

"You've made an impression here, Layla. People like you at the Hotel." Rikyava chuckled. "And... you had another visitor this morning. One who was *very* sad you'd not woken up yet."

"Adrian?" Layla frowned, noting that Rikyava hadn't mentioned him coming to visit her.

"Not that sexy cousin. The other one." A twist of humor graced Rikyava's lips.

"Fuck! Adam." Layla suddenly realized she had missed their dinner appointment two nights ago, where Adam was going to answer her questions about the Desert Dragon clan. She fell back against the pillows with a curse.

"Don't worry," Rikyava chuckled, re-crossing her boots, teasing rampant in her frank lavender gaze. "Adam knows about your condition. He's happy to reschedule anytime. Though you should have seen his face two nights ago when I told him you were still unconscious and wouldn't be coming to dinner. Priceless. Kinda seems like he was hoping to get in your pants."

"I'm not hopping into bed with Adam, Rikyava." Layla snorted, having another bite of soup. "He's a jackass."

"Don't I know it," Rikyava teased back, her gaze sly. "But you have to admit, that orchard-sweet energy of his is pretty charming."

"I think Adrian would have my head, or Adam's, if that ever happened." But Layla frowned, wondering again why Adrian hadn't come to visit while she was out.

"So?" Rikyava slapped the bed as a scent of scorch lifted in the air around her suddenly. "Fuck Adrian! After that stunt he pulled three nights ago, you're well within your rights to tell him to go fuck himself, Layla. Almost causing you to shift for the first time on Hotel grounds? That's bad news. He's a Royal, he's supposed to have better control of his magic than that. But the moment he saw you in the hall, his energy went roaring out to you. And when he kissed you it was a hundred times that. He basically poured his magic into your body through that damn Bind you two have."

"I don't remember it," Layla tried to push herself back through those memories, but found only blackness. "What happened?"

"You collapsed." Rikyava's gaze was intense, something dark and worried in it now. "Adrian's magic hit you so hard when he kissed you, that you went down in seizures. It was only by Dusk's fast action that you weren't seriously injured, or shifted. Your skin was rippling with light – a pre-shift aura. You were lucky Dusk was standing right beside you when it happened and that crystal is his channeling medium. He took all his power and rang that fucking cathedral like a bell, hammering your magics back inside your body. Dusk acted quickly, but Adrian was stupid. I wouldn't be surprised if Adrian gets canned by the Board of Owners if they hear of it. Unfortunately, the shiftee tends to get blamed in situations like this, even if it's triggered by someone else. Like I said, you were lucky."

"Dusk really did save my life, didn't he?" Layla sat back upon the pillows, her brows knit as a deeper realization of the danger sank in. "He wasn't just mad when he blew up at Adrian as I was recovering. He was afraid. Terrified that he might not have been able to stop my shift and that I'd be a goner by now. So he was justified in how pissed he was at Adrian for triggering it."

"He really was." Rikyava's gaze was sober. She was about to say something else, when a soft knock came at the door.

"I'll get it." Rikyava rose, moving to the door and opening it with one hand on her rapier. Layla couldn't see who it was, but Rikyava startled. A low voice issued through the open doorway, susurrating with the song of a thousand birds, and Layla came instantly alert. She already knew who it was when Rikyava made a motion for the man to wait, then closed the door, returning to Layla with astonishment on her face.

"Layla! King Falliro Arini of the Phoenix has come to pay his respects."

"Should I see him?" Layla blinked, stunned that the King of anything would come to her room to inquire about her health.

"I mean, technically you're not well, so you could send him away, but he is the Phoenix King." Rikyava cocked her head, her blonde brows knitting. "You'd be within your rights to refuse to see him, but… King Falliro is exceptionally choosy with those he befriends. His visit is pretty unprecedented."

"Then I guess I should see him." Layla tried to swing her legs out of bed to stand, but was immediately swamped by pain surging through her spine. She gasped, her breath catching as Rikyava gave her a tough-love smile and waved her back into bed.

"It's ok. He's a shapeshifter. He'll understand. Just sit tight and look adorable in your robe and I'll show him in."

"Is my hair ok?" Layla fretted suddenly, worried that she looked like hell from her convalescence and that it might be a bad way to receive a King.

"Comb twice with your fingers, and then you're all good." Rikyava winked, then went to the door.

Layla hastily combed her fingers through her loose curls, getting the snarls out enough that she could brush her long hair over her shoulder, then set her breakfast tray aside upon the bed. Rikyava opened the door and stepped back with a crisp bow, admitting the Phoenix King into the room. Tall and slender, he wasn't gloriously naked with his gaping feather-robe today but instead was clad in an embroidered robe of midnight-blue silk, woven soft and thick, that covered him fully. The high collar framed his elegant neck, the draping sleeves and long hem reminding Layla of a classic North African men's caftan, though it was fit slender at the torso and more flared below.

With airy grace, King Falliro moved into the room on his high-arched bare feet, nodding to Rikyava as she closed the door behind him. She moved off, settling in a chair near the fireplace well out of earshot, though she watched their interaction attentively like a bodyguard. King Falliro moved to Layla's bedside, not sitting but clasping his black-taloned hands and gazing at her. Raising his bright blue crest of feathers, King Falliro's pale yellow lips eased into a smile as his golden eyes swept Layla. The cobalt down over his face and longer glossy feathers at his temples and cheekbones were similar to Dusk's Dragon-scale pattern, though a lighter shade. In her mind, Layla heard the call of birds again, though she had a sense King Falliro wasn't using his active magics – what she felt from him was merely a product of his strange otherness.

"Ms. Price," King Falliro Arini breathed, the sound of a thousand birds in his hushed, singsong voice. "You are looking very much better than I might have thought. May I sit?"

He gestured elegantly at the bed with one taloned hand, and Layla nodded. "Sure."

As he sank to a seat, turning so he could face Layla where she rested against the pillows, he set a taloned hand lightly to her leg. A sweet energy like a whispering wind filled with birds chorused through her and Layla took a deep breath. It was calm and elevating, and when she opened her eyes she felt a gentle joy surging through her from the Phoenix King's magic. He smiled, his cheeks crinkling up until she could see lines at the corners of his eyes beneath his cobalt down, the only thing that belied his age.

"Better?"

"Yes, thank you." Layla breathed, astounded at the Phoenix King's amazing energy.

"Good." He spoke, watching Layla with his strange all-gold eyes. "Though you are unwell and I have come to pay my respects for your illness, I have also come today on a more political matter, Ms. Price. If you would hear me out?"

"Political?" Layla raised her brows. She saw Rikyava tense in her chair by the fireplace, as if she could hear the conversation, but Layla didn't mind if the Guardswoman was listening. Layla glanced back to King Falliro. "I'll hear what you have to say, but what do you mean?"

"Good." His eyes crinkled up again in that wizened, amazing smile, before they sobered. "I have come to speak with you today because I believe you are in danger, Ms. Price. I have not lived three thousand years as King of my Lineage without learning a few things, and from what I felt three nights ago at the Dragon party, I believe that danger lurks in this Hotel. And it is revolving around you."

"You're three *thousand* years old?" Layla blinked, befuddled. "And what do you mean, danger?"

"Phoenix can regenerate in ash and flame when we die." He gave a gentle smile. "I have had nearly a dozen bodies. If you ever wonder how old a Phoenix truly is, gaze upon the color of their plumage. The oldest have feathers of dark violet, midnight blue, and black, the youngest are white and gold with reds and oranges. Our plumage shows our wisdom-age, not the age of our current body."

Layla swallowed, unnerved that she sat before a three thousand year old being. She couldn't even comprehend that much time. Falliro Arini had been a king of his people when Egypt was still in its golden age. "And you feel I'm in danger?"

"Yes." He gave a nod, watching her with his piercing eagle-eyes. "All Phoenix have a talent for reading the currents of the air, Ms. Price, much like a Crystal Dragon can read the vibrations of the earth. With it comes an ability to read magical scent. Every Lineage of the Twilight Realm gives off a magical scent, like a fingerprint. I walk in a constant flow of scent-currents, breathing around me as they move. And sometimes, I feel a void in the air."

"A void?" Layla's brows knit, not understanding. "What do you mean?"

"I mean," King Falliro smoothed one hand over the duvet, rippling his black talons across it, "that sometimes I feel a hole in all that motion. As if a black void suddenly swallowed all the scents of the wild leaving nothing but emptiness, a place where all the energy stops. Where all the scent and flow on the wind just dies. And in that place, I feel a Royal Dragon *shift visage*, before they manifest again as someone new."

"A Royal Dragon who can take on other faces and bodies?" Layla sat up straight, very interested now but still confused. "You mean Adrian?"

"Not Adrian; he is far too young." The Phoenix King shook his head, his feathered blue crest rising. "What I am describing is a far older phenomenon than your young drake. A phenomenon I have felt since my very first lifetime. And where it manifests... death follows."

"So you're saying it's a Royal Dragon with visage-shifting abilities that you feel when you sense this void – and that it's over three thousand years old? And what, it's here in the Hotel, stalking me?"

"Precisely." King Falliro's golden gaze pierced Layla, cunning and very sober. "Ever since I arrived four days ago, I have felt it lurking about the Hotel. I catch a moment of the void somewhere in the Hotel and the next moment it is gone. I am unable to pinpoint its whereabouts; it comes and goes very suddenly as the Royal Dragon shifts its appearance. But it was present at the party. I felt it open right near you at one point, and though I turned my head quickly, you were surrounded by a throng, so the person's exact location was hidden from me. But it has walked your hallway, Layla Price. It has stalked you these past three days while you were recovering. And where this ancient thing goes – misfortune happens."

"How do you know it so well?" Layla breathed, a dark fear sweeping through her and chilling her to her core. "How do you know that misfortune follows it?"

"Because like you, Ms. Price, I have the ability of a Royal Dragon Bind." King Falliro's demeanor was level, his presence utterly frank. "Or I once did, before I killed that body and re-birthed myself in ash and flame to be rid of the void-shadow creature that hunted me down night and day. And caused ruin wherever it went."

CHAPTER 10 – SOLACE

Layla gaped at the Phoenix King Falliro Arini, knowing her mouth had fallen open; unable to close it. He had just professed to being a Royal Dragon Bind – in one of his past bodies, at least. As they watched each other, him sitting on her bed and Layla still propped up against the pillows, she suddenly realized why the Phoenix King had made a point to meet her at the Dragon party and had come here to her apartment now. He understood what Layla was going through. He understood the dangers and risks of what she was.

Because he had been one also.

"You were a Bind?"

"I was." King Falliro nodded serenely, though his golden gaze was still piercing upon Layla. "Every time I regenerate, I have Royal Phoenix magic in one variation or another. But once, two thousand years ago, I regenerated into a new body that had very unique abilities. It happens sometimes as Phoenix magic matures, that our bodies do not have quite the same skills from life to life. And in that particular body, I acquired Bind magic. It was strong, highly unpredictable, and I made myself a fortress off the coast of Manarola at that time, to keep my magics from roaring out and binding all the strongest Dragons around me against their will."

"Your Aviary."

"Quite so." He nodded his crested head with elegant precision. "It has been my stronghold ever since, but at that time, it was a refuge. A place I could go with my most trusted, to hone and experiment with my

Bind powers. For, as you have been told already, a Bind's magic develops from their experiences in life, and the flavor of their heart."

"So you retreated there so your magic wouldn't reach out and bind other Dragons?" Layla queried, fascinated.

"Indeed." King Falliro's gaze was intent upon her. "I have always enjoyed my freedom as a person, and my privacy, and both were severely challenged by having Bind magic. As you are experiencing already, it calls to others, reaching out to Bind strong Dragons long before either you or them realize it consciously. With the wrong people... such a bond can be disastrous."

"Which was why you created your Aviary."

"It was a place of solace." He nodded with a secret smile. "A place I could go, already fortified with some of the strongest hiding-magics known in the entire Twilight Realm, a place used by others long before I discovered it. But when I found that it could stop my bind-magics from reaching out and bringing unwanted mates to my door, I disappeared for a while from my duties as King, entrusting the Lineage to one of my most accomplished Firsts at that time."

"But you had to come out of hiding eventually," Layla guessed.

"Eventually. But before that happened, I began to sense the *void-shadow* following me. I was still in hiding at that time, untraceable even by the strongest trackers of the Intercessoria, but the void-shadow had somehow found me when all others failed. It surfaced in the streets of the village on the coast – and people died. It surfaced inside my stronghold, and a terrible case of betrayal took my dearest beloved and ten of my most loyal servants. It followed me when the Phoenix were summoned to war against the Seven Giants, when I came out of hiding to lead one of the most difficult campaigns of my battle career."

"What happened?" Layla asked, riveted even though a terrible, dark sensation of fear had opened up inside her.

"Where the void-shadow went, slaughter followed." King Arini eyed her pointedly. "I could not escape this predator, for it tracked me everywhere. And so I took my own life, regenerating in fire in the hopes that the next body would not have Bind magic. It didn't. I have been safe from the void-shadow ever since, though I have felt it watch me from time to time, especially when I regenerate in a new body. And now I feel it here, stalking you like a hunter in the darkness. Out beyond where you can feel it or reach with your very young abilities."

"What are you saying?" Layla breathed, horrified. "That I should kill myself?"

"No!" King Falliro gave a soft smile. Reaching out, his black-taloned hand clutched Layla's reassuringly. "I am merely offering you wisdom, and a warning. You are a bright breath of air through my lungs, Ms. Price, and from the moment I saw you, I felt deep goodness in you. Scorch you may have within your scent, but there is also the brightness of citrus. Citrus is a happy scent; a flavor that brings joy. I would not see that joy darkened by the hunting of this void-shadow."

"Did you ever discover a way to track it? To find this Royal Dragon?" Layla asked, needing to know. Something dark moved through her, knowing this thing was on her trail now, and her Dragon coiled up tight inside her; afraid.

"I did not. For how do you track a nothing? Like a devouring maw in my mind, I feel it only when it is close by, and it is gone so quickly it is impossible to locate."

Rising with a sad smile, King Falliro moved from the bed. Layla frowned as he went to her side-bar. She thought he was going to pour them both drinks, but instead the Phoenix King lifted up the crystal decanter of bourbon, easing his fingers underneath and retrieving something from under the bottle. Layla blinked to see it was the cobalt feather he had given her at the party three nights ago – that Dusk had hidden it under her bourbon, the one place she was certain to find it since he couldn't access her wall-safe.

Moving back to the bed, King Falliro set the feather in Layla's palm, closing her fingers around it. He gave a soft smile, gazing down upon her. "Come to me when you wish, at my Aviary in Manarola. And I will tell you everything about my life with Bind magic. And we will sing songs of woe and joy until dawn."

With those strange, archaic words, he departed, easing through the door and closing it softly behind himself. A last twitter of birdsong left with him, and Layla realized it had been in the air the entire time, as if she'd stood in a high-morning forest after a sweet rain. Her body felt strange now, jangled with the departure of the Phoenix King's calming presence. Layla closed her hand on his feather, feeling a small hum of birdsong echo through her. Reclining back upon the pillows, she stared out the windows as Rikyava rose from her chair.

"Holy shit." Rikyava breathed as she neared, settling to a seat at Layla's bedside. From her wide lavender eyes and alert posture, Layla was certain the Guardswoman had heard the entire conversation. "Are you ok?"

"I don't even know how to begin answering that." Layla blinked, focusing on Rikyava. "Is this something you know about? This *void-shadow*?"

"No." Rikyava shook her head, her blonde brows scowling. "And that's a *very* big problem for Hotel security. If we have a Royal Dragon among us who is able to shift its visage so completely that we can't even pick it up with our security systems... damn. I'll need to speak to Dusk about that. He monitors the Orb of Cephalus for the Hotel."

"The what?" Layla's brows knit, not understanding.

"The big bad backup security system that can pick up on shadowy shit." Rikyava gave her a wry smile. "Crystal Dragon-made. Not something you need to be concerned about. But believe me, I am going to look into this, deeply. If something is stalking you – maybe a ridiculously strong visage-shifting Royal Dragon, maybe a member of some ancient Lineage that's not even on the books anywhere – then the Hotel has a very big problem. The safety of everyone at this establishment, including you, is my job and Dusk's. And King Falliro's words have me worried that something bad might happen if we can't find this void-shadow. Soon."

"Bad like my Dragon almost rising in the middle of a party bad?" Layla breathed.

"That was entirely Adrian's fault." Rikyava gave her a look with sympathy in it. "But I wonder… who told Adrian about your cuff? Who told him about the Hamsa Bind, the only artifact that could bind a Bind, and where to find it? Adrian's clearly not mature enough to handle the way it coiled you two together. And you don't know anything about your own magics yet… it's practically a recipe for disaster, if you both can't learn your shit, fast."

"What do you mean?" Layla's heart thudded in her chest. Even thinking of Adrian brought a memory of his searing aqua eyes to her mind. Her skin was suddenly crawling with the desire to see him again, to feel his touch. A bourbon-orange scent rose around her and Rikyava raised a blonde eyebrow.

"I mean *that*." Rikyava nodded to the air pointedly. "You're flaring with magic just thinking about Adrian. And clearly he's got no equilibrium around you. You have to understand, Layla. Adrian is a renegade, he plays by his own rules, but he still has them. He's not only powerful, he's also *calculating*. Adrian does nothing without a motive, and a damn good one, even though nobody can generally predict his wild chess-moves. He's like a grandmaster savant at playing the game of power, Layla, which is why he's risen so high so fast in a number of

111

dangerous games."

"I feel like I've seen that side of Adrian," Layla murmured, "but he seems so… rash and passionate around me that people tell me these things about him and I don't believe them."

"That's because he's behaving differently since your Bind happened." Rikyava lifted a blonde eyebrow, her face serious. "I've never seen Adrian lose his shit so fast as he did at the party, and I'm certain it's because of the Bind. There wasn't anyone home for a moment in Adrian's eyes as Dusk separated you both and whisked you from the hall. I wasn't just afraid you'd shift – but that Adrian was going to, and that he'd wreck ruin trying to get to you. Fortunately, Adam was there. He has a way with Adrian. It's one of the reasons Adam's Clan Second. Because when Adrian goes death-metal sandstorm, Adam can play pastoral pan-pipes in his ear."

"Pastoral pan-pipes." Layla's lips quirked, glad for Rikyava's humor. It helped ease the situation, and she sat back on the pillows, feeling tired. "Fuck. What am I going to do?"

"Heal first. We'll figure everything else out later." Rikyava gave the duvet a swift pat, then rose. "I need to go find Dusk and tell him about this new development. I'm sure he'll want to question King Falliro personally about this void-shadow. You ok sitting tight? I've got six guards on your door. Anything happens in here, you just shout and they'll be in fast."

"Sure. Go do your thing." Layla smiled. "And thanks for being here."

"No problem. You – eat." Reaching out, Rikyava thunked Layla's soup-tray back over her knees, then gave a big smile and departed, whisking out through the doors and opening them wide enough that Layla could see Guards upon the other side. It made her feel better as Rikyava left. But as Layla spooned up Rake's soup again, she found herself wishing Adrian was there with her. Even though his magic had made her flare, she suddenly wanted his arms around her, his warm heat against her back, holding her through all this uncertainty. But even as she sighed, feeling a dark hole open in her chest, another knock came at the door. Layla set the tray aside but didn't rise, not caring anymore if someone saw her looking weak.

"Who is it?"

"Sylvania, dear," a lovely silver alto voice breathed through the door.

"And Rake." A man's calm tenor followed the Head Courtesan's, and Layla recognized it.

"Come in."

They pushed in through the door, a duo of excellent and intriguing grace. Sylvania Eroganis, Head Courtesan of the Hotel, was willowy and tall, her pale skin luminous with moonlight as she swept forward. Her unbound white-silver locks were smooth as a river at midnight, her high-collared robe made of a white diaphanous material that showed far more of Sylvania's willowy body than it obscured. Her lovely breasts were pierced with strings of pearls that trickled like waterfalls from her nipples, the same pierced through her abdomen and down to her groin, scintillating and decadent.

Rake André could have passed for human, even though he was ridiculously good-looking. Tall and built in a yoga-fit way, he wore a long-sleeved emerald silk shirt with crossover toggles and high Tibetan collar. His pants were tan rough silk, his usual attire for yoga class rather than the crisp waistcoat he wore bartending. His ash-blond hair was short, a blond stubble on his defined chin. His calm green eyes shone with gentleness as the duo came to Layla's bed, one on either side.

"Poor dear! Such fatigue runs through you!" Sylvania crooned as she came close. Lifting the duvet and sheet, she slid beneath the covers, reclining and pressing her sensual body close to Layla's. Before she knew it, Layla found herself pulled back against the Head Courtesan, her blue robe being shed by Sylvania's elegant hands as Sylvania's robe also disappeared – Layla's bare back suddenly pressed against the Head Courtesan's amazingly warm and luscious front.

"Um, what's happening?" Layla blinked as Sylvania's arms came around her, cradling her close. But then a soothing balm of light began pouring through Layla from all her skin contact with the Head Courtesan, and she relaxed. She found herself staring up at Rake André like an idiot as he moved in with a chuckle, taking her tray off the bed, then stripping off his shirt and baring his amazingly cut body as he slid under the covers also. Gathering her close from the front, Rake slid a hand over her bare hip, and Layla's breath caught as he eased in close – his warm exhalation and sweet lips a mere breath away.

Silver light curled through Layla's body from Sylvania. And gazing up at Rake, snuggled in so close their hips touched, Layla found herself fascinated by the golden color of his stubble. She had never been this up close and personal with Rake, and she suddenly had the urge to touch him. Sliding out a hand, she stroked his impossibly soft stubble. It was as smooth as it looked and Rake chuckled, stroking back Layla's bed-tousled curls with a kind smile in return.

"So… what are we doing?" Layla asked again, her mind not quite working anymore as the sexy, luminous duo snuggled in close with her.

"Sylvania and I wanted to come help you feel better," Rake murmured, his tenor voice gentle. "But Rikyava said we couldn't until you woke up. We heard you were awake. So we're here."

"What? I mean, that's nice…" Sylvania's ethereal light was pouring through Layla from their skin contact, making her feel like she danced upon fairy dust now, calm and blissful.

Rake stroked her cheek with his knuckles, his calm green eyes knowing. "Just breathe, Layla. Close your eyes and breathe like we do in yoga class. Let Sylvania and I do the rest."

"Ok." Layla didn't know what else to say. She could already feel Rake's sweet energy breathing out from his parted lips, curling in through hers as they breathed together. Once she noticed it, their breaths were suddenly in synch, slow and deep with Sylvania's silvery bliss pouring through Layla's sinews also.

As Rake exhaled, Layla inhaled, taking his out-breath and letting it wash over her tongue and down her throat, deep in to her lungs. Normally, she got claustrophobic breathing someone else's exhalation, but Rake's breath was sweetened like dawn over the Himalayas, fresh and cool. Spreading out inside her in wave after wave of peaceful ecstasy, Layla made a sound of enjoyment as Rake's breath synched to Sylvania's luminous surges. Layla let their combined ministrations sweep her – taking her away from her tired, painful body as they sweetened her in slow waves of delight.

Layla drifted, caught in their magics. She didn't know how far she drifted, but in her blissful trance, she began seeing visions. A Moroccan palace of blue tiles; a fountain-courtyard with potted palms and a kitchen with good scents of spiced meats, citrus, and honey. Adrian's face. Sitting on his bed up in his Moroccan-styled apartment on the fourth floor of the Hotel, he thumbed through texts on his phone when his head suddenly lifted. He inhaled, his aqua eyes piercing her – as if he could see her also. Her heart beat hard as he looked right at her and whispered, *Layla?*

But a surge from Sylvania and Rake pushed the vision away. Layla drifted, luminous and fuzzy. She didn't feel fatigued or painful anymore, only a blissful languor as Rake's hand slipped up her hip and he closed the distance to her lips, kissing her gentle and sweet. As they

115

kissed, he pulled her close, his silk-clad hips flush with hers. She could feel his arousal, but she also knew as he stroked her hip with his fingertips, that passion didn't drive Rake André. He kissed Layla sweetly, opening her mouth with his tongue and exhaling his next breath gently down her throat. Layla sighed, swept away in pleasure – her Dragon rolling over with a contented smile, letting his energy play within her like sunlight.

And it was play, that moved the three of them upon the sweet tides of the morning. Layla found herself undulating in a quiet passion as Rake kissed her, pleasurable and slow, and as Sylvania flushed her with silver-gold light. It was divine, and they were divinity in her flesh, breathing through her in rippling waves.

But rather than feel devoured by their energies, Layla felt energized. Rake's breath was in her throat, surging deep inside her. Sylvania's light was building in her heart and sex, powerful with sunlit pleasure. As Layla and Rake kissed, he drew her closer, pressing his lips to hers and driving that morning warmth deep inside her. His hardness brushed her and she cried out at his mouth, surging in a wave of golden bliss.

As if they had planned the moment, Sylvania suddenly flared like a star at Layla's back – flooding all through Layla in a wave of ecstasy. Golden light filled Layla. She exploded into climax, crying out into Rake's mouth as he pressed another wave of ecstasy deep inside her, then another. Layla came again and again, arching in Sylvania's arms as her lips and body pressed hard against Rake – joining them in a circle of radiant bliss.

Layla shuddered bonelessly as the power finally waned, undone by golden pleasure and light. The Head Courtesan cradled her, kissing her neck as she gradually drew her sunlit energy back. Rake's smile was amazing as he pulled away also, setting one last kiss to Layla's lips.

"Beautiful," he murmured as Layla undulated against him in a sweet wave. He was still rock-hard, and the sensation of it made Layla surge one last time. Golden sunlight poured through her a final time and she cried out, arching as Rake clasped her close. And then Layla was finished, gasping gently in their arms, feeling like she glowed from head to heels and not giving a damn what Adrian might think.

"You are so beautiful, Layla Price." Rake eased his hips away. Lifting a hand, he stroked Layla's curls back from her face as he gave her another sweet kiss, though this one had none of his magics in it. "How do you feel?"

"Like someone filled me up with sunlight," Layla breathed, not ever wanting to lose this luminous feeling. Her lips curled in pleasure, and she realized it was her Dragon smiling deep inside her, inundated with bliss.

"Good." Rake stroked her curls again, and the soothing sensation plus the warm light still washing through Layla made her sleepy. She closed her eyes with a smile and Rake chuckled as he kissed her forehead, then Layla felt him nod to Sylvania. They slid gently out of bed and pulled the covers up around Layla's chin, swaddling her in golden sunlight and warmth. Layla heard them dress, but stayed where she was; cozy and blissful.

Sylvania pressed her lips to Layla's brow as Rake left one more gentle kiss upon her lips. And then the duo eased from the room, the door-latch clicking softly behind them.

CHAPTER 11 – FRIENDS

It was much later when Layla finally woke. Feeling ridiculously well, but her bladder also ridiculously full, she glanced around the room and found she was alone, then slipped from bed and padded to the bathroom. Peeing with the door open, she heaved a sigh as she relieved herself, her eyes tearing from sweet relief. She was pulling toilet paper and wiping when the door to her apartment was suddenly slung open – Dusk bustling in dressed in one of his usual impeccable Italian suits with a black laptop tucked under his arm.

Layla was hasty with the toilet paper, but Dusk's glance was faster, seeing she was not in bed and flicking quickly to the wide-open bathroom door. Their gazes connected and Layla froze like a rabbit on the toilet, one arm covering her breasts but all too obvious what she was up to – entirely naked. Dusk blinked, and then an enormous grin split his lovely lips and he laughed, full and merry. Setting the laptop upon her bed, he gathered up Layla's royal blue silk robe from where Sylvania had draped it over the headboard, then strode to the bathroom, offering it to Layla as he grinned at her with merry summer-blue eyes.

"Nothing I haven't already seen." He chuckled genially, his eyes twinkling with mischief as Layla snatched her robe from his hand, turning to flush the toilet and slinging the silk on quickly.

"You could try knocking when you bust into a woman's room." Layla grumped sourly as she tied the sash. Though it was rather funny now as Dusk grinned at her like a lecherous old man.

"Glad to see you're up and about." He chuckled, still grinning and playful. "Sylvania told me about her and Rake's little visit. I see it helped."

"None of your business." Layla's cheeks burned; she couldn't control the blush that rolled through her in a hot wave. But she could tell her Dragon was feeling better as it raised hackles high to either fight with Dusk or fuck him – clearly her passions were back online.

"You're not the only person those two have healed, Layla." Dusk smiled at her, lifting one dark eyebrow.

"You?" Layla blinked at him.

"Many times." Dusk nodded genially, but offered no explanation as he made a welcoming gesture to Layla's breakfast table. She saw a steaming dinner of chicken soup and steak with a chimichurri sauce plus a side of asparagus already set upon the table, and wondered that she'd not heard the Catering staff when they'd set it all up. She must have been sleeping deeply, and though Layla knew something had woken her, she frowned, not able to place what it had been.

Perhaps the Catering staff on their way out the door.

Layla sat and began to eat; famished. Her Dragon seemed to be making up for lost days as she piled her plate high and ladled an enormous bowl of soup, tucking in with her belly roaring.

"Did you bring all this?" Layla eyeballed Dusk as he sat in the chair at corners to hers – it was becoming a thing with them, sharing a meal. But he only cut a piece of steak for his plate, shaking his head as he poured a bottle of cabernet.

"No, Catering brought all this, though I was specific about what to bring. Chicken soup to replenish electrolytes from your fever, steak to fortify your blood, and asparagus to clean out your kidneys from your near-change."

"And the wine?" Layla grinned as she reached out to collect her wineglass and have a sip. It was full and mellow, a lovely bold cabernet that complemented the steak perfectly.

"Well, who doesn't like a little wine with dinner?" Dusk grinned with delight, then had a sip of wine also. Setting it aside, he reached for the laptop, lifting it and placing it beside Layla's plate with a knowing quirk of one dark eyebrow.

"What's this?" Layla asked, glancing at the laptop.

"*This*," Dusk spoke with a little smile, "is something the Madame approved for you."

"Your doing?" Layla raised an eyebrow, wondering what this new scheme of his was.

"Maybe." Dusk gave her a pleased smile, a flash of iridescence moving through his hair. "Open it."

"Okay." Taking another gulp of wine, Layla set her glass a reasonable distance away from the laptop, then opened it. It turned on instantly, already open to what she realized was some sort of odd Skype session. There were no apps open, though a series of strange symbols flowed along the bottom of the view, like if Arabic and old Norse runes had a bastard language-child. Blinking at the view, Layla saw the kitchen of her old house on Capitol Hill in Seattle through an arched craftsman-style room ingress. She saw the scarred wood of their well-used dining table, and chairs waiting at the table. On the other side of the connection, Layla heard an odd series of chimes, similar to the gongs the Hotel used to announce formal dinners.

And then she heard yelling in the background, her housemate and best friend Arron Jacobs' strong tenor voice yelling out, "Off your asses, kids! She's online!"

"*Layloo!!*"

A chorus of happy voices squealed her name and Layla's eyes filled with tears as her housemates in Seattle suddenly poured into view, eagerly thumping down into the stout dining chairs with bright eyes and smiles.

Layla couldn't see. Her eyes were filled with tears as she laughed, feeling a joy stronger even than Sylvania and Rake's blissful healing. There they were, her human friends. The people she loved; the ones she'd left behind to protect from her Dragon's catastrophic magic. They'd spoken on the phone these past weeks, but she'd not seen their faces. And now she laughed, wiping away tears even as they spilled, her heart flooding with warmth – her Dragon exploding sunlight through Layla's veins as she roared with joy.

"Ohmigod, Layloo!!" Celia Carron laughed brightly, a smiling pout on her cute Hispanic lips as she pushed her chunky horn-rimmed glasses up her button nose. Wearing an artsy smock, her long dark hair was bundled up into a messy bun atop her head with crimson chopsticks. "Are you crying?! You're gonna make me cry!! Ohmigod! Don't do that!"

Layla laughed, feeling better than she had in weeks, still wiping away tears. "I can't help it! It's just…" Layla hiccoughed, laughing again, unable to speak.

"You, girl, are in big trouble." Arron Jacobs lifted an ash-blond eyebrow at her, though he was grinning also. Wearing a white collared shirt with pink and blue birds printed on it, he had on a dark charcoal waistcoat and a hot pink silk cravatte tucked in his open collar.

"What did I do now?" Layla laughed, finally not crying anymore as she rubbed away tears.

"We heard you got in some kind of magical accident." Arron lifted an eyebrow at her, though his smile was kind. "Laid you up for *days* and made you miss our regular phone call. What were you thinking? Playing with magic all Katy Perry style. You dark horse."

Layla laughed again. She and Arron had made fun of Katy Perry's ridiculous music video to no end, though they both secretly loved it. "If

I'm a dark horse, you're a flamingo! Where did you get those swanky duds?"

"Oh this?" Arron stroked his glaringly pink cravatte with a reckless grin – obviously silk and obviously expensive. "*Someone* sent ridiculous amounts of money from her quarterly paycheck, straight into our accounts."

"Your first deposit from the Hotel went through two days ago," Dusk coughed with a pleased grin. "I distributed ninety percent of it among your housemates' personal accounts, just as you specified. The untraceable ones we set up for them."

"Charlie bought a boat!" Celia laughed brightly.

The housemate in question, big buff Charlie Avondale who looked like Adonis and Cupid had the most beautiful lovechild, tousled his blond curls with a sheepish smile. "I wanted a boat, yo. We live in Seattle! It'll be fun for Seafair."

"Don't tell me you're taking up sailing!" Layla laughed.

"Speedboat, yo." Charlie grinned, reckless and fun. "I just wanna rev that engine!"

"At least it was used." A fourth voice spoke as someone else took the final chair. "Charlie didn't blow all his money in one go, I made sure he got a good deal on it."

And there he was. Layla's heart stopped for a moment, seeing her ex-boyfriend, the one her magic had almost killed two months ago. Luke Murphy was Layla's first true love. Dark-haired with bright emerald eyes, he was as handsome as men got – and just as tempestuous. Luke had a critical streak a mile wide, but even he seemed happy right now, his emerald eyes glittering with humor as he and Layla gazed at each other.

He looked good, she realized. She'd known he was recovering well from what her Dragon had done to him, but Layla didn't know she'd still carried that last image of him spasming upon his bed and bleeding out of his eyes, until now. Something released inside her, something that had been tight for months. And as she gazed at him, her eyes teared up all over again.

"Good to see you, Luke." She swallowed, blinking away tears.

"Hey." Kindness took his face, and for a moment Layla felt like they were the only ones on the call as they held each other with their eyes. "I'm ok, Layla. Glad to see you are, too."

"Thanks."

"Dusk said you were healing," Arron jumped in, his gaze flicking to Layla's left. "Is that the man himself?"

Leaning into the camera's view, Dusk gave a grin, flashing his white teeth as a ripple of pleasure lit the midnight scales at his temples and his artfully-styled dark hair. "Arron. Good to see you at last."

"My god!" Arron's grey eyes got huge. Even Celia and Charlie were gaping in astonishment, though Luke merely gave a wry smile. Dusk had visited Luke in the hospital once, and Luke had memories of Dusk healing him when Layla's magic had attacked. But the rest of the housemates had never seen Dusk, only heard his voice on the phone, and their reactions were priceless. Arron in particular, gave a sudden amazing smile three miles wide.

"Layla! You didn't tell me your boss was the handsomest rogue I'd ever meet!" Arron grinned, beguiling and flirty as hell.

Layla saw a wash of color pass through Dusk's hair again as he laughed, bright and utterly amused. Dusk loved attention, in all forms and from anyone, gay or straight. "Arron Jacobs, in the flesh. I've heard about your proclivities. Are you sure you aren't a Dragon?"

"Are you sure you're not hopping on the next plane out of Paris to come be my next beau?" Arron was lewd and disastrously sexy as he raised a blond eyebrow at Dusk. Arron was a hot mess, in a good way.

Dusk laughed, shaking his head. Layla actually saw him blush in his dusky-tanned skin, which was rare for the Crystal Dragon. "I have too many duties to leave right now. But if you'd like to take a trip to the Hotel… it could be arranged."

"Seriously?" Arron's eyes went wide.

Dusk nodded, and even Layla was astonished by his next words. "Seriously. I've already had it pre-approved by the Madame and the Hotel Head. Four complimentary guest passes for a ten-day stay, for whenever you all would like to come visit. Meals, transportation, and Hotel events are complimentary… as well as three Assignations of your choice during your time here. Of course, the confidentiality agreements you four signed already about the Hotel and the Twilight Realm would stay in strict observance."

"Of course." It was Luke who answered, the other three too astounded to speak. And though Layla saw a flash of wariness in Luke's Irish-green eyes, she saw he was also impressed. Luke had confided in Layla over the phone that Dusk was growing on him ever since the accident. She knew the two had even spoken one-on-one by phone, though neither had told her what it had been about.

Turning, Layla regarded Dusk. "You didn't tell me about this."

"I wanted it to be a surprise." His sapphire eyes gleamed with pleasure, and Layla felt a low rumble of his magics suddenly slip out. He didn't have his invisible barrier up, and his magic shivered Layla for a moment, disrupting the connection of the computer into a fuzzy mess before Dusk got ahold of himself again. His lower-than-sound rumble disappeared, and the video connection stabilized.

"How about Christmas break!" Celia pounced on the idea immediately, beaming as she pushed her chunky glasses up her button nose. "Luke's got two weeks off from clinic and classes, and Charlie, Arron, and I can get time off work, I'm sure of it. Ohmigod, Paris here we come!"

"Ohmigod, blow-your-mind to smithereens here we come," Arron corrected, still gaping at Dusk. "Why did you arrange this?"

"Layla needs her friends." Dusk's smile was pleased, but Layla saw his calculating problem-solving mind deeply at work as he slipped into Head Concierge mode now. "The Hotel has not had a Royal Dragon Bind on the premises in decades, and hasn't had one working here in over a thousand years. Layla's magic develops based on her experiences, and since the four of you are a large part of those experiences, the Madame and I thought it best to provide you all with some time together. Time where you four can deepen in your understanding of Layla's new world, and remain a part of her life."

"You did this for me?" Layla stared at Dusk as she blinked.

"The Hotel needs you healthy." His words were professional, but his gaze was deep with concern and unspoken things. Dusk gave a soft smile and Layla saw him almost reach out to touch her hand, then hesitate with her four housemates on the video link. He smiled wryly, pushing up from the table instead and stepping behind Layla's chair so he could still be seen in the video.

"You can arrange the trip for whenever you like. Luke, just use that special smartphone I gave you, set your intention and touch the call button – it will call the Reservations department. It's attuned to all four of your harmonics, so it will work for any of you, but to anyone else it will be just a dead phone. Your own electronics won't dial out on Hotel premises, but feel free to bring them if you have any personal work to do while you're here. I need to go. Arron – pleasure finally meeting you."

"Likewise." Arron's voice was soft now, awed, and Layla could tell by the big dopey smile on his face that he was falling for her artfully sexy boss – hard. Dusk could charm the pants off anyone, and

Arron never had difficulty taking off his pants.

But there was no more time for flirting as Dusk gave a quick bow by Layla's chair, then winked at her and whisked from the room, closing her apartment doors behind himself. Layla was left on the line with her housemates, Arron laughing incredulously as he shook his head.

"That man is *brutally* handsome, Layla Price!"

"Don't I know it." Layla grumped, though she was smiling. "He knows it, too. Don't stroke his ego any more than it already has been."

"Oh, I want to stroke far more than just his ego," Arron spoke with a devilish smile.

"Be my guest." Layla made a welcoming gesture and Arron, Celia, and Charlie all laughed. But Luke was more sober as he regarded her, something knowing in his emerald gaze.

"So how is it going between you and your boss?"

"Fine." Layla found herself suddenly not smiling. Luke and his petty jealousy could be too much sometimes. She felt something rise inside her, heated, and all at once the housemates were looking from her to Luke and back again.

"Aaaand… that's our cue." Arron rose from the table, beckoning Charlie and Celia up also. They went with a laugh and a wave, making her promise to call again soon. Apparently, Dusk had set up these exclusive computers on both ends so they could securely FaceTime anytime, rather than using phones. Layla left them with a promise she'd check in over the next few days, and the three departed from view.

Leaving only Luke. But rather than get severe with her, crossing his arms over his godly chest and leaning back like he usually did, instead Luke leaned forward toward the computer screen, lacing his hands atop the table and gazing at her intently.

"So, truth. Are you ok, Layla?" Luke's emerald eyes were deep with concern as he looked at her – *really* looked at her, seeing far more than the others could.

"I'm ok." Her words were subdued; she really didn't know how to answer that.

"You're not." Luke's gaze was searching.

Lifting a wry eyebrow, Layla shook her head. "I never could hide from you. You're right – I'm rattled, Luke."

"What happened?" Luke's demeanor was intent, watching her. "Dusk said you collapsed at a Dragon party, some kind of magical accident."

"It was bad." Layla swallowed, feeling like she wanted to pour her heart out to Luke but not knowing quite what to say. They weren't lovers now, and couldn't ever be again based on the way her Dragon had nearly killed him the last time. But she still felt love for Luke, and watching him be sincere now and non-judgemental, she suddenly missed him. "I had some kind of magical resonance with someone at the party. It sparked my Dragon and it tried to shift inside me. Dusk stopped it, thank god. But I was pretty ill for a number of days because of it."

"He told me shifting was dangerous." Luke's gaze was knowing. "That if you shifted on Hotel premises, out in public... that there were consequences."

"Death." Layla swallowed, feeling ill. "By execution. Euthanasia."

"Jesus." Luke cursed low, a deep wariness in his eyes now. "Are you sure the Hotel is where you want to be right now, Layla?"

"I'm sure." She nodded stubbornly. "Dusk and Rikyava and a few others here are the only ones who can help me learn to control my new magics, Luke. They can't leave their duties. So I need to be here."

"As long as you're sure."

"I have a feeling I'd be dangerous any place I went," Layla spoke softly. "But at least being here, there's a chance at safety. Did you know I met another Bind? The King of the Phoenix. He's offered to teach me about my power, though he's not a Bind anymore."

"Dusk told me." Luke's gaze was penetrating, and Layla wondered how much had been shared between King Falliro Arini and Dusk, then Dusk to Luke. And whether any of it had been shared with Adrian. "If I could have any affect on your safety... you know I'd do anything to make that happen."

"I know." Layla spoke softly.

"Dusk said this is probably the only way we can help you," Luke spoke gently, "by coming to visit, showing our support. I would come right now, but—"

"The university hospital wouldn't understand this kind of thing. I know, Luke. You need to continue your medical studies. That's important."

His smile was wry, something sad in it. "He paid off my house mortgage, you know. And my student debt. All our student debt, actually. None of the money you sent us is going towards our student loans, just into those private accounts now."

"Who paid off your student loans? Dusk?" Layla blinked, confused. That had been her first promise to her housemates when she'd gotten her job at the Hotel, that she would pay off all their student debt.

"Not Dusk. Adrian." Luke's words were soft. But his green eyes burned as he held Layla's gaze through the video-link. "He pre-paid all the rest of my grad school tuition, also. I almost called the school and the bank and told them to reject the money."

"Don't do that." Layla spoke quickly, hoping Luke wouldn't throw the opportunity away. Adrian was flagrant with his money, and even though Layla saw the manipulation in this move, it had also been extremely generous.

"I'm not going to. But Adrian can't just buy my allegiance where you're concerned. I hope he knows that."

"Adrian's not very good at relationships," Layla sighed, feeling suddenly tired again.

"Do you love him?" Luke spoke softly.

"Yes." Layla and Luke had never bullshitted each other, and she wasn't about to start now.

But Luke didn't blow up, merely nodded, then gave a deep sigh as he closed his eyes. "Fuck, this hurts."

"I know." Layla watched him process, feeling for him. At last, Luke opened his eyes with another deep sigh, then gave her one of the loveliest, most honest smiles Layla had ever seen from him.

"I am going to see you at Christmastime. And if Adrian fucks with you, I'll give him a piece of my mind, money or no. Maybe even a piece of my fist."

Layla laughed. Suddenly, the world didn't feel quite so dark with Luke's fighting spirit and fuck-the-world Irish attitude. She was still smiling as he grinned at her, in that way that had first made her love him so many years ago.

"I love you Layla Price." He spoke solidly. "Even if we can't be together, even if we suck as partners, I'm always gonna love you."

"I know. I love you too, Luke," she smiled, meaning it to her core. They smiled at each other a moment longer and Layla felt all their history, all the beautiful sadness of it. With a light slap on the table, Luke broke the moment.

"I gotta get going – gotta bike to class in ten minutes. But I will be keeping this computer open and at my elbow when I'm home, to catch your call any time of day or night, ok?"

129

"Thanks." Layla meant it. With feeling, she set her fingers to her lips, blowing him a kiss like she'd once done when she'd been away traveling the world while they were dating. He caught it, slapping it to his cheek in a way that made her laugh and always had. They beamed at each other another moment, before he waved.

"Bye, Layloo."

"Bye, Luke."

Her fingers slid out as his did, and she wasn't sure who ended the call, but it just suddenly cut out. Layla was left staring at a blank screen, the sigils along the bottom gradually dimming out as they slowed to a stop.

With a sigh, Layla closed the laptop and slid it away on the table. Gazing at her plate, half-full of food, she felt her Dragon stir within her. Her heart still hurt, but she was also hungry. Reaching out, Layla took up her fork and began to eat, chewing slowly.

CHAPTER 12 – DRAGONS

The next morning, Layla dressed fast at her walk-in closet. As Dusk zoomed around her apartment, unveiling breakfast and pouring coffee, Layla shimmied on a new riding-dress in desert duns, somewhere between a modern frock and a Victorian style, preparing for a morning hunt with the Moroccan Dragons. Since none of them had gotten a chance to meet her yet except Adam, Dusk had arranged an outing today on Layla's last day off from Concierge Services.

An event Layla was looking forward to.

The ride had been planned early, as it was supposed to thunderstorm by noon. As Layla dressed, she glanced out the open closet doors to the high windows, watching grey clouds churn. The corseted plaid dress was wool and would be warm, a mix of modern and antique that was short at the knees with a long bustle in back. Layla was feeling tremendously better today, knowing her friends were coming to visit for Christmas. Lightheartedness moved through her despite the grey day as she zipped on fawn boots with faux-Victorian buttons. Pulling on leather kid-gloves, she pinned a hat with long pheasant feathers up on her sable curls. Gazing at herself in the mirror, Layla had to laugh.

She looked like a Harper's Bazaar model out for an English country ride.

"Layla? Are you presentable?" Dusk called from beyond the closet doors as he arranged the table. "We need to get a move on!"

"Coming!" Layla sashayed out of the closet with a grin, making her short bustle sway. Busy this morning in his usual daytime way, Dusk glanced up from the breakfast table and eyed her with a critical Head Concierge look. He gestured for her to turn, then gave a pleased smile.

"Excellent. Food, quickly!"

He beckoned and Layla approached, loving the ease with which she could walk in the Victorian riding boots with their stout hourglass heels. Gesturing for her to sit at the table, already set with bacon and eggs, grilled tomato, and english muffins, Dusk poured coffee, mixing Layla's with a generous amount of heavy cream just the way she liked it.

"So. About this ride. Is there anything specific I should know about the Moroccan Dragons before I meet them today?" Layla asked as she sipped her coffee, then tucked in quickly. "I missed my meeting with Adam where he was supposed to answer my questions about the clan."

"Regrettable, but it can't be helped." Dusk answered as he sipped his own coffee, then snapped a napkin out in his lap and began to eat also. "And yes, there are a few things about the Moroccan clan you need to know before we see them today. You already know Adam, the Clan Second. Even though he's a pain in the ass sometimes, he is actually quite supportive of Adrian, though he's also probably the clan's most outspoken member."

"Obviously." Layla snorted with a smile as she dug into her eggs. "Who else?"

"Clan Third is Adrian's great-aunt Rachida Rhakvir, Adam's foster-mother," Dusk smiled as he continued, sipping his coffee. "She is Adrian's grandfather's sister. Rachida is judgemental, and her judgement of you, good or bad, will influence the clan. But the only thing you can do about it is be truthful. She appreciates honesty but she's also feisty, so use your usual wit and you'll be fine."

"Anyone else significantly high-up to be aware of?" Layla asked, chewing her bacon.

"Emir Tousk is Adrian's Battle-Lord, as he was for Adrian's mother." Dusk continued with a frown. "He's a hard man but decent, and his opinion carries weight. The rest you don't need to know right now. There are some powerful rivals for Adrian's throne – though most of those aren't here at the Hotel. Adrian has had a number of dominance-battles to get where he is. Fortunately, both Rachida and Emir have never wanted the clan leader position. If they ever did, Adrian would be in for the fight of his life."

"Will Adrian be there?" Layla's heart leapt to her throat and clenched at the same time.

"Yes." Dusk gave her a look. "And for all that's holy, do *not* let him touch you today."

"Have you briefed him on the plan?" Layla grumped, taking another bite of eggs. "He was the one who kissed my neck at the Dragon party, not the other way around."

Dusk's smile tried to not be amused and failed. "Adrian has been slapped up one side and down the other by Rikyava and the Madame for that, not to mention Rachida and Emir. He'll likely behave himself today."

"Why does he have so little control around me? Rikyava said she thinks it's the Bind." Layla lifted her left wrist, the silver Moroccan cuff in place on her arm.

Dusk sobered, wiping his lips with his napkin, then gave a hard sigh as he pushed his finished plate away. "Royal Dragons are temperamental in the extreme, Layla. Adrian's not come into his full power yet, or the control that comes with it. At 150 years, he's still technically young. And though he's calculating in the arts of power,

Adrian has had a reckless streak since we were kids. He's learned to be calculating because of what it gets him, but his recklessness is more natural. Though, he got cold for a long time, empty in some deep part of his heart. Until—"

But Dusk cut off suddenly, eyeing Layla.

"Until what?" Layla prompted.

"Until he saw you again. At Mimi's funeral." Dusk spoke quietly. "And when that Bind between you two happened in the art gallery, I believe it caused you both to resonate with each other's magics. It's destabilizing Adrian's control over his Dragon."

"What?" Layla blinked, worrying for the first time that the Bind between her and Adrian was actually hurting him, destabilizing him in a way she'd never considered before. Suddenly, the conversation he'd hinted at, that she was somehow dangerous to him like Superman's kryptonite, made a lot more sense. "What do you mean?"

"Finish up and I'll tell you as we walk."

Dusk was already rising, downing his coffee. His fit frame looked excellent today in a dove-grey riding jacket and breeches that was part sleek Victorian, part modern, a fox-fur collar on his jacket and a white cravat pinned at his throat. Marching to the apartment doors in his black riding boots, he raised his eyebrows and Layla downed her coffee. With a smile, Dusk opened one door and Layla joined him, moving out into the hall and down a stairwell. They exited the Hotel to the gardens, moving past burbling fountains and bare topiaries, the heavy sky churning above. Rounding a row of hedges, they marched past the crystal cathedral where the Dragon party had been. Skirting the bower of willows where Dusk had saved her life, they entered the woods, golden leaves of alder and oak swirling down all around.

"So you were saying about Adrian?" Layla prompted as they took a gravel path through the forest to the far stables. The Hotel had more parkland than the human Palace of Versailles, with miles of trails for riding and dense forests, which was where the hunt would be today.

"Yes. Right." Dusk blinked as he surfaced from deep thoughts. "Based on what I've observed, I have a theory on why Adrian's been so volcanic lately."

"Because of the Bind. What have you noticed?" Layla asked, curious.

"Since you two were bound together by that cuff," Dusk nodded at the talisman on Layla's wrist, "I've sensed a change in Adrian's resonance. It's as if his energy is… vibrating along a similar frequency as yours now."

"What do you mean?"

"I mean," Dusk glanced at her, "that since you both have hot-tempered, sand-funnel Desert Dragon passions that are easily triggered, it's like you're constantly spinning each other up when you're around each other. Ever see the video of the 1940 Tacoma Narrows Bridge collapse?"

"Sure. Everyone in Seattle knows about that." Layla smiled.

"Well, that's what I think your energy is doing to Adrian's and vice versa, ever since you two were bound." Dusk glanced at her again, his handsome features sober. "Like the both of you are producing some kind of harmonic resonance, it causes you to vibrate too fast when you're around each other – producing skyrocketing tempers and passion. It's been a long while since I've seen Adrian lose control like he did the night of the Dragon party. I'm beginning to wonder if this Bind is not entirely good for him."

"Or me." Layla read between the lines as they stepped out from the trees onto a greensward lined by Victorian-style gas lamps. The day was so grey that the lamps were lit, even though it was full morning. As they rounded a hedge, a pavilion of crimson and white silk erected in a

135

tumbled stone ruin near the woods came into view. The Hotel's stables sprawled to their left, and Layla heard a whinny of horses being prepared for their pheasant-hunt.

Layla's heart was in her throat as they moved toward the pavilion, realizing that she could feel Adrian already. Like a press of heat through her body, the closer she came, the more she felt him. As they neared, Layla's pulse was pounding, a cold sweat on her hands. Dusk glanced over, then reached out to touch Layla's fingers, pouring a bolstering vibration through her. It steadied her and she smiled. He nodded as they continued toward the elegant silk structure snapping in the breeze, the sky now burgeoning with impending rain.

As they mounted the stone steps, Layla heard laughter and the clinking of glassware. Arriving at the top, she finally saw inside the open-sided pavilion, noting fifteen people lounging in chaises and rattan chairs around brightly tiled Moroccan tables set with a decimated breakfast spread, coffee urns, and alcoholic mixers. Adrian held court in a rattan chair to the left, chatting with Adam in the seat next to him. Dressed in riding attire and breeches, Adrian's long legs were stretched out, his russet riding boots crossed at the ankles. Swirling an Old Fashioned with three cherries and a curl of orange peel, his piercing aqua eyes found Layla as she moved up the steps.

Adrian's aqua eyes held far more green today, stormy like the sky. Wearing a crisp white shirt, a pinstriped charcoal waistcoat and a cobalt ascot, Adrian was slender deliciousness in his charcoal breeches. As Layla arrived, she felt their magics connect, swirling around each other though the reaction was quieter today. Whether it was because they'd already had an explosive moment four nights ago, or because Adrian was controlling himself, she felt only a brief brush of scales and heat over her skin, giving her a shiver before it passed away.

Adrian set his drink aside and rose as she approached, Adam

doing the same, dressed in tans with a hunter-green ascot perfect for his blond coloring. All eyes turned to them, conversation pausing as the Moroccan Dragons gave intrigued smiles. But Adrian's eyes held a hardness today, and Layla felt an iron-clad cold tingle across her skin. Her heart hit her throat and she swallowed, feeling like he was angry with her – though she had no idea why.

"Layla Price, Royal Dragon Bind of our clan, be welcome." Adrian's speech was stiff and formal as he gave a crisp bow. He didn't reach out to touch Layla's hand, and kept his distance as he greeted her.

Layla swallowed, feeling like this was bad. Something was wrong but she had no idea what. "Adrian Rhakvir, Clan First. Thank you for inviting me today." Layla spoke back, in the formal way Dusk had taught her when meeting the head of any clan.

It felt wrong. So wrong for them to be this formal, this cold. Layla had felt passion between them, recklessness, even fury, but she'd never felt Adrian so chill and unapproachable. Adrian's smile was bitter as he stared her down, silent. Others gathered with their drinks, evaluating the situation with clever fire in their aqua, green, and blue eyes. Tall and elegant with dark hair like Layla's or cinnamon-blonde, most of the Desert Dragons had stunning olive or golden-tanned complexions – their clan including all of Italy, Greece, Spain, and North Africa.

Adam was the only ash-blond, Layla noted, his handsome jade-violet eyes watching Layla with a subtle smile, his features distinctly Italian mixed with Norse. One woman commanded attention, a fantastic redhead with rich olive skin and masses of luminous red-gold waves cascading down her back. Wearing a spring-green caftan beaded with emeralds over her elegant curves, she sipped a martini, watching Adrian and Layla's interaction closely. A man beside her was built like a Roman warrior, his distinctly Spanish features a complement to his brush-cut black hair. Dressed in all-black riding gear with a martial feel, he had dark onyx eyes – eyes that watched Layla with a ready attention.

"Is Layla not of our clan, Adrian?" The woman with the red hair moved forward in her elegant caftan. "Do you not wish to welcome her more formally?"

"Forgive my intrusion, Matron Rachida," Dusk answered with a clearing of his throat. "Layla has been quite startled by skin contact with Dragons recently. Her magic is new and needs culturing. I wouldn't recommend it."

"*Startled*, that's one way of putting it." Adam moved forward with a bourbon on the rocks, giving Layla a teasing grin, his tenor voice resonant with laughter. "Practically shifted right on the dance floor four nights ago. Quite the event, Ms. Price, one that none of us is likely to forget. Though I suppose it excuses you from skipping out on our dinner date." He saluted her with his drink, his eyes glowing with humor.

"Yeah, we agreed it wasn't a date, bucko." Layla flushed, mortified that he'd said that in front of Adrian, though she realized Adam's elegance in breaking the ice. He'd made plain everything that had happened that night, with humor and wit. And though Adrian set his jaw, scowling at his Clan Second, others were smiling. But before Adrian could speak, the red-haired woman moved forward.

"So this is Mimi Zakir's daughter." Rachida Rhakvir's voice was low and resonant, though it held sharp, decisive tones. A mature woman, she had thin lines at her eyes and mouth, though she was still stunning. "I heard of your mother's demise. From all our hearts, I pass on my condolences. Mimi was a great light."

"Thank you Ms. Rhakvir." Layla gave a nod as emotions cascaded through her.

"Call me Rachida, child. Any friend of my dear boys Dusk and

Adrian is a friend of mine." The woman reached out, setting a warm palm to Layla's face. A breath of brisk spice wind flavored with sandalwood stirred through Layla and her magic responded, but it was like two enormous beasts just sliding around each other in acquaintance; nothing that flared her passion. Layla shivered at the sensation but it was mild. Holding Layla's gaze, Rachida's Mediterranean-blue eyes brightened. Copper flecks stood out in their depths, and she gave a smile.

"You are just like your mother, so lovely." Rachida murmured, her hand slipping away. Sipping her martini, she turned toward Adrian, raising her eyebrows as if prodding him to be a good host. Adrian paused, uncertainty on his lips. And it was Adam who moved forward, smiling as he deftly angled a rattan chair in beside his and beckoned for Layla to claim it.

"Ms. Price, please come sit with us."

Adam didn't touch Layla, only stepped to her side, inviting her with his bourbon glass to join their group. Layla moved forward as Dusk took a rattan love-seat on the other side of hers. Adam reclaimed his chair by Adrian, Rachida settling her tall elegance on the other side of Adrian as the rest took seats or migrated to the table for a last round of drinks.

"So tell me, Layla," Adam leaned forward, swirling his bourbon as he began casual conversation, "you were raised in Seattle? Do you remember anything of Morocco? Rachida tells us you were born at Riad Rhakvir, Adrian's family home."

"I don't remember much," Layla spoke, her hands restless in her lap. Rachida noticed it and gestured to a handsome young man with dark Greek curls and midnight blue eyes who hovered by her shoulder like a valet. Moving to the table and quickly mixing a drink, he returned, settling the drink in Layla's hands – an Old Fashioned like

Adrian's. Layla took a sip gratefully, feeling the mellow liquor, orange peel, and cherry smooth her jangled nerves, nodding her thanks to Rachida. The older woman gave a smile, as if she'd known exactly what Layla had needed.

"So what do you recall of Riad Rhakvir, child?" She asked genially, though her gaze was piercing like talons.

"Desert winds." Layla answered, seeing again the dreams she'd had back in Seattle when she'd first been marked by the hamsa-cuff. Though her talisman was a symbol of legitimacy in her Lineage, Layla felt like a fraud sitting here among her clan – knowing hardly anything about them and not having been back to Morocco since her infancy. "I remember a blue courtyard, with a fountain and tall potted ferns and palms. A view out over the evening desert; maybe a chasm in the distance. I remember my mother cooking in the kitchen, and how good it smelled. Her singing to me. That's all, really."

"She does remember her birth-home," Rachida's gaze sparkled, something approving in it. "And Mimi never told you that you were birthed of her loins?"

"I didn't find out until recently. After she died." Layla gave Adrian a pointed look. He looked away, sipping his drink.

Rachida's brows raised as she looked to Adrian with an accusatory glint in her eyes. "Adrian, how much about her history and clan have you told Layla?"

"Not enough, clearly." Adam snorted as he gestured with his bourbon. "Layla feels alienated among us; it's written all over her scent. You're too goddamn cagey, Adrian, not sharing more with her. No wonder she's pissed! Tell her some truths and maybe she'll trust you more. And then your budding relationship might not be so rocky so soon."

It was a scathing tirade. Layla gaped at Adam's frankness as

Adrian scowled, a hot flush of cinnamon-jasmine wind swirling through the pavilion. The rest of his clan shifted uncomfortably at Adrian's sudden rise in magic, but there were a few who didn't budge. Rachida for one, clearly the old matriarch of the clan. The black-eyed man for two, whom Layla was certain was Emir Tousk the Battle-Lord, watching with a wary scowl. And Dusk, lounging comfortably at Layla's side, though his sapphire gaze was piercing upon Adrian.

"Informing Layla about her clan was her mother's responsibility." Adrian spoke pointedly at Adam, his swirl of cinnamon-jasmine scent still stinging through the air.

"Yeah, well, Mimi Zakir passed on, and she didn't tell her daughter a damn thing." Adam snorted, nonplussed with Adrian's response or his magic. "As our Clan First and the first person to re-establish contact with Layla when Mimi died, it was your responsibility to tell her the truth. You didn't; she suffered. And because she suffered, our clan has suffered, Adrian. You don't treat family that way. And if you won't fill her in about us, I welcome the opportunity. Over a nice dinner that befits the hospitality of our proud heritage."

Adam sat back in his chair, his legs crossed ankle to knee and his hands spread on the arms of his rattan chair. His bourbon was set aside, and his position was one of challenge. A sweet current of air whirled out from him like apple-blossoms in a hot summer wind, facing off with Adrian's cinnamon scent. The two locked gazes and Layla felt the opposition there. Adam might have been Adrian's cousin and supportive of his Clan First, but he was also a Royal and wasn't about to let someone fuck up the clan's ethics.

"Is that what you want, Adam? Be my guest. Take Layla out to dinner. By all means, *fill her in.*"

As he spoke, Adrian set aside his highball glass with a precise motion, his eyes searing with a gold that was so cold now it burned. His cruel innuendo wasn't lost on anyone. Layla had to clench her hands into fists to not just get up and slap his face as glances were exchanged beneath the pavilion. Adam's eyes went wide, his ash-blond brows rising at Adrian's comment. Layla felt Dusk's crystalline shield swirl up around her, cutting her and himself off from Adrian and Adam's sudden pissing-match.

Tension rippled between the two cousins as Adam set his jaw and Adrian lifted his chin, giving Adam the full weight of those burning gold eyes. Magic seethed so hot and thick between them that Layla saw a mirage waver in the air, bursting with small curls of red, aqua, and hunter-green flames. As Adam stared Adrian down, Layla realized that Dusk was worried of a dominance challenge; right here, right now – though she didn't know what a Dragon dominance challenge looked like.

Or how devastating it might be.

But at last, Adam took a deep inhalation, letting it sigh out. His summer orchard scent eased until it was only Adrian's whirling cinnamon and jasmine flavor in the air and all the curls of flame had ceased. Layla felt Dusk's invisible barrier fall as the tension in the pavilion did. Turning towards Layla, the fury in Adam's eyes bled out to apology.

"Ms. Price. Please forgive our magical demonstration. As per his words, my Clan First permits me to answer your questions over dinner. I humbly request permission to reschedule our previously arranged dinner for tonight. I will answer any and all questions you can think to ask, and even ones you don't know to ask, about our clan. Do you accept?"

Layla's gaze flicked to Adrian, knowing now that he'd be pissed if she had dinner with Adam. To make it worse, Adam had clearly twisted the situation so that his Clan First had given him sarcastic permission to take Layla to dinner – though it was still technically permission. As Layla looked to Adrian, he looked away, gazing off to the woods with a bite of tension in his jaw, reclaiming his drink and sipping it.

Fury rose in Layla suddenly. A hot, bright fury that Adrian was acting like an asshole. She couldn't control the surge of wrath that washed through her, and Dusk did not reach over to touch her and contain it. Like a flash of heat-lightning, Layla's orange spice wind whipped the pavilion, surging out from her in a rolling tirade. It wasn't nice. It was brutal and it came with no eroticism, only a sensation like daggers seething out from her skin and hurling at Adrian.

Adam's nostrils flared and he jerked his head back with wide eyes as that hot wind seared by him. But Adrian got the brunt of it, flinching in his rattan chair as if he'd just been stabbed in the gut. He turned molten eyes upon Layla, and the look was pure fury. That wasn't Adrian's look, not the man she was bound to. It was the look of a Clan First – that someone so new to the clan had dared attack their leader.

But Layla didn't care. She gave that blisteringly cold look right back, her orange-spice wind whipping out at him again. Adrian made a quick gesture with his drink, as if casting aside her energy and Layla felt her instinctive attack turned away harmlessly over the greensward – but there was more where that had come from.

And if Adrian wanted to be a dick and see it, he would.

"Adam Rhakvir." Layla turned back to Adam, not missing the smug smile that curled Dusk's lips beside her. "I would be honored to accept your invitation for dinner."

"Wonderful. I look forward to it, Ms. Price."

Adam's jade-violet eyes glowed with dark humor. Adrian gave a low growl but Layla didn't look over. She knew he couldn't go back on his offer, even made in deep sarcasm as it had been. She saw Adam knew it, too. As their eyes locked, Layla felt a curl of orchard-wind ease out from him, caressing her cheek. Her lips fell open, surprised at his touch as her Dragon raised its head, rippling with eagerness. But Adam said nothing, only gave her a salute with his drink. No one else reacted to what had just happened between them – not even Adrian or Dusk.

Layla wondered if anyone else had felt it.

Or if Adam had such precise control of his magic as to direct a caress to her and her alone.

CHAPTER 13 – HUNT

"Well!" In a flourish of elegance, Rachida Rhakvir stood, setting down her martini on a side-table and smoothing the long folds of her spring green caftan. All eyes moved to her as a brisk wind rippled the pavilion. "Now that we are all properly entertained, and the issue of Layla getting to know her clan has been solved, I suggest we set off on our ride. The weather gathers, children, and as much as I would like to dally, I think we'd better get moving if we are to have any fun this morning. Soukos! My riding crop."

The handsome Greek valet who had served Layla her drink rushed to Rachida's side, escorting her toward the pavilion egress as he handed Rachida a black leather riding crop. The rest of the clan rose as the wind whirled again, setting aside drinks or downing them as they set out after their matriarch. As everyone departed, Adrian made a move toward Layla's side, his eyes pinning her – but Adam stepped in suddenly as they moved down the stone stairs.

"So. Fun first day in the family?" Adam grinned as he walked.

"If it's as dysfunctional as it seems, we're going to get along splendidly." Layla sassed with a scowl. "If Adrian can ever shake the shit out of his boots, that is." She gave a pointed glance past Dusk to where Adrian now walked with the dark-eyed Battle-Lord. Adrian glanced over, his brows knitting in a frown, though Layla didn't think he'd heard her.

"Well, shit can only be cleared out of one's boots two ways." Adam laughed brightly. "One: by stopping what you're doing to see how much shit you've put in there, then wiping all that out. Or two: by not shitting in your boots in the first place. I'd tell you the course of action Adrian favors if I knew it."

"I felt your magic back there." Layla glanced at Adam, seeing now how much he loved to play games. "Some might think you're strong enough to be Clan First."

"Alas," he gave her a sly grin, "Adrian's a stronger Royal than I am. I'm a Royal Dragon Chimeric, not a Royal Dragon with visage-shifting abilities like Adrian."

"What's a Royal Dragon Chimeric?"

Adam chuckled, though something in his eyes held pain; the second time Layla had seen it. "Adrian will be able to take the appearance of any humanoid or creature once his magic fully matures. Me, I can only take the shape of animals. Royal Dragon Chimerics are what you see carved all over the Hotel; shape-shifted into mixed creatures like Sphinxes, Gryphons, and so on. My talent manifested when my parents died, but becoming a dog is not the only creature I can do now. I've mastered all sorts of farm animals – pigs, turkeys, mice, gophers…"

Layla laughed, enjoying Adam's cheeky wit. She suddenly felt like punching him in the shoulder, so she did. Adam grinned, raising his eyebrows at the punch though he kept walking. "Anyway, my power's not a match to Adrian's. Never was."

"Seems like you were doing well enough back there," Layla lifted an eyebrow at him.

"Adrian's temper needs a little spanking now and then," Adam chuckled. "As his cousin, I've been his sounding-board for years. He gets hot about something; I get inquisitive. I smooth out the problems Adrian's too proud to address directly. We need someone direct in the clan. And we need someone dominant. I'm no dominant – that's

Adrian's job. But I am direct."

Though his words were demure, Layla felt another secret curl of power caress her neck as he spoke. Adam glanced at her with a rakish smile, but again, no one around Layla responded. Clearly he had exquisite control of his magics, and something about his cheeky ways reminded her of someone else she knew.

"You remind me of Dusk."

"Do I?" Adam grinned wide, glancing back to where Adrian and Dusk walked. Heads together as they approached the stables, Dusk and Adrian spoke low about something with serious faces. "I'll take that as a compliment. Dusk and Adrian and I were basically raised together when I was adopted by Rachida, who was quite close with Adrian's mother Juliette. We hung out as boys a lot at Riad Rhakvir in Morocco, though I was less in the mix of brotherly hatred and sibling rivalry. I was the baby of that group-hatch."

"Group-hatch?" Layla asked as they arrived at the stables, grooms from the Hotel leading out sleek steeds already saddled and bridled, hitching them up at cross-ties for the party to mount up. Layla would have thought there'd be shotguns or crossbows for the hunt, but looking around, she saw not a single weapon. Her brows furrowed as she watched the Dragons walk through the horses and select steeds, passing their hand over a horse's nostrils and letting the animal smell them before they decided on their mount.

"Dragons tend to give birth in groups." Adam chuckled as Layla watched the proceedings. "It's called a group-hatch, though we give live birth. Every fifty years or so, a new generation gets birthed, usually within ten years of each other. Adrian and I are part of our generation. The previous hatch was forty years before us, and the one before that was almost seventy years. It's a pheromone thing. Dragons aren't often fertile. We get almost no magical or human diseases so we can live a long time, but our women don't get pregnant unless they're in estrus. Talk to Rachida; she'll be able to advise you on what to look for when that happens."

Layla blinked; some of that was way too personal. But it was good information, and looking at Adam, she decided it hadn't been meant as innuendo, just explanation of how her biology worked. She hadn't had a period since her magics opened. She'd missed periods before so it wasn't alarming, but Layla made a mental note to talk to Rachida about it. The Hotel had methods of keeping guests and staff disease-free and clear of pregnancy, though it sounded like being a Dragon would have additional benefits.

"Thanks. I'll make sure to ask her."

Almost everyone was mounted now, only five or six people without steeds yet. Horses were getting un-hitched from the cross-ties, prancing eagerly beneath their riders and tossing their heads. Adrian had claimed an impressively tall black gelding with a flowing mane and tail – a Friesian. Layla had spent some time riding as a girl, and moved up to a dappled grey mare that looked just like her stuffed comfort toy, holding out her hand. The mare snuffled Layla but then her eyes rolled back, wild. She whinnied, shying sideways in the traces.

"Not that one. She's afraid of your Dragon-scent." Adam moved up beside her, indicating a bay gelding to Layla's right. "Try him."

Dusk had stepped to the dappled mare, soothing her with low vibrations. She calmed beneath his touch and he was soon mounted up, reining his horse around to follow Adam and Layla as they stepped to the bay gelding. Holding out her hand, Layla let the bay snuffle her. His nostrils flared and then the big horse gave a deep groan, his eyes settling half-closed. With a languid movement, the gelding pressed his forehead to Layla's chest, practically falling asleep on her. His black eyelashes closed and Layla realized she could feel a deep serenity coursing through the animal as he smelled her orange-bourbon scent.

"You've made a friend." Adam grinned with a wink. Stepping to a white mare beside Layla's besotted gelding, he held out his hand and was immediately rewarded by an excited whinny. Her ears perked and she pranced, practically jumping with delight as Adam mounted up. He stroked her neck and she calmed, though her body still shivered as if she was eager to run like the wind for him.

"Looks like you have, too," Layla smiled.

"Horses love me." He grinned back with a rapier wit. "Apples in my scent, you know."

Layla laughed. She took up the bay's reins and set her hands to the saddle, needing no help mounting, though not flashing anyone in her skirt was a bit of a problem. But the skirt was pleated, and tucking the long bustle beneath her thighs, she found she was protected from chafing. The call of a hunting-horn blared and hounds were brought out by the grooms, yipping on their leashes. These were handed over to three younger Dragons including Rachida's Greek valet. Just like that, the party began to move into the trees – Layla clicking her sleepy bay into a walk between Dusk and Adam.

The day was darkening as they selected a well-used trail through the dappled underbrush and thick moss. They soon left the trail and the horses spread out, moving down into fern-filled hollows and up rises, the dogs sniffing through the brush in front. Adam rode at Layla's left, Dusk on her right. Adrian had pulled his horse up next to his cousin, though he was quiet as they ambled through the shadowy forest. Above, Layla could see the sky blackening; clouds roiled in a charcoal mass as the brisk autumn wind blew the storm closer. Even though Adrian had rained on everyone's parade with his cutting attitude earlier, it looked like it was going to rain again.

Beating through the brush, the dogs suddenly bayed. Unclipping their leashes, the men gave them release and the dogs rushed into a thicket, baying and snarling. With a whirring of wings, six pheasant flew up into the grey sky. As they did, a brutal roar exploded from dozens of throats; magic thickening so fast around Layla that she felt like she was breathing molten glass. Whipping her horse forward, Rachida dashed up a rise after the pheasants. Suddenly, the Dragon-matron stood in her stirrups and screamed into the burgeoning sky – her body bending like a bow from the force. Like a lance, that scream tore the air, hurtling up toward the birds.

And like they'd been skewered, all six suddenly fell out of the sky; dead.

Rachida laughed like a girl, clapping her hands at her kill. Wheeling her horse, she gave it a flick with her quirt and laughed with bravado at the group. "*That's* how you bring down a brace of birds, children! Quickly, off to gather them!"

The party wheeled their horses in the direction the birds had fallen, but Layla reined in atop a rise, stunned at what she had just seen. Like an eagle or a falcon, Rachida's scream had pierced her ears with fierce talons. Layla had felt Rachida's Dragon-essence in it; she'd actually seen a fiery red streak of magic lance up through the darkening sky to make that kill.

"Showoff." Adam reined his horse up next to Layla's with a chuckle. "Gods, that woman loves to kill things. It's always the meanest old drakainas who love a good slaughter."

"How old is she, your adopted mother?" Layla glanced at Adam.

"Rachida?" He seemed to think about it as if doing mental calculations. "Well, she did give birth to Gaius Julius Caesar, so pretty damn old."

"Come on." Layla smiled wryly at him. "Really?"

"You think I'm pulling your leg." Adam tilted his head, a bemused smile on his face. He nodded at Rachida, now laughing with a number of young men who ogled her with delight, including the Greek. "Gaius was her first son, a Royal Desert Dragon in our Italian clan. Conquered half the known human world and got famous for it. Marcus Junius Brutus was also a Royal Desert Dragon, Gaius' Second. Brutus was the only one strong enough in his magic to bring Rachida's son down when Gaius became too power-hungry. Check your history books, Layla Price. A lot of world events attributed to humans weren't human at all. Twilight Lineage-wars spill out all over the human realm. Constantly."

Layla gave Adam a slow blink, then looked back to Rachida. Her pheasants had arrived and she took them up, slinging the dead birds over her saddle like trophies. Slapping her horse with the quirt, they walked on. "What did she do after her son was killed?"

"Found the Dragons who conspired against him," Adam's words were low, solemn. "Challenged them to a dominance battle. It was seven on one. None of them survived – she tore them all apart. But that was long before my time."

A strange energy went reeling through Layla at the horrific, incredible tale. She had that same sensation she'd had back in Seattle, as if she was watching herself from the outside. Seeing herself here, living history as she learned about her clan. A heated citrus scent wafted off her and she smelled an answering cinnamon-jasmine scorch on the wind. Looking over, she saw Adrian upon his big black horse on a separate rise, watching her, his gaze burning with gold-aqua fire. Their surroundings disappeared and for a moment all Layla could see was him – as if those eyes called to her soul just like their first night in Seattle. The party trailed after Rachida, but Adrian lingered – devouring her with his steady, molten gaze.

"We should keep up." Beside Layla, Dusk urged his horse on, gesturing for Adam and Layla as he went. Up the rise, Adrian walked his horse on also, moving though the brush. Adam kept his white mare beside Layla's, apparently not concerned about joining the hunt.

"Dusk said that Adrian has fought dominance battles." Layla glanced over to Adam.

"He has." Adam responded with a sober nod. "Adrian didn't become the clan's leader by being soft, Layla. Just because he's a Royal doesn't guarantee him a place at the top of the slashing-order. Adrian fought seven dominance battles to be where he is. The most recent one almost killed him – his challenger, one of the Sahara nomads, was a fucking brute. But Adrian managed to win, god only knows how."

"Has Adrian hurt people?" Layla asked, wondering.

"Dominance battles over the Clan First position generally end in death, Layla." Adam's voice was gentle, his gaze honest. "Some Dragons concede when they're losing, but most don't. It's one of the reasons Dragon-battles are fucking impressive. Once a man or woman goes full-Dragon for a fight, someone's going to die. The beast doesn't understand mercy, or surrender. It wants to fuck and it wants to kill. And that's about it."

Layla felt sick. Something inside her clenched, and she could smell Adrian's jasmine scent on the air as a roll of thunder boomed over the forest. Adam glanced at her, and then a soothing orchard scent rolled over her and Layla could breathe again.

"I'm sorry – did I upset you?"

"I just never thought of Adrian as a killer." Layla answered truthfully, glancing over at Adrian on the top of the rise. He watched them, then turned his horse and walked around a copse of trees, Dusk following with a deep frown. Up ahead, they heard the dogs bay. Again, Layla felt a massive bloom of power as she saw a trio of pheasants clear the trees and be swiftly brought down – this time, by two separate spears of golden light and one that was opal. A third dark navy shimmer missed the pheasants entirely, and at her side, Adam chuckled.

"Poor Soukos. Rachida's little paramour is *really* trying. Boy's just not a killer, though."

"The navy energy spear?" Layla glanced at him.

"Good, you can see them." Adam nodded with approval. "What you're seeing is a Dragon killing-strike. Small ones and tightly controlled, but effective for small prey. Soukos has enough strength to send a killing-strike to bring down small prey, but he always sends them wide. Either he's got terrible vision or he's sending them wide on purpose. Dragons don't generally miss their targets once they learn how to kill. Come on. We'd better catch up."

Adam urged his horse through a thicket of golden alder and Layla moved her horse in behind his. Dusk waited for them on his dappled mare and fell into step beside Layla, and she saw Adrian move his horse to the rear of their group, following.

Slowing her horse, Layla nodded for Dusk to ride ahead with Adam. Dusk lifted his eyebrows but acquiesced, not about to gainsay her in front of her clan. Layla appreciated that, and it made her smile a little. Slowing her horse so Adrian could catch up, she let him draw alongside. He glanced over but did not slow his black gelding. Layla clucked her tongue and her horse stepped on, keeping pace alongside Adrian's.

CHAPTER 14 – STORM

Layla paced her horse beside Adrian's, lagging behind Adam and Dusk, who had ranged on ahead through the golden-dark forest. A boom of thunder rolled in the clouds as rain began to spatter the leaves and ferns. Though the drops were still sparse, the gloom was finally winning. Layla felt heat in her veins from her ire with Adrian's attitude today, but the cold was also getting to her – as if her heart ached like a black pit, not able to combat the dreary chill.

"So are you ever going to talk to me?" She asked, glancing over at Adrian as her patience finally snapped. "Or are we just going to continue this stalemate in perpetuity?"

"I thought you didn't want me to talk to you." Adrian blinked as he looked over also, something surprised on his face. He reined his horse to a stop and Layla did the same in a low hollow crowded with ferns. Another roll of thunder sounded, though the rain kept its slim patter, not yet ready to drown their day.

Yet.

"Why wouldn't I want you to talk to me, Adrian?" Layla frowned, feeling confused, wanting to touch him and also wanting to slap him for being an idiot. "And why did you not come visit me while I was ill?"

"Because you told me not to," he murmured, his aqua eyes aching. "After you almost shifted… you told me to go away, to not touch you or talk to you. So I did. I tried to stay away so we wouldn't touch or speak with each other. So I wouldn't raise your Dragon again through our Bind."

"Oh, Adrian." Layla's heart broke to hear his words even as she stared at him, dumbfounded. She could feel the Bind between them as the beast inside her roared for his touch; roared to be recognized and included even in his idiocy. Layla's eyes stung; too hot. A desperate look came over Adrian's face as the first of her tears fell. He reached out between their horses, hesitated, then finally cupped her cheek in his hand. Layla hitched a breath, but Adrian was controlling his powers like a sonofabitch – she didn't smell even a whiff of cinnamon, didn't feel a single brush of scales from him. He just set his warm palm to her cheek as her tears slid down, his aqua gaze raw with apology.

"I'm so sorry, Layla," he grated, watching her. "I've been such an asshole."

"Yeah, you have been!" She half-laughed, half-sobbed, relishing his touch. Turning her face into his hand, she pressed her lips to his palm. She heard Adrian sigh, his eyes too bright now just like hers. "Don't you know that when a woman you're in a relationship with tells you to get lost, you're supposed to apologize and try to work it out, rather than give her the cold shoulder?"

He flushed, a beautiful look coming over his face as his jasmine-spice scent whirled through the drizzle, shaking the leaves and showering them in gold. "Are we in a relationship?"

"You tell me!" Layla laughed, shaking her head with incredulity. "I want to be in a relationship with you, Adrian. I want to get to know *you*, not just be mystically bound to you. But so far, all you've given me are half-cocked romantic evenings where you run out on me for weeks at a time, too-hot-to-process passion, or the deep cold shoulder. It's driving me insane!"

"I just… I go crazy around you," he rasped, annihilation taking his handsome face.

"I know." Layla laughed again, another tear blinking down her face. "I go crazy around you, too. Did Dusk tell you his theory?"

"He did." Adrian spoke, gazing at Layla with longing. "I'm starting to think I never should have bound that talisman on your wrist, Layla. That I did us both more harm than good. Dusk's right. I didn't research the Hamsa Bind talisman thoroughly enough – I didn't question the magic it contained as deeply as I should have. I bound us together with it and now we're both paying the price of that dire magic. I hate that you're paying for my impetuous stupidity. I can't stand seeing you suffer – and knowing I'm the cause."

"Are you always this volcanic in relationships?" Layla laughed again, rubbing away her tears though the rain was spattering more now, fat drops hitting her face.

"I didn't used to be." Adrian gave a sad, sincere smile. Removing his hunting jacket and leaning over from his horse, he settled it around Layla's shoulders as the rain pattered down, snugging it close around her to keep her warm. "I'm rusty on being close to people, and the Bind isn't helping. Would it make a difference if you knew I was trying?"

"Maybe." Layla shrugged his jacket around her, breathing deep of his heady desert-spice scent in the soft wool and satin. "Dusk said you've been celibate since we met."

"Dusk has a big mouth that he needs to keep shut." But the way Adrian's straight dark brows furrowed let Layla know it was true. He drew a deep breath, his aqua eyes locking to hers, deepening with gold. "I've had a lot of women in my time, Layla. But you slay me in a way I've never experienced before. I dream of citrus groves at midnight, tossing and turning in bed while seeing your eyes. I lose track of time when I sip a bourbon twisted with orange peel. I pause when I see women with hourglass curves and dark hair on the street. I turn, hoping to see your face. Hoping that you somehow figured out where I was and hopped the next flight searching for me. I didn't just bind you because it would raise my power, Layla. I bound you… because from the moment I saw you again at Mimi's funeral a few years ago, I couldn't bear to not have you in my life. I searched for the Hamsa Bind talisman not just to wrangle your power, but because I needed you beside me, *with* me. *These pains you feel are messengers. Listen to them.*"

Adrian's tirade and his final Rumi quote whirled in Layla's mind as his energy swirled around her, raw and passionate. The scent of jasmine was thick in the rain, drowning her. He reached his hands up, cupping her face in his palms and Layla's tears fell harder, wanting him so badly. But he was touching her, and it was so good through the hurt. Her power roiled in deep waves, responding to his and sending a spiced orange scent twining through the trees – coiling deep into his magics in a bright cord.

With a sigh, Adrian leaned close. Sliding his hands down around Layla's waist, he hauled her up from her saddle. In a smooth, powerful movement, he'd lifted her from her horse and slid her down his body astride his own saddle. Facing each other with her in front, Layla's power ranged out now that they were close – tasting his energy, devouring it, needing it as the rain soaked their clothes, a flash of lightning illuminating the black clouds as thunder boomed.

"How in the hell are we ever going to figure this out?" Layla spoke, needing him. Needing his energy, needing to smell him, to taste him – to inhale and touch every part of him.

"One step at a time," he breathed, kissing her shoulder, brushing his lips over the skin of her neck. Layla's heart raced at the touch of his lips, so smooth, so impossibly soft. A deep passion thrummed in him as he gathered her close to his lean, strong frame – though she could tell he was being exquisitely good, still holding most of his magic back from affecting her.

"I want you," Layla breathed, turning her face up to his.

157

"I want you, too." Adrian's breath was harder now, his chest starting to heave. Cinnamon flavored the air with jasmine now, and clove and sandalwood and more as his lips whispered over her neck and collarbones. Even as he pressed those soft, hot lips to her skin, she could feel him hauling his energy back – more in control than she had ever felt him.

"You're controlling your magic," she spoke, hating it but also grateful.

"I made a mistake at the party, acting on rash impulse." Adrian kissed her neck gently, though his breathing was hard now. "Adam and Dusk are right. I harmed you. I won't let it happen again."

"But I want it to." Layla breathed, arching in his arms as he kissed his way up her neck – feeling his strong, warm body pressed against hers. "I want it to unleash. For us to unleash together. I want to feel it, to ride it... to have it. Together."

"Layla... you don't know what you're asking..."

Adrian's heart was beating fast against her body, his breath ragged in his chest as he kissed her neck again. She could feel him struggling for control as he wrapped his arms tighter around her. Another roll of thunder moved through the heavy clouds. The rain was chill on Layla's skin, Adrian's energy so hot. With a growl, he heaved his hands up under her thighs, hauling her thighs up over his and pressing his body even closer to hers in the saddle.

She could feel the tip of him, so hard and hot, straining against his breeches and pressing through her skirt. With another deep growl, Adrian swiped the fabric of the skirt aside and tilted his pelvis, hauling her thighs up around his waist so Layla's boots were on the saddle as he pulled her hips in tight with his hands. His hardness found her, delved into her lace panties as if it would rip them apart and Layla cried out, shuddering hard as her bourbon-citrus scent surged from her, her veins racing with delicious heat.

Adrian cried out also, his head thrown back as his power roared around her now like the rain had caught fire. Crushing her close with one hand cradling her head and the other gripping her low back, Adrian trapped her to his powerful body. Losing his careful control, his energy roared out, scalding in the thunder and rain. Chain lightning ripped across the sky and a wind whipped, shedding golden leaves all around them. Layla gasped as Adrian pressed himself hard at her opening; her body all but bared to him and his barely contained. Controlling her by her hair, Adrian made her look down and meet his gaze as he pressed up deep, straining the small amount of fabric between them.

A hurricane of energy poured down around Layla as she stared into Adrian's amazing, vivid eyes. He gazed down at her with an incredible look, his eyes simmering a bright aqua-gold through the downpour. Water sluiced down his lovely face, highlighting his elegant cheekbones and black hair like diamonds on obsidian. His scalding hands were gripped firmly on her hair and back; steam whipped into vapor all around them from their burning hot magics. Emptying from the black sky and from Adrian, power roared through the shedding curtains of rain. As lightning flashed and thunder boomed, Layla felt her own heat flood out also – every drop of rain upon her skin another opportunity to shed her furious tensions and let her true passion flow free.

Layla felt Adrian surge; she felt an incredible power unfurl from him like some massive spread of wings all around her, scalding and roaring and bright. In the rain and cold, Layla felt her own power expand in response to Adrian's – filling the forest. Rolling out from her body, her magics expanded with an enormous heat – dancing with Adrian's; matching it coil for coil and scale for scale in a simmering mirage of vapor and wind and lightning all around them.

"God, I feel you, Layla..." Adrian's lips were so close; a hot breath from hers in the downpour.

"I feel you, too, Adrian..." Layla breathed, arching, reaching for him.

"I want you..." He breathed back, his arms tightening around her. Crushing her deliciously with all that enormous power and renegade heat. Rocking his hips, he thrust up; making Layla's spine bow with pleasure and a ruined sound of ecstasy, her eyelashes fluttering as she trembled deep inside – nothing separating them now but fabric.

"Then take me," she breathed back. "Please... this heat. We've postponed this too long. I can't wait any longer."

With a dark growl, Adrian abandoned his restraint – completely. His power roared, surging out so thick and fast around Layla that she screamed with pleasure; driving so deep inside her body that she convulsed with it. A wave of aqua and crimson flames burst upon the air with a nimbus of golden ones, her magic and his twined together in a massive coil of muscle and barbs and power.

And then they were kissing, lips hard upon lips, hands hard upon each other.

They drove into each other, they twisted; they coiled. Every kiss deeper, every gripping of hands more unrestrained. In the pouring rain, Layla's heat was devouring, rabid for him. Adrian's voracious power thrust through her in a mad drive as he ripped his breeches open. But the whinny of a horse up on the ridge made their heads turn. Surging, panting, Layla looked up to see Dusk on his grey mare in the downpour, his face a mixture of shock and fury as he watched her and Adrian down below. As their gazes connected, Layla felt a wall of crystal energy slammed up between them. And then Dusk's expression changed. As if he'd gone dead inside and all that was left was a beautiful shell – lovely as a diamond and just as hard.

Adam reined his horse up next to Dusk on the ridge, his hunter-green eyes bled dark. There was something furious in the set of Adam's tall, lean body also. Something so tight that Layla blinked as she palmed rain from her face, Adrian still holding her close.

"Having a good fuck?" Adam called out as he palmed his wet hair back with a laugh.

"Dammit, Adam!" Adrian laughed back, breathless.

But Layla knew Adrian had missed the coldness in Adam's eyes as he reached up, wiping rain from his face so he could see, his lungs heaving as his heart hammered as hard as Layla's. Adrian was smiling with reckless delight; the same smile Layla had seen the day they'd met. It was the smile she would have done anything for – luminous. His gaze returned to Layla and he growled a hot sigh, setting his forehead to hers. But they could both feel it; the storm was passing. Even now, the thunder was distant as the sky lightened. Adrian used one hand to surreptitiously zip his breeches, though he growled into Layla's neck as he did it. She shuddered, aching, needing him to finish it.

But Dusk and Adam were still at the top of the ridge. As Layla looked up, Dusk turned his horse and clicked his tongue – moving on over the ridge and out of sight beyond the trees. Adam watched him go, then turned back, reaching up to wipe rain from his short blond beard.

"Everyone's gone back to the barn, Adrian!" Adam called down. "They've called the hunt. Some of the clan are planning a party tonight, but they wanted to check with you. Otherwise, I really would have left you two alone."

Though his words were glib, Adam's smile said otherwise. Something in his energy was hard-edged, and though Layla couldn't smell his scent from this distance, she watched his eyes go ferociously dark as the cousins grinned at each other. Layla glanced from one to the other, suddenly feeling like those grins were snarls. But there were no magical pyrotechnics like before, and though Adrian's energy was still flowing wide around her, enormous, it seemed smooth now and didn't rush up the slope to fight with Adam.

"We're coming." Adrian called back. "No thanks to you!"

"No problem, asshole." Adam laughed as he flicked water out of his hair and beard again. "Really though, rain sucks. You guys coming back?"

"Go on! We'll be back soon."

"Sure you will."

Adam gave another dark grin then turned his horse, disappearing the way Dusk had gone. Turning to Layla, Adrian cradled her with a low growl. But the storm was over, only a patter of rain sparkling down from the golden leaves now as the sun began to strike through the clouds. Their moment had been broken and the power with it, though curls of vapor still breathed up around their bodies on the chill autumn air. Adrian heaved a sigh of content frustration and Layla matched it, winding her arms up around his neck and gazing into his amazing eyes.

"To be continued?" Adrian smiled down at her, sexy and utterly delightful.

"Absolutely." Layla spoke back, though something inside her still worried at both Dusk and Adam's reaction to their tryst.

But then Adrian lowered his lips and kissed her, and Layla forgot everything else.

CHAPTER 15 – ADRIAN

Adrian escorted Layla back from the hunt. Dusk wasn't anywhere to be found once they got back to the barn and relinquished their horses, though Adam was standing just inside the open barn-doors flirting with a pretty blonde groomswoman as he helped brush down the horses. He looked up as they arrived and hailed them, then stepped over as they dismounted and turned their horses over to be unsaddled and wiped dry.

"So, any more fun out in the woods, kids?" Adam grinned, his green eyes still dark though the violet ring around them was present now.

"One more word and you are so going to get canned from your position as my Second." Adrian glanced over with a grin as he turned the reins of his black Friesian over to the groomswoman, still in a soaring mood after he and Layla's tryst even though they hadn't been able to finish it. Layla felt herself blush, but Dragons were merciless teases she was learning, especially about sex. She straightened her spine and decided to deal with it without embarrassment as Adam laughed.

"You can't can me," he grinned, accompanying them as Layla gave her sleepy bay gelding one last scratch and they turned toward the barn doors.

"I could," Adrian grinned at his cousin as they reached the sliding-barn doors.

"You wouldn't." Adam grinned wickedly. "No one controls your reckless pleasures like I do."

"I couldn't have said it better."

Adrian laughed his infectious, spontaneous laugh, the same as the first day he and Layla had met. Her energy soared to hear it and a feeling of joy spread through her. He glanced over, his eyebrows raised at her wash of sweet bourbon scent. But Layla just shook her head, reaching out and tucking her hand around his elbow. He was soaked, his shirtsleeves rolled up now as Layla still wore his hunting jacket. But Adrian's skin was scalding, his shirt and vest already drying as Layla cuddled close and they walked away from the barn along the gravel path. She slid her fingers down, stroking the crimson, black, and gold dragon-tattoo that coiled around his left forearm.

He glanced at her, sexy and dark and bright all at once.

The sun was striking through the heavy clouds now as they walked back to the Hotel. Light sparkled from every golden leaf and blade of grass, making the world seem ultra-vibrant. Colors were richer and scents more stunning here in the Twilight Realm – all the senses enhanced. Even though the scenery was ordinary, every play of light on shadow had a clarity and intensity to it that made Layla catch her breath as she gazed around in the aftermath of her and Adrian's ardor.

And she realized suddenly that she hadn't seen anything of the Twilight Realm besides the Hotel grounds.

"So, what is the rest of the Twilight Realm like?" She asked Adrian and Adam as they ambled peaceably along the path. It seemed whatever tension had existed between the cousins was over now as both of them looked over at her with surprisingly similar motions. Layla blinked, realizing that Adrian and Adam had a shared way about them, even though Adrian was a searing sand-funnel to Adam's roguish pastoral orchard.

Dusk didn't share whatever it was, even though he'd been raised with them, and Layla realized that it was a similar cinnabar-spice scent that lingered around all the Desert Dragons she'd met today. They were more casual than Dusk, more relaxed – and more unpredictable. For all his teasing and sexuality, Dusk was highly predictable, something about his nature almost rigid compared to the chaos Layla felt moving through her own kind. She noted it as Adrian and Adam both opened their mouths to respond at the exact same moment, then Adam grinned, making a conceding gesture to his Clan First.

"The rest of the Twilight Realm is a lot like this," Adrian answered, glancing down at Layla as they walked through manicured woods, the crystal cathedral up ahead. "Some places seem as ordinary as the human world, though you'll always have a sense of heightened experience, while other places are about as wild as you can imagine."

"The heightened experience," Layla commented, seeing the facets of the crystal cathedral shine with color as they passed the enormous structure. Rain had only accentuated its vividness. "Why is that?"

"This whole realm vibrates at a different frequency than the human world," Adam chimed in. "It's sort of like being high. You know that feeling you have when you smoke a lot of weed or do mushrooms? How everything becomes crystalline and enhanced? It's like that."

"Do drugs much?" Layla grinned at him.

"As often as I can." Adam laughed brightly, a rogue to his core. "No, but really. This place is like stepping out of the regular frequency of your brain and all your senses and re-tuning them to a higher functionality. Its not uncommon for humans who spend a lot of time here to become psychic, actually. You know Edgar Cayce? He spent a lot of time in the Twilight Realm when he was young, and it opened up his ability to read people's bodies and make prognostications about their health. Not magic necessarily, but a different frequency of the body and mind."

"I wouldn't think someone like you would be interested in Edgar

165

Cayce," Layla lifted an eyebrow at Adam as they walked through the manicured gardens now. The lilacs were dead on their trees finally, as if they had given up their last the other night.

"Get to know me a little and you might be surprised, Layla Price." Adam chuckled.

"Don't get to know him too well." Adrian grinned.

"Asshole." Adam grumped pleasantly.

"Dick." Adrian grinned back.

"Alright boys," Layla admonished with a laugh. "No fighting now."

"Yes, Matron." Adam sassed her as they stepped over the flagstones that wound through the ponds. "No, but really. Our mothers insisted on Adrian, Dusk, and I having an intelligent upbringing. We studied all the poets, the prophets, mathematics, astrology, classical literature, you name it. People like Edgar Cayce and Ken Kesey and such strike my interest. They're iconoclasts; they push the envelope and make people see things in a new way."

"Well, well, the bad boy with the motorcycle thinks." Layla grinned at him.

"Hey. Don't knock my bike. It's pretty badass." Adam gave her teasing eyes, vibrant with both purple and green now. They had arrived at the Hotel and Adrian held the door open. Layla moved through, drowning in his eyes for a moment as they sparkled like sunlight on the deepest blue of the Mediterranean. He stepped behind her as they moved in, setting a hand to the small of her back and giving her a pleasant shiver. Adam was left to follow as they took a gilded staircase up two levels to Layla's room.

When they arrived, she didn't want to go. She didn't want to leave Adrian as he stepped in front of her, taking up her hands. His eyes were so beautiful, his handsome height so perfect, his short black hair sexily mussed from the rain. Layla couldn't stand it suddenly, how stunning he was. And now he beamed down at her, a smile softly curling his full lips as Adam stepped off a pace and pretended to be interested in the decorations on a Ming vase.

"The way you're looking at me right now," Adrian breathed down, his breath spiced with desert fragrance. "I feel like I don't deserve a look like that."

"Maybe not yet, but it's what I feel." Layla spoke, enjoying the smooth currents coiling between them. Adrian stepped closer, pressing one of Layla's hands with a soft kiss as he watched her, one hand curling around her waist. Gripping her just a little; just enough to catch her breath and remember everything they had shared out in the woods.

"Don't forget we have something to finish," he growled as he pulled her close, cupping her hand to his chest.

"I haven't."

"Good." Holding her hand to his chest, Layla could feel the burning heat of his skin radiating through his shirt. Adrian's hand kneaded her waist like he wanted to manifest talons and dig them into her, to pin her against him. Layla's breath caught and Adrian gave a wickedly alluring smile as he gazed down. She felt their beasts slide along each other, impossibly intimate like coils and hot scales. She felt their energies entwine and it was suddenly overwhelming – feeling so much of Adrian's body touching her even though he hardly touched her at all.

It was like what he had done the night he stood outside her window; when he had slid his wind-heat up her ankles, then made it dive in through her lips. But this was more like their time at the opera; stronger, like that sliding, sensual wind had muscle and girth to it. Power, as it coiled around her. Power, as it slid in through her lips, kissing her and licking deep into her mouth like a tongue.

Power, as it slid up her inner thighs and pressed deep into her body – as Adrian held himself carefully away, watching her with his annihilating aqua gaze.

Layla trembled against him as that meaty deliciousness delved into her both above and below; lifting her chin and making her knees weak as she practically begged for him to finish it with his real mouth and phallus. But he gave a handsomely dark smile and left her like that, lifting her hand to his lips and giving her the full force of his burning aqua eyes.

"Until later, Layla Price."

"Until later, Adrian Rhakvir."

She was unsteady as he let her go, his magics slipping away as his hand did also. Everything surged with pleasure and Layla shivered again, loving it. The things he could do to her without doing anything at all. It flooded her with the possibility of what they might enjoy together and she flushed. An orange-bourbon scent swirled up around her and Adrian smiled, flaring his nostrils to inhale it – then turned, beckoning to Adam.

"Come on, you. Let's discuss this shindig our clan wants to have later."

But Adam cleared his throat, his gaze darting to Layla then back to his Clan First. "Um, Adrian. I did promise Layla to meet for dinner tonight and answer her questions about the clan."

"Right." Adrian blinked, and Layla watched him surface from sexy, smoldering mode to clan leader mode. He glanced at Layla, his brows knit though he didn't simmer with mean energy against Adam's suggestion anymore. "I suppose it's your choice, Layla. Dinner with Adam, or do you want to party with the clan tonight? We can always do a clan-party tomorrow."

He was being intensely reasonable, and for a moment Layla

thought it was a trap. But his eyes were so luminous, so serene and clear, that she realized suddenly this was the normal Adrian – the Adrian everyone else saw regularly but whom she barely knew. An effortless leader, calm and collected without being rash, weighing the benefits and pitfalls of any action and taking into account the health of his clan. With a blink, Layla realized that she was seeing the real Adrian – and she liked it, tremendously.

"I would love to get some questions answered tonight, actually." She spoke, some part of her still wondering if Adrian was going to be angry about her decision.

But he only smiled, continuing to beam at her with those amazing aqua eyes. "Sure. Adam, Layla's case takes priority. Tell the clan they can get drunk together tomorrow night. They can do other things tonight. Dusk always has a number of evening activities planned at the Hotel – they can check with him and do whatever they wish this evening."

"Clan First." Adam gave a nod to Adrian, but a pleased smile to Layla. He was looking forward to dinner with her.

Smiling gently at Layla, Adrian spoke again. "Enjoy your evening; get your questions answered. I have some business to attend to, but I'll be up in residence on the fourth floor for the next week. I would love to schedule a dinner with you also – or a few, if you'll have me."

"Of course." Layla smiled at him, feeling her heart smile also.

Adrian saw it and beamed. With a chuckling laugh, he beckoned for Adam, then turned away, moving off with his Second down the hall. Layla watched them go, smiling, then ducked in through her door, closing it softly behind her.

Leaning back against the door, Layla let out a long breath. Her body still roiled with heat from how Adrian had kissed her before his departure. As if his energy still poured through her, Layla felt a deep, hot sensuality curl through her again, stroking through her body like a hand. She closed her eyes in the afterglow, feeling like that warm hand stroked up her neck, playing over her throat; gripping her gently. Layla gasped, making a pleasured sound as she leaned back against the door. That warm energy spilled up and in through her lips; kissing her. And then it dissipated on a cinnamon-spice breeze – as Adrian's baritone chuckle rolled through her ears.

She saw a flash of aqua eyes in her mind.

And then he was gone.

"You bastard." Layla breathed to the empty room, her lips curling into a smile.

But he was well and truly gone now, and did not answer. Smiling more, Layla pushed away from the door and stepped to the walk-in closet to shuck her sodden riding attire. It was only then she realized she was still wearing Adrian's riding jacket and she lifted one lapel, inhaling his scent. It made her smile again and she undressed quickly, taking her silk robe from its peg and sliding into it, cinching the sash.

Still smiling, Layla headed for her gilded bathroom. At the last moment, she picked up Adrian's jacket, taking it with her. Settling to a silk ottoman beside the claw-foot tub, she turned the chromed handles and started water for a bath, balancing the hot and cold. Remembering how the storm had balanced her and Adrian's heat earlier, Layla shed her silk robe, then stepped over the porcelain rim of the tub. Sinking into the water, she heaved a sigh, settling her head on the angled backrest.

Her fingers stole out, lifting Adrian's jacket from the ottoman. Bringing it to her lips, she inhaled his scent. Cinnamon-jasmine musk eased up into the curling steam, reminding Layla of the mirage of heat and rain that had risen up around her and Adrian earlier.

Her lips smiled more and she set the jacket aside.

Sliding a hand under the water, she sank into the bath, making the pleasure of the morning last.

CHAPTER 16 – JULIS

Down at the employee's bar for cocktail hour, Layla stepped through a gauntlet of Hotel Guards with pikes in the vaulted glass atrium and into the soaring Egyptian art deco lounge. All around, Hotel employees chatted at colorful silk chaises scattered through the vaulted hall of stone Buddhas, potted palms, and Egyptian-painted columns. It was the same place where she'd had her Hotel debut back in August, and though the space had been foreign then, it was well-known now. Layla hardly needed to glance around before she spotted Adam, sitting on a barstool at the classy copper bar tucked into the potted palms where Rake André normally worked.

Adam raised a hand, hailing her with a pleasant smile. Casual tonight, Layla had worn one of her cocktail dresses from Concierge Services, her sable curls up in a side-chignon. She didn't even realize she'd chosen the same dress Adam had first met her in until he grinned with obvious pleasure. The stretchy cream dress with burgundy lace shoulders was one of her favorites, and Adam's eyes glowed as she slid up to a barstool next to him, propping her burgundy heels on the stool's rung and crossing her legs. She'd worn some of Mimi's jewelry tonight just to keep it classy, the sapphire and diamond teardrop set winking in the overhead spotlights.

The bartender, a woman named Amira that Layla knew from yoga class, came up with a big smile, her chocolate skin hailing from India but in the Twilight Realm. Amira was a Dakini and one of Rake's regular partners, but beyond that, Layla didn't know her much.

"Hey, Layla." Amira moved up with a lovely smile, her honey-brown eyes entrancing. "What can I get you tonight?"

"Your best bourbon, with a small splash of water. And don't bullshit me," Layla grinned. "I know Rake keeps the good stuff under the bar."

"Coming right up!"

With a laugh Amira moved off, leaving Adam and Layla alone at the end of the bar. He was grinning at her, but there was something more in those jade-violet eyes of his as a sweet apple and honey scent rolled off him. Dressed in a snappy ensemble of charcoal pants and a matching vest, complete with a hunter-green silk tie that brought out his eyes, he had an honest-to god pocket watch on a gold chain clipped to his vest, which he tucked away as Layla settled. Russet leather wrist-bracers studded with antique brass rivets matched his russet Oxfords, making his entire outfit pop, elegantly punk-chic.

"Hey, sexy." Adam grinned as Layla settled in, receiving her drink from Amira.

"Hey, yourself." Layla sassed, feeling suddenly awkward at his greeting like maybe they were on a date after all.

"I'm not sexy?" Adam grinned, making big eyes and batting his blond eyelashes.

"You know you are." Layla gave him an eyebrow lift, turning on her barstool and taking up her glass. She hated to admit it but Adam had style, and he was damn sexy. But before she could sip to cover her attraction to him, Adam smiled like a rogue, lifting his Tom Collins and clinking glasses with a chuckle.

"Yeah, I know I'm sexy. Deal with it."

"And so suave."

"That's just my shampoo."

Layla laughed. Despite his asinine tendencies, Adam had wit, and

Layla had to admit she actually liked it. She shook her head, though she couldn't stop a grin. Sipping her bourbon, she found it was the same one she had up in her rooms, Rake's secret stash from New Orleans. Mellow and sweet, it filled her with a blissful ease, and Layla sighed with delight as she sipped. Whoever made it created nectar of the gods.

"That smells good," Adam eyeballed her drink, setting his own back down on the polished copper bar. "What is it?"

"Rake's secret sauce. Not my secret to divulge." Setting her drink down also, Layla faced Adam with a professional brusqueness. "So where do we start, talking about the clan?"

"Whoa! No foreplay?" He grinned like a brigand.

Layla flushed scarlet. A wave of heat rolled off her skin, scented with citrus. She opened her mouth to protest his teasing and tell him that in no uncertain terms was this a date, when he laughed and shook his head, holding up a hand to forestall her.

"I'm kidding! I'm kidding. You really haven't been around Dragons much, have you?"

"I just imagine the most asshat frat boys I used to serve at the bar in Seattle, and it works pretty well." Layla grumped sourly, though a sip from her bourbon immediately cured her sourness.

"Not all Dragons are asshats." Adam sipped his drink in a decidedly lurid fashion, still grinning at her. "Just me."

"Great. So I have full permission to toss my drink in your face at some point tonight?" Layla sassed, wondering if her little prophecy might just come true.

"Absolutely." Adam grinned back. "Others surely have."

The conversation halted suddenly, and they were left staring at each other. Layla felt Adam's honey-smooth energy falter as his green eyes deepened and the smile on his face slipped. He covered his intensity by sipping his drink, but Layla had felt it. Something deep lingered inside him. Like Dusk, Adam was far more than he seemed, and had learned how to cover it up with a blithe, teasing demeanor as much as Dusk covered his depth with brusque, affable do-it-all camaraderie. Layla cocked her head, a smile touching her lips as she suddenly understood far more about Adam.

"Are you nervous about meeting me tonight?" She asked, though she already knew the answer.

Adam's blond eyebrows lifted, but rather than bullshit her, he set his drink down to the copper bar with a sigh, meeting her gaze. "I am, actually."

"Why?" Layla's brows knit, curious to know more about the real Adam she was seeing now. It was the same person who had faced off with Adrian in the pavilion, she realized suddenly. The feel of his power was soft yet strong in a way she couldn't quite describe, like a good perfume. She felt it curling around her as Adam gave a soft laugh. Turning his Tom Collins glass on the bar with his fingertips, his ornate emerald and platinum dragon-ring flashed in the light of the beaten-copper spots overhead.

"Well, I could start with the obvious." He smiled wryly, though his green eyes darkened. "I'm insanely attracted to my cousin's girl. She compels me like no-one I've ever met. And she's sitting right here looking like a fucking Dragon Queen, shooting the shit with me and sipping good bourbon. Not to mention the fact that her *skin* smells better than the best bourbon I've ever had, which is fucking hot as shit. Do you want me to continue?"

His directness made Layla blush hard. Her citrus scent wafted up around her and she shifted on her barstool. But rather than back down, she set her bourbon on the bar and dug in with her talons. "So is this a date? Is that why you invited me here, Adam?"

"Not unless you want it to be." He grinned, rapacious, though his gaze was still dark, simmering with that new energy Layla was discovering about him.

"Adam." Layla gave him a withering look.

"No, it's not a date." Adam gave her a more subdued smile, then sighed. "If it was, Adrian would eat me alive. But I can't help liking what I like, Layla. Just thought I'd clear the air before we go any further. I'm jealous of Adrian. I want you; he knows it. I'm not going to make a move and destabilize our clan, but I need to be honest."

"You really are like Dusk, aren't you?" Layla cocked her head at him. "Brutal honesty is also his M.O. And covering his true nature with another one."

"Sometimes." Adam smiled wryly, though his gaze sharpened on her now, alert as if she'd hit just a little too close to home. "Dusk is his own creature, though. I'm sure you haven't even seen the tip of that buried diamond yet. He pretends he's devil-may-care, but just wait until you see him really pissed off."

"I saw some of that when I nearly shifted the other day."

"Some." Adam eyeballed her with a dark intensity, setting his drink aside on the glossy copper bar. "Layla. Do you know anything about this world you've just entered? How dangerous it is – how intense? Do you know the full repercussions of what nearly happened during that party the other night?"

"Dusk has told me a fair bit." She shifted on her seat, trying not to fidget. "How about you fill me in on the rest?"

She thought he might speak, but instead Adam just sat there, watching her. With a frown narrowing his straight blond brows and a dark intensity in his hunter-green eyes, he swirled his Tom Collins, then downed it and set the glass decisively aside on the bar. "Finish your drink."

"What?" Layla blinked.

"Finish your drink." Sliding off his barstool, Adam nodded in thanks to the bartender and pinned Layla again with his eyes, a truly dark green now. "We're going somewhere else."

"Do I get to know where that is?" Layla asked suspiciously, taking a deeper drink of her bourbon, though it was a shame to sip something this good so quickly. Something in Adam's manner had raised her hackles a little, and deep inside, her Dragon shifted, watchful.

"You want me to fill you in on our world?" Adam cocked his head, something piercing in his eyes now. But despite that, he was calm, and Layla sensed nothing dark in his intentions.

"Yeah." Layla frowned, still not sure, but intrigued.

"Then finish your drink and get up off your ass."

Layla blinked at him. Her Dragon roared inside her, affronted at his demanding language. A whip-hot heat surged from her, and she was about to open her lips and give him an earful when Adam's hand suddenly flashed out to her bourbon glass. In one fell swoop, he'd downed her drink, clapping the glass to the bar and grinning like a Roman devil.

"Hey!" Layla growled, pushing to her feet to get right up in his tall, smug face. "You suck!"

"Got you up off your ass, didn't it?" Adam grinned like a brigand, something much lighter in him now as he gave a laugh. "Come on. Evening's not going to party by itself."

He was suddenly moving off, striding through the atrium and down the hallway with a long, purposeful stride. Layla growled as she picked up her feet, trotting across the marble floor in her high heels to catch up. She was quickly deciding that Adam was far more of a pain in her ass than Dusk. And as a Desert Dragon, he was far more unpredictable – which Layla began to realize she found both contentious and alluring.

Finally catching up as he turned the corner, Layla kept pace as he strode to a side-door that led out to a courtyard north of the sprawling main building. Marching to a sleek wine-red and black cafe-racer Harley in the motorcycle parking area, Adam lifted a black leather jacket from the seat and tossed it at Layla, then handed over a matching helmet.

"Ever ride on a bike?" He grinned, picking up his own helmet from the seat. "A real bike, I mean, not those fucking push-pedal scooters that hipsters drive around in Seattle?"

"Enough times." Layla couldn't help herself, she grinned as she donned the black jacket. Though it was far too big, clearly made to fit Adam's tall, fit physique. "Ok, now you've got me curious. Where the fuck are we going?"

"You know Paris?" Adam slung on his helmet, the visor up so he could see her. Slinging a leg over the cafe-racer, he wheeled it back out of its parking spot.

"Are we going into the city?" Layla asked as she donned her own helmet.

"Something like that. Hop on." Adam twisted, patting the seat behind him.

Layla was hesitant, but something inside her boiled for an adventure tonight. Adrian was too busy to show her a good time, Dusk was too proper in his boss / employee relationship, and also too damn busy. And though Adam wasn't Layla's first choice to go out on the town with, she realized that a night out of the Hotel would be just the thing tonight. Tensions had been high lately, and Layla could use a little fun.

With a conceding laugh, she stepped to the bike, slinging a leg over and settling in behind Adam. She could practically feel him grin as he secured her arms around his middle, then fired up the bike, revving it. Turning it, he put on the gas hard enough that Layla had to grip him tight as they peeled out into the evening.

Exhilaration filled her as they raced through the courtyard along the Hotel's wrought-iron fence. Adam was a natural, guiding his bike in fast, smooth arcs around planters and lampposts, zooming them in delight to the gilded Hotel gates. The gates barely parted in time as they roared through. But as they raced through the stone posts that acted as a portal from the Twilight Realm to the human world, Layla experienced no disorientation like she expected passing between Realms. As they zoomed along the avenue, she found it turned into a country lane surrounded by a thick forest rather than the busy city of Versailles. Flying along a deserted nighttime road now, Layla understood with a jolt that they weren't going anyplace in the human world.

Adam was taking her out in the Twilight Realm tonight – the City of Julis rather than Paris.

The motorcycle's headlight was bright in the forested darkness as they roared around turn after turn. Layla heard a waterfall as they took a tight hairpin turn, heading down into a ravine she was certain didn't exist in the human world, before they roared up the other side. A vehicle approached but as the headlights passed, Layla's eyes widened to see it was some kind of mechanized brass and copper carriage with arching brass lamps and a shockingly purple velour interior. It galloped with eight legs like a spider-horse, passing with a jingle of bronze bells. Layla was still blinking, astounded, as a very normal-looking yellow Ferrari zoomed past next. And then Adam roared the bike up another slope and around a bend – giving a broad view over a wide valley surrounded by jagged cliffs.

A city sprawled through the valley, in the same place Paris would have occupied, but it was unlike any Paris Layla had ever seen. There was a broad river like the Seine but it curved through the land differently, and all around the city's margin wasn't the sprawl of suburbia but the darkness of a forest, glowing under a high sickle moon and a wide sky of autumnal stars. The lights along the avenues were of every hue, and as they zoomed down from their vantage, wrought-iron Gothic lampposts began along both sides of the road.

Swirling with lights like fireflies, every lamppost featured a snarling gryphon or dragon or mythical creature coiled around the base. Another odd carriage approached, a double-decker clockwork Gypsy caravan. Layla gaped as it passed, pulled by eight massive lions, each with enormous leathery wings tucked tight to their backs as they pulled in their traces. The lions snarled as Adam passed and one swiped out at the bike, which he dodged with a fast maneuver. As they zoomed by, Layla saw scorpion tails whipping behind them, and she heard Adam shout back through the wind.

"I fucking hate manticores! Worse than potholes!"

But as they raced along a watercourse into the city, the isolation suddenly broke to houses and sidewalks. The City of Julis was like a city time had forgotten, antique and fantastical. Similar to Paris in the Victorian era, Gothic mansions stood side-by-side with Victorian row-houses and French Baroque chateaus. Shops and restaurants of stone lined the streets with wide plazas surrounded by cathedrals even more gargantuan than Notre Dame. Everything was wrought-iron, gilded, and cobblestoned, and they zoomed past all manner of vehicles on the evening avenue; from horse-and-carriage, to Teslas, to huge-wheeled bicycles.

Turning down a side street, they headed through a Gothic neighborhood past a wooded park and into a gayly colorful quarter. Wrought-iron and brick apartments crowded close, bars were packed with evening revelers spilling out onto the streets. Wineshops were bursting with song and music on every corner. Many people looked human, but Layla also saw bird-men and cat-people, Satyrs and Phoenix out and about, even a group of Faunus laughing with smoke rising from their nostrils as they stumbled from a bawdy hookah bar.

The dress in Julis was no less astounding than its vehicles. Layla saw everything from Victorian corseted frocks to 1700's couture with white-curled wigs, to waistcoats and trousers straight out of the movie Newsies. Modern fashions looked like they'd been curated from the pages of Vogue and Harper's Bazaar, and Layla suddenly realized where the Hotel's Head Clothier got her gregarious designs. Dressing like Cirque du Soleil met Victorian steampunk was the norm, and as Adam pulled up before a lively bar on the corner of a broad cobblestoned plaza strung with multi-colored lights, a feisty gypsy-band playing within, Layla felt out-of-place in her cream cocktail dress and burgundy heels.

As they slung off the bike and Adam reached out to take her helmet, he gave her a rapacious grin. "Welcome to the City of Julis, Layla Price. What say you?"

"I say wow." Layla stared around like a drunk person. If she'd thought the vibrance of the Hotel had inundated her when she'd first arrived in the Twilight Realm, it was quadruply so here. The air was super-saturated with fragrance; music broke upon her ears from every street. The lights were so bright they seemed like rose-crystal flooded with starlight. The bar before her glowed with warmth, people laughing as they spilled out to wrought-iron balconies and a sprawling porch. They smoked pipes in the potted greenery, hookahs, and cigarettes. They drank red wine, cocktails, and moon-silver *sileth*-wine. They clapped as musicians finished their lively tune through the open windows, they stomped cloven hooves, they rubbed fingers together producing a chirring sound like grasshoppers.

It was a wonderful cacophony of sound and motion and color –

and Layla felt instantly at home, like she once had in the vibrant Capitol Hill neighborhood of Seattle.

With a bow, Adam motioned her up the steps of the bar and past the crowded front porch, then in through the open wrought-iron doors. The space was so packed they had to push their way inside, turning sideways to squeeze up to the long mahogany bar. Shining beneath bright Tiffany lamps and crystal chandeliers, the bar was welcoming, with stout padded booths of crimson leather lining the walls and a rickety Victorian staircase leading up to the second level.

The musicians were taking a break, settling their gypsy-band instruments near a roaring river-stone fireplace. Gothic and Victorian mirrors threw the light, making the bar seem enormous though it was actually cozy. Fortunately, a couple vacated their leather-padded barstools just as Layla and Adam pushed in. Sliding up to a seat, Layla grinned at the beautiful melee as a handsome bartender noticed them, and beamed as he recognized Adam.

"Adam Rhakvir, be still my beating heart!" The tall bartender laughed as he came over, in a bright baritone that made Layla feel instantly happy. He wore a charcoal waistcoat and a black collared shirt, his sleeves rolled to his elbows with charcoal trousers. A white bar-towel was slung over one shoulder, sleek black curls pulled back from his face in a stylish man-bun. Black stubble graced his chin, his lean good looks and high cheekbones as stunning as any Courtier of the Hotel. Dark eyes the color of coffee laughed to see them, and Layla instantly adored him.

"Jessup Rohalle! Thought you might be working tonight!" Adam extended a hand and they clasped wrists like old friends.

"Marnet's got me working every night this week until Samhain on the thirty-first – Rollows Eve, you know. I'm never free of that old goat this time of year!" Jessup laughed with an infectious good humor.

"I heard that, you miscreant!" A booming male voice yelled from around a wooden doorway that led back to steaming kitchens. "Rollows is our most important night of the year! I need you here, working!"

"I meant for you to hear!" Jessup yelled back over his shoulder in the way of family. "I need a day off! You can't just work me to death, old man."

"When you're dead, *then* you get a day off! Until then – work!"

Jessup laughed, clearly on good terms with whomever was in the back cooking. He chuckled, then tossed out two coasters before Layla and Adam, decorated with a laughing jester. "So what'll it be, Adam? You two in town for Rollows?"

"Rollows?" Layla glanced at Adam, her eyebrows lifted in question.

"It's like Mardi Gras, but twenty times more decadent. It's a saint's day here in the City of Julis, something they celebrate rather than Halloween or Samhain." Adam grinned at her, then looked back to Jessup. "No, we're just here for the night, for dinner. And make sure Marnet doesn't spit in it, will you?"

"I heard that, Adam Rhakvir, you little dog!" Rounding the ingress to the kitchen came a man just as fat as he was tall, not sloppy but burly with serious muscle. His pate was shining bald on top with short dark curls around the outside, his black mustachios curled up with wax. He chuckled heartily, his black eyes glittering as he wiped enormous, filthy hands on his equally filthy white apron. Roaring laughter, he extended a hand to Adam and they shook before the man spied Layla.

"Well!" He boomed over the bustle of the bar. "And who's this?"

"Layla Price." She stuck a hand out without waiting to be introduced. "I'm a friend of Adam's."

"A *friend*, eh? *Enchanté!*" The man grinned at her lecherously, taking her hand in his enormous one and pressing it with a kiss. "I am

183

Marnet Lousoutte, the owner of this fine establishment! Anything you need, beautiful *mademoiselle*, you have just to yell it through the thick skull of my nephew Jessup here, and he'll mess it up at least six times before I fix it!"

"I heard that." Jessup crossed his arms, grinning in a pleasant way as he leaned a hip against the bar.

"I meant for you to hear, miscreant." Marnet gave his nephew a teasing grin. "In any case, good to see you Adam, and Adam's Hotel Courtesan for the evening. The kitchen is busy tonight and my *pot-du-vin* won't wait! Do excuse me."

With that, the big man bustled back to the kitchen. Layla blinked, turning beet-red as a flavor of scorched bourbon lifted from her skin. "He thinks I'm a Hotel Courtesan?" She looked to the bartender. "Will you please tell him I'm not?"

"Could have fooled me. You're lovely enough to be one." Jessup's dark gaze was sexily deviant as he poured them a pair of waters from a copper pitcher.

"Watch it, Jessup. She's Adrian's." Adam spoke with a sly grin as he took a sip of water.

"Adrian!" A look of terror suddenly washed over Jessup's handsome face. He flushed across his high cheekbones and when he spoke again, it was with a very professional courtesy. "Forgive me, Ms. Price. If I had known you were Adrian's, I never would have—"

"It's fine." Layla held up a hand, forestalling Jessup's cute blustering. He was flushing so hard he looked like he might just crawl underneath the bar, and it was damn adorable. Layla realized he was young for a Twilight Realm person, probably no more than twenty-five, and still had that sprightly embarrassment of youth. "Adrian doesn't own me. He and I are complicated, that's all."

"Welcome to the Gypsun Quarter, where *everything* is

complicated." With a grin, Adam raised his water in a toast. "And welcome to the City of Julis. You think Paris is eccentric? The City of Julis is thrice as decadent, and far more fun."

CHAPTER 17 – ADAM

Adam ordered dinner at Marnet's bar, requesting whatever the heavenly smell was issuing from the kitchen plus dessert. Their food arrived promptly, personally delivered by Marnet with a wink and a twirl of one waxed mustachio. A delicious-looking stew of red wine and beef so expertly cooked it was falling off the bone, the meal was accented by sprigs of rosemary, thyme, and a fragrant purple peppercorn. Jessup brought them two glasses of Marnet's best bourbon, plus something called a *gin-lemon fizz* for Adam as Layla set her spoon to the heavenly broth and began to eat.

"A gin-lemon fizz?" Layla lifted an eyebrow at Adam as she dug into the tender beef. "Is that like a Sloe Gin Fizz?"

"No, it's a Tom Collins." He grinned at her as he began to eat also. "They don't know my favorite drink by that name here in the Twilight Realm, except at the Hotel."

"I met someone recently in Seattle who said a Tom Collins was their favorite drink." Pausing her meal, Layla frowned at Adam. "You sure that wasn't you in disguise?"

Adam blinked at her, confused though he was still smiling as he set down his spoon. "You know I can't visage-shift, Layla. Ask anyone in the clan. If you met someone in Seattle who loves the same drink I do, I'm sure it's just blind coincidence. Unless it was Adrian, imitating one of my habits for an alter-persona."

"No, it couldn't have been him," Layla shook her head as their drinks arrived. Jessup handed her bourbon over with a handsome smile, then whisked away to another group. Layla watched him go as she sipped her drink, a fabulously smooth bourbon though not as good as Rake's secret sauce. The atmosphere was high inside the bar now, like someone had spiked the air with uppers. Bawdy singing had begun outside on the porch and people were dancing in ecstatic frenzy to the band's music, laughing gregariously. The bar held a wildly happy intoxication and as Jessup passed by again, Layla felt a bold yet innocent aura pouring out of him – whirling that happy frenzy higher. He sang under his breath as he mixed drinks, an enormous smile on his face as if he was loving every moment of wildness inside the establishment.

He winked at Layla as he passed by again, delivering a tray of drinks to the end of the bar, apparently no longer concerned about Adrian.

"Jessup is just sunshine in a bottle, isn't he?" Layla laughed, watching their cute bartender.

"Not always." Adam gave her a knowing glance over his bourbon. "Wait until the music changes later. You'll find no higher highs and no sadder woes anyplace else on earth than inside a Gypsun bar."

"Gypsun? Is that Jessup's Lineage, and Marnet's?" She asked Adam, glancing at him.

"Jessup and Marnet are *Tempesti gypsonii,* Gypsun Tempests." Adam smiled at her genially as he swirled his bourbon, then tucked into his stew also, blowing on the spoon. "Most of the people who live in this Quarter of Julis are. They're part of the Tempest Lineages, which include Furies and Valkyries. Gypsun Tempests are the most mild-mannered of the Tempests, though. They love the arts; music, song, cooking, dance, painting – any profession where they can channel their emotions into creativity and help others emote. And they tend to wander like the human Romani, with which they've historically

187

interbred. Of all the Tempest breeds, only the Gypsun have the additional abilities of being Seers. In highly intense emotional states, they can talk to the dead, communicate with non-physical entities in the demonic or higher realms. Though that's a fairly rare ability."

"So do people come to this bar so they can emote?" Everyone was having a heady, ecstatic time as the band struck up another fast tune by the fireplace.

"Damn straight." Adam grinned, tracking Layla's gaze to the enthusiastic band. "Why do you think Adrian and I come here? Because when our emotions come out here, we don't need to apologize for them. Laughter, tears, ecstasy – nothing is forbidden in the Gypsun Quarter of Julis."

As if on cue, the music suddenly changed. The energy inside the bar became deliciously moody as the musicians began playing a darkly sexual song with a rhythm like a Spanish flamenco. As if a spinning top had clattered over, Layla felt it sweep up the bar's frenzy and cast it out through the open windows with a curl of night-breeze. She instantly relaxed as the lights turned low and dancers took the floor, beginning an intimate partner dance very much like the flamenco.

Layla watched as she and Adam ate, feeling her veins heat with fire. Like the blaze that roared in the river-stone hearth, her Dragon began to stir inside her with a sweet-bold heat. Smoke curled through the bar, teased by the October breeze, and Layla breathed deep of intensely sexual scents now issuing from couples kissing in booths all around. It was moody and divine, and Layla drew a deep inhalation, enjoying the atmosphere more than opium. Turning to Adam, whom she could feel watching her as she devoured the bar's change, she gestured with her bourbon.

"You know what this is doing to me, don't you?"

"It's not just you." He smiled rakishly, something darkly pleased in it as his hunter-green irises flashed in the Tiffany lights. "Look around. This is what a world of magic feels like, Layla. The highs, the lows, the intensity of it is more than you could have ever dreamed in the human world. The Hotel provides exquisite experiences, but for someone raised human, simply living in a city like Julis is experience enough."

"So why did you really bring me here?" Layla asked, setting her drink aside as the music changed to a mournful tune that dug her heart from her chest and ate it raw.

"Because this is the kind of place Adrian wouldn't know to show you." Adam turned towards her on his barstool, his gaze deep with his inner persona now as he set down his spoon and pushed his meal away. "It's the kind of visceral experience Adrian forgets about the Twilight Realm – a place where a Dragon can feel everything we are, safely. Can feel it and accept that sex and blood and battle run in our veins. Dragons are carnal creatures, Layla. Moreso than almost any other Lineage. And the sooner you accept that, the sooner you'll accept yourself. Because I know you don't yet. And if you're going to control your magic, you need to accept that your passions and rages are simply what you feel – and that they're ok. That they're a part of you. Something to be embraced, not rallied against. To let wash over you like the music in a Gypsun bar, rather than fight so damn hard."

Layla took an inhalation, surprised that Adam could read her so well, yet not surprised. Like Dusk, Adam seemed immensely intuitive in his deep inner persona, though he covered it with his daily charade. She found herself impressed by his frankness and also challenged by it. When the mournful Gypsun chanteuse began a new song, Layla sobered. She'd never been comfortable with the passion that lived inside her. Her volcanic temper had been a hard thing when she was young, with too many tough lessons. Fire roared in Layla's veins and it always had. She knew that now, but it hadn't made life any easier.

"I've always felt it," she murmured, taking up her drink for comfort. "The blood and battle inside me. The passion."

"We all do." Adam's dark gaze was kind, but he didn't try to console her. "Even for Dragons raised around magic, sometimes their true abilities don't open up until late. For younglings with no magical outlet for their temper and passion, it can be a wild, tough ride."

"But you opened up early."

"I did, but only because of dire circumstance." Adam's gaze was level, holding hers with deep emotion. "Dusk was the same. Adrian didn't see his family killed in front of him like Dusk and I, but his parents nearly tore each other apart from fighting, which is worse in some ways. It caused him to open young to his magics also. Living our life is hard, Layla. Mimi tried to save you from that by taking you to the human world. She thought it would protect you. But now you've hit your late twenties with a total naïveté about your own urges. Which is why I decided to bring you here – so you can see you're not alone in your frustrations and the epic emotions your magic brings."

"Epic emotions." Layla snorted, swirling her bourbon. "That sounds about right."

Adam smiled, taking up his Tom Collins now that his bourbon was done and pushing away his finished bowl of stew. "In any case, I'm here to answer your questions. Hit me. What do you want to know about our clan or about your magic?"

Suddenly there were too many questions. Layla had come here tonight wanting answers about her clan, but now felt like she wanted to ask more personal questions. And getting personal suddenly brought Dusk to mind. These past days, she'd felt something far more personal rising between her boss and her. He'd mentioned that Layla's magic was seeking powerful mates to bind in Adrian's absence – and Layla knew the first question she needed an answer to.

"You mentioned that Dusk is a powerful Royal but that he hides it." She spoke plainly. "I've heard others say similar things but I've never seen him do anything particularly stunning at the Hotel, other than the night I almost shifted. How powerful is he, Adam, really?"

Adam's eyebrows rose at the topic but he gave a dark smile, as if he enjoyed outing his adopted cousin's personal business. "Dusk is a force of nature, Layla." Adam spoke as he set his drink down on the bar. "He only shows a small sliver of it at the Hotel because he doesn't want to offend anyone – problem-solving is his M.O., and him getting his panties in a twist at something is against his intent as Head Concierge. But let's put it this way: you know the earthquake that fucked Fukushima? Dusk could have caused that if he'd been angry enough. Crystal Dragons are strong, but Dusk is a Royal Crystal Dragon, and a powerful one to boot. Even if his Egyptian clan wasn't dead, he'd still be their First, hands down. It's no secret that the Crystal King Markus Ambrose is watching Dusk carefully – because he's afraid Dusk may rival his own power someday. Maybe sooner than later."

Layla's eyebrows rose, so much about Dusk making sense suddenly – and why Layla's Royal Bind magic was reaching out to him. "If that's the case, then why does Dusk hide how strong he is? Is it because of his position at the Hotel?"

"Not exactly. It's because he's not done growing." Adam gave her a look, sipping his drink.

"What do you mean?"

"I mean that Dusk is *actually* like a crystal or a diamond." Adam nodded up at the crystal chandeliers above. "They're never done maturing. And the older Crystal Dragons get, the stronger they get. Like Adrian and I, Dusk is only one hundred and fifty years old. I'm nearly finished maturing in my magic. Adrian's got a ways to go; he's still surprising everyone. But Dusk will never be done growing in his magics. His power will never stop getting more formidable. There are people out there, not just King Markus, who would slit Dusk's throat in his sleep if they had any idea how powerful he really is. Even Adrian's afraid of it, I think. Or he should be. I'd hate to see it if they ever had a real fight."

Layla blinked at what Adam had said. It painted Dusk in a whole new light, and she believed it. How effortlessly Dusk had used his powers to stop her beast from shifting. That invisible crystal wall he could slam up against other people's magics like an armored shield. The way even the slightest rumble from him could shudder the earth. Layla sipped her drink, thinking about it. "They've fought pretty badly before, haven't they, Dusk and Adrian?"

"As kids." Adam nodded, his face serious. "It landed them both in the hospital more than once."

"That bad?" Layla's brows rose.

"Their biggest fight was in their early twenties," Adam continued, "over a girl Adrian had fallen in love with and Dusk then charmed and fucked for fun. Adrian could shift into his beast by then but Dusk couldn't. Adrian attacked as his Dragon, roaring and slamming Dusk with tail and talons, whipping sand-funnels like a fucking hurricane. But Dusk was in human form. And still, he managed to not only weather that storm, but get Adrian's beast pinned and choked at the throat by a noose of crystal magic. Rachida had to knock them both out to stop the fight. The girl left them both and Adrian left home in a rage to go find himself traveling the world. They haven't fought like that since, but it simmers sometimes."

"Jesus." Layla blinked, trying to imagine it. "What does Dusk's Dragon-form look like?"

"It doesn't." Adam set down his glass with a frown. "He still can't shift."

"But I thought all Dragons could shift."

"Generally. It comes at some point as our magics mature." Adam nodded, still looking strangely concerned. "But Dusk has never changed – not yet. It's a scary thought, actually. It means he's still quite juvenile in his power. Like a fucking Pokemon, what we see is far from his final shape."

"Wow."

"Yeah." Adam's eyes had gone a deep hunter-green, dark with thoughts Layla couldn't even come close to interpreting. Like he'd looked on the ridge when he'd come across Adrian and Layla's tryst in the forest, there was something deep inside Adam that simmered in darkness. As if he'd seen too much war, Layla suddenly realized her perception of him as a WWII flyboy or a Roman conqueror was strangely accurate. On the surface he was blithe. But deep down, Adam was scarred – in a way that Dusk and Adrian, for all their conflict, just weren't.

Looking up as the mournful song ended and the musicians took a break, Adam's haunted look cleared. "What else would you like to know about our clan, Layla?"

"What in the hell does Adrian really do for a living?" The second question of the night was already on the tip of Layla's tongue. "And why can't he ever stay in one place?"

Adam laughed his good, bright laugh, his former moodiness banished. Taking up his Tom Collins, he downed the rest of it in one fell swoop, then set it back to the bar. "A better question is: what *doesn't* Adrian do for a living? Adrian's a business mogul, Layla. He invests money in a lot of places, heads up a number of boards for international companies, is a part-owner in the Hotel, which is a far more elite and difficult position than you might think. He trades stock, he invests in alternative energy and clean-earth tech. He's a primary investor in Space-X and Tesla and a number of companies you'd recognize. He's been involved in zero-point energy development and holds an *enormous* amount of Bitcoin and different cryptocurrencies. He's also part of a ring of Twilight tycoons that find genius inventors and whisk them away into the Twilight Realm so they can continue their work safe from deep-state persecution."

"So that's why he's never around." Layla stilled on her barstool, wondering if she had been too hard on Adrian. She'd imagined some of the things Adam had said just now, but hearing it all laid out in one long list was overwhelming. She couldn't imagine how one man could manage so much and have any life at all. But it was still difficult, learning all this about Adrian from other people – never from the Royal Desert Dragon himself.

"It's rare for Adrian to be in one place for even a handful of days." Adam's expression softened as he watched her. "He's a nomad, Layla. A business nomad, but a nomad all the same. Our ancient Desert Dragon ancestors roamed the deserts like the wind, similar to the Gypsun Tempests. He's like that. But I think…I think somewhere underneath it all, he's looking for something real. Something to give him a home."

"Are you saying I could pin him down?" Adam's direct gaze was not lost upon Layla.

"Maybe." Adam shrugged. "But I think the question you should ask yourself is – do you want to?"

"What do you mean?" Layla frowned, sipping her drink.

"I mean – is Adrian worth your heartbreak and rage?" Adam's gaze was penetrating. "Desert Dragons are passionate creatures, and the two of you spin each other up like like nothing I've ever seen. Maybe not in a good way."

It was far more than insightful. It was as if Adam could do that trick Dusk did, of climbing inside Layla's heart far more than she wanted anyone to, and coming to the same conclusions. She shifted on her barstool, re-crossing her legs as she cradled her bourbon glass.

"I don't know. The connection I feel to him…"

"All magic can be broken, Layla." Adam's voice was sincere, his green eyes deep. "The Bind Adrian placed on you was criminal. I didn't know about his scheme until after he succeeded. But if I had known…" Adam took a deep breath and sighed, rubbing a hand over his trim blond beard. "I would have told Adrian not to do it. Ancient magics like that cuff of yours come with dark prices. Things no one should have to pay. Least of all you."

"Thank you." Layla found herself speechless from Adam's honesty. She glanced down at the silver hamsa-cuff on her left wrist, watching the bloody coral teardrop catch the chandelier lights. It seemed like it was grinning at her and Layla adjusted the cuff, turning it over so she looked at the enameled patterns on the back. But all the same, her wrist throbbed beneath the cuff as if her magic was calling to be recognized. "Do you really think the Bind could be broken?"

Adam shrugged. "Before she died, my real mother Gallatea used to tell me that all magic could be undone. She didn't believe in magical ultimatums. She'd seen a lot of binding-magics in her time, that she'd worked to break. Did I tell you my true mother was a Jud?"

Layla had heard the term before from a conversation with Rikyava, but still didn't really know what that was. "What's a Jud again?"

"Intercessoria Judiciary," Adam explained. "Twilight Realm police – special forces. They get called in when someone's magic does bad things. They're the ones who undo bad shit, Layla, and help people who have been bound or harmed against their will."

"Are you saying Adrian did something worthy of the attention of the Twilight Realm's special forces when he bound me?" Layla frowned, feeling uneasy now.

"It wouldn't be the first time." Adam gave a shrug, though his gaze was dark. Adam leaned back with his elbows on the bar, watching her intently. "How much of this do you want to hear?"

"How much of what?"

"How much of what Adrian does is so not by the books." Adam pinned her with his eyes, his teasing manner gone now as the green in his eyes darkened beneath the chandelier lights. "Adrian's got ventures in a number of places, Layla. Some of those are supported by not-so-legal means. Tech espionage using various forms of magic. Smuggling rings for hard-to-get magical items. Private security in remote areas who use lethal force. I'm not party to most of it. But he's called me in a time or two when he was in a bad spot because of a shady deal gone wrong. He deals with some *very* bad people at times, Layla. He's made enemies… and not all his enemies are the bad guys."

"Are you saying Adrian's one of the bad guys?" Layla hoped to god it wasn't true, her heart writhing in her chest at Adam's words, a black pit of darkness opening inside her.

"I'm saying Adrian does what he has to, to get the results he wants." Adam leaned forward, intense. "Like he did with you: tricking you in the gallery. Binding you to himself before you had any say in it. Making you think he was John LeVeque so he could get to know you. Yeah, I heard about that awful series of lies from Dusk. But you have to realize – that's all par for the course with Adrian."

Taking a deep breath, Layla watched Adam in the dim lights of the Gypsun bar. She took a drink not because she was nervous, but because the conversation troubled her. Either Adrian was as shady as Adam said and Adam was trying to be a friend, or… Adam had it in for Adrian, and this was a strong move to try and take Layla out of the game between himself and his Clan First.

Staring at Adam, Layla felt a moment breathe around them in the tight space of the bar as the singer, violist, and accordion player took up a new tune. The dinner crowd was thinning, moving out to the porch as the trio began a sad song that twisted Layla's emotions into dark places. She felt something swirl between her and Adam – felt her energy caught in Adam's smooth magics. But they were dark now rather than bright, like moonlight pouring over an autumn orchard where the fruit had already begun to fall.

She felt Adam's energy caress her collarbone in that moment, like he had actually reached out and smoothed his fingers over her skin. Layla's breath caught as she felt her Dragon stir deep inside her, allured by Adam's honey-dark energy. His ethereal fingers eased over her shoulder, stroking her gently, sliding up under her chignon to caress her neck. It was erotic, and Layla's eyelashes fluttered as she felt him caressing her nape with his smooth fingers of magic.

"I don't want to see you get hurt, Layla," Adam breathed, his hunter-green eyes penetrating as he touched her slowly with his power. "People tend to get hurt around Adrian. Especially those closest to him."

"What do you mean?" Layla murmured, feeling a deep, slow eroticism surge inside her as the singer mourned her song. The sensuality of the Gypsun music released her into Adam's passions, and Layla was breathing hard now from his touch as he stroked her neck with his orchard-dark magic. The scent of blossoms eased up around her, and Layla was suddenly drowning in Adam's touch – and his power. Tendrils of wind curled around her; power breathed along her skin in a scintillating ripple. As good as Adrian could make his power feel, Adam could do also. And as he touched her with those ethereal hands, his actual hands still idle as he rested his elbows on the bar, Layla found herself surrendering to it, lifting her chin and closing her eyes at that gentle, dark power stroked her throat.

"I mean that you wouldn't be the first girlfriend of Adrian's to meet an untimely death." Adam breathed gently as she succumbed to his touch. "Not even the fifth."

Layla's eyes blinked open. His words hit her like a punch and Layla's throat gripped, her heart squeezing as the music's sway intensified. Adam wasn't threatening her, only trying to protect her – and yet. What he'd said undid his attentions, shocking Layla back to a hard reality. Her eyes stung suddenly, her heart screaming for a good cry over Adrian, but she didn't want to give in to that here. Taking deep breath, Layla slid off her barstool to standing. Adam watched her, his green eyes deep. He rose also, his magics paused from stroking her neck.

"Please take me back." Layla spoke low.

"I'm sorry if I upset you." Adam's gaze was deep as he reached out, stroking her cheek with his real fingers now, warm and smelling of a sweet apple-orchard in October.

"It isn't your fault." Layla gave a wry smile.

"Still." Adam lowered his hand, his touch slipping from her skin. Reaching down, he cradled her left hand, gazing at the hamsa-cuff as he stroked his fingers over the red coral. "I would break this thing in a heartbeat. Set you free. Maybe we could find a way. If you want it."

"Maybe." Layla knit her brows. "I don't know yet, Adam."

"Of course." He gave a wry smile then let her go, gesturing toward the doors. "Shall we?"

But in that moment, Layla paused, not quite knowing what she wanted. She wanted Adrian so hard it hurt. She wished it was him with her right now; that she could touch him and kiss him, or maybe hit him with all the tortured emotions rolling through her right now. She wanted to stay, to revel in the mournful music and sip bourbon and let it release her inner passions; release her Dragon so she could accept it.

But that would mean releasing herself into Adam's arms – not Adrian's.

Layla's heart twisted. Some part of her just wanted to be back out in the night, riding on Adam's motorcycle as the cold wind blew by. Riding far from the Hotel and Adrian and never looking back.

But most her just wanted to be home.

"Just take me home." She spoke solidly. "Take me back to the Hotel."

"Sure. Let's go." Adam spoke gently, watching her process. "But if you have any more questions, know that I'm here, Layla. I will always be here for you. All you have to do is ask."

Adam gave her a low bow, formal and deep. Layla nodded and they turned, heading towards the door – her heart churning with far more questions than she'd started with.

CHAPTER 18 – SHADOWS

The next morning, as she was absorbed in updating the Samhain schedule, Layla was startled by a presence stepping up to the Concierge desk. Cinnamon-jasmine musk hit her with a smooth shot of desert wind and she caught her breath, her fingers paused at the keyboard. Her gaze tracked up; from Adrian's charcoal vest with its light blue pin stripes to his rolled-up shirtsleeves, to his open collar and exquisite collarbones, to the light stubble on his jaw. His sensual lips smiled at her as her eyes finally made it all the way past his achingly high cheekbones – getting arrested at his amazing aqua eyes.

He was smiling at her, bemusement on his face as Layla fell into his eyes. Rich and deep like a sunny Mediterranean ocean, Adrian's irises shifted to azure, then emerald – then flaring gold. Currents heated between them and Layla's body was suddenly scalding. Her Dragon raised its head with an eager stir, coils simmering through her veins as Layla's pulse hammered, a scent of spiced citrus easing up around her.

Dusk was off about other matters, but Jenna and Lars were busy at the other end of the desk and Layla straightened, pushing away her keyboard on its adjustable stand and staring Adrian down. His enigmatic smile wilted, his straight dark brows knitting.

"Have I done something wrong again?" He asked, his gaze searching.

"Not yet." Layla crossed her arms over her slinky royal-blue cocktail dress with the beige lace shoulders, a twin to the one she had in cream and burgundy but darker. She wanted more than anything to reach out and touch him, her Dragon roaring at her to vault up onto the desk and deposit herself in Adrian's arms. But that was so not going to happen until they got a few things sorted out first.

Things Adam had told her the night before but which Adrian had never brought up.

"What's *not yet* supposed to mean?" Consternation took Adrian's handsome face as his smile evaporated.

"It means," Layla lifted an eyebrow, "that I had the opportunity to ask Adam a *lot* of questions last night at dinner."

"I haven't spoken to Adam yet today. Why do I have the feeling your dinner didn't go well?" Adrian's speech was low, his eyes careful now, and dark.

"Oh, it went fine." Layla sassed, shifting her stance. "Adam answered all my questions to the best of his ability."

"About?"

"You. And Dusk." Layla stared Adrian down.

"I see." Adrian's fingertips skated over the polished wood of the desk, his brows deeply knit now. He slid his fingertips over the wood in a circle, blinking a few times as he frowned. And then he tapped the desk quickly, as if coming to a decision. "Layla. Would you be able to step away a moment?"

"Is it urgent?" Layla re-adjusted her arms. It was a tight posture, but she needed some real answers out of Adrian. She also wasn't at his beck and call. She was at work and she took her work seriously.

"Defending my honor is urgent for me." Adrian's aqua eyes were penetrating as he stared her down. "You can decide if knowing some deeper truths about me is worth your time or not. Adam knows some of the truth about Dusk and I, but he doesn't know everything."

"Does anyone know everything about you?" Layla sassed viciously, feeling irritated.

"Layla. Please. I'm trying. Take a break for a moment and come hear what I have to say."

Layla took a deep breath, then sighed. Deep inside her veins, her Dragon roiled with a mix of anger, irritation, eagerness, and flat-out desire. She wanted to listen to him, she wanted to jump his bones, and she also wanted to not be interrupted with private shit while she was at work. At last, curiosity won. With a look at Adrian, she stepped over to Lars and Jenna. Jenna looked up as she approached, her gaze flicking to Adrian as her white-blonde brows rose.

"Do you need to step away a moment, Layla?" Jenna assessed the situation perfectly. She knew Adrian and Layla weren't exactly a couple, but she wasn't a fool.

"Yeah, I do."

"Take all the time you need." Jenna's smile was kind. Furies were friendly despite their reputation, and Jenna clasped Layla's hand then gave her a peck on the lips. Layla was used to it – even Lars kissed her on the lips most of the time. She smiled, then returned to where Adrian waited near the end of the broad, curved mahogany desk.

Stepping around the side, Layla lifted an eyebrow and Adrian led the way up the grand double staircase. Setting a hand to the smooth railing, Layla stepped up after him. Adrian was quiet until they reached the second level, then gestured to an empty meeting-room with mermaids and the Hotel's emblem carved upon the doors. Layla entered and Adrian shut the doors, locking them so they wouldn't be disturbed. A fire crackled in the ample fireplace, a small but elegant spread of food in the room as if it was to be used soon for a Hotel departmental meeting. Those were scheduled with Events not Concierge Services, so Layla didn't know which department or how soon.

But all that mattered was that she and Adrian were alone for the moment. He stood before her almost awkwardly, his hands thrust in his pockets, his gaze still thoughtful. At last, he stepped to where an urn of coffee waited on a side-table. Pouring two cups and mixing cream into both, he handed one to Layla. She'd had plenty today but it was a nice gesture and she accepted it. Adrian stepped to a set of high-backed blue velvet chairs near the fireplace and sat. Layla followed, sipping her coffee. Damn that Adrian – he'd mixed it in the perfect ratio. He knew her, had researched her in so many ways, and yet she knew almost nothing about him still.

Something she hoped to remedy right now.

"So, defend your honor." Layla spoke as she sat. A brisk autumnal wind rattled the windows, swirling up dead leaves outside. Adrian's gaze was determined as he set his coffee on a gilded end-table, then faced her.

"First, I want to know what Adam told you last night." He spoke, leaning forward with his elbows on his knees and lacing his long fingers.

"Well, it wasn't good." Layla sipped her coffee then set it aside also, knowing this was going to be a doozy of a conversation if anything Adam had said was true. Even if it wasn't, it was still going to be illuminating concerning the politics internal to Adrian's clan. "Adam told me about some of your more clandestine activities, Adrian. Said you deal with bad guys. Tech espionage, smuggling, private security teams that use lethal force."

Adrian paled, but just like when she'd confronted him about the Hotel's activities in the restaurant Lark back in Seattle, he didn't immediately refute Layla's statements. Her brows climbed her forehead, but before she could say anything, he spoke.

"What Adam said is true. But it's not the whole truth." Adrian's gaze was hard, anger in it now – and desperation. His fingers tightened together, so hard they were turning white as his gaze went complex, his straight brows knit. Layla realized he was trying to hold something in, yet another of his secrets that he thought was too dangerous to tell her. But all it made him look was guilty, and they both knew it.

"Aren't you even going to try to defend yourself?" Layla asked, astounded.

"I want to." Adrian's gaze was dark but honest as he watched her. "But if I tell you the truth, I can't protect you. You'll be too far in – you'll know too much. It will put you directly in the line of fire with my enemies."

"Aren't I already?" Layla answered, knowing they were approaching something deep that was integral to the whole of Adrian's secrets. "Adam says the people you're close to tend to die. He said more than five women who were close to you have wound up dead."

"It's true." Adrian's voice was a hard rasp, his eyes terrible as his hands wrung each other again, tight. "It's one of the reasons I don't let myself—"

"Let yourself what?"

"Fall in love." Adrian finished softly. His gaze held hers, deep. Sincere. Scared. The haunted honesty in that gaze was terrible: so open and raw. Layla had never seen Adrian like this, and it struck her suddenly, exactly what he was trying to say.

"You love me?" Layla blinked, not having expected the conversation to go this way.

Adrian didn't answer. But as he held her gaze with that deep, haunted honesty, his energy swirled, caressing Layla like a warm, protective cocoon. Holding her close inside his gentle power, she felt as if he was cradling her in his arms, even though his hands were still laced tight together. She could feel him, as if they weren't sitting apart but he'd stood and pulled her close. Smoothing his warm hands over her back; nuzzling his lips into her neck and hair. Breathing her in as he held her close to his strong, lean chest. Layla could feel Adrian's deep heat as he brought her into the circle of his arms and his power, protecting her.

As if she were the most precious thing in the world.

"I would do anything for you," he spoke at last, his eyes luminous and dark all at once. "And if my enemies find that out, if they find out how much I… they'll kill you, Layla. They'll move against me, by striking at my heart – again. I can't let that happen. I just can't."

Adrian wrung his hands. As he took a deep breath, his gaze moving to the windows and watching the autumn leaves whirl, Layla's heart broke for him. This was the truth; this was what tortured Adrian night and day and made him cagey with secrets. Layla could still feel his energy around her, protecting her as if cocooning her away from the rest of the world. And watching him, she knew that he'd tried to stay distant from her for a reason. Because she was safer that way. Because she'd be protected if the forces that hunted him thought he didn't love her, that he was only using her for her power, and for the power it gave him.

But love didn't work that way.

Suddenly, Layla understood that Adrian was in an impossible situation. With a smooth movement, she rose, stepping to him. Adrian looked up as she neared but didn't rise, his hands still clenched as if he was trying to hold the entire world from breaking. Layla watched his eyes flare gold; desperation in them as she stepped close.

Gazing down at him, feeling her own love and her desire to help, Layla felt a warm, soothing energy ease out from her body. Caressing over his clenched hands, her energy held his fingers – pressed them in the unseen way that his power normally did with her. But it was Layla reaching out this time with her Dragon's power – touching him, stroking him, soothing him rather than the opposite.

Adrian's eyes widened; his breath caught. His face opened in shock at her etheric touch as he gazed up at her, his eyes luminous even as much as they were bleak. "Layla..."

"Shh..." Layla knelt before his chair. Clasping his hands, she smoothed her real hands over his, warming his tension with her Dragon's energy. Reaching out, she ran her fingers through his brush-cut black hair, feeling its silky texture.

Watching Adrian's eyes become astonished as she touched him.

"Layla, please... don't."

"No." She firmed her resolve, understanding that this was the piece she had been missing about Adrian. It wasn't that he was an asshole, or that he was clueless about relationships, or that he was purposefully trying to be unkind. It wasn't that he was a tycoon and didn't tell her about his dealings because they were shady. It was that he was afraid – for his life and for hers.

And he couldn't tell her why because it might get her killed.

"Do you trust me, Adrian?" Layla spoke, stroking her hand down his cheek, caressing her thumb over his cheekbone. He didn't say anything for a moment, staring at her with obliterated longing in his eyes as she touched him.

"Yes." He breathed at last, and Layla saw his raw honesty.

"Can you trust that I'm stronger than your fears?"

"I want to. But you don't know our world, Layla."

"And if you shut me out, I'll never know." Layla answered. "You trusted me in the forest to feel your real power, your real feelings. How is this any different?"

"It's not different." He spoke quietly. "It's just that I have so much I'm afraid of. Both with my power and how little of it I still have to protect you with."

They were hitting the sweet, painful spot of radical honesty now –

for perhaps the very first time. Just like they had found abandon in the forest before, it was real and it was deep. It was the stuff true relationships were built on. And even as painful as it was, it made Layla's heart sing. Deep inside, her Dragon took a tremendous breath. Coils loosened, barbs were set down. Layla put away her fangs, feeling her way into that tender place, wanting to be there with him. For the first time, she felt her energy and Adrian's swirl together, not in passion but in depth and kindness; achingly tender and raw.

And for the first time, Layla felt truly close to Adrian, as they stared deep into each other's eyes.

"Last night," she spoke quietly, moving into that space, "Adam took me to the Gypsun bar in the City of Julis – Marnet's."

"He took you to Marnet's?" Something brightened in Adrian, as if he remembered the exquisite emotion of that place. And then darkened. "I wish I had been the first to take you there."

"You could have been." Layla's gaze was honest upon Adrian. "You could have been the first to show me Julis, to show me the true nature of the Twilight Realm beyond the Hotel, if you had trusted me. My magic may be newly opened, but I'm still me, Adrian. Everything you've read in my dossier; every reason you hired me to take this position at the Hotel in the first place. What Adam showed me last night is that this magic has always been inside me, always strong. I've always been furious, and passionate. You were right when we spoke at that restaurant in Seattle; my rage does make me strong, Adrian. My Dragon has always been here, and just like I've learned to live with it these past twenty-eight years, I can learn to master it and aid us. I'm not stupid to my power, Adrian. And you don't have to protect me the way you think you do. Trust me. Trust that whatever it is – I can help."

"You sound like Dusk." Adrian's lips quirked, sadness in his gaze. "He said exactly the same thing to me... years ago."

"Does Dusk know about all of this? About whatever it is you're still hiding from me?"

"Far more than Adam." Adrian drew a breath, then let it out shakily. "I trust Dusk with my life, Layla, and with yours. It's one of the reasons I left you in his care all these months. He and I have never really gotten along, but Dusk is honest to his bones. Dusk is the man you see everyday, and has been ever since we were young. He just has many facets to him that come out at different times, like turning a cut gemstone through the light. It used to heat me so badly, his blunt, crystalline reflection of my every wrong, his judgement of me. But I trust it. Adam, however…"

Layla's brows rose as Adrian trailed off, understanding something profound. "You don't trust your Clan Second. Your own cousin."

"Adam smiles, but there's something dark behind his smile, Layla." Adrian's visage was terrible, brooding now. "He's never given me reason to not trust him—"

"But you don't." Layla inhaled, thinking of how Adam had snuck out tendrils of energy multiple times now, touching her in a clandestine way no one else noticed. She thought about how his eyes had darkened on the ridge, and in the Gypsun bar last night. That look, as if he'd seen terrible things he could never recover from – as if it had darkened his very soul somehow. Adrian must have seen something on her face, because his brows furrowed. Layla's hand slipped from his cheek and he readjusted his hands, clasping hers.

"Are you alright?" He asked.

"It's just Adam…" Layla murmured. "Did Dusk tell you what Adam did when he and I first met at the Concierge desk?"

"Dusk told me Adam tried to mate-taste you." Adrian's eyes darkened again, and he set his jaw. "He's done it before with Dragon women I've dated. He has a jealous streak in him, Layla. Something he doesn't like to show."

"He also touched me… during the hunt. And again at the Gypsun bar last night."

"Touched you *how*?" Layla felt the first heat of Adrian's scorched temper surge around her.

"Just a caress of energy on my cheek, and on my neck," Layla found herself being vague at Adrian's sudden whip of jealousy. "But no one else noticed."

"Adam has impeccable control of his power." Adrian's gaze had darkened considerably, as his hands pressed hers a little too tightly now. "I've heard second-hand accounts of how my cousin can wield his magic without anyone else knowing. I didn't think they were true until there were too many of them to be ignored. As a Royal Dragon Chimeric, he doesn't have my ability to visage-shift, but he's got a stealth to his energy I could never hope to match. Be careful around Adam, Layla. Dusk trusts him, but…"

"You keep your friends close and your enemies closer."

"Adam's not my enemy." Adrian's face was drawn.

"But if he was your friend, would he have told me the things he did last night?" Layla adjusted her hands so Adrian's fingers weren't gripping her quite so hard. He noticed and eased his touch; smoothing his fingers over hers gently now.

"Adam's like Dusk, he doesn't appreciate secrets."

"And yet he keeps secrets from his Clan First." Layla lifted an eyebrow pointedly.

"I don't know that for certain." Adrian's gaze held a tinge of warning now. "Though Adam has a dimension to his magics I can't feel, Layla, it doesn't mean he's a problem for the clan. He's a capable Second and keeps me in line more often than not. Don't be so quick to judge a situation you are new to. Dusk is far more of a loose cannon than Adam and always has been."

"That I don't believe." Layla snorted, remembering Adam's energy hitting her fast and hard at the desk.

"Trust me." Adrian's gaze was intense, his smile hard. "Dusk has his passions. Just because you haven't seen them in action yet doesn't mean they don't exist. And when he erupts, you better hope there is someone around who can whip that crystal energy back and control him. Crystals are hard until they shatter. And when they do, they explode into a million razor-sharp shards."

Layla sobered, considering it. Dusk's energy was so busy, like he never gave himself a chance to get to that place where he might explode in anger. But Layla had felt him shake the ground the night she'd almost shifted. She had felt his tremendous strength; as if Dusk was a live fault line ready to crack and release a hundred years of stress. Everyone had warned her that he was more formidable than he seemed. Everyone but Dusk himself – as if he didn't even know quite how deep his own power went.

"So what do we do now?" Layla asked, meeting Adrian's beautiful eyes.

"We?" He gave a wry twist of lips, though there was humor there now. "You mean you still want me after all the shit you heard from Adam?"

"Maybe." Layla's lips twisted into a small smile also. "It depends."

"On?"

"On," Layla stroked his fingers, still feeling her and Adrian together in that tender space. "Whether you can trust me or not."

Adrian drew a deep breath. His nostrils flared and Layla felt him draw a curl of her scent deep into his lungs. His eyes softened, something amazed in them as a complex smile touched his lips. "I do trust you, Layla. More than anyone in my life, strangely enough, excepting Dusk and my own mother, rest her soul."

"Good." A smile beamed from Layla as she gripped Adrian's hands, feeling their Bind strengthen in a way she couldn't describe. But it was as if her own scent contained cinnamon in it suddenly, and Adrian's held a trace of sweet bourbon. "Then trust me to be strong, Adrian. Dusk is teaching me about the Twilight Realm; I'm making capable friends. When you first told me about this job, you said it would use every skill I have. I just didn't know the job was actually understanding the complexity of my new life, and navigating yours. I'm not weak, Adrian. Not as a human and not as a Dragon. Teach me. Help me, so we can hold your secrets together. Whatever it is you're afraid of —"

"I'm afraid of losing you," he breathed, reaching a hand out to cup her cheek tenderly.

"You're afraid of more than that." Layla's gaze was honest as she reached up, cradling his hand to her cheek.

"I am." His words were low, his eyes raw and dark. As he stared at her, she felt his energy swirl into a tense knot. Like a ball of snakes writhing in and in upon each other, it was a sensation Layla knew well. It was the same feeling she had when she was terrified, like her Dragon was coiling in and in upon itself, descending into a deep, black pit. Adrian was terrified and he was letting her feel it – letting her experience his true fear for the very first time.

Trusting her with it.

"I'm afraid of the… the thing I can't see in the darkness, Layla." He breathed at last. "I'm afraid of the shadow in the void."

Layla blinked. Her lips fell open. Adrian's words echoed precisely the Phoenix King when he'd spoken about the void-shadow that had once hunted him, and now was hunting Layla. Her world reeled as her body contracted, as tense and fierce as the snakes she still felt writhing in Adrian's energy. And suddenly, so much about Adrian came clear – and why he'd kept her in the dark about the dangers he faced.

"The void-shadow. You know about it." She breathed. "The visage-shifting Royal Dragon that King Falliro Arini warned me about. The thing he once committed suicide to escape…"

"Why do you think the Phoenix King and I are allies?" Adrian breathed back. His demeanor was dire as his tense energy whirled the air inside the vaulted drawing-room, just like the October winds whirled the leaves outside. "That thing killed my mother five years ago, Layla. It's killed every woman I've ever let myself get close to. I've been hunting it all my life – just like it's been hunting me. And just like it's been hunting you."

CHAPTER 19 – VOID

Layla stared at Adrian from where she knelt, her mouth fallen open, her mind spinning as autumn winds whirled outside the vaulted drawing-room. Adrian had just revealed that the void-shadow the Phoenix King had warned her about had been hunting Adrian all his life. Layla settled to her heels on the thick carpet before the fireplace, stunned, her hands fallen to Adrian's knees where he sat in his high-backed chair.

"That thing is here at the Hotel, Adrian. It's been tracking me. King Falliro said he's felt it a few times since he's been here."

"I know. It's the real reason I organized the Dragon gathering. Because I've been feeling it too, ever since we got you here." Adrian spoke darkly. Reaching out, he brushed his fingers tenderly over her cheek, his aqua-gold gaze deep.

"You knew this void-shadow was following me?"

"It's been around for years, Layla." Adrian wrung his hands and Layla set her hands over his. He stopped, but truthfulness was suddenly pouring from him in a wave of intense cinnamon-jasmine musk. "It's been haunting my home in Morocco since the day you were born. Since you arrived in this world, it's been stalking you. And Dusk and I."

"This thing has been hunting the three of us since I was *born*?" Layla breathed, incredulous.

"It was the strongest reason Mimi spirited you away to the States." Adrian murmured, intensity simmering from him along with his honesty. "Only a few people knew about the creature. Me, my mother Juliette, your mother Mimi, and Dusk. I didn't find out until

213

later about King Arini. Dusk was the first one to feel the void-shadow back when you were born. He was there the day you were born, same as me. He had intense nightmares for the next month, feeling a black presence watching our palace of Riad Rhakvir from the dunes. He experienced its nightmares – of the world before civilization. Of the *Twilight Realm* before civilization, which goes back at least fifty thousand years."

"My god." Layla breathed.

"This thing is old, Layla." Adrian continued. "Dusk found out he was resonating with its dreams, though at some point it realized a powerful young Crystal Dragon was reading its nightmares and it started guarding its mind. But not before Dusk saw an infant in those dreams. You. And he felt the void-creature's intention – that it wanted you. That it would plow through Dusk and I, and anyone else who tried to protect you, to get to you. Dusk told Mimi, and the rest was put in motion quickly to get you away from Morocco. What I told you about the High Council wanting to eliminate Royal Dragon Binds is also true, and that was an additional reason Mimi took you away from our home. But this was the deepest reason."

"But it found me." Layla breathed, fear flooding her as her Dragon coiled tight into her stomach, making her want to vomit.

"It did." Adrian reached out, brushing a curl of Layla's hair back from her face. "The same way I found you. Mimi was reckless in not using a pseudonym when she went into hiding. Though she had a powerful magical talisman that obscured her imprint from being found, and yours, she had hubris about her life as the Twilight Realm's most prominent chanteuse. She kept her real name. And when that name showed up in the Seattle obituaries after her death, her talisman no longer working to hide you after she died, Dusk and I were able to find out where you were. And so did the void-shadow."

214

"And it's been following me ever since." With a dark, sinking sensation deep inside her, Layla suddenly understood everything. "That's the real reason you pushed the Hamsa Bind on me. So you could feel me if I was in trouble. So our magics could be bound together, stronger as one. Against this thing."

"It was getting too close." Adrian breathed, dire truth in his eyes. "Dusk and I felt it near you a number of times after Mimi died. You were exposed; I had to act. I had to do something to protect us all. My one regret is that I didn't come clean to Dusk about which talisman I was about to use – and I didn't come clean to you about it, either."

"But... why did you leave me after we were bound together?" Layla spoke, trying to understand. "Wouldn't we have been stronger against this thing if you'd stayed at the Hotel with me?"

"I tried leaving you alone, to see if it was following me," Adrian spoke, a terrible apology and sorrow in his eyes now. "But Dusk said it stayed here, though it did follow me to Morocco at one point, though I can't figure out why. So I came back, and devised a plan to use the four of us as bait to try and draw it out."

"Four of us?" Layla's brows knit.

"You, me, Dusk, and Arini," Adrian spoke softly, "the only four people we know it's hunted. It both worked and it didn't. The void-shadow is here in the Hotel, but it's so sporadic that Dusk and I can't trace it, and neither can Arini."

Adrian's gaze was level with Layla as her world spun like a badly thrown top. She had that lightheaded sensation again of standing outside her body looking down from the highest corner of the room as she felt her blood wash with a dark cold. It was her own terror she was feeling now rather than Adrian's, her Dragon coiling over and over upon itself and baring fangs.

Layla drew back. Pushing up from the floor, she stood. Too many emotions rioted through her, but when Adrian stood, smoothing his hands down her shoulders, Layla found herself leaning into his touch, wanting to be held. Needing it. Adrian curled her into his arms, holding her tenderly and Layla breathed in his warm spice scent at his collarbones. Adrian wound her closer in his arms, breathing softly by her temple.

"Are you alright?" He murmured.

"No. I'm terrified." Layla spoke bluntly, feeling her Dragon still churning inside her, coiling tighter and tighter. Black and sinister like a void of Layla's own had opened up deep inside her, the cold would have been overwhelming had it not been for her hamsa-cuff sending pulses of warmth into her body. "Is this the reason you've been away from the Hotel so much?"

"Partly," Adrian breathed at her cheek, "the other part is all the investments I hold, and being an owner in the Red Letter Hotel. But the void-shadow is why I've been a madman about building my empire these past twenty-eight years. Especially after all the things Arini's told me."

Layla glanced up. Adrian still held her close, but she pulled away slightly, needing to read the truth in his face. It was there in his eyes; plain and honest. "All this time, you've been building your wealth to be able to find this thing?"

"Why do you think I invest in all the newest tech, both Twilight and human?" Adrian watched her, something careful on his face though he was relaxed now, relieved to be telling her the truth. "New tech, brilliant inventors, tracking down ancient artifacts in lost ruins – that yes, I do protect with Twilight mercenaries who will keep those discoveries safe with lethal force. I deal with mafia, I steal and smuggle anything illegal that my inventors need. I build my empire just so I can pay all those people, Layla. People who are trying to find something –

anything – that will be able to track this void-shadow. Or capture it."

"Why?" Layla breathed, the scope of Adrian's machinations boggling her mind.

"To turn us into the hunters rather than it." Adrian's eyes flashed, the gold in them molten. "King Arini asserts that it's a visage-shifting Royal Dragon like me, but I can sense others with my ability when they're around, even when they try to shift to escape my notice. It's something I'm trying to achieve – shifting without betraying my scent, or the power of the shift – but it's goddamn impossible. Even so, I only use my alter-egos for low-level work. As myself, I have the status and power to infiltrate the highest echelons of Twilight and human society, and I do. So I can find this thing."

"Like being a part-owner of the Red Letter Hotel," Layla murmured, understanding so much at last. "It gives you access behind closed doors."

"And I put up with the Hotel Board's vicious dealings – most of which are ten times more illegal than mine," Adrian agreed with a nod, "to pump the elite for any information they have on this thing. Casually and discreetly, of course. If one of them is the void-shadow, if it masquerades as someone at the very top – and I have the feeling it might – I will find it, Layla. I will find it and so help me, I will bring it down in flames before it harms you or Dusk or anyone else I love. It's already taken too many."

"Your lovers," Layla breathed, everything finally making sense. "It wasn't just your mother it killed. It's not just targeting me… it's targeting you. By killing people you love, over the years."

"Yes." Adrian spoke softly, with wrath in his voice. "I've discovered from some of the patterns in the deaths that have surrounded my life, that it was targeting me long before you arrived, all the way back to my early twenties. But its efforts have become worse now. And that is why I have to bring it down."

Vehemence was in Adrian's eyes. Cold, hard ruin, and Layla saw the brutal grace she'd glimpsed when he'd commanded at her Hotel interview. Adrian was a force of nature, and Layla saw it burning from his eyes as he stood strong in his determination. Heat blossomed from him – enormous coils curling around Layla in a protective shield. She actually saw it: a shimmering mirage that coiled around her in the solar, made of wind and heat and curls of aqua and crimson flame that burst suddenly upon the air. Layla's breath caught as that simmering magic encased her, licks of etheric, unburning flame easing up her skin as Adrian held her.

He stared down at her, something fierce upon his face and in his eyes.

And then he bent, pressing his lips to hers.

His kiss was gentle. And like it had been in the forest, Layla's heat leapt to his, surging up her throat, twining with his. Layla felt herself swallow him like liquid flame upon her tongue, as if the Mediterranean Sea could be made into nectar. She made a sound as she felt him inhale her upon his tongue also; shuddering as he twined her closer in his arms and magic. His magic licked across her skin like a thousand caresses now, touching her everywhere. Layla gasped in his arms and Adrian shuddered hard – devouring her deeper.

Desert fire surged down Layla's throat, deep into her body as Adrian poured himself into their kiss. Caresses slipped up her thighs as his magics slid between her legs, buckling her knees as he caught her. Layla cried into his mouth as his magics slipped inside her; delving deep, hard. Plunging in, Adrian was suddenly inside her without any clothing shed; driven into her as deep as he could go. Layla cried out, breaking from their kiss and screaming her pleasure into his neck. She shuddered as he hardened within her, so wild – feeling him so deep,

218

needing him to finish what he'd started.

But a brisk knock at the locked door suddenly interrupted them, Dusk's diamond-hard voice coring through the wood. "Whatever you two are doing in there, stop it! The entire Bartending staff is waiting out here to use this meeting room, and though Head Bartender Rake André is polite, I am far from it. Break it up or take it upstairs to Adrian's suite, but for god's sake get the fuck out of this room, *clothed*, and don't make me bust the door down!"

Adrian pulled back from Layla with a gasp. The sensation of his body plunging inside her released and Layla gave a hard shudder and a cry. Cradled against his chest and weak with tremors, her body was a tower of heat, wetness thick in the wake of Adrian's ecstatic plunge. He shuddered against her in an answering annihilation. But though he was as shaken as she, his smile was enormous as he turned toward the door, raising his voice. "I'm Head of this Hotel, not you, Dusk. I can do as I like in its rooms."

"Test *that* theory and get banned, I don't care who the fuck you think you are, Adrian!" Dusk's voice was still hard as diamonds and thrice as cold in his ire. But Adrian's gaze was scaldingly brilliant as he turned away from the door and kissed Layla lips again. She breathed him in and he breathed her, and Dusk's voice came through the door again.

"I mean it, Adrian. Layla."

With a wry smile, Adrian finally let her go, though his gaze scalded her with all the passion of everything they still had yet to consummate properly. Layla breathed unsteadily, Adrian's hand at the small of her back. But she was smiling, beaming even though they had been interrupted yet again. Some truth was finally out between her and Adrian, at last. A truth that made them stronger together, rather than weaker. It was real intimacy, the kind that Layla had been looking for with him.

Which they were truly finding now.

Though now Layla had a million questions for Dusk, which she was going to make him answer come hell or high water. He'd not been lying to her exactly, just holding out, and to Layla they were basically the same thing. Steadying herself with one final out-breath, she moved to the door and unlocked it. The room hadn't been disturbed except for two cups of coffee, and though Layla and Adrian were flushed from the magics that had poured through them, Layla was learning that metaphysical sex wasn't nearly as messy as the real thing.

Magic had its advantages.

Dressed in an impeccable dove-grey Italian suit, Dusk gave her a withering stare as she opened the door, probably the coldest she had ever gotten from him. Layla could feel his crystal wall firmly in place against her and Adrian's involvement, and he raised a dark eyebrow as his gaze pinned her, merciless.

"Layla Price. You are needed back at the main Concierge desk, if you are *quite* finished?"

Dressed in a smart black vest, emerald shirt, and trousers, Head Bartender Rake André stood beside Dusk with his emerald eyes sparkling and amused, not something Layla normally saw from him. The other members of the Bartending staff had made the most of their time, pulling one of the mobile copper bars close and having an impromptu mix-off. Layla stepped out and Rake ducked in with a wink, summoning his staff. They poured into the room after him – leaving Adrian, Layla, and Dusk out in the hall.

"Try to be a little more discreet with your sexcapades, will you?" Dusk lifted a dark eyebrow at Layla and Adrian, his jaw set and his lips in a furious line. "I could feel that ten rooms down and on the first floor."

"I can't promise anything." Adrian's gaze was simmering as he took up Layla's hand and kissed it, making her flush. "Layla and I came to an understanding just now."

"Adrian, goddammit!" Dusk made a hard scoff in his throat, his gaze hot like sapphires in a volcano. "Half the Dragons have rooms down this hall right now! You invited the clans here for a reason, and that reason is *not* stirring them all up by making them feel you and Layla's Bind at all hours!"

"I know." Adrian sobered, giving Layla's fingers a squeeze. "Layla and I were talking about King Falliro, and things Adam told her last night. I came clean with her, about why you and I are guarding her, Dusk. So you can leave off being a judgemental asshole and start thinking about how we're going to move forward now that she knows. Take Layla off Concierge until Samhain. This takes priority. Say she's sick, say anything to the rest of the Hotel, but you and she need to talk – and then we need to strategize. Layla wants to be in, and I'm not going to hold her back from it. Not anymore."

Dusk was gaping at Adrian. His sapphire eyes were wide, his beautiful lips fallen open. He blinked at Adrian, then his gaze swung to Layla. "So you know."

"I know." She spoke back, watching his face. "I don't know everything yet, but I've heard the gist of it."

Dusk took a deep breath, then let it out. His gaze swung to Adrian and they shared a long look as Adrian nodded with a wry twist of lips, his face hard. Dusk closed his eyes as if gathering himself and Layla felt his crystal wall slip. At last, it came down completely as he looked back to Layla. The sapphire in his eyes was brilliant as if they'd turned to blue diamonds. He was tense as he spoke, though calm and collected finally.

"Layla. You're off Concierge starting now. You'll still get paid for the week, but until the Samhain Masquerade, you will be at my side. I have to stop by the desk and re-arrange the schedule, then we'll go to your room and get you properly outfitted. Yoga clothes will do for our aims in the next few days."

"Doing what?" Layla lifted an eyebrow, astounded at his change and intensely curious about what was going on now.

"Teaching you how to fight, Dragon-style." Dusk gave her hard eyes back. "If you're going to be in on this secret, then you need to be able to protect yourself by Samhain. Come on, step lively. I want to make sure you're at least able to shield before midnight."

Dusk flicked his fingers in his usual brisk way, though it had a military commander's efficiency in it now rather than his usual grace. Astounded, Layla could only nod with big eyes as she glanced at Adrian.

"Go," he murmured. "I'll join you when I can. Maybe not tonight, but soon. I promise. And Dusk's right. If you're going to be involved in hunting the void-shadow with us, Layla… you need to know how to fight."

Layla nodded, reaching out to clasp Adrian's hand. His fingers smoothed over hers and Dusk watched them a moment, something strange on his face. At last, Dusk stepped away, back down the hall in the direction of the Concierge desk. Releasing Layla's hand, Adrian nodded for her to follow.

Layla followed, even though a part of her screamed to leave Adrian. But squaring her shoulders, a vicious kind of elation filled her at the prospect of learning to fight with her magic. Recalling the lances of color she had seen during the hunt, Layla felt an eager swirl of coils and talons inside her body.

Her Dragon reared its head and snarled, baring fangs as if excited to kill. A scorched citrus scent curled up from her skin and Dusk glanced back, slowing his stride to let her come abreast of him. He watched her with piercing, sapphire-bright eyes – and then a subtle smile curled his lips before he marched on.

CHAPTER 20 – GUARD

A half-hour later, Layla was dressed in a green yoga top, grey leggings, and black flats, a cream wrap sweater tied on over everything as she walked through the Hotel at Dusk's side. He'd been quiet since they'd left Adrian, a deep intensity vibrating from him that Layla could feel shivering through her body as they walked, though not in a sexual way. She didn't think he was doing it on purpose, his pensive frown not directed at her as they strode to the south wing of the Hotel.

Mostly personnel apartments and meeting rooms, the south wing didn't have any guest suites, though Layla had been through these halls to visit the Hive of the Head Clothier. But Dusk took them a different direction now, turning a corner and marching down a broad series of stone stairs to the sub-basements where the Hotel Guard trained. A few off-duty Guardsmen strode up the stairs toward them, sweaty and bruised but laughing. With towels around their necks and their crossover crimson jerkins unbuckled, they showed brawny chests blossoming with bruises from training. The quartet gave Layla hot gazes as they passed, but smart nods for their Head Concierge.

"Dusk," one of them growled genially, a broad fellow built like a shield who was older than the rest. Still handsome, he had grey in his short-trimmed beard and wavy blonde hair. Missing an eye, a ragged scar extended from beneath a stylish black eyepatch.

"Lorio," Dusk nodded back as they paused to clasp wrists on the stairs.

"Training tonight?" The older man gave Dusk a knowing look,

though he glanced curiously at Layla. "Rikyava's busy with some new recruits, but she should be able to join you in an hour."

"Thanks, but I'm not here to spar with Rikyava tonight."

Layla's brows rose at this information, that Dusk and Rikyava didn't just spar together in the bedroom, but she kept silent.

"Do you need a sparring partner?" Lorio asked. "I could stay awhile. I'm off shift."

"No, but thanks. I'm actually training Layla tonight. Is the Vault open?"

The man lifted an eyebrow, then dismissed the younger Guardsmen with a lift of his chin. They continued up the stairs, though they had grins for Layla. None were guys she had met yet, and she gave them a frosty eyeball like she'd once done at the bar in Seattle. They laughed and continued up, buckling their jerkins and shucking their towels into a laundry chute before being seen in the Hotel proper. Lorio gestured for Dusk and Layla to follow, then turned down the long staircase to a set of massive stone doors at the bottom.

Carved with martial scenes, the doors swung in easily at Lorio's touch. Opening to an enormous underground space that Layla had only seen on her tour, they entered Rikyava's domain – the Hall of the Guard. Entirely underground, the vaulted atrium was like a medieval catacomb. Tasteful lighting filled the vaults and niches, showing off porticos devoid of decoration. There was nothing down here to distract a person from what this was: a war-hall, a training-area, and an armory.

Closed steel doors like bank-vaults flanked the ingress, massive vaults that Layla knew contained magical weaponry, though she had never been inside. The next set of steel doors were open, though, showing enormous well-lit rooms protected by steely-eyed Guards and containing polished racks of swords and pikes, and velvet dummies of armor. Not to mention lit walls of knives displayed in shining perfection alongside military-issue handguns, rifles, kevlar, and other modern war-making accoutrement.

The next set of doors were closed, leading to tunnels that warrened deep beneath the grounds. Those led to the Safehouse, Layla knew, a series of enormous underground halls that could protect the entire staff and a full contingent of guests if the Hotel were ever attacked. Cleaned once a month, the Safehouse was kept stocked with magically-preserved goods. Layla knew it connected to an underground aquifer, but hadn't been down there as it was off-limits.

The next series of rooms contained deliciously-honed men and women moving in and out, clad in sports-bras, shorts, gym shoes, and workout gear. The enormous weight-lifting area and functional fitness gym was in constant use, Guardsmen and women sweating and heaving as they worked out in teams. Beyond that, Layla saw climbing-walls and other athletic equipment used in the Guard's drills. Through another vault was a sauna facility with steam-rooms and hot pools, Guards laughing naked in the pools as others lounged quietly after a long day.

Beyond the steam rooms were fight-halls with glass view-panes set into their doors. These were dedicated to sword and pike practice, and the next few were shooting ranges, muted pops issuing from within as Guards trained with modern firearms. But the last seven halls were dedicated to magical fighting. Five of the six doors were open, displaying enormous gymnasium spaces entirely made of natural amethyst and rose quartz crystal – magical insulation. Any staff member could come down here to let off magical steam, Layla knew. But the last room at the end was the Hotel's deepest and most secure, known as the Vault – a place they put prisoners if someone did something severely out-of-line.

Glancing in the first closed magic-hall door, the window

reinforced with a thick shield of rose quartz, Layla saw Rikyava inside with a group of Guardsmen and women. Magic simmered as she watched, one of the trainees heaving a blast of fire at another who slammed up her hands, forming a shield-wall that burst into the air with a furious scream. The wall shrieked as much as the woman who had cast it, her head crested with gold-black feathers; a Harpy. The screams devoured the fire from her partner who sagged to his knees, screaming as he covered his ears.

Rikyava shouted and the Guardswoman ceased, breathing hard from her exertions. Dressed in her crimson uniform but with the jacket casually unbuckled, Rikyava removed earplugs. Seeing them at the window, Rikyava waved, then marched toward the door. Layla heard a complex latching mechanism and Rikyava heaved the door inward.

"Hey guys! What brings you down to my dungeon realm?" The Head Guardswoman grinned, though her violet gaze flicked from Layla to Dusk with a measure of curiosity.

"We need to get into the Vault, Rikyava. Layla and I need to practice down there tonight." Dusk spoke with his usual efficiency, but Layla saw Rikyava's blonde brows climb her forehead.

"Training?" Rikyava glanced to Layla's Moroccan cuff. "You'll have to remove that first if you want to have Layla do any training, Dusk."

"I know." His words were quiet. "Hence, needing the Vault."

"You think she'll shift?" Rikyava's eyes narrowed, shrewd.

"I'm not taking any chances." Dusk glanced at Layla with something sober in his eyes – and Layla realized that tonight was going to be a lot more challenging than she had initially thought. Suddenly, learning how to fight with her magic didn't seem like so much of an adventure as worry began to gnaw Layla's gut. The last thing she wanted to do was shift into her Dragon, or almost shift again. That had been fucking painful and had taken days to recover.

"You need backup? I can be done soon." Rikyava stated, watching Dusk.

"No, thanks." Dusk smiled and it was kind, something tender in it for Rikyava. "Layla and I need to do this alone."

"Ok, whatever." Rikyava glanced between them, though her gaze was searching. It was clear she wasn't about to just let them waltz down to the Hotel's strongest maximum-security room without a thorough explanation. She was good at her job, and her job included asking questions when something was out of the ordinary. Which Layla was realizing this little visit truly was. "You want to tell me what this is all about?" Rikyava quipped, though her violet gaze was penetrating.

"Personal protection." Dusk was slightly curt with Rikyava. He was smiling, but had essentially told Rikyava that she didn't need to know why Dusk was training Layla all of a sudden. It struck Layla that Rikyava wasn't party to Dusk and Adrian's plans. Though she had heard everything King Arini had spoken in Layla's room about the void-shadow, Rikyava wasn't in on the whole meal deal – and from Dusk's stonewalling, Layla realized he wasn't going to tell her right now.

"Oh-kay." Rikyava's lavender gaze soured on Dusk, though she turned to Layla with a tight smile. "Clearly I'm not going to get any answers out of this asshole. But Layla, if you need anything, just ask. If you want to learn how to spar magically or physically, or learn to use firearms or whatever, I'm happy to help. We've got a lot of guys down here who would absolutely love to train with the Royal Dragon Bind."

Rikyava gave a wink, but glanced one last time at Dusk, pointedly. Something passed between them, bristling like a lover's quarrel. But when it was obvious that Dusk wasn't going to be forthcoming, Rikyava at last gave a hard sigh. Rolling her eyes, she beckoned for them to follow her as she proceeded to the last door in the hall, set into the furthermost wall of the vaulted catacomb.

Made of solid sapphire rather than steel, this door showed a small softly-lit grotto through the blue, with steps that corkscrewed down to darkness. Setting a hand to the door's smooth surface, Rikyava closed her eyes and murmured a phrase, then breathed on the door. The sapphire door seemed to ripple in its frame, like a giant version of the mirror-trick that hid the safe in Layla's room. With a mighty crack, the sapphire suddenly split in the middle, sliding back into its frame on both sides. Blue sigils flowed through its depths, curling like fire in the sea.

Dusk nodded his thanks, then stepped into the dim grotto beyond. Beckoning for Layla, he glanced to Rikyava. "Lock it. I'll let you know when we're done."

The Head Guardswoman's eyebrows climbed her forehead as her gaze moved to Layla. "Layla. I need your permission to lock this door. Once you're inside… if I magically lock this door behind you, I'm the only person who can open it. Not you, not Dusk, not anyone else. If something happens in there and this door is locked… you get the idea."

"So what you're really asking me is how much do I trust Dusk?" Layla glanced to him. He kept silent, watching her.

"And how much you trust me." Rikyava nodded, her violet eyes careful.

Glancing between them, Layla realized she did trust them both. Dusk had been her ally since the moment she had set foot inside the Hotel. Other than testing her and withholding a few truths because of Adrian, Dusk had been stalwart and honest with her. And Rikyava had been a friend since the beginning. Upright, protective, kind; Rikyava and Layla had bonded tremendously. As Head of the Guard, the Blood Dragon had earned her position here at the Hotel, and Layla knew it was merited.

"I trust you. Both of you." Layla murmured. "If Dusk says lock the door, then lock it."

"As you like." Rikyava's lips curled in a smile, her eyes pleased. She reached out, squeezing Layla's hand. "If you need anything, if anything happens, just run back up the stairs and signal at the door. I'll station two guards here, and I'll be close by. They'll come get me if anything goes wrong in there, ok?"

"Ok." Layla breathed easier, nodding at Rikyava, glad that her friend had her back.

"Ok." The Blood Dragon squeezed her hand. She let go with a pointed look at Dusk, basically saying that he was so on her shit list if anything bad happened during their training. Then she turned, whistling for two grizzled veterans standing by watching – one of which was Lorio.

"Lorio, Ben. Watch this door. Anything goes wrong, come get me *immediately.*"

"Yes, Captain."

She gave them a stern eyeball, then a last one for Dusk, then beckoned Layla inside past the sapphire doors. Layla went, stepping into the cool of the Vault, Dusk just behind her. Rikyava beckoned Layla and Dusk back a few steps, then set her palm to the sapphire still visible at the edge of the stone door-frame. Closing her eyes, she murmured a phrase, then breathed on the door. With a rumbling, grinding sound, the door slid shut.

Layla could still see Rikyava and the Guards on the other side through the smooth blue depths, though sigils still curled through the massive gem. Rikyava locked her gaze to Layla, then lifted her palm and slapped it hard to the gem's surface. A shockwave blasted through the stone, igniting the sigils to a pure blue-white fire. Blazing, they dazzled Layla, then bled to a deep, murky red. The central seam in the stone disappeared and Layla felt a cool mist roll off the gem, as if she'd been locked inside a medieval dungeon.

Her heart panicked, racing, her stomach in her throat. She was locked in. Locked up.

But Dusk's hand found hers in the bloody blue half-light and Layla felt a smooth vibration ease into her from their touch. Stepping close, he took up her other hand also, gazing down. "I'm not going to let anything happen to you while we're training, Layla. I promise."

"But what if I shift down here? What if my Dragon rises?" She spoke, fear coiling though her gut and tightening everything inside her body – not in a good way.

"I won't let that happen. And if it does…" Something dire eased through his sapphire eyes in the murky light. "If it does, I can protect myself. And make sure you don't get hurt either."

"Are you sure?"

"Almost."

Layla was about to protest and tell him to get Rikyava in here plus a few other Guards just in case, but Dusk stepped close. Pulling her in by the hands, he lowered his chin, pressing a soft kiss to her lips. Layla's breath caught as something delicious rolled through her; feeling him, knowing him, understanding him in a deep, indescribable way. Entranced by the feel of Dusk's soft lips, it was a moment before she realized he wasn't using his magics – it was simply the feel of him kissing her that had caught her so suddenly.

Smooth, gentle, Dusk's lips were an exploration of dark sweetness in the half-light. Layla felt herself falling into it as her Dragon stirred inside her, sensual and pleased in a way that even Adrian couldn't match. She could taste river-water in Dusk's kiss, clear and refreshing like it had been purified in a waterfall. Layla found herself lost in it as he kissed her, that deep pull like a golden cord rekindled between their bodies as had happened before the Dragon party.

She kissed him back.

It felt good. So good and so right. And Layla understood that whatever was happening between them wasn't just because Adrian had been absent from her life for weeks. Something was happening between Dusk and her, separate from her lust for Adrian. When at last Dusk pulled back, Layla found herself paused, not even able to breathe as she stared up at his lovely sapphire eyes in the half-light.

He gazed down, something determined on his face. Reaching up, he stroked Layla's cheek and she took a deep breath, realizing she'd not been breathing. The moment stretched between them as she stood there, lost in his beautiful energy. Like the sapphire door behind them, Dusk pulled her with a deep, ineffable nature – like she'd been grounded in the earth itself. And as she felt his power, the depth and enormity of it, she suddenly understood what he hid with his brisk do-it-all daytime presence and his witty, debonair nighttime self.

Emotion. True emotion. All of it, the good, the bad, and the ugly – and the power that came with it. As he gazed down at her now, Dusk let her see his emotion just as Adrian had let Layla see his fear. But Dusk wasn't afraid. As Layla gazed up into those beautiful sapphire eyes, she saw his power. A depth of emotion in his heart that she had never seen in anyone before, deep like the very caverns of the earth.

And the strength it gave him.

"I will not let anything happen to you, Layla Price, I swear it." Dusk breathed, lifting his lips to kiss her forehead gently in the half-light. "Come on. It's time to let your Dragon stretch her coils at last."

CHAPTER 21 – FIGHT

Layla moved down the stone stairwell as if in a dream, still feeling Dusk's kiss as they descended deep underground, into the Vault. Moving down the corkscrewing stairs, crystal firefly-globes in niches brightened at their approach. At the bottom, the stairwell opened into a cavernous space. As Layla stepped out onto a smooth flow of pure rose quartz, she realized the cold, black space was actually a cavern – an ancient place beneath the Hotel that breathed with cool energy and flooding darkness.

She could see nothing beyond the light of the stairwell, though she could hear water in an underground stream, echoing through what felt like an enormous cavern. Layla had never been permitted down in the Vault, not even on her tour, and was about to ask Dusk how someone turned on the lights – when she felt more than heard a massive rumble issue from him.

Dusk's vibration rushed through Layla, invigorating, thrusting out in a massive wave through the black. Slamming through the cavern, it hammered crystal stalactites and quartz columns all around, making them ring like a symphony of bells. Columns sang with resonance as Dusk's vibration cast back again and again. In a flooding wave, the entire space was suddenly glowing bright as day, crystals all around shedding light from their core.

For a moment, the cavern was pure sound, a symphony of vibration and life. Until at last, Layla felt the energy stabilize, looping around the cavern and keeping the crystals bright. It wasn't a solid light, but a washing surge that twisted in an unearthly way as it flowed from pillar to pillar. And beneath it all, Layla could still hear a faint resonance, as if the earth itself sang.

Layla's breath was stolen as she stood, mesmerized.

"Shall we?" Dusk gestured to a space on the rose quartz flow, where stalagmites and stalactites gave way to a flat, glassy surface. Firefly lights on crystal pedestals lit as Layla and Dusk moved forward, but the enormity of whatever Dusk had done to brighten the crystal columns trumped them, making their meager light obsolete. Reaching the center of the expanse, the size of a small amphitheater with the cavern's ceiling arching overhead, Layla turned to Dusk.

"So, I'm guessing that's not the normal way to turn on the lights."

"Crystal Dragon," he spoke with a mischievous glint in his sapphire eyes. "I don't do anything the normal way."

"I guess so." Layla grinned and got an answering one from Dusk. It was clear he was pleased with his feat of magic, and Layla remembered all the things people had been saying about him. Turning to face him, she decided it was time to play twenty questions at last.

"So, everyone's been telling me things about you – Adam, Adrian, Rikyava." Layla spoke as she faced him. "That you're a powerful Royal but you're hiding it, and that's why my Bind-magic has been resonating so strongly with you. Why? What are you hiding from? And why won't you tell anyone how powerful you are?"

Dusk eyed her with one eyebrow lifted, but didn't refute anything she'd said as he sat on the smooth flow of pink crystal and started taking off his shoes. He nodded at Layla and she sat and began doing the same. Still watching her, he set his black Oxfords near a collection of upthrust stalagmites. The stalagmites were a mixture of rose quartz and amethyst, but also with green spikes like emerald or amazonite. If some of those actually were emerald, Layla couldn't even imagine the value down here. Far off, she could see clear blue columns of sapphire. Clearly though, this space had more value for its magical properties than its retail cost.

"Do you really want to know why I hide my ability?" Dusk spoke at last.

"Of course." Layla countered, setting her flats aside.

"It's because my life is in danger, if I show how powerful I am." Dusk's eyes held no lie as he slung his arms around his knees, watching her.

"What do you mean?"

"My King will kill me if he thinks I'm a challenger."

"King Markus Ambrose?" Layla blinked, an angle of Dragon-politics hitting her that she'd never considered before. "He kills off anyone he thinks is a threat to his power?"

"Yes." Dusk held her gaze with a level intensity. "Anyone who seems like their power will rise to the same level as his gets an invitation to his palace in the Czech Republic. From which they don't return. My mother went to his palace when I was only three. She cried as she left. I remember how passionate my parents were with each other before she went. She knew she wasn't coming home – and she didn't."

"My god." Layla didn't know what to say. "How awful."

"All Crystal Dragons of sufficient ability know to hide their power from Markus as long as they can. Until they think they have a chance of standing up to him."

"Have any succeeded?"

"Not in the last thousand years." Dusk's gaze was deep.

"Could you?"

"No." And though Dusk's words were succinct, Layla saw a question gleaming in his eyes.

"You're lying. You think you might be strong enough to challenge him."

"It doesn't matter," he sighed as if tired. "If I get an invitation to Markus' palace, I'm dead, Layla. I'm only a hundred and fifty years old, and I haven't even changed into my Dragon yet. I don't have a chance of staying alive if I face Markus in a dominance battle. And I kind of like being alive."

"But there are other things you can do," Layla pushed, wanting to know the extent of Dusk's abilities. "You can cause earthquakes. You can stop other Dragons from shifting. You can encase other Dragons in crystal prisons. You can infiltrate people's dreams."

"Who told you that I can spy on people's dreams?" Dusk's eyes hardened; that last tidbit was clearly not something he shared.

"Adrian. He told me it was you who sensed the void-shadow first, by accidentally tapping into its nightmares. Way back when I was born."

"Fuck." Dusk suddenly looked tired as he wiped a hand down his face. Gazing off into the crystal pillars, he was distant for a moment, something he rarely did. And suddenly, Layla realized he was stressed. It wasn't something Dusk ever showed, and Layla watched him, realizing that it wasn't just her who felt over her head right now.

"The void-shadow is nothing to trifle with, Layla," Dusk spoke at last as he looked back to her. "And neither is King Ambrose. There's a reason I don't associate with other Crystal Dragons, because I don't want any of them knowing a damn thing about me. My friends know to keep anything they learn about my power to themselves, as do my lovers here at the Hotel. I appreciate that Adam and Adrian are just trying to help you get to know me better, but if you want to know anything from now on, just ask me. And then keep it to yourself."

"Sure." Layla felt strange suddenly; they were probably the strongest words Dusk had ever used with her, without Adrian driving his ire. Even though he was a tough boss, he was always fair and positive. But now she was seeing a side of him he rarely showed – a hard-edged fury that could have cut diamonds. It made the crystal pillars around him resonate harder, brightening like Dusk was some kind of battery even though he wasn't actively using his magics.

With a deep breath, Dusk mastered himself. Layla felt that simmering rage calm, and his posture softened. "Sorry. I didn't mean for you to feel all that. It's just… living on the lam for over a hundred years gets to a person."

"Can't you ever go home?" Layla spoke softly. "To Egypt?"

"Egypt isn't my home anymore," Dusk spoke just as quietly, something bleak in his eyes. "Riad Rhakvir is, in Morocco. And the Paris Hotel."

"What about your clan?"

"My clan is dead." Dusk sighed, something bleak in his eyes. "I wouldn't dare re-start it, even though I have that right. It would be too obvious a challenge to Markus' power, if I began sending out quakes from our temples on the Upper Nile to attract mates and fighters. No, my place is here, protecting my friends. Which is why we're down here tonight trying to get you some skills in fighting. Which we really should start doing."

Dusk was back in his regular know-it-all teaching mode now as he stood and offered Layla a hand. She felt him lock all his emotions back down again, encasing them in crystal and stuffing them away deep inside his body for another time. As Layla took his hand and faced him, she suddenly wondered what it would take to break him. To shatter that impeccable container around his rage – and send those shards flying out in every direction.

But she was distracted from those thoughts as Dusk began stripping off his jacket and tie.

"Whoa, nobody mentioned getting naked, cowboy!" Layla blinked.

"You've got comfy clothes." He gave her a pointed look, though there was humor in it now. "I don't. So you have to deal with my sexy."

"Hey, we could have stopped to get you some yoga clothes, too." Layla crossed her arms, lifting an eyebrow though a smile crept in around her lips.

"Don't worry. You like my hot body." He grinned at her, back to his usual off-work antics. "Besides, yoga's not how I stay in shape, Layla."

Layla frowned. She realized suddenly that in all their conversations, she'd not once asked what Dusk did to stay fit. Apparently, he sparred with Rikyava now and again, but that couldn't be all of it. "How do you stay in shape, then?"

Dusk gave her a sideways grin that spoke volumes. "Body by sex."

"Oh." Layla blinked, trying not to blush and failing.

Suddenly, she was thinking about that kiss he had given her as Dusk began to strip off his jacket and unbutton his shirt – with a dark smile that said he knew exactly what he did to her. Layla watched him, mesmerized as he stripped the shirt away. Adrian was lean and mean but Dusk was fit as shit, and as the shirt went, out came the body. She couldn't help but stare at the defined muscles rippling beneath Dusk's sleek dusky-tanned skin. Built like a World Cup soccer player but taller, his waist was a lean dream, his shoulders and chest strong and his abs washboard-ridged. Small lines of midnight-blue scales curled over his broad shoulders and defined hipbones, catching the light of the cavern as he turned and cast his shirt gracefully to the rose quartz floor. Lacing his hands behind his head, Dusk stretched into them, rolling his chiseled shoulders – showing off a decadent spread of lats and biceps.

"You're ogling me again, Layla Price." Dusk gave her a sinfully knowing look as he stretched again.

"Shut up." Layla turned away, trying to hide her blush and failing as a rush of heat washed through her, her Dragon stirring eagerly. Jesus, hadn't she just been hot for Adrian this same afternoon? But her Dragon didn't care, roaring inside her veins like blistering gold. It didn't give a shit whom Layla felt bound to. It wasn't just Adrian her Dragon was hunting, and it wasn't just anyone powerful. It was hunting Dragons who were stronger than all the rest, who could Bind her and protect her – and teach her how to protect herself.

A fiery scent wafted up from her skin and Layla heard Dusk chuckle. "Your turn. Strip."

"I thought you said I was dressed properly for this!" Layla turned in protest. But Dusk held up his left arm, jiggling his wrist at her.

"The hamsa-cuff, Layla. Off with the cuff. You can't fight with a talisman on, not very well at least. We need you to take the leash off your Dragon. So strip it."

"Oh. Right." Layla flushed harder, feeling idiotic. Setting her right hand to her left wrist, she hesitated over the long silver pin that would unbind her antique Berber wrist-cuff. She'd not been without it since almost killing Luke back in Seattle. That episode had scared Layla straight, and now the cuff felt far less like a manacle and more like a safety blanket, able to contain her magics whenever her passions rose. Now, a series of worries poured through her, having no idea what would happen once she took it off. She didn't have any clue how strong her Dragon really was after two months of being awake – nor what might happen once it was free.

Dusk saw her hesitation and moved forward. Suddenly, all that hard, honed muscle was standing close to her and Layla shivered, gazing up into his lovely sapphire eyes. They glinted with humor, but also understanding as he reached out, setting smooth hands to her wrist. His skin was silky as he held her wrist and the cuff. "Would you like me to do it?"

"I don't know what's going to happen, Dusk." Layla spoke, letting him see her fear. She trusted Dusk – it was herself she didn't trust.

"I don't either," he spoke reassuringly, his blue eyes kind. "But you'll never know what you're capable of until you try."

Cradling her hand in his, Dusk nodded at the long silver pin. Him being there, helping her through this, suddenly made gratefulness wash through Layla. Here he was helping solve her problems just like he always did – even though he had plenty of his own to worry about. Gazing into his eyes with his warm hands on hers, Layla realized that that was who he was. He was a problem-solver, and a kind heart. He loved his friends with the same depth of passion Layla had, and he would always be there for her. Just like this, with patience and tenderness, something neither Adrian nor Adam could do. In that moment, she felt Dusk's depth and crystalline surety – and as she did, she smelled a curl of his scent steady her like a clear river purified by crystals.

Bolstering her. Holding her hand as she faced the unknown.

With a swift in-breath, Layla nodded. And then she pulled the silver pin, letting the Moroccan cuff fall into Dusk's waiting hand.

There was nothing for a moment, except silence. A cool flow of air moved through the cavern as Layla's Dragon went utterly still inside her. Silence stretched between her and Dusk as he watched her, still holding her hand and the cuff, touching her skin.

And then a roaring sensation spilled out from Layla so fast and hot she screamed. A tirade of energy rushed out from her, flaring through the unbound silver cuff into Dusk where he still touched her.

With a short cry, Dusk collapsed to his knees and Layla went with him, falling onto his body and bowling him over backwards to the floor. Dusk roared and Layla echoed it as she felt her blistering power slam through him – from the silver cuff still trapped between his hand and her wrist.

The red mark of the hamsa burned upon Layla's inner wrist, flaring like lava. She felt that scorching flow rush into Dusk everywhere their skin touched – spearing him like a thousand harpoons. Dusk arched in pain, roaring. Sprawled over him, Layla saw and felt his body erupt in luminescence beneath her, like sunlight through a prism. The midnight ridges along Dusk's arms and around his hips flared with light, shuddering him in waves. Spears of light shot from his shoulders and his spine so hard it thrust him up. Light rushed through his body beneath Layla, blue-white talons shooting from his fingertips as a flare of diamond brilliance rushed through him from head to heels.

Their hands still clasped, their bodies entwined upon the crystal floor, power rushed through Layla also. Waves of fury and passion bent her backwards atop him, making her cry out in vast pleasure now. Heat blossomed from her; too much to contain. A drowning orange-bourbon scent swirled into Dusk's clear river-water fragrance – flooding the cavern with the scent of oranges chilled in a river of diamonds. Their hands were clasped hard together, Dusk's body pulsing with light as he vibrated like an over-tuned harpstring. Pleasure flooded Layla in an obliterating wave to his power and music, cresting her instantly – again and again. Dusk spasmed beneath her, crying out now with incredible, overwhelming pleasure as their thundering power brought him also.

And somehow through her passion, Layla knew what was happening. As Dusk shuddered hard to match her last obliterated cry, she knew they had been bound together – just like she had been with Adrian. Gasping for breath as she fell back to his chest, tears leaked from Layla's eyes as the power finally flooded away. It was pain, but it was also so much pleasure as her orgasms finally left her. Beneath her, Dusk coughed, his body shuddering and his fingers still laced tight through hers. Her right hand had clamped behind his neck in their glory, and Layla gasped as she looked up, moving her head so she could see him.

Though he'd returned from his strange half-shift, Layla found Dusk changed, his body more astoundingly vicious and elegant than before. Extensive ridges of midnight scales curled over him where there had only been thin lines before. Serrated now, the scales were honed, accentuating the exquisitely cut muscles of his body. His skin was slightly darker, rippling with iridescent lines that edged his muscles and chiseled him out to perfection, etching him like midnight rivers. The spines of light that had appeared during his transformation were gone, but hinted at what he would one day become.

A Crystal Dragon, sleek and powerful like a diamond.

An obliterated half-laugh came from Dusk as he rolled his head to look at Layla. As their gazes connected, she felt a rush of power roar through her again – a smelted hot and cold fever that blazed like a star. She gasped and Dusk echoed it, his eyes scorching from sapphire to diamond in an instant. Layla felt the brilliant fury of those eyes coursing through her. She felt her Dragon roar, matching that light with heat, thundering through her body and his.

In that moment, Dusk moved. Lightning-fast like a sidewinder in the sands, he rolled Layla down with a surge of powerful muscles, pinning her to the crystal floor.

And then he kissed her – like there would never be another dawn.

Starlight fever rushed through Layla, swirling up inside her body and deep into his as they kissed. Rushing from Dusk's lips into her, making her Dragon shudder with pleasure, their kiss was a bond as they devoured each other's breath, lips, and tongues. Layla's mind fled – all she could see was stars, standing out diamond-bright in a black night sky. Endless. His power was endless, and she felt it in that moment, in the passion of his kiss. As strong as the earth, as wide as the night sky, Dusk's power was his heart. And as he poured all of that passion and glory through Layla she found herself obliterated by it – rushing out far into the universe like a shooting star.

There was no limit. There was no stopping point. There was no way to stop it, how far she would go with him, surging with his passion roaring through her like an underground river and hers scalding that river into a roaring boil. But it was Dusk who broke from their kiss with a gasp, his eyes blazing with all colors in the white – just like a diamond.

"Stop!"

Layla felt Dusk slam up his shield-wall between their endless passion. Layla gasped; it was painful, her energy so deeply entwined in his that it felt like he'd hacked through it like a battlefield surgeon. She cried out, spasming upon the stone – and gripping her neck so she wouldn't whack her head, Dusk moved her up to a crosslegged seat, holding her in his arms. Cradling her close, he heaved with hard breaths, shaking just as much as she was – yet still maintaining his barrier between them. It was an effort; she could feel his Dragon screaming for her touch just as much as hers did for him, to taste that endless power again.

To shoot through the sky like a falling star.

And yet, through all that passionate annihilation, Dusk held himself back – solving their mutual problem even as they both shuddered, pressed close to each other and gasping.

"My god!" He laughed at last, unsteady.

"Holy shit!" Layla heaved also, still annihilated.

"Did we just…?"

"Yup." Layla laughed back, completely undone. Dusk clutched her closer to his chest, still heaving as she inhaled his cool river-water scent. It was different now, holding a fragrance of crystallized orange peel and chilled bourbon. Whether Layla's Dragon had bound him when they'd touched with the hamsa-cuff or if the cuff had done it, Layla didn't know.

But the truth was in Dusk's scent now, and hers.

"You smell like me." Dusk's nose was in her hair, confirming it as he drew a breath and let it out in a deep sigh – as if nothing had ever made him more content.

"You smell like me." Layla murmured back, a smile curling her lips. Snugging his arms around her, Dusk pulled her close in his lap, a rumbling pleasure rolling through her now as he growled low, kissing her neck gently. It was heaven to Layla, feeling his slow rumble course through her, wrapped tight in his arms with his smooth lips at her neck. Her Dragon had been hot with passion but now it settled, listening to a symphony pour through her bones. She should have been angry. She should have been pissed that the cuff had bound her to someone other than Adrian. Yet she wasn't. Being held in Dusk's arms after that explosive moment was the safest she'd ever felt – and the deepest.

"Adrian's going to be pissed." As if reading her thoughts, Dusk's growl was dark – though Layla felt him smile by her ear.

"Did you plan that?" She asked, suddenly wondering.

But Dusk's next laugh, bright and startled, assuaged her fears. "Gods, no! I thought the cuff had one Bind in it and one Bind only! I assumed it would only bind you to the first Royal Dragon who clapped it on your wrist. Not one trying to take it *off* you."

"So I guess you are an actual Royal Dragon then," Layla spoke with a small smile.

"I guess I am."

"Are you sorry?" Pulling back, Layla gazed up at him, needing to see his eyes.

"That we've been bound? No. I'm not sorry." Gazing down, Dusk's eyes had returned to their clear sapphire color, though Layla saw lighter flecks in his irises now as if the diamond-brilliance would never quite recede. His face was serious, something beautifully amazed in his eyes. "I didn't know this would happen, but I don't regret it, Layla. This sensation with you...gods! I'm almost afraid to let down my wall and feel the fullness of it."

"Because you don't know what we'll do." Layla spoke softly. "I know what you mean."

Layla felt it, too – the intensity of their Bind, as if it was more solid and earth-shaking than her Bind with Adrian. Layla and Adrian swirled like two sand-funnels roaring into a burning desert sky. But this sensation with Dusk was deep and passionate. As if his cavern-bright energy anchored her sand-funnel heat, making everything flow in a tremendous roar of coordinated power rather than chaotic eruption. It was deeply grounding and erotic, as much as it caused her to soar through the sky – and Layla loved everything about it.

Dusk's eyes were luminous as he watched her; and she knew he felt the same way.

"What are we going to do?"

"Well," Dusk smiled, though Layla saw strain there. "Now we do what we came here to do. You're going to learn how to shield, just like I'm doing now. Because if it's just me shielding from you, Layla, I'll end up jumping your bones right in front of Adrian and then we'll have a real Dragon-fight on our hands. And with my power increase just now..."

"You gained power from our Bind?" Layla wondered about his

half-shift. Gazing at him, it was obvious Dusk had changed. If he'd been handsome before, the changes had made him ridiculously so – something no one would miss at the Hotel. As Layla watched, a flare of light went rippling through his body, following his stark ridges but also spreading out in an opalescent wave. He'd never refracted like that before and Layla watched it, mesmerized – like watching light shining through diamonds in a stream.

"I gained a *lot* of power, Layla," Dusk eyes were serious as the light passed away. "I nearly shifted all the way. I could feel it, coursing through every part of me. It was only my fear for your safety that kept me human tonight. And if Adrian gained this much power from binding you back in Seattle – then he's playing small right now. *Very* small, to try and trick his enemies. If he's gained as much power as what I'm feeling... then I don't want to see what happens when he decides to show it."

But his words suddenly made Layla's heart clench and her Dragon coil up. Setting her lips to Dusk's skin, she inhaled her scent running through his flows. "Dusk? Do you think Adrian would try to kill you for what happened just now?"

"I don't know." Dusk spoke softly. Setting his lips to her temple, he kissed her, letting his smooth lips linger. "I won't pick a fight with Adrian, but if he takes this out on either of us, what happened just now by accident, I will rise in defense. That said, I think it's best if we both learn control. Let's work on shielding. Hopefully, we can get us both some passable control over this Bind by dawn."

"And if we can't?"

"Then we face the fire," he breathed softly.

CHAPTER 22 – FOCUS

There was no clock down in the crystal Vault deep beneath the Hotel, though Layla was certain it was well past midnight and probably honing in on one or two a.m. Dusk had been trying to teach her shielding for hours, but ever since their Bind, it was proving impossible to separate their energies long enough to practice. Shielding necessitated a desire to resist the magics of another person – but all Layla's magic wanted to do these past hours was to coil its way into Dusk and stay there, permanently.

They'd tried everything. Dusk had taught her over a hundred movements in the past hours to create various kinds of magical shields and wards. With an exhausted huff, Layla sat on the glassy flow of rose quartz in the center of the cavern, massaging out a cramp in her hand from all the sigils and shielding movements he'd been guiding her through. Magical fighting was far more physical than she'd expected, like a martial art, with precise hand and body motions for everything.

And Layla had failed at every single one.

"This is useless, Dusk." She sighed, as irritated as she was exhausted. "Maybe I can learn to shield against someone else, but our energies are so intertwined now…"

"I know. I feel it, too. Let's take a break."

With a wry smile, Dusk flopped to a seat beside Layla. They had been working so long that the crystals in the cavern had begun to dim and he sent out a low rumble, flooding the cavern with resonance again. As if woken from slumber, the twisting luminescence in the crystal pillars flared in rings outward from the central space. With a start, Layla realized she could feel it as Dusk's vibration surged into the pillars – like her own awareness suddenly expanded, diving into the earth and spreading out in a ring. A vicious vertigo took her, of being everywhere in the cavern at once, staring at herself from every pillar and stalactite.

She swayed and Dusk caught her, his hands warm on her shoulders.

"Whoa! Easy." He spoke gently, though his voice had no vibration in it now. Layla could still feel his barrier preventing their energies from touching, though it seemed brittle now as if he'd held it too long. "What just happened?"

"I felt it when you lit the pillars." Layla blinked at him, shaking her head a little to clear it. "Like I was inside them; my consciousness watching us here in the center from a thousand different locations."

"That's what it feels like for me." Dusk narrowed his eyes, watching her with interest. "When I send my vibration somewhere, especially into crystals, I usually have a brief moment of vertigo like I'm in two or more locations at once. Bi-locational, or multi-locational. You felt that just now?"

"I guess so."

"Interesting." Dusk's brows narrowed and he slung his arms around his knees, thoughtful. "It sounds like you're starting to experience my magic like I do – you're resonating with it just like you do with Adrian's magic."

"Great, awesome. Now I get to have vertigo a lot in addition to feeling like a raging sandstorm all the time." Layla's mouth felt dry and she suddenly wished she had brought a water bottle. Listening to the stream somewhere in the cavern, she looked at Dusk. "Hey, is that water I hear drinkable?"

"It's a wellspring, comes up from deep beneath the Hotel. It's clean. Knock yourself out." Dusk nodded to a location behind a trio of sapphire pillars thirty paces away. But as Layla stood to get a drink, he rose in a fluid movement. "Actually, I could use some too. Shall we?"

He gestured and Layla took the lead, stepping off the rose quartz and winding through stalagmites until they reached the sapphire pillars. They were enormous, tall as trees, and just beyond them Layla saw a stream curling around their roots, flowing down over a drop into a small waterfall. Stepping down carefully on the slick rock, Layla knelt at the base of the falls and cupped her hands. The water was cool and sweet as she drank, reminding her of Dusk's scent. She eyeballed him as he knelt beside her, drinking also. Her Dragon stirred despite Dusk's firm wall between them, sending licks of deep heat in his direction.

Dusk shivered at Layla's side. Currying water through his elegant dark hair, he gave her a sidelong smile. "I felt that."

"Sorry." Layla blushed, internally exacerbated with her Dragon. For hours, Dusk had been trying to teach her how to focus her energy and throw up a shield, any kind of shield, but the only thing her Dragon had been interested in doing was trying to break through Dusk's diamond-hard wall and fuck him.

As Layla blushed, heating again, her magic licked out, finding chinks in Dusk's barrier and seeping in like a determined wind through a fortress wall. Dusk shivered, his lips falling open as his head tilted back, his eyes closed. He took deep breaths and Layla felt him try to firm that invisible barrier between them – and fail. With a slow out-breath, Dusk opened his eyes and looked at her. The sapphire in them was hot with flecks of diamond, as if gems could burn like phosphorus.

"You don't even know how hard it is to resist that," he growled, and Layla felt a dark rumble of his magics shudder the air. The water in the falls rippled as she felt the first teasing edge of those dark, delicious magics.

"Sorry." Layla spoke again, softer now.

But she really wasn't sorry as she stared at him, at how impossibly handsome he was. She wanted to touch him. She wanted to stroke her fingers over every inch of that body, to feel every ridged scale and smooth contour, every hard crevasse. She wanted to lick all that delicious skin, exploring it with lips and teeth and tongue.

As she had that thought, a languid stroke of heat rolled out from her, sliding over Dusk's barrier like a snake's coils trying to find purchase on stone. A tongue of hot energy licked from those coils, finding a weak spot in his barrier – licking deep into that crevasse. As if her tongue had found his actual skin, she could suddenly feel him and taste him; a delicious spot where his abdomen delved into the edge of his hip, where a scintillating line of midnight-blue scales rode his hipbone down beneath his pants. Layla rode that energy, licking along that ridge; feeling like her tongue was actually touching Dusk's skin. She could taste him as she licked along the serrated hardness of his scales and into the smooth hollow that delved towards his groin.

Dusk cried out softly, shuddering, the skin and muscles in his lower abdomen shivering as if she'd actually licked him. He breathed hard and Layla felt his barrier become spiderwebbed with cracks. As if his resolve to resist her had been hit with a bomb, those cracks rushed out, consuming the barrier. Dusk cried out again as Layla's energy sent eager talons into those cracks, tearing at them with a fast, passionate wind.

"Layla, stop! I can't...!" He shuddered, his hands gripping into fists as if it was the only thing that could stop him from reaching out and seizing her.

But Layla didn't know how to stop, as she became swept away in her Dragon's passions. Freed from her hamsa-cuff while they were practicing, her Dragon knew what it wanted. It was riding her and she couldn't stop it; every sinew alight, every muscle trembling. Layla fell to her back upon the crystal floes, writhing with pleasure and need. As her Dragon stretched its coils, she wrestled with the enormous energy pouring from her, surging against Dusk's barrier like a roaring ocean.

Wanting to tear down his limitations.

With a deep shudder, Dusk suddenly heaved up from his knees. Lurching across the cavern, he moved quickly to the central area and snatched up something. And then he heaved his way back, trembling as if every movement was a struggle.

A broad mirage of heat curling with golden flames surged around Layla as Dusk came staggering back. She felt him come, as if he pushed through a sea of hot wind and drowning citrus scent to reach her. His eyes were wild, his irises entirely taken by diamond-light as he fell to his knees beside her inside that ring of etheric golden fire.

His body was refracting again, light pouring through his Dragon-scales. Layla's body was not her own, surging and arching with passion, everything that was human inside her obliterated by how much she needed him – needed to mate with him. Moving over her, Dusk braced himself on trembling arms to either side of her ecstatic roiling. Layla could feel him, so cool and clear to her desperate heat.

But he was breaking, his crystal wall fracturing. And as it burst, as the dam broke and Layla's raging heat swept through his wall, Dusk seized her left hand – clapping the Moroccan cuff upon her wrist and binding her magics tight.

Something screamed inside Layla as he set the silver pin – as all that blissful heat was suddenly slammed into a cage. She cried out in pain and frustration as her Dragon roared inside her, furious. Thrashing with claws and fangs, raking her insides, her Dragon cut her up in its fury and Layla cried out in terrible pain, thrashing against the stone.

Dusk recovered quickly, now that he was no longer under assault from Layla's magics. Hauling her up from the crystal floor, he held her close, pouring a cooling vibration like a river into her until her Dragon quieted. Layla breathed hard, tears leaking from her eyes as her body shuddered with a morass of pain and heat and desire.

"How am I ever going to control this?!" She gasped, feeling wretched.

"I'm so sorry, Layla," Dusk gasped as he cradled her. "If it's any consolation, wrangling our Dragons is not any easier for Adrian and I. We just have more practice."

His words made Layla set her jaw against the tears, feeling awful that controlling her Dragon's passions might never get any easier. Rage and fury, heat and sex still ripped through her, her scent turned to scorch though the majority of her magic had been stuffed away again.

At last, Layla was able to re-gain some modicum of control. She still felt wild, but it was more manageable as she wiped tears away with the heels of her hands. Reaching up, she wound her hands around Dusk's neck as he held her. Breathing at his bare chest, she inhaled his cool scent, relaxing.

Dusk pulled back a little. Nuzzling her lips, he sighed and Layla drank his sigh. She inhaled it, touching her lips to his again – so impossibly silken. Closing her eyes, she felt his breath fill her as he smiled now, kissing her more.

It was smooth and kind, soothing vibrations easing from his lips down into Layla's tortured body. Her Dragon stirred in long, languid movements as Dusk kissed her and she kissed him back; a thing of slow fire and deep rushing rivers as their lips pressed, as their tongues explored. As they kissed, Layla felt his heart; as if it spilled up through his body like a crystal river, passing in through hers. Layla felt a golden pleasure fill her like her Dragon was beaming, like its scales could

252

shine with glory to feel the tenderness and purity of everything Dusk was.

At last, they parted. Opening their eyes, they stared at each other, and it seemed to Layla as if she could see inside Dusk's soul, crystalline and perfect – and he could see into hers, luminous and golden. Dusk breathed hard as he stared down at her in amazement, his blue eyes alight. A soft smile touched his lips as he reached up, stroking back one of Layla's wayward curls.

"I could kiss you like that forever, Layla Price." He spoke quietly.

"Why don't you?" She breathed, still feeling that delicious ecstasy swirling through her.

"Because someone else would be mad." Dusk whispered, pressing her lips again with his. Layla arched up into him, pulling him close. He wound his arms around her, crushing her gently to his body. Breaking the kiss, he moved his head so his lips nuzzled her ear. "God, I want you."

"Then take me."

"I don't think that's wise." Dusk kissed her neck now, oh-so-softly.

Layla shivered with pleasure, her chin lifting and her eyes closing. "Wasn't it you who told me Dragons have multiple lovers?"

"Yes." She felt Dusk smile into her neck as he kissed her again.

"So why can't you and I be lovers in addition to me and Adrian?"

"Because Adrian and I would tear each other apart." Dusk kissed her neck again. "We've fought over women before. It wasn't good."

"Adam told me." Layla sighed as Dusk kissed her neck again. Holding her, he squeezed her waist, kneading her with his strong hands as he buried his nose in her shoulder. Layla felt a graze of teeth on her neck. She shuddered as Dusk bit her lightly, as if marking his right to be exactly where he was – as her bound mate.

Dusk growled into her neck and Layla's entire body shuddered, needing him. Without warning, he scooped her up in his arms, pushing up from the cavern floor in a powerful thrust of muscles and striding back over the stream. Moving quickly to the central flow, she thought he was taking her to the rose quartz to fuck her rotten – when he suddenly deposited her on her feet. With a kiss to her nose as she blinked in surprise, he pulled away, laughing his way over to his clothes and scooping up his shirt. Turning, he was still laughing as he slung his shirt on, grinning at her with rogue merriment.

Which pissed Layla off. Feeling like he was suddenly laughing at her, her Dragon coiled up in anger – breathing a stiff scorch through her veins and making her cross her arms. "What?"

"Nothing." Dusk grinned like a devil as he buttoned his shirt and tucked it into his pants, retrieving his jacket from the cavern floor. "You're just so cute when you're pissed, Layla Price. When you want me and I won't give it to you."

"Wow. You *so* did not patronize me like that after everything we just shared." Layla lifted an eyebrow, simmering with a fury that was now overcoming her passion – quickly.

"Yes, I did." Slipping on his shoes, Dusk faced her. Still grinning, he palmed his hands back over his dark hair, styling it into place perfectly as if it'd never been mussed. "And you're going to take it – every little bit of patronization I can give you. Because if I know one thing about you yet, Layla, it's this: you've got a weakness for me. Because underneath all the smarts and can-do attitude, you're really just a desperate girl who likes to fuck. And what you like to fuck, is bad boys. Well, congratulations. I'm a very bad boy and we can fuck all you want. But first... I want you to beg me for it. And then we'll see about a good, hard fuck to calm your blistering loins."

"*Excuse* me?!" Layla's fury reached its boiling point, incredulity filling her. Dusk had gone from tender lover to frat-guy asshat like Adam in two-point-five seconds – and it scalded Layla in a way she hadn't felt since he'd first tried to mess with her at her welcome banquet. She seethed with fury, suddenly wondering if Dusk's tenderness and friendship with her over the past few months had all been a ruse. If it had all been a big game – a long-con, to bind her and steal her away from Adrian at last.

Not to mention, to get in her pants.

"You *fucking asshole!*" Layla shouted, rage rising so hot and fast inside her that her body broke out in goosebumps, a surging wrath of heat blossoming up all around her now in a mirage.

"Yes, I am an asshole. Heads up."

With a rakishly mean glint in his eyes, Dusk suddenly hurled a hand at her like throwing a fastball. Something broke from his palm, a diamond-bright spear of energy now barreling at Layla, fast. Her eyes widened; shock smote her as her Dragon roared in fury. Her palm came up on instinct with all five fingers together in a warding gesture like her hamsa-cuff. Layla felt something slam up before her – a barrier of swirling, molten wind that sundered the diamond-bright lance in a flash of light.

Bursting it into crystal shards so small they looked like glittering snow as they scattered over the rose quartz floor.

Shock smote Layla as she took in all those glittering pieces, not invisible energy now but thousands of actual shards of white crystal, each one sharper than a blade. Her barrier dissipated, her scalding mirage blowing away to nothing as the danger passed, leaving her breathing hard with her left hand still raised in her ward. It was something she'd done on instinct, not a gesture Dusk had taught her over the past many hours. And as she stared at him in astonishment, she saw Dusk grin – a dark light of pride in his eyes as Layla breathed hard, realizing what had just happened.

She'd had a problem of not being able to protect herself while she was hot for him.

So Dusk had solved it like the clever bastard he was – by making her furious instead.

CHAPTER 23 – MORNING

Layla blinked at Dusk incredulously in the cavern of crystal pillars. Thousands of crystal shards coated the rose quartz floor from his killing-strike, like someone had exploded a crystal pillar into tiny daggers of snow, each like a bladed toothpick. And though Layla's rational mind said she should be infuriated, her Dragon-mind was laughing, roaring with delight as if fighting and death was just some big game. Layla breathed hard as she slowly lowered her palm – stunned at what Dusk had done and also impressed at his cunning.

Not to mention her own response.

"You just tried to kill me!"

"It worked, didn't it?" He grinned, scooping up Layla's sweater and flats from the crystal floor and shaking crystal shards out of them, his sapphire eyes alight with merriment. "Congratulations, you just cast a protective barrier with your magics. And you did it with your hamsa-cuff in place. Not a small thing."

Gone was Dusk's frat-boy attitude, replaced by his usual self. He was tender and kind as he moved close, setting a warm palm to her cheek, his eyes luminous with delight. With a huff, Layla batted his hand away, slinging on her sweater and eyeing her shoes for crystal shards before stepping into them.

"Fuck you." She spat.

"Are you mad at me?" Dusk cocked his head, his lips curled up at the edges in amusement.

"Yes. No. Hell, I don't know." Layla growled, her Dragon jubilant inside her though her mind was still trying to come to grips with the fact that Dusk had just thrown a potentially lethal bolt of energy at her. She threw up her hands in exasperation, though she was smiling now as she shook her head. "You seriously just tried to kill me, Dusk!"

"There was a chance it wouldn't have harmed you. It was more of a stunning-strike than a killing one." He lifted an eyebrow like a devil – a ridiculously handsome devil Layla still wanted to pounce with every inch of her body.

"Damn you." Layla shook her head again, though she was smiling now as she headed for the stairs. They'd achieved their aims: she'd cast a shield. She was so done with training tonight and wanted the softness of her bed at whatever ungodly hour it now was. Dusk trotted up, gaining her side. Grinning at her, he lifted a dark eyebrow as they started up the corkscrewing stairwell.

"That was a great shield, Layla."

"Fuck off."

"I mean it. You didn't just turn my lance away, you blasted my strike apart. It takes a lot of energy to make my blows shatter into real crystals, I hope you know."

"So?" Layla sassed, still not knowing what exactly to make of it. She was tired; her body hurt. Her Dragon still wanted sex, but all Layla wanted now was to be done for the night.

"So." Reaching out, Dusk stopped Layla's ascent with a hand to her arm. She paused, feeling her energy leap to his again, even though he was solidly back behind a new shield-wall and she was contained by her hamsa-cuff.

But his face was serious, imposing his lesson. "You have power, Layla. Maybe you don't know what to do with it yet, but you executed on instinct what it takes other Dragons weeks to learn. Not only did you learn shielding in one night, you did it with so much panache that you exploded a strike from a far older and more powerful Dragon – *with* your talisman on. And with a *personal* ward, something that's learned only on instinct and is different for each Dragon. That's more impressive than you know. If you were on Rikyava's Guard, she'd fast-track you for combat. Ask her yourself – she'll tell you the same thing. You have power, Layla. And even if you don't know what to do with it yet, your Dragon does."

Layla stood there, wanting to believe him yet not believing it. But Dusk was so serious in his intensity that Layla began to ponder it. What if her Dragon did have power? The power of not just passion and sex, but the ability to hone her fury into battle. Her beast roiled inside her as if eager to try, and though Layla had only ever taken self-defense classes, the adrenaline she'd gotten just now from warding off that strike had been exhilarating. She'd always been an adrenaline aficionado; roller coasters, downhill skiing, skydiving. Hell, even her relationships with Luke and Gavin had been adrenaline highs – fighting one minute, fucking the next.

Her beast rolled over eagerly as she thought about it. And though Layla had never willingly put herself in a combat situation, she suddenly wondered if she might just like it.

"I need to get some sleep." Layla started back up the stairs. "Not everybody is a stress junkie like you are, Dusk."

"I'm not a stress junkie, I just never quit. There's a difference." He smiled at her, lurid and lovely.

"Are you seriously saying you have energy for *sex* right now?" Layla laughed, feeling something inside her slither restlessly at the idea.

"Maybe." He was renegade, grinning as they ascended the top landing. The sapphire door was still glowing with red sigils as they approached, and Layla saw the two Guards idling outside. They glanced up as Layla and Dusk arrived. She could barely hear Lorio's sharp whistle, but she saw him beckon. Rikyava stepped out from one of the training halls, her face a relieved smile. Setting her palm to the sapphire door, Rikyava's lips moved in an incantation. A shockwave of energy went through the door again, except this one flared the sigils from red to a searing white before they faded to blue. The crack appeared in the sapphire like magic and the two halves of the door sighed back into the wall.

"Whew! You guys were in there a long time! I was beginning to wor—what in the actual fuck?!" Rikyava blinked, scenting the air. Her violet eyes went wide as Layla and Dusk exited the chamber, her gaze taking in Dusk's new appearance. "You... you both..."

"Smell like each other? Yeah. So that happened in the past few hours." Dusk's smile was wry, something careful in his eyes as he faced Rikyava. Layla suddenly remembered the two were lovers as she saw a long scowl devour Rikyava's lovely face.

"He's bound to you." Her tone was icy as she turned to stare at Layla. "Him and Adrian. Both."

"It was an accident, Rikyava—" Dusk protested, but the Guardswoman cut him off.

"Accident my ass." Her eyes whipped from Layla back to Dusk. "Was this your plan? Take her down there and touch the cuff so she would *bind* you? Make her life more impossible than it already is? Way to go, asshole. You've just won *boss of the year* award. Jesus!"

"Rikyava, it's ok—" Layla protested, realizing that the ferocious Blood Dragon was actually taking her side rather than Dusk's. She had thought because Rikyava and Dusk were lovers that Rikyava would have been pissed at her. But instead, the Head Guardswoman's fury was boiling up at Dusk. Rikyava held up a palm to Layla, then faced Dusk, thunderclouds building in her eyes as they began to turn a stormy red.

"How could you, Dusk?"

"Rikyava, it really was an accident." Dusk looked chagrined. "I didn't know the cuff would bind me to Layla when I helped her take it off."

"Good thing you and Adrian did your research when you went hunting that thing. Good thing arcane artifacts never have strange *surprises*." Rikyava's eyes were a deep red now, fury in the set of her stern jaw and the narrowing of her eyes above her high Swedish cheekbones.

"You helped Adrian find my cuff? You never told me that." Layla turned to Dusk, her eyebrows raised at this new tidbit.

"I did." Dusk sighed, his humor gone. He looked as tired as Layla felt now as he passed a hand over his lips, then rubbed his cheek. "We'd researched the Hamsa Bind along with a number of other talismans for you, ever since Mimi's funeral. And though the Hamsa Bind was the most promising one, I'd told Adrian under no circumstances would I let him Bind you with that thing. But he got swept up in the moment at the gallery. I swear, that wasn't how we'd planned it. We can talk about it later."

"We *will* talk about it later." Layla spoke, making it plain with her glance.

"You're really going to let this slide, Layla?" Rikyava turned incredulous eyes to her. "What they both did to you? Tricking you, *trapping* you into relationships with them?"

"I believe Dusk when he says he didn't plan this, Rikyava," Layla returned, exhausted to her bones and not wanting to stay here arguing about a bruised sense of honor she didn't really feel. "Adrian has his own machinations to answer for. And he will."

"Yeah, after you tell him you're also hitched up to Dusk now, too. Good luck with that."

"Could you be any more sympathetic?" Layla snapped at her friend now, feeling irate suddenly after such a long and complicated night. "It's not like any of us understands this magic! I don't. Hell, you don't. Dusk doesn't, but he's trying. He just spent an *entire night* trying to teach me how to shield so I can protect myself from that goddamn void-shadow King Falliro Arini told us about, for Christ's sake! And now you're ripping us both a new one, acting like it was you who was slighted that Dusk and I managed to get ourselves accidentally bound together by some magical resonance we don't understand! What's with you? This is my problem, Rikyava, but you're acting like I just shat in your porridge."

Rikyava's pretty lips had fallen open. She stared at Layla, the red in her eyes clearing back to violet. She blinked, and then her eyes filled with tears. Layla stared at her, astounded as tears shed down Rikyava's austere cheeks. The Guardsmen behind her shifted uneasily and Layla was willing to bet they'd never seen their Captain cry before. With a hard huff, Rikyava flicked her tears away, then squared her shoulders. "I'm sorry. I was out of line. Forgive me."

Sympathy filled Layla suddenly. Her heart reached out to her friend and she moved forward, taking up the Guardswoman's hands. "What's wrong? What's going on? Is this really about me and Dusk?"

She thought Rikyava would draw away from her, but after a moment the woman relaxed, letting Layla clasp her hands. "I just... I wish I could Bind the man I want, that's all. Like you have with Adrian and Dusk."

"Is it Dusk you want?" Layla asked, hoping to god it wasn't. She'd never seen the proud Rikyava so dejected, and it worried Layla suddenly that the man she wanted might be the same man Layla had just bound.

But Rikyava only laughed, her gaze flitting embarrassedly to

Dusk. "No, gods no! You're a good lay, Dusk, and a great sparring partner, but my heart lies elsewhere. No offense."

"None taken." Dusk moved forward, settling an arm about Rikyava's shoulders in a kindly way. It was clear they were far more than familiar; they were friends, no matter how Rikyava tried to deny it. And it was also clear that Dusk wasn't upset with her saying she was in love with someone other than him. "You want to talk? Layla and I were just about to get some breakfast. We'd love for you to join us."

"We were?" Layla blinked. "I mean... want to come chat about whatever's bothering you?" More than anything else, Layla wanted sleep – but if her friend was hurting, that took priority. Friends just did, period.

Rikyava opened her lips and it looked like she was about to say yes, when her blonde brows knit. She sighed, then shook her head. "No. You guys go ahead. I need to work it out with the man in question, not anybody else. My problems aren't going to get solved over coffee and beignets. But you're both sweet to offer."

"Hey, our offer stands," Dusk reiterated, jostling Rikyava about the shoulders. "Anytime; anything you need. We're here."

Layla nodded at his words and Rikyava laughed sadly, glancing between the two of them with ruefulness in her eyes. "God! It's like you're an old married couple now. I feel this... harmony flowing between you. I'm jealous, really. But it merits the question: what are you going to do about Adrian?"

Dusk and Layla shared a look.

"We don't know yet." Layla answered – realizing suddenly that she had answered like an old married couple, using *we* instead of *I*.

"I am so going to station extra Guard at all your rooms for a while." Rikyava shook her head, a ready look in her eyes now. "This feels like it could get ugly, fast. If you didn't know this second Bind could happen, Dusk, then Adrian's *really* not going to be expecting it. And we all know he doesn't take surprises well."

"I agree with a little extra caution," Dusk was suddenly in business mode as he turned to Rikyava. "Keep a detail on Adrian, discreetly. I want extra Guards ready at all times if he gets out of hand. Layla's going to have to break the news to him eventually, or he might scent it out on his own like you did. Either way…"

"Either way, we're going to have sparks," Rikyava agreed, back to her usual Guardswoman brusqueness as if her emotional breakdown had never happened. "I'll spread the news and get back to you later this morning."

"Not too early. I need to sleep in." Dusk grimaced and Layla suddenly realized he was tired. She'd never really seen Dusk tired before, and the man never slept in. Layla found herself watching him closely as she realized he'd expended more energy tonight than he was telling. His posture wasn't quite as upright as usual; his smile was dragging. As Layla watched, a fine tremor shuddered him, and he leaned on the wall rather than stand up straight.

The Crystal Dragon did have limits to his never-ending boisterousness.

"Sure." Rikyava gave a brief smile, something like sympathy in her violet eyes. Stepping away, she flicked her fingers to her Guardsmen. Lorio and Ben stepped up with smart attention, and Rikyava beckoned for them to follow toward her Captain's office by the gym. Layla watched them go, and when Dusk motioned her toward the egress of the underground hall, she went.

Moving through a more subdued Guard-hall in the deep hours of the night, they reached the exit and ascended the broad stairs back to the south wing. Dusk was quiet as they moved through the somber halls of the Hotel. He seemed lost in thought and extremely tired as they ascended a broad staircase to the third floor. Turning the bend, he was about to ascend the staircase to the fourth floor when he suddenly stopped.

He glanced at Layla, his hand on the railing. "Would you like to come up?"

Layla paused, realizing he'd just asked if she'd like to come up to his apartment with him. And then she realized something even more strange – that she'd never seen Dusk's apartment. She'd always assumed he had rooms on the fourth floor, but for all the times they'd had drinks or dinner together, Dusk had always come to her. Layla hesitated, wanting to see how he lived – yet feeling suddenly shy about it.

"For breakfast, or something else?" She murmured, not wanting anyone to hear though the hall was quiet.

"Breakfast," Dusk spoke with a soft smile. "Maybe a little sleep."

"Just sleep?" Layla didn't know why it mattered, but it suddenly did.

"Just sleep." Dusk spoke gently, though his eyes spoke more.

Layla paused. Her hand strayed to the railing; to him. Wanting to touch him again but fearing it. Dusk saw her hesitation and turned, sliding his hand down the rail to touch her fingers. Their fingertips met and caressed. A soft sigh issued from Dusk's lips as Layla's lips opened also – feeling that gold-diamond light ease through them both again.

"I don't know if I can." She murmured. "Adrian—"

"I understand."

Dusk's words were low in the empty hall. He hesitated, then moved back down the stairs. Their gazes connected, but before Layla could say anything, he stepped in – gathering her close. As he did, he let his shield drop. Golden light surged through Layla, and her body was suddenly searing with bliss, held in his arms. Her Dragon turned over inside her, filled with pleasure as he clutched her close, breathing softly at her ear. Small tremors wracked him also. Dusk was feeling their melded diamond-gold energy, rushing through him as much as it did her. Layla felt lightheaded as her energy expanded and she swooned. Dusk caught her fast so she wouldn't collapse, one hand cradling her head. It left her looking up at him, meeting those handsome sapphire eyes – watching them burn with flecks of diamond in the night.

"You slay me, Layla Price," Dusk murmured, moving his lips softly over hers. "You slay the heart of this Crystal drake. I don't care what Adrian says; I'm not sorry you bound me. But I will do what you ask of me…whatever makes your life easier. Tell me to stay or go—"

"I don't want you to go," Layla breathed, feeling herself lift up, as if for a kiss.

"But you don't want to come home with me." Dusk's smile was wry.

"I can't right now. Please."

"You'll miss me when I'm gone." He breathed back, smoothing his lips over hers.

"I miss you already."

Dusk chuckled at her lips. And then he pressed her with a kiss, right out in the open for anyone to see. It was warm and sensual and Layla reveled in it, swirling with golden light until he finally let her go. His eyes drove into her like diamond lances as he slowly released her. He licked her taste from his lower lip, taking it gently into his mouth and sucking with a devilishly handsome smile curling the edges of his lips before speaking again.

"Goodnight, Layla Price. Dream of me." A smooth rumble slid through the floor, sliding up Layla's ankles and thighs, deep into her body. She gasped, her eyelashes fluttering, one hand clutching the railing of the stairs so she wouldn't collapse.

"Damn you," she breathed.

"Damn us both." And with a last rumbling glance, he was gone up the stairs.

Layla shivered from Dusk's lingering pleasure. She could still feel it, as if their Bind left a tingle of his delicious energies still rushing through her, and always would now. Steadying herself on the wall, Layla turned and walked back toward her rooms, exhausted and languid, and pleased.

CHAPTER 24 – BIND

Layla had slept in long past her usual five a.m. wake-up and well into the mid-afternoon. She'd woken with a tremendous amount of energy, bounding out of bed, and had slung on her yoga clothes from the night before. Filling a water bottle and grabbing her orange yoga mat, she was out the door with only a bite of bacon and a sip of cold coffee – down to her favorite spot in the gardens with a spring in her step.

Rolling out her yoga mat on a smooth expanse of flagstone near a leaping fish-fountain, Layla breathed deep of the chill autumn air as she stepped onto her mat. Sunshine flooded her nook as the October wind whirled by the fountain carrying golden leaves, but Layla wasn't cold. She felt invigorated, trying inverted balancing poses today that she never usually attempted without a wall. As she moved, she realized that a diamond-gold energy filled her still – an echo of what had passed between her and Dusk the night before.

She knew she should have been thinking about Adrian. She should have been worried about how he would react to her Bind with Dusk. But she found she just couldn't be upset today, as if binding Dusk last night had somehow changed her. Today everything was perfect, and as Layla held her unsupported handstand strong, she realized she could do more. Lifting her right hand, she adjusted to balance one-handed, something she'd never done. Glowing with energy, she missed the soft step behind her until someone spoke.

"Well, someone's vibrant today."

With a startled *eep*, Layla lost her balance and fell, barely controlling her tumble and catching herself on the balls of her feet. Her inner Dragon growled to be so rudely interrupted and Layla growled with it, whirling to face her intruder.

Except that her intruder was Rachida Rhakvir, Third of her clan and Adam's foster-mother, not to mention Adrian's great-aunt. Layla paused the tirade she had been about to unleash, closing her mouth in surprise. Rachida was dressed in yoga clothes also, and the fierce drakaina had her exquisite copper hair pulled back in clips today, showing stark cheekbones and a lovely jaw that looked like it could crack bones.

"May I join you?"

Rachida's alto voice was like buttercream over molasses, rich and full. Unlike the Storm Queen, Rachida Rhakvir was still in her prime, and her curvy, strong body betrayed no infirmity. As those knowing emerald eyes pierced her, Layla realized it was Rachida's presence that felt ancient, as she slung a yoga mat down off her shoulder. Power pushed out from Rachida in a battle-ready way, like her aura was so full of strength that she couldn't contain it. Layla blinked, recalling Adam's words that this was the woman who had birthed Julius Caesar.

"Be my guest." Layla gestured to an open spot on the flagstones. Rachida smiled, moving forward with grace and rolling out her mat.

Rachida didn't speak again as she began her routine. Layla resumed her own practice and the two women moved through their flows as the chill day blustered around them. But Rachida performed a strange series of postures Layla had never seen, then eventually sat and began pranayama breathing, fast pants with long holds that heated her like a forge-fire. Sweat was soon cascading off Layla's body from the woman's scalding energy, though Rachida remained cool and composed. But whatever she was doing was flaring her magic like a bellows, and Layla's own Dragon roared inside, wanting to understand it.

Layla sat. Watching Rachida, she learned the breathing, then gave it a try. Immediately, her body flared with heat and she felt her magics expand, like her body was a bellows powering a volcano. Her inner Dragon coiled in an ecstatic way that had nothing to do with sex and everything to do with power as a flood of energy roared through Layla. It made her dizzy and she had to cease – humming with energy like she could fight a hundred men.

"So. The Bind has battle in her veins and not just sex." Rachida had ceased her breathing and was watching Layla, a small smile on her lips. "I feel your beast, child. It is a wild animal. But it can be tamed."

"What were you doing just now, that breathing pattern?" Layla asked, feeling like Rachida was a wealth of untapped information.

"It's called *Feeding the Dragon*." Rachida smiled, taking her copper waves down from their clips and combing them out. "I learned it during my first sojourn to Tibet as a young woman. An old Crystal Dragon matron taught it to me. I practice it daily."

"I feel like battle filled me as I was doing it. This enormous fire," Layla spoke, curious.

"Indeed," the elegant Dragon matron smiled, her emerald eyes twinkling. "How do you think I bested seven drakes in an open fight once? I wasn't bigger than them. I wasn't stronger, or older. I was faster and more vicious, and my magic roared through them like a battering ram. Because I practice strength, subtlety – and control."

"Your battle when your son was murdered. Julius Caesar?" Layla felt bad questioning the Dragon matron, but she couldn't help it.

"Indeed." Rachida smiled peaceably. "But we are not here to talk about that son of mine, long dead and gone. We're here to speak about my living sons. Though Adrian is not mine and neither is Dusk, they are as sons to me. And I wish to ask your intentions with both of them.

And perhaps with my adopted son Adam, also."

"Ms. Rhakvir—" Layla protested. "I don't mean your sons any harm."

"Royal Dragon Binds have a way about them, Layla Price." Rachida lifted an eyebrow, her green eyes intense. "I've known quite a few in my lifetime. You flood my sons with power; don't think I can't feel your Binds on them. Adrian and Dusk hum like twin suns today, and *you* are the source behind it. That talisman is a poor piece of trash in its ability to contain you. Ask yourself one question: did it Bind you to Adrian and Dusk because they touched it – or did *you Bind them* through your talisman, because you wanted it to do your will?"

Layla was struck mute at Rachida's words – though a little voice inside her had been wondering same thing. "I'm assuming you know the answer."

"I do." Rachida gave a vicious smile. "All talismans magnify the wearer's deepest desires. This is something Adrian and Dusk chose to overlook when they went searching for yours. Adrian had heard stories of the Hamsa Bind's uniqueness, and he can be very headstrong when he discovers something that will give him power. What he and Dusk would not listen to me about, is that talismans amplify the wearer's inner urges. You wish to have your magic contained because it is wild and frightening; so it is contained. You wish to feel in control, because being out-of-control with passion and rage is terrifying; so you are controlled. But you also wish to be bound by men who strike you with fury and passion. Beautiful men who would go to the ends of the earth with you. And so the cuff Binds them for you – when you are too afraid to admit what you want and do it yourself."

"And what exactly is it that I want?" Layla breathed, stunned.

"Two powerful Royal Dragons and possibly a third," Rachida's gaze was deep. "I've seen Dusk today. He is bedridden from the events of last night; how you bound him and flared him into a partial shift. My young Crystal Dragon can barely move, yet he stays abed with a tremendous grin on his face. Because you bound him; because he feels the golden light of your nature pouring through him still."

"Dusk's sick today?" Layla suddenly felt terrible, her heart aching.

"Adrian was the same after the art gallery." Rachida gave Layla a knowing look. "He called me that night; he'd nearly shifted and did everything in his ability to stop it. He was in excruciating pain for days."

"He never told me. He never let it show," Layla breathed, feeling truly awful now.

"Adrian is a master at deception," Rachida lifted an eyebrow. "But Dusk does not care for deception. And so he languishes in bed today, enjoying his day off and dreaming of a certain woman even though his bones scream like ground glass."

Layla recalled the horrible sensation she had been beleaguered with after she had nearly shifted. Adrian and Dusk were powerful enough to stop their own shifts, but apparently it still cost them.

Layla rose, rolling up her yoga mat.

"Where are you off to, child?"

"I need to see Dusk." Layla tucked her mat in its carry-bag and zipped it. "And if that happened to Adrian also when we met, then I need to apologize. If it's truly my magic binding them rather than just the cuff… I need to make amends. And find a way to unbind them. If they want it." Layla added, feeling terrible that they might choose to be unbound from her but wanting to give them a choice. If Rachida was right and it was Layla's magic doing the binding rather than the talisman itself, then Layla had a lot of apologizing to do.

And a lot more control to learn.

"Good." Rachida flowed to standing, taking up Layla hands. "If you wish my sons no harm and want to make amends for your wild magic, then your heart is worthy. I give you my permission to Bind and mate with my sons – all three of them if you like. And I am here, if you wish to learn the arts of war. Dusk is a challenging teacher, but what he cannot teach you is the prowess of fighting like a drakaina. A drake uses power and muscles when fighting; a drakaina uses cunning. Come to me if you wish to learn a little cunning, child. And I will teach you."

Layla blinked, not sure if she should say thanks or if she should feel offended that Rachida felt she needed permission to date. "If I hadn't gotten your permission, if you'd judged me unworthy of Adrian, Dusk, or Adam—"

"Then I would have torn you apart." Rachida's gaze was unapologetic, and terrifying. "Maybe not today, maybe not tomorrow. But when your back was turned I would have ripped my talons through your chest and bitten out your heart, child. I shall suffer no weakling to Bind my sons. They may date and fuck as they like. But a true mate gives her partner challenge, heart, and strength. And only a true mate will do."

Layla blinked, realizing that Rachida meant every word of what she'd just said. If she'd judged Layla unworthy, she truly would have killed Layla – no matter Adrian's or Dusk's feelings about it. And Layla realized suddenly that she was standing before a real Dragon matriarch. Others held stronger positions in the clan, but Rachida was the one they turned to when things went bad.

The one who wouldn't hesitate to do what had to be done.

"Are we clear, young woman?" Rachida spoke again, lifting one russet eyebrow.

"Crystal." Layla breathed, terrified of the Dragon matriarch yet also impressed.

"Speaking of crystals," Rachida clasped her hands with a softer smile now. "I know a Crystal Dragon who would very much like to see you. I can show you to his rooms."

"I would like that." Layla tried to smile. Rachida intimidated her to no end, though she also realized the woman could be a powerful ally if Layla played her cards right.

"Come, then. You and I will speak of the arts of war at a later time."

With that, Rachida turned, taking up her mat. In a short moment, the two drakainas stepped from the secluded patio, moving back toward the Hotel. They didn't speak as they ascended to the fourth floor. Moving down the hall, they stopped at the third door on the left, carved with a crystal cavern scene. Rachida knocked and announced herself through the door, and they heard a muffled, "Come in."

Moving into the apartment, Layla was surprised by Dusk's decor. Modern and elegant, Dusk's apartment was bright and clean, late afternoon sunshine flooding through the vaulted windows to highlight a pale ashwood floor. The space was done in blacks and taupes with accents of royal purple, saffron, and forest green. Ebony furniture in a 1930's style decorated the space, the apartment fengshuied so it breathed with openness.

But what astounded Layla were the crystals. Enormous rock gardens of sapphire, jade, and amazonite surrounded pillars of rose quartz. Huge geodes of amethyst that Layla could have crawled into like a hot tub were nestled in groups of potted palms. Altars decorated every corner with smoky quartz, labradorite slabs, and living trees full of live orchids. An obsidian Anubis statue occupied a prominent spot, water flowing from its outstretched palms into a pond of lazy koi-fish. White crystals formed the basin, creating a starkly luminous effect against the effigy.

It was incredible, and Layla found herself amazed at the space Dusk had created. As she entered, she saw the vaulted apartment had a modern kitchen and dining area. And though Dusk's four-post ebony bed was off to the left, it was artfully screened off by a wall of see-through shelves holding crystals and potted orchids. As Layla moved left with Rachida, she saw a white duvet with something purple beneath. Moving closer, Layla saw it was a pad of crushed amethyst crystals under the bedding.

As they entered, Rachida announced, "I have someone to see you, Dusk."

"If it's Adrian, tell him to go away," Layla heard Dusk's muffled voice come from the bed. "I'm in no shape to fight him today."

"It's not Adrian." Rachida spoke chidingly as she and Layla moved to the bed, which contained a form curled up beneath the fluffy duvet. "And if you'd get your face out of the pillows, you might just be surprised."

Layla saw movement. And then a face peered out from the covers, before Dusk sat straight up, his sapphire eyes wide. "Layla!"

"Hey." She stepped forward to the massive bed, big enough to sleep five or six people. "I heard you weren't feeling well."

"You're not supposed to see me like this." Dusk flopped back to the pillows as if it was too much effort to stay up. But he grinned as Layla sat at his bedside and reached out to take his hand. A golden light tingled through Layla as their hands connected and she saw Dusk shiver, his eyes brightening.

"I'll take my leave." With a small smile, Rachida backed out of the apartment, shutting the double-doors. And then it was just Layla and Dusk. His hand was scalding compared to how he usually felt, and Layla clasped his fingers as she listened to the burble of the Anubis waterfall echoing through the space.

"You've got a fever."

"I'm fine." But even as he said it, Dusk cast the covers off his upper body with a smooth movement, drawing the cool air of his apartment deep into his lungs. Casting the covers down had bared him to the hips, and as the late afternoon sunlight played over the palatial bed, Layla saw his body, chiseled with those perfect lines of iridescent scale. His groin was barely covered and Layla found herself staring, wondering if the ridges went down all the way. She'd been with fit men but Dusk put other men to shame, and she couldn't help but stare, caught in the play of light on his incredible nakedness. He was like some Adonis carved of marble and decorated with all the best details.

"You're ogling me, Layla Price." Dusk chuckled as she stared at his rock-hard body. He patted the bed beside him. "Come here."

Layla didn't need to be asked twice. Dusk's low rumble was pleased as she cuddled in under his arm, moulding close to his side and slinging one leg over his. But being so close, her body pressed to all that sexy heat and her leg up over his naked thigh, suddenly made Layla viciously intrigued. Her Dragon stirred inside her, roiling with the urge to writhe all over that chiseled muscle and feel it hard and silky beneath her. She flushed, a riot of orange-peel and bourbon scent rising up around her and Dusk laughed. Setting his fingers under her chin, he lifted her head so she was no longer staring at his nearly-exposed groin, but at his face.

"Hey, I'm up here."

"Sorry." Layla flushed harder.

"I'm not. I like it when you stare at me."

Dusk lifted her chin further with his fingertips. Their lips connected and Layla melted into him as they kissed slowly in the waning sunshine. His lips were warm and beautifully soft. Even Adrian's lips couldn't match the exquisite silken texture of Dusk's skin, as if a smooth river flowed through the Crystal Dragon's very nature.

Their kiss was slow and decadent, with an echo of that diamond-gold sensation they'd found the night before. Layla felt herself smiling as Dusk licked his tongue into her mouth; tasting her and exploring. They had time; they had privacy. And kissing him back, she found she was breathless as her Dragon stirred within her – reveling in the exquisite sensations.

Suddenly, Dusk made a rumbling sound that shuddered Layla with delight. In a powerful movement he rolled her, pressing her to the bed with his hard body atop hers. Trapping her with his mouth and hips, he moved against her slowly as he kissed her. Their hips rocked together with a slow-burn passion as they reveled in each other's bodies, warmed by the play of sunlight on skin. Dusk pressed his hips down and Layla felt him against her clothed thigh, hard and ready. She writhed, enjoying it with a delicious need as they kissed – as he moved her arms up above her head and pressed his hands down on her wrists.

Lifting her legs as they kissed, Layla wound them around Dusk's hips and he made a dark growl in his throat that thundered all the way through her. Heat built between them, like a rushing river in the last of the light. Layla cried out as Dusk growled into their kiss, pouring his lower-than-sound vibrations deep inside her like the thundering flow of a waterfall. Layla cried out, breaking their kiss as she spasmed with pleasure – driving her hips hard against his.

Bracing his hands upon her wrists, Dusk slid his body up so his hardness was pressed against Layla's groin. Lowering a hand, he slid down her yoga pants so she could feel all that silken hardness pressed against her skin. She gasped as he thrust, pressing that hard heat just above her groin and making her arch – breaking their kiss with a gasp as passion shuddered through her.

"I want you…" He growled in her ear, thrusting his hips again.

Tasting her deep, though in the wrong place.

"Please…" Layla's Dragon roared with lust as scent pummeled the air; a river of oranges flowing through a cavern of clear water.

"I'm not well, Layla," Dusk growled into her neck, biting her gently. "I want to do this when I'm better. I want to show you how I can really take you, at my best."

"What if I can't wait?" She gasped, her legs locked around his naked hips, her body raising to meet his next powerful thrust. Dusk shuddered as he pressed her again, but his arms were shaking now as he braced himself – and not from passion. His brow was beaded with sweat; his lips were ashen rather than their usual luscious blue-grey. And as he drove into her again, he gasped, trembling as if it was both ecstatic but also painful.

That gasp made Layla alert. Her lust evaporated as she saw Dusk's pain. With a shock she struggled up, halting their moment. Dusk fell to the bed with both loss and relief on his face as Layla sat up next to him. Reaching out, she cupped his face in her hands, staring into his sapphire eyes, concern flooding her.

"Should I call Rake and Sylvania?"

"No… no." Dusk fell back to the bed with a tired sigh, then winced as he shifted position, drawing the covers back up as if he was chilly. The last of the day's light faded, casting the apartment in a sudden gloom. "I'm so sorry, Layla… I want to. You have no idea how much—"

"Shh." Layla stilled his words with her fingertips. With a smile, she cuddled back down, pulling the coverlet up. They lay as they had begun, him on his back with her under his arm, kissing his chest as the apartment was swallowed in shadows. "I'm sorry I did this."

"I'm not." She felt him smile as he nosed his lips into her hair. "Even if my bones do feel like they've been through a wood chipper."

"That bad?" Layla asked.

"On a scale of one to ten? It's an eleven. Maybe a twenty, actually. Probably because I came so close to my first true shift… if I had let myself."

"I'm so sorry, Dusk."

"Stop apologizing." He turned his head so he could look down at her, his eyes luminous in the fading light. "I told you already. I'm not sorry the talisman bound us, Layla. Sure, it complicates our lives. Sure, I almost shifted for real and I have to endure the consequences. But you're safe, and I'll be fine. Besides, it's fucking incredible what I can feel now. Like someone lit me up from the inside like a falling star."

He reached out, stroking her cheek as he watched her with a small smile. Cupping her hand to his cheek, Layla watched him back, feeling that golden sensation pouring through her. His description of their Bind was just like she'd seen in her vision. And suddenly Layla wondered if they were cursed or blessed. She pushed up to sitting and Dusk frowned, then set his hands to the bed, pushing up also – though leaning back against the pillows.

"Did I say something wrong?" He murmured, his sapphire eyes watchful.

"I don't know." Layla spoke as her mind spun back to the things Rachida had said. "What if this Bind was just me, Dusk? Rachida said something to me earlier, that perhaps it was my power that bound you and Adrian. That it might have been *my will* which encouraged the talisman to act as it did, not the talisman itself."

Dusk blinked. Still blinking, he settled back to the pillows. "Talismans magnify the wearer's will. Fuck, I remember Rachida telling me that while we were searching for a talisman for you. I just never considered that a talisman could amplify your *Bind* power."

"Maybe it's stronger with the Hamsa Bind talisman," Layla

breathed, something wary racing through her. "Maybe what happened with you and Adrian and I is stronger because of the unique nature of the specific talisman I bound you through."

"Shit." Dusk's eyes had cleared to a keen diamond-sapphire color. He blinked, then let out a breath as his gaze tracked to Layla. "I told Adrian to not search for that thing."

"But if it gives us all power, bound this close…" Layla set her hand to Dusk's abdomen with the sudden feeling that she couldn't bear to be parted from him.

"Adam's going to want a piece of the action." Dusk's face had gone thoughtful.

"What?" Layla blinked, frowning.

"Adam." Dusk glanced at her. "I saw his face in the forest, when you and Adrian were… exploring. I remember his eyes. A darkness like I've never known shone from Adam's eyes as he watched you two. It was pure jealousy – like you were supposed to be his and not Adrian's. He snarled under his breath up on the ridge. I thought he was going to rush down and fight Adrian for you right then and there, but he didn't. But I've never seen Adam like that before. I've felt him jealous before, and lord knows I was too in that moment, but Adam's reaction to you two being together was almost unholy."

"What if my Bind powers are calling Adam also?" Layla breathed. "What if his reaction was because my power is calling him like it did you and Adrian?"

"Or what if it's making Adam unstable?" Dusk gave a long, slow blink. Turning his head, he stared at Layla. "We need to talk to Adrian. Now. I don't trust Adam to not unleash a full dominance challenge over this."

"Not yet." Layla pressed a hand to his chest. "You're not well."

"Are you going to be my guardian now, woman?" A small smile

lifted his lips.

"Yes, if you need it." Layla sassed him, smiling also.

"I might. Because if Adrian doesn't buy our theory about your Bind powers being amplified by the talisman, calling Royal Dragons harder because of the nature of the cuff... he might just kill me for what happened last night."

Dusk's eyes were serious as he held Layla's gaze in the settling evening. Layla returned the look, an understanding stretching between them.

"I'll talk to Adrian." She spoke, smoothing her fingers over Dusk's chest. "He'll probably take the revelation better from me rather than you. In the meantime, I'll cover your shifts in Concierge, and we can talk to Adrian after the Samhain Masquerade."

"Be careful." Dusk trapped her hand to his skin. "You and Adrian wind each other up."

"I'll try to stay cool, I promise."

But Dusk was serious, not about to let her go without impressing this lesson. "Please, Layla. Be careful when and just what you tell him. I really don't want to be in pieces anytime soon."

And though Dusk was teasing, he was also deadly serious. Worry shone from his eyes and Layla reached out, cupping his cheek in her palm. Smoothing her thumb over the midnight ridge on his outer cheekbone, she tried to smile. But it was her Dragon that bolstered her, swirling up with a roaring orange spice scent as if ready to do battle in the darkening evening.

"I won't let Adrian hurt you, Dusk. He can fume and rage about this... but you mean too much to me. Just like I wouldn't let you attack Adrian, either. So let's find a better way to solve our current conundrum, huh?"

"What about Adam?" Dusk reached up, taking her hand, his

sapphire eyes deep.

Thinking about Adam, about his clandestine nature and the darkness of his eyes when he truly showed himself, Layla felt her Dragon's coils twist, raising a white-hot heat in her veins. It wasn't a pleasant feeling. And Layla suddenly knew that Adam was an outsider. He wasn't hers; he wasn't supposed to be. Layla's magic had chosen Dusk and for whatever reason, it balked at the thought of binding Adam. For the first time, Layla could feel it deep inside her. A sensation that she would go to battle for both her bound men – but she wouldn't go to battle for Adam.

"What about Adam?" Layla spoke as she stroked her thumb over Dusk's smooth lips. "He's hot… but I have a feeling my Dragon doesn't want him."

"Better for me," Dusk smiled, though it was tired as he kissed her fingers. "I don't want a fight with Adrian or Adam, and certainly not in my current condition. Speaking of – were you serious about taking my shifts these next few days?"

"Serious as a nun on Sunday." Layla smiled. "You rest. Layla Price has got this. You always solve everyone else's problems. Let me solve this for once."

"My savior." Dusk grinned, kissing her fingers again. And then he pulled her in with strong arms. Layla fell against his body and he gave a very pleased, very masculine chuckle. But it had none of his usual rumblings as he lifted his lips, kissing her. As Layla kissed him back, she realized she could feel his deep fatigue. As if tiredness swamped his every sinew, she felt it heavy like lead in her veins.

"Go to sleep," she murmured, pulling away. "I'll come back and check on you later."

"My hero," he growled again, though he was already rucking down into the duvet. He gave a fatigued smile, his eyes closing as he fought exhaustion and lost. Layla smiled as she pulled the covers up. But his fingers shot out from beneath the duvet as she tried to rise, clasping her hand. Weaving his fingers into hers, Dusk gave her a last sleepy smile and a roguish lift of one eyebrow. "Promise me you'll be back."

"I promise."

"You still owe me breakfast."

"Do I?" Layla laughed.

"You do."

And with that, Dusk cuddled down in the duvet, letting her go. Layla watched him; she saw the beautiful smile that curled his lips as he drifted off. Suddenly, she wanted nothing more than to slide back under the covers with him. To stay beside him all night, feeling his delicious warmth and easing her hands over his muscles as they breathed together, listening to the fountain burble in his crystal apartment.

But she had duties to attend, and problems to solve.

With a small smile, Layla turned – moving out through the doors and shutting them quietly, heading back down to the main Concierge desk.

CHAPTER 25 – SAMHAIN

Dusk had been out for three days. Layla had been up to his apartment a few times to check on him, but he'd generally been asleep, recovering. Rachida had stayed there watching over him – though after she and Layla's talk, Rachida had been pleasant rather than disturbingly intimidating. Layla had resumed her shifts at Concierge Services and also taken Dusk's, working eighteen hour days to finish the Samhain preparations. But tonight, she'd been relieved of her duties by Jenna and Lars.

Because one of the biggest parties of the year had arrived – the Samhain Masquerade.

It was an event Layla had heard stories about, of debauchery and excellence, scintillation and fascination. The Hotel had four masqued balls a year, the Grand Masquerades – the Samhain Masquerade in the fall, the Yule Ball at Winter Solstice, the Beltane Bacchanalia on May first, and the Litha Bonfire at Midsummer Solstice. Each ball was an ostentatious event and the Hotel was full, every suite and outbuilding stuffed with patrons. Tonight, the entire palace would be lit from stem to stern, every ballroom flooded with dancing, every dining-hall and bar lively with drink and laughter and an unholy excess of food.

Every staff member could choose to attend two Masquerades per year, working the other two. But the Dragons were still in the Hotel, minus Rachida and Emir Tousk, who had left upon an errand for the clan this morning. But most of the Dragons were still in attendance, and Dusk had impressed Layla that under no circumstances was she to work this event.

She was to take this one off – her first Masquerade at the Hotel – to drink and make merry.

Layla was looking forward to it. Stepping back up to her apartment, she watched the Hotel in its final transformations. All the decorations were up, the entire palace glowing from stem to stern. Every marble pillar had been wreathed with garlands of autumn leaves, every French Baroque niche had been set with cornucopias of real pumpkins, gourds, pears, and grapes. Sheaves of wheat braided with autumn berries and corkscrewing willow-branches had been woven across every arch, laurel and bay leaves entwined through it all with a glossy artistry. Firefly-globes lit every hall, kindled just for this event. Niches for debauchery had been created with screens of vines and autumn marigolds. Scents of cinnamon and clove, harvest berries and sandalwood perfumed the air, with the delicious musk of nag champa straight from Nepal.

The autumnal indulgence lifted Layla's spirits and hurrying up to her rooms, she shut the gilded doors quickly. A sparse dinner waited on her table; chicken soup with sautéed kale. Far from extravagant, her dinner was a only snack – the real manifesto that Catering had been working on all week would be served in the banquet halls and ballrooms.

After a few hasty bites, Layla went to her closet and threw open the doors. Head Clothier Amalia DuFane had outdone herself with Layla's gown for tonight. Though Layla hadn't heard from Adrian in the past three days, Dusk was feeling better and had asked Layla to be his partner for the evening. She was looking forward to it, and as she unlatched the crystal honeycomb case of her gown, a thrill of anticipation rioted through her.

Whether or not Adrian showed tonight, Layla was going to have a *very* good time.

Her gown didn't fit the autumnal decor. A royal midnight color, it was entirely beaded in dark sapphire, labradorite, and midnight Swarovski crystals – that shone with the oilslick iridescence of Dusk's scales, in a swirling pattern reminiscent of Dragon-scale ridges as well as crystal stalactites. Amalia's magic made the gems come alive on the sleek gown, the tight corset giving way to a beaded silk wrap-skirt that slithered out in a long train.

Layla shed her work dress quickly, shimmying into the gown. It slid on like a waterfall, cooling her skin. The sweetheart bodice with its plunging cleavage was beautiful armor for the evening, hard with beadwork and gems. Because it was armor tonight – armor against Adrian, whom Layla had still not been able to find and tell about Dusk.

Slipping on midnight silk heels, then donning Mimi's diamond and sapphire jewelry, Layla stepped to the bathroom. Her makeup and hair had been professionally done after her shift, her sable curls in a chignon at the side of her neck with 1940's waves, her makeup in gentle blues and purples, her eyes smoky and lips crimson.

Moving back to her bathroom vanity, Layla took up her masque for the night. Made from a plaster cast of her face, the half-masque was an incredible representation of Dusk's serrated midnight oilslick ridges, though far more extensive. Arching over the cheekbones and temples, the scaled ridges were interspersed with lines of gold that also ran through the gown, the scales on both the gown and masque created with Swarovski crystals, sapphires, and labradorite gemstones. Long spines corkscrewed back and up from the masque, done in diamonds and gold – the same as Layla had seen when Dusk had nearly changed in the Vault.

As Layla donned it, the half-masque seemed to snarl at Layla with power and grace; Amalia's artistic representation of a Crystal Dragon drakaina. Layla's eyes shone jade and smoky from the eyeholes, and as she watched herself in the mirror, she felt a smooth tremor shiver her. As if Dusk was somehow with her, Layla felt a lower-than-sound vibration ripple through her body in a scintillating wave.

Observing herself in the mirror, Layla suddenly saw Adrian's aqua eyes widen in her mind – like he'd been slapped. As if he was with her also, watching her get ready, Layla caught her breath in a moment of vertigo. She felt Adrian's fury as he saw every detail of her costume and knew precisely what it meant.

Adrian's heated, roaring energy was suddenly pouring through Layla, as if he were right there with her. It staggered her, one hand against her gilded mirror as she breathed hard from the scalding wind lashing through her body. Triggering her own rage in a wave, her combined heat with Adrian's staggered her – causing vertigo along with a sudden spike of hot pain through Layla's body. Breathing deeply, Layla struggled against their Bind – to fold all that power and heat back down beneath her hamsa-cuff.

The Dragon was out of the bag, apparently.

And he was pissed.

It wasn't the way Layla would have preferred to tell Adrian about her and Dusk. But even as a dark worry poured through her, that maybe she should skip the evening and avoid trouble, a polite knock came at the door. Layla shuddered back to standing, using the hamsa-cuff to aid her control over her Dragon's heat and banish her connection to Adrian. Moving to the door, she threw it wide. She had almost expected it to be Adrian at her door, but it was Dusk – looking more splendid than Layla had ever seen him.

He took her breath away. Dressed in a white tuxedo jacket and black tux trousers in his preferred well-fitted style, Dusk's shirt was an iridescent midnight color the same as his scales and Layla's dress. Open at the neck without a bow-tie, Dusk's shirt showed the ridges of midnight scales cascading over his collarbones, glinting in the bright chandeliers. His incredible skin was both his costume and jewelry; rippling with subtle light, his sapphire-diamond eyes were vibrant behind a half-masque that left his beautiful jaw and lips visible.

An amazing creation, Dusk's masque was a twin of Layla's but with starker lines, deeper colors, and more serrated, cruel-looking scales. A male version of Layla's female one, two sets of corkscrewing diamond and oilslick-dark spines cascaded up from Dusk's masque like a flared mantle, arching back and up. His only jewelry was his sapphire and diamond Rolex, plus matching cufflinks on his French-cuffed shirt. But as he dazzled Layla, standing there nonchalantly and grinning at her, she realized his costume merely echoed what he would one day become.

A powerful Crystal Dragon – a force to reckon with.

Grinning to beat the band, Dusk gave a low courtier's bow – though his vibrant eyes never left hers. Layla felt herself heat at how amazing he looked, how masculine and seething with dangerous, luminous energy. "Layla Price," he whistled at her, low and wolfish, "you look stunning."

"Right back at you." She quipped, floored by him. "Someone stole my costume idea, I see."

"Amalia might have leaked a few details about your outfit," he grinned, sly. "I asked her to improve upon the idea, slightly."

"I think she outdid herself," Layla blinked, still amazed.

"For both of us."

"Are you ready?" Dusk sobered, his clear blue eyes penetrating through his masque. He offered his arm, watching Layla. And suddenly, she knew this was it. Once she took his arm, she would be showing the entire Hotel that she was bound to Dusk now. And though that made her heart race with exhilaration and fear to be so bold, Layla knew it was the right choice. Dusk had been more than a friend these past months. He'd been a mentor and a confidante, a helping hand and a shoulder to cry on. He'd been her teacher in Twilight Realm politics, and her guide through harrowing magical engagements. He was a Clan First and a powerful force.

And though Adrian was bound to Layla's heart, Dusk was no less. Not by a long shot.

"I do believe you're ogling me again, Layla Price," Dusk spoke low, a curl of pleasure on his lips as a smooth vibration thrummed Layla.

"I am ogling you," Layla spoke, "because you deserve to be ogled, Dusk Arlohaim. Always."

Moving forward, she took his arm – then lifted to her toes, setting her lips to his. She had to be careful with their masques, to not accidentally twine their diamond-spire horns together, but as her lips met Dusk's, she felt him smile. They kissed gently, a delightful thing of slow presses and subtle licks. He used none of his magics, but as they eased away, Layla found herself breathing hard, her pulse fast just from the feel and taste of him. Dusk breathed his pleasure out upon her lips in a sigh, a renegade darkness to his beaming light. As Layla watched, a ripple of illumination curled through his skin and artfully-styled dark hair.

Lighting his scales up like a night full of stars – that the diamonds on his masque could never hope to match.

"You slay this Crystal drake, Layla Price," he breathed at her lips. "Are you ready to go show the world what we are?"

"A power couple?" Layla grinned at his lips, nuzzling his nose.

"A power to be reckoned with." Dusk spoke back, intensity radiating from his gaze. "Couple or no."

"Absolutely."

Reaching up, Layla kissed his lips once more, feeling that blissful diamond-gold light cascade through them both. She loved it that Dusk didn't need to define what they were to each other. And as Layla kissed him, she felt something open up deep inside her, simply because he didn't need to possess her. As they kissed, something like a thread of diamond light eased down her lips and throat, into the deepest part of her. Layla inhaled, feeling that beautiful energy curl into her heart. As their kiss broke, she breathed quietly, stunned – feeling Dusk touching a part of her that no one, not even Adrian, had ever touched.

Gazing up at him, Layla was brought to silence by whatever had just passed between them. For a moment Dusk was also, his eyes closed as he set his forehead against hers, a look of bliss upon his face beneath the masque. At last he surfaced, coming back with a deep inhalation as his eyes opened – entirely diamond-white around his dark pupils.

"Ready to take the world by storm, Layla Price?"

"Don't you mean by diamond light?" She quipped back, grinning.

"Absolutely."

With a rakish gleam in his amazing eyes, Dusk set her hand on his arm. They set out down the hall, ready to claim the night as they headed down the grand main staircase. As they neared the first floor, Layla saw the party was already in full swing. Orchestral music curled through the air with unearthly sounds. The main floor of the Hotel was packed with people – eating hors d'oeuvres by the fountains, getting drinks at the copper bars, laughing gregariously. All were clad in masqued costumes, the men in tuxes or sexually ostentatious outfits like David Bowie in Labyrinth. The women were no less wildly arrayed – elegant evening gowns accented by bird feathers, animal hides, scales, tree branches, and every manner of precious gems.

Twilight folk spared no expense for the Grand Masquerades.

But none were so instantly striking as Layla and her date. Heads turned, watching Layla and Dusk descend the sweeping grand staircase beside the main Concierge desk. Applause began in the crowd, and it took Layla a moment to realize that the Hotel was applauding their Head Concierge and his date in their exquisitely impressive costuming. Though Layla and Dusk's creations were made of cool midnight colors, they glowed beneath the bright chandeliers. Either by Amalia's magic or Dusk's thundering intensity, which Layla suddenly felt him roll out in a wave through the crowd, Dusk and Layla were suddenly the toast of the evening as they stepped off the crimson-carpeted stairs into the masses below.

Masques and magic swirled around Layla, people pressing in, touching her dress and caressing her skin, laughing – all of it instantly overwhelming. But though Layla froze in the sudden attention, panic creeping up her throat, Dusk was effortlessly effete. His rolling laugh was jubilant as he clasped hands, his smile gregarious, his quips witty. Navigating expertly through the crowd with his usual panache, Dusk kept Layla close as he steered them through a swirl of magic she could barely breathe in.

Tucking his arm around her waist, he escorted them out of the throng and into the Grand Ballroom – into breathing space at last. Layla was finally able to look around, relieved from the intensity of the Hotel's packed main hall. Still early in the festivities, the main hall had been where everyone bottlenecked, and as they entered the Grand Ballroom, Layla found that although it was busy with a crowd and dancing, there was space to catch her breath.

Glowing from stem to stern, the Grand Ballroom was the site of the main revelry, even though dozens of events were happening all around the grounds tonight. Enormous, the ballroom was half a football field in size and decorated like the mirror-hall of the Palace of

Versailles. The ballroom where the Hotel held its grandest celebrations, it glowed with light, laughter, and music tonight, Catering staff whisking around in special gold and crimson uniforms as they served gilded trays of drinks and small bites.

Hundreds of crystal chandeliers threw the light, magnified by gilded mirrors upon every wall. Enormous floor-candelabra shone against gold-veined marble columns, the columns curling in fanciful designs like ostrich feathers as they rose to the high-domed crystal ceiling and the bright autumnal stars beyond. Like being inside an enormous Victorian Gothic candy-dish, the entire space glittered with opulence so great it was disorienting, and Layla swayed against Dusk's arm as she looked up, trying to fix her sight on the stars above and failing.

But Dusk guided her through it all, gracious with his rumbling wit. The ballroom was a who's-who of the Twilight Realm tonight, and Dusk greeted everyone by name with a clasping of hands, regardless of how impossible they were to recognize in their costumes and masques. Layla soon found herself maneuvered to the bar, an Old Fashioned deposited in her hands and Dusk holding the same. He'd somehow got them out of the worst of the shuffle, and as he clinked crystal glasses with her and they drank, Layla downed hers in one go.

Dusk gave her a grin from behind his masque, then downed his and signaled for two more.

Layla sipped her second drink, the whiskey firing her throat and helping her breathe at last. She'd never been claustrophobic before and it took her a moment before she realized the unease she was experiencing was actually because there was so much magical energy in the hall. She had felt individuals or groups unleash their magic in the Hotel before, but this was thousands of people doing so at once. Practically drowning in waves of magic, Layla's skin was crawling, shuddering with exuberance so high she felt like she'd taken mushrooms, ecstasy, and cocaine simultaneously – and had been transported to a whole new Wonderland.

A world where her inner Dragon felt right at home.

Fire flooded Layla's veins, as if her Dragon was feeding off the abandon in the hall – and for the first time, she let herself sink into it. Like she'd felt at the Gypsun bar, she felt the magics of others become unrestrained here in the revelry. As if everyone had permission tonight to be as passionate as their magics always wished to be, like the patrons of Marnet's bar, no scent or flare of magic was being controlled tonight.

Though reined in by her hamsa-cuff, Layla's own Dragon-magic raged out, eager to indulge in the game of hedonism and abandon. Devouring the energies around her and expanding, Layla's magic uncoiled, caressing those nearby with scintillating curls of orange and bourbon-spiced wind. A number of people shivered, looking her way with startled laughs.

But the mood of the night was far more permissive and scandalous even than the *bacchanalia*. Layla instantly understood that tonight would supply the epitome of what the Hotel provided its guests – a mind-blowing experience of passion and ecstasy. Already, she saw people coupling off, kissing and fondling as they danced and drank. As if she needed any more confirmation that containment was not necessary tonight, Dusk suddenly downed his second drink, stepped behind her, and wrapped her in his arms – trapping her close to his smoldering body.

"Go wild, Layla," he murmured at her ear, his soft lips smoothing deliciously over her skin. "Nothing is impermissible tonight. The Grand Masquerades at the Hotel are the four nights of all the year where anyone may do as they wish. Let your magic do what it wants tonight. I'll be here to catch you. I promise."

293

With that, Dusk set his impossibly smooth lips to her neck, kissing her. Layla felt a spear of crystal-bright power sunder her – Dusk's magic at its most unrestrained. As if he knew her deepest intimate places, Dusk's power was suddenly flooding Layla – lighting her up like a golden twilight. As Layla gasped, she felt her Dragon inhale like a demon, devouring Dusk's beautiful crystal energy.

And then her magic burst outward in a roaring wind of heat, sex, and passion – flooding the hall with wild energy.

As her unbound lust surged out, tasting everyone around her, Layla's knees buckled. Turning into Dusk, she let him devour her with his kiss until their night exploded into diamond brilliance – and Layla knew nothing more except power and passion as she was swept away into the stars.

CHAPTER 26 – MASQUES

Spinning. Layla's only sensation was that she was spinning in a vortex of heat and power, passion and lust. Her head whirled as she spun upon Dusk's arm through a dance, moving through a sea of glitter and debauchery. They were on the ballroom floor, dancing in the middle of whirling couples, and Layla had no memory of how they'd gotten there or how long they'd been there. She was music, she was heat and energy and sound, she was the flow of every breathless laugh. She was muscle and movement, coil and release as Dusk spun her again, whirling her through the dance with grace as cool as a river's sparkling flow.

She was spun – into the arms of another partner. The dance was pure movement, the eyes of her partner a vibrant gold, and Layla recognized the indigo plumage of the Phoenix King beneath a snarling ruby Gryphon masque as he dipped her in his strong, lean arms. Bending his incredible height to brush a kiss over her collarbones, Layla was a feather in his arms as his zephyrs teased her. The chirring of birds was in her ears and the flapping of a thousand wings as he kissed her lips – and then spun her away into the arms of another partner.

Layla felt storms and thunder as her new partner took her. Eyes the color of moody skies clashing with lightning beamed at her from beneath an art-nouveau masque like exploding raindrops. She realized it was a woman dressed as a man in a feminine tuxedo, power blazing from the woman's skin with the smell of ozone in a thunderstorm. It was the Storm Dragon Queen Justine Toulet who spun her, and Layla saw them dancing all around her now, the Desert Clan and the Storm, the Phoenix and the Blood Dragons with Rikyava in Dusk's arms now, dressed in a long silver gown. But Layla barely had a moment to breathe Queen Justine's rainwater fragrance before she was spun away to yet another partner.

Tall and perfect in an all-white ensemble over three centuries out-of-date, Head Courtier Reginald Durant had no powdered wig on tonight, his own shining golden hair bound back in a club, luminous as sunlight on an arctic sea. His masque was a snarling white ocean-dragon decorated with pearls and glittering diamonds, flowing tendrils cascading up from the masque like some leviathan come to drown unlucky ships. His long jacket and waistcoat were embroidered with shells, diamonds, and pearls.

Reginald's eyes pressed her with the weight of the ocean, deep and drowning as they danced. As had happened when he'd danced with her on her first day at the Hotel, Layla felt her Dragon's heat rolled beneath his chill northern sea, the call of gulls and salt spray drowning everything else out. For a brief eternity, the hall faded until there was nothing but the feel of ocean mist on Layla's skin and the breath of sea air in her lungs. Her lips fell open as she spun, mesmerized by the Head Courtier as she stared up into his impeccable ice-blue eyes.

Until he released her like a ship upon high ocean winds – straight into the arms of the one person who could break her.

Adrian caught her hard against his chest, and the dance stopped. For everyone else it continued, whirling all around them, but for Layla and Adrian, the world of glittering delight suddenly came crashing down. His hands burned her like firebrands where they gripped her bare shoulders; his eyes seared with reds and oranges through the aqua and gold, a seething fury that Layla had never seen. Dressed in a white tux jacket but with a Chinese fu lion masque with a stunning mane,

Adrian's gaze raked Layla's costume – his beautiful lips curling up into a snarl.

"Dusk. I should have fucking known."

Adrian's eyes burned from behind his masque, his voice grating. Fury radiated from him, flaring with the sensation of fire-ants and stinging sand. People cried out, backing away, and the dance fractured. As Layla stared up at Adrian, caught in his seething magics, a spike of furious red-hot wind suddenly burned her from his hands – straight into her core.

Pain exploded through Layla and she cried out, convulsing from whatever Adrian had done. With a roar, he hauled her close, terrifying in his snarling lion masque. His hands were clamped so hard on her arms they were bruising and as Layla tried to wrench herself away, he sent that red-hot spike through her again, spearing her deep.

Her Dragon roiled, writhing in pain and Layla actually screamed this time, feeling like every nerve was on fire from whatever Adrian was doing. Struggling, she tried to knee him in the groin, desperate to get away. But as he sent a third spike of blistering rage into her body, she felt something tear inside her – something that shouldn't have torn; something not physical but magical. As Layla screamed again and Adrian roared in pain also, she realized what he was doing. He was trying to tear apart their Bind.

He was trying to rip himself free of her.

Adrian tried again, sending a burning spike of magic deep into Layla and she screamed again, collapsing though he still gripped her close. The tearing of their Bind rebounded on him and she felt him convulse as he screamed in pain also. Hands were suddenly there – so many hands, trying to haul them apart. But something was happening. Magic was seething around Layla like a sandstorm. Layla felt Adrian's hands change shape; becoming talons. Massive black talons that pierced her arms like daggers; blood flowing from the wounds.

But she couldn't feel that pain, only a dark agony rioting inside her as Adrian tore at their Bind. Hands were hauling her away now; Dusk's strong body cradled her, pouring his soothing music through her bones as Adrian roared, his lion-masque ripped away but his handsome face just as terrible. He was roaring like a mad thing, with bass notes and overtones that men just didn't have – and Dusk was roaring back the same way. Shuddering with convulsions in Dusk's arms, Layla saw magic manifest upon the air – a liquid-red and aqua fire coiling out around Adrian and an answering nimbus of vibrant crystal shards beginning around Dusk.

Shuddering with agony, Layla watched Rikyava, Adam, Reginald, even the Phoenix King seize Adrian, trying to haul him away from Dusk and Layla. But Adrian was fighting them all. With a roar, Adrian sent a hard pulse of energy through his captors, staggering them – except Reginald. The Head Courtier had an iron grip on Adrian and as Adrian whirled, leveling a punch at him, the Siren ducked and inhaled a massive breath. Something whirled out around him like a leviathan, and with a roar that shredded Layla's ears like grinding ice, Reginald backhanded Adrian across the face, spilling Adrian to his hands and knees on the ballroom floor.

Layla cried out – feeling Reginald's power as it hit Adrian like the rage of the entire ocean. Though Reginald's Siren-slap had been meant for Adrian, it was Layla who was inundated by it. Ice water flooded her through the Bind and she gasped, drowning. Reginald's slap had stumbled Adrian; but the Siren's ice was drowning Layla. As she spasmed from the sluicing chill, Adrian did also – glancing over to her from where he had fallen.

Cradled in Dusk's arms, she was in rigors, shuddering like liquid nitrogen filled her veins. Terror filled Layla as the world went black around the edges and she gasped for breath; drowning in the Siren's floes. Someone had torn away her masque and her eyes met Adrian's. Seeing her gasp, tears leaking from her eyes as she drowned, Adrian surged to standing with horror in his beautiful eyes, but Dusk was already scooping Layla up.

Dusk whisked her from the hall, fast. Reginald's oceanic energy was still pummeling Adrian – and through him, into Layla. But though Adrian was a match for Reginald, resisting his inundation, Layla wasn't. Her lungs felt filled up with seawater; her pulse was slowing as she choked. Though they were out in the gardens now, Layla couldn't hear, couldn't see – the weight of the ocean pressing her down.

"Reginald, stop! You're killing her!" Dusk's roar, raging with lower-than-sound vibrations, cut though Layla's crushing darkness like a thin beam of light. She could barely feel his hands on her, pouring light and warmth through her as fast as he could, her body laid out on the patio's flagstones.

"I can't release Adrian until he gets his rage under control!" Reginald's cold snarl sounded like a tsunami inside her mind and Layla screamed, though all that came out was a struggling gasp. She felt distant from the surface; from oxygen. Layla flailed, but her body wouldn't respond; even her Dragon seemed like a tiny spark now – crushed in a leviathan's blackwater coils.

"Reginald – release her!" Adrian's cry was tortured with fury and pain; Layla felt him fall to his knees beside her, clutching her hand. But he was cold from Reginald's inundating power and Layla was even more ice-chill as she gasped now in tiny sips.

"Control your Dragon, Adrian Rhakvir," the Head Courtier snarled low, his voice pounding through Layla's ears, "or she dies through your Bind! You have the strength to resist me; Layla does not. Decide now if your rage is worth her life."

"Adrian, please!" Dusk's voice was grating where he knelt at Layla's side. "Don't let your anger over Layla's and my Bind kill her! It was an accident, by all the gods I swear it!"

"Adrian, don't let her die, my god!" Adam's voice came also, and Layla felt his gentle touch upon her hand, a smooth curl of summer-orchard scent easing around her. Tracing to her lips, that small flow was precise; pouring sunlight and warmth in through Layla's lips into her lungs. It wasn't much, but Layla seized on that small drip of warmth and air, gasping, holding onto it like a lifeline. She felt Adam shudder, falling against her as if feeding her his very life though their breath. The blackness receded enough that Layla could see him kneeling by Dusk, his hunter-green eyes devastated in the night.

The moment stretched – Layla gasping with the last of her life, Adam feeding her the barest breath to keep her from dying, Dusk pouring his crystal vibrations through Layla's body in an attempt to push back Reginald's black tide. As she gasped the meager life Adam and Dusk provided, her gaze found Adrian's – seeing the fury evaporate from his eyes at last.

With a heart-wrenching sob, Adrian moved in, seizing her face tenderly in his hands. As he pressed her with his kiss, a surge of smooth, hot wind poured down Layla's throat and deep into her lungs – letting her gasp a real breath at last. As Adrian's love for her poured in, filling her to the brim, the crushing cold of the ocean poured out. Layla felt Reginald's power washed away as Adrian poured all his heat and power into her through his kiss.

And his love.

Layla's Dragon woke in a rush of fire and golden light, flooding upwards to meet Adrian's kiss just as much as Layla wanted to sob from it. She felt their beasts surge deep into each other's bodies. And though Adrian's kiss stole her breath just as much as it gave her life,

Layla suddenly roared inside. With a twisting surge of coils, a hard wave of heat rushed out from her in a flood of golden ether – hammering Adrian in the chest, hard.

It hit him like a battering ram and he was shoved off her as she snapped up to sitting on the flagstones, her left hand making the same palm-out gesture like she'd done in the Vault. Adrian's lips fell open, his beautiful aquamarine eyes shocked that she'd warded him away. He surged forward again as if to embrace her and Layla's hand slammed out a second time – that same wave of power hammering Adrian so hard he was hurled to his ass on the flagstones. Coils seething through her body in fury, Layla rose to standing – staring down at Adrian with wrath burning in her heart.

"Layla, I—" he stammered.

"I don't want to hear it." Layla's voice was colder than midnight sands; a voice she didn't know – the wrathful voice of her Dragon. "You could have given me a chance to tell you about Dusk and I and the accident that caused our Bind, Adrian. You could have shown up *anytime* in the past three days and spoken with either of us. Instead you show up now, like *this*. Trying to *rip your Bind with me apart* because you were too unhinged to act like a human being. Well, I'm done. I'm done with your games. I'm done with you putting your fears and cold-hearted secrets before the people in your life that you say you love. You say you're *protecting* me? Us? I call bullshit. From what I've experienced tonight… you're only protecting yourself."

"Layla!"

But Layla was already turning, walking away into the night. Adrian lurched to follow her and Layla just held up a hand in warning, ready to blast his ass all the way to the north pole if she had to. He stopped and watched her go, devastation upon his handsome face. Adam stepped to her side, but Layla waved him back also. Reginald just watched her, but as Dusk stepped forward to take her arm, Layla heaved a deep breath.

"Not right now, Dusk. I need to be alone. Please. This just... this fucking sucks, and I need to think."

Dusk's luminous gaze was crestfallen as she rejected him, but he stepped back with a low bow, understanding in the way she knew he would. "Take all the time you need. I'll be here."

A crowd had gathered at the entrance to the gardens, mostly Dragons watching the scene but quite a few Hotel staff also. Layla saw the Madame hurry out through the doors, bustling to Reginald's side and speaking low words. Layla didn't want to be anywhere near any of them at the moment. Turning from the Hotel, she walked off into the night. She didn't know where she was going, she just chose a path. Her eyes stung and it was a moment before she realized she was crying – reaching up to wipe tears away as she moved off through the chill October night.

Silence shrouded her with the rustling of dry leaves as she made it to the edge of the manicured grounds. She didn't know where she was going until she wound up at the horse barns near the edge of the forest where the pheasant-hunt had been. Sliding in the barn doors, Layla could barely see as she moved through the quiet stables, not caring that the train of her silk gown trailed through straw and dry horse shit.

Without knowing what she needed until she was there, Layla collapsed upon the wooden stall-gate of her big bay gelding, sobbing. The bay's nose came out to meet her, nuzzling her hair as he whickered, resting his forehead against hers – which only made Layla cry harder. She hadn't noticed anyone was in the barn with her until a hand settled to her shoulder. Layla startled, but the orchard-sweet scent of the man beside her gave him away.

"I thought you might come here. Are you alright?"

Adam's eyes were deep like a forest as he gazed at her. His sweet orchard scent blossomed out around Layla, surrounding her like the world's most comforting blanket. Before she knew it, she was turning, throwing herself into his arms as she sobbed. She didn't care if her Bind-magic was calling him, or that her Dragon was conflicted about him. She needed someone unrelated to her problems right now, just to hold her.

Adam did, his warm hands lifting to stroke her back. He cradled her close and she could smell his apple-orchard scent. So vivid, so intense; Layla was drowning in honey and blossoms as it soothed her. But suddenly, it seemed like too much. As if his scent was swamping her, Layla felt a strange lightheadedness, like a cloying perfume surrounded her now rather than a summer's day. It was something she couldn't push away; couldn't escape. Easing through her muscles, it made Layla lethargic as Adam's warm hands cradled her. The world didn't make sense as she felt him gaze down at her with a strange look in his eyes, his hunter-green irises impossibly dark. Layla suddenly smelled lemons in his scent, and gin. She blinked, having a vision of her dark-haired Tom Collins from the bar in Seattle months ago.

"Your scent. What...?" Layla looked up, feeling fuzzy.

"Rest, Layla." Adam breathed, a smooth curl of lemon-gin scent easing from his lips and diving down Layla's throat – deep into her body. "Don't fight it. Just sleep..."

Layla blinked, feeling a forest-dark fugue pour through her. Her mind quieted as her muscles relaxed. Her Dragon coiled up, tucking its nose beneath its tail. And Layla was suddenly melting against Adam's strong body, held effortlessly in his arms.

She couldn't keep her eyes open. Layla felt Adam Rhakvir lift her into his arms as she slid sideways into darkness.

CHAPTER 27 – VISAGES

Blinking blearily, Layla surfaced from a fugue of white sands and black oceans, of dark forests in a land where prehistoric things walked. Finding herself in a world as strange as her dream, crystal towers rose up around her, glowing with a low, soothing light. Blinking, Layla realized she was back in the Vault where she had practiced shielding with Dusk three nights ago – though she couldn't recall getting here.

Her head felt fuzzy as she realized she was still wearing her beaded gown from the evening. Blinking around, Layla saw she lay on a pile of feather duvets and ornate throw-pillows, plus an assortment of soft fur rugs. It was like a makeshift nest, pelts of alpaca and lambswool beneath the pillows. A slide of coils moved inside her as her Dragon woke. It stretched and Layla felt its contentment; as if there was no place it would rather be than in this cozy, dark space.

As she reached up to touch her head, wondering if it was Dusk who had brought her down here, Layla suddenly realized someone reclined next to her in the half-dark. But rather than Dusk's clear river-water scent, a smell of orchard blossoms and honey lingered in the air and Layla inhaled, knowing who it was.

"Adam… what happened?"

She turned toward him as she pushed slowly up to a seat so her head didn't reel, making out Adam's face in the half-light. He reclined on one elbow beside her, his green eyes dark as he watched her. Still dressed in his tux from the party, he wore a classic black jacket, his black bow-tie undone over his white shirt. His collar was open and

Layla could smell his apple-sweet scent easing from his tanned skin, his ash-blond hair mussed. His French cuffs were pinned with glossy onyx stones, and he wore his malachite and emerald ring but that was all – the luminous darkness of his eyes his only true ornament.

As those eyes devoured Layla, taking her in, he reached out, smoothing his fingers over her thigh where her leg was bared from the slit in her gown. A soft sigh came from his lips. Soothing and deep, his energy was like a combination of Dusk's patience and Adrian's ardor, though with a strange, ancient stillness. Layla thought she saw beasts of legend roar in his eyes for a moment; dark and green like the deepest forest. His fingers caressed her skin in long, flowing movements – and for some reason, Layla didn't want to pull away.

"Your men were fighting again, after you left."

Adam spoke softly, not with his usual bravado but a smooth voice and deep tones that Layla could have listened to forever. That calm voice eased between the crystal columns with his orchard-blossom scent; soothing. She found herself recalling everything that had happened after Adrian's wrath and Reginald's power. Layla remembered leaving for the horse barn and how Adam had found her. And the strange fugue he'd put her in to bring her down here. But as if her fugue wasn't entirely gone, Layla found herself mesmerized by Adam's presence now and his touch, and it took two tries before she could speak.

"So you brought me down here to keep me safe?"

"I brought you down here so we could be alone, Layla."

"Why do you want to be alone with me?" Layla still felt like she reeled in a nexus world of heady magics and strange dreams. Somehow, Adam had brought this nest of fluffy stuff from the Hotel down into its deepest basement – not on the flat rose quartz flow, but tucked deep within the forest of columns near the underground stream. Water burbled nearby, a simmering light easing through the crystal pillars. Layla realized the nest was set between pillars of pure emerald, though it was a strange, dark shade like Adam's eyes.

Adam gave a soft laugh at her question, a smile lifting his lips. His gaze flicked down to where he brushed his fingertips over Layla's bare thigh, watching his fingers trail over her skin. Layla shivered, the sensation suddenly deeply erotic. He'd not done anything, yet now Layla's Dragon was on high alert, a luscious sensation of energized sensuality pouring through her. Dusk could shiver her into thinking about sex, Adrian could scald her there, but Adam simply heightened her awareness – until every molecule of her skin was suddenly drinking in his presence and his smooth, intoxicating scent.

He watched her as he kept tracing patterns on her thigh. Layla was breathing hard now, her heartbeat rapid, her pulse pounding in her throat and groin. Adam had done nothing, yet her body suddenly wanted him with the kind of rushing pleasure she'd previously only felt with Adrian and Dusk. Yet here he was, the third of three Royal Dragons whom her magic was calling – stirring her body into the most intense pleasure she'd ever known.

Layla's breath caught as Adam's hand slid up her thigh, stopping just short of the beaded hem. Slipping out, he caressed his fingertips over the fabric and Layla stiffened with a gasp, a ripple of pleasure sliding through her so hard it made her eyelids flutter.

"I want to be alone with you," Adam murmured, watching her, "because I want to show you who I am."

"Adam… what?" Layla blinked, confused and inundated with pleasure from his touch. "What's going on?"

"My name is not Adam," he breathed softly, in a strange accent that was quite suddenly not Adam's at all. "And I never was part of the Rhakvir family."

With that, his face suddenly changed. Layla watched it morph in a ripple of light, until it was the young financial guy from the bar in Seattle. The one with kind hazel eyes and black shaggy hair who'd ordered a Tom Collins and apologized for his asshat coworkers. She was staring at the same man who had offered her a ride home that night and whom she had seen again at Club Havana. Layla blinked hard, realizing Adam's scent had changed to odors of whisky and shampoo and aftershave and all the normal things human men smelled of.

And lemons swirled into gin.

Layla's breath caught and his face rippled again – to the sexy young chauffeur who had been there to greet Adrian's Learjet as it landed at the Paris airport. And then it rippled again, to the one-eyed Lorio with the fierce scar and silver streaks at his temples and beard. And then his face rippled to a man Layla didn't recognize – an austere man with silver-white eyes that reminded Layla of a combination of Reginald and Sylvania. And then back to Adam – his apple-blossom scent returning in a curl of honey-soft wind.

His hand paused on her thigh, as Adam's dark eyes watched her once more.

"You're the void-shadow!" Layla breathed, afraid now, though he'd made no move to harm her.

"I am the shadow in the evening." His gaze was level as he spoke, his voice low and smooth. "I am the void in the darkness. I am the man with a thousand faces. I am the Hunter in the night. And I would very much like to make your acquaintance, Royal Dragon Bind. First true resurgence of my Lineage in a thousand years."

Layla's breath stopped. Her mind stopped. She could do nothing but stare at him, all thought and emotions fled. This was the man the Phoenix King had warned her about. This was the shadow that had killed Adrian's mother and his lovers and had haunted Layla's birth.

307

This was the Royal Dragon that could make himself disappear so utterly from notice that he left only a sensation of a shadow upon the vibrations of the world.

And he had just told Layla he was a Royal Dragon Bind.

"*Your* Lineage?" Layla breathed, astounded.

"My Lineage." He agreed. Adam's eyes lit with delight, pleasure shining from him. "For I am its oldest living member, and you are the most recent birth of that Lineage, Layla Price. Mimi Zakir renewed our ancient magics in her mixed blood, mating with the renegade Dragon of Seven Winters as she did. But our Lineage is as old as the roots of the mountains. Only because of being hunted have we diminished. The Royals of your Lineage still exist, hidden through the faceless ages. And where we were once hunted, we have become the Hunters. I have come here tonight to ask you – will you join with the Hunters, your own ancient kin? Or will you side with those who tear us down – and become the Hunted?"

Layla reeled, taking it in. Knowing suddenly that this creature before her was millennia old, and that he was both a Royal Dragon and a Royal Dragon Bind. Something elegant and ancient, dangerous and cunning – something that had survived the purges and persecution against Layla's Lineage down through the ages.

Power, so much power surged around her from the Hunter's body. And all of it so carefully contained that he could send a curl of wind sighing delicately over her lips, brushing them like a kiss, before disappearing.

Layla's breath stopped; her heart stopped – wondering just what exactly he was asking of her. "But... you murdered Adrian's mother. You tried to kill the Phoenix King. You hunted me when I was a baby, terrifying Dusk with your dreams. Why? What do you want?"

His green eyes darkened, to a look that shivered Layla with

tension, though he'd changed nothing about his posture. "I want you to think about where you belong, Layla. The young drakes have bound you; they were clever in their machinations to chain a creature of power to their hearts. But to a drakaina of rage and purpose such as I feel flowing through you, those Binds are a paltry thing. Miscalculate your way through the world, stumbling and burning hearts… or come stand by my side. Learn what your magic can truly do, from a teacher who has lived all the mistakes you will ever make. Come to me, and I will show you how to make others sing to your magic. So we can make a world that will never harm another one of us, ever again."

"You speak words of benevolence, but I hear only vigilantism." Layla breathed. "How long have you been masquerading as Adam Rhakvir? How long have you been deceiving Adrian and Dusk and Rachida?"

"Adam Rhakvir never made it out of his family's stronghold alive." For the first time, Layla saw sympathy in the Hunter's dark eyes. "He died as a child, cowering under a bed as a dog."

"You killed him?" Layla breathed, horrified, her mind spinning.

"I witnessed his death." Hunter spoke low. "But it was convenient for my purposes, so I did not stop it. Before Rachida Rhakvir arrived at the fortress in Florence, I had burned Adam's body and assumed his identity. His adult persona would never be known – only my version of Adam Rhakvir ever truly existed."

Layla's world spun. Her breath was stolen as if she'd been punched. "So you've been Adam all this time. And what is it that you actually call yourself?"

His smile was wry and Layla saw a moment of confusion there, though it was covered quickly by steadiness. "You may call me Hunter."

"Is that your real name?"

"No."

"Will you tell me your real name?"

"Perhaps. Eventually."

"Will you show me your real face?"

"They are all my real face. Every one of the men I have come to you as."

But again, Layla saw a deep pain flicker through Hunter's eyes before it was gone. The conversation paused and Layla breathed into that silence, trying to wrap her head around the depth of Hunter's lies. If Adrian was difficult with his secrets and other identities, Hunter was a mastermind of manipulation and deceit.

Layla felt sick inside, realizing that it had been Hunter who had mate-tasted her at the Concierge desk. Hunter, who had watched her nearly fuck Adrian from that ridge-line, his eyes dark and full of wrath. Hunter, who had taken Layla to the Gypsun bar in Julis, wooing her with his orchard-blossom scent and trying to align her against Adrian.

Hunter, who had kept her alive when Reginald's oceanic power had nearly killed her tonight.

As if his very presence was swaying, Layla could feel his magics surrounding her in a wave, easing her worries, convincing her to side with his story. Inhaling a breath, Layla's left palm flashed up to slam that sensation back, to clear her mind from his subtle influence. With a renegade roar of her Dragon, a wash of furious power suddenly flared from her. It didn't hammer Hunter back like it had done Adrian, but it whisked away that cloud of convincing orchard-sweet vapor – casting it back like shadows upon the wind.

Hunter's eyes widened. His green irises sharpened, becoming vertically slit like a cat. And though Layla felt him gather power, a roaring sound in her ears like a forest when a cyclone hits, he did not attack. Instead, he let her blow his scintillating magics away, a slow smile lifting his lips as the shape of his pupils gradually returned to human.

And then he laughed – deep and bright, his green eyes sparkling with colors Layla had never before seen.

With a smooth movement, he rose. Before Layla could do anything, his deft fingers had pulled the pin of her silver wrist-cuff, collecting the cuff into his quick hand so that her magics buffeting him were completely unleashed. Increasing a hundredfold, Layla felt her power roar out as it was freed, felt her Dragon rush outward in a heave of muscled coil and fang, talons of immense power ripping through the crystal cavern. Golden flames of ether surged out from her as a gale surged up inside the cavern while she held her hamsa-ward at Hunter. Smashing the crystal pillars, making a howling sound like a demon as it rushed through the space, hurling the bedding of the nest up and setting it afire in her golden flames.

But Hunter merely stood in her sudden gale, laughing – her winds and sand-funnel heat and flames harming him not at all.

He'd thrown up no shield; he'd used nothing to counter her blistering rage. Though Layla's power, increased to catastrophic heights by her bonds to Dusk and Adrian, cracked three emerald pillars in a series of hammering blows, and something far up near the staircase burst with a sudden deafening concussion, Hunter merely stood in her cyclone winds and golden fire – unaffected and admiring her with his intensely dark eyes.

"Fight me with your fury, beautiful drakaina," he spoke, his handsomeness arresting as he stood untouched. "Fight me and feel our truth – know that *this* is what you were meant to be, to the depths of your scalding sinews. This power, this rage, this roar of passion and battle. This is *who you are*. Become your truth, Layla. Come with me – and I can teach you how to become everything you should be."

311

"You mean a murderer, like you?" Layla seethed as her gale roared, furious that he was trying to seduce her into joining him in some arcane quest against all of the Twilight Realm.

"Become a conqueror." He spoke back, watching her with level eyes through her gale. "With more right to rule than those who hold thrones in any land. I could show you how to make your gales penetrate my sways, Layla. I could show you so much."

"I'd rather go back to bartending." Layla growled, her fury intensifying. She shuddered with it now, both hands up as she held the power of her hamsa-ward. A scalding wrath poured through her, raging around the cavern in a powerful wind.

Now that the silver cuff was gone from her wrist, Layla could feel the full force of her rage, like molten lava and stinging sand in her veins. She had always been passionate; she had always had a temper. She had chosen men in her life who were trouble, and some part of her knew it was because something inside her needed a conflict. Needed to gnash her fangs and spit fire and lash her tail at the world.

But Hunter's words were poison in her fire. Layla wouldn't believe that her passion made her a vigilante like him. Or that the world would be a better place if she used her Bind magics to seduce others into submission. As they watched each other through her gale, she saw a slow smile curl Hunter's lips. As if he could read her mind; as if he knew how much she detested the thought of being like him.

"Very well." He spoke at last through her storm, still smiling with dark eyes. "I can see you need more time. But know that my offer stands. Watch for me, Layla Price. Watch the shadows, the dark forests and deep places of the world. For the Hunter will come to you again, eager to show you what you truly are. And in the meantime… I require that you never again Bind your glory to the hearts of lesser men."

Holding up the silver hamsa-cuff, he curled his fingers around it –

312

and it was suddenly seeping with hot red through the silver. As Layla watched, a sensation of horror rising in her, the Hamsa Bind began to melt, smelted into steaming silver and burning gemstones in Hunter's palm and dripping through his fingers. The bone hamsa-hand stared at Layla a moment longer with its red coral teardrop, as if begging her to stop Hunter's horror.

And then he curled his hand into a tight fist.

With a sharp *crack* like the wishbone of a turkey breaking after a Thanksgiving meal, the white bone hamsa split in two. Opening his hand, Hunter showed that the coral teardrop had also burst as the bone cracked – shattering through the smelted silver.

Layla felt something break inside her as the Hamsa Bind did. As she watched Hunter turn his hand over, scattering smelted silver to the floor of the crystal cavern with broken gemstones and destroyed enamel, a sensation of loss filled Layla. Her world tilted; her hands holding their ward faltered. And as had happened before, she was suddenly outside herself, watching from the shadows of the cavern.

Watching something precious in her life be destroyed.

Suddenly, Layla heard sounds high above in the stairwell. She regained focus as the sound of blasting hit her ears – enormous concussions coming from the sapphire door far above.

"Your lovers have arrived," the Hunter spoke, a dark knowing in his eyes. "I must go. Look for me, Layla. For I will be haunting your steps when the shadows move, watching your progress. When the time is right, I will come again. And the Hunted and the Hunter will not be such strangers to each other next time; I promise it."

Layla heard a deafening blast up above, shuddering the foundations of the crystal cave. The man of void and shadow suddenly swirled away in a flash of wind and darkness. As he snuffed out right before her eyes, Layla's furious energy suddenly had nothing to duel.

Her hands were still up, but with no cuff upon her wrist now and no enemy to face off with, her roaring gale began rushing around the cavern, unrestrained and murderous. Hitting pillars, surging up the river, it cracked stalagmites and exploded columns – Layla's furious attack a writhing monster with no end.

And nothing she could possibly stop.

Layla saw Dusk and Adrian hit the bottom landing of the stairwell at a run, their hands up to deal with the storm surging through the cavern from her abductor. Murderous with power and magic, they smashed into flying shards of shattered quartz, ready for her kidnapper's attack now ricocheting through the hall as they sprinted onto the flow of rose quartz.

But even as their gazes found Layla's, it was too late. Dusk's and Adrian's eyes both widened to see it was not her abductor, but Layla herself casting the screaming gale around the crystal cave.

But they had already thrown their attacks meant for Hunter – twin killing strikes of fire-gold and midnight-diamond energy – straight to Layla's heart.

CHAPTER 28 – TRANSFORMATION

Scents blasted Layla as her world exploded into a jasmine, cinnamon, and river-water fury. Cries slit her ears – two dismayed men's voices. Her Dragon was motionless inside her as she fell, pierced by some terrible energy as crystal shards shattered on a shield of diamond-light far above. Someone rushed up, laying his body atop hers and pouring sound and light though her as he cradled her close. Someone else exhaled down her throat with scorching winds, sweet jasmine-cinnamon scent giving her breath.

She breathed. And breathed. And breathed.

Her world faded. And then it came back as she was being rushed up a flight of stairs in someone's strong arms. And then returned again as someone did CPR on her, cussing a blue streak. And then it faded again, but not as far as before.

Layla surfaced, feeling strong hands holding her; warm flesh cocooning her. She was naked in a bed and a naked man lay behind her, breathing quietly. Curled close with one arm cradling her ribs, his palm was pressed to her heart. Another lay before her, his hips pressed to hers, one hand palming her waist as he exhaled spiced breath at her lips. Soothing, the man behind her rolled a lower-than-sound vibration through her body, pressing it into her heart. The warm scent of jasmine swirled around her as the man before her fed her sips of life each time she inhaled. Her lips parting, she breathed him in – sharing wind and fire, spice and heat.

Spinning her up into a bright funnel as they lay breathing together.

But the force at her back held her safe, in ancient caverns where time moved slow and strange. Layla nestled back into that strong body, feeling him curl around her, molding to her flesh like he belonged there. He did belong there. As the man before her reached out, stroking her face with his fingertips as their lips and life breathed together as one, Layla knew they both belonged there; breathing in time with her as if all three had been yoked together. One impossible loop smelted together like a figure-eight, bound through Layla's own body.

Sharing energy, sharing breath – sharing everything.

A rumble of pleasure rolled through Layla, the man's hand on her chest resonating love deep into her heart, healing her damaged body. The other one breathed with her, pulling her close by his hand at her hip, melding their bodies together as his lips softly touched hers; pouring life gently down her throat. They were everything Layla wanted; everything she needed. They were the perfect balance to the roaring winds that raged through her.

They were the balm to her heart, and the fire in her veins.

Her hands shifted, the only part of her that could move – one to clasp Dusk's hand at her heart, the other to twine her fingers into Adrian's at her hip. She felt them startle; then smooth out as they settled back into a gentle bliss.

* * *

Layla woke to clinking cutlery. Blinking back to awareness, she stretched in her canopied bed, the cobalt drapes drawn so the world was shut out from her blessed cocoon. Alone in bed now, her silk sheets were twisted from sleep, though she could still smell cinnamon-musk and river-water lingering on her pillows and skin. A smile lifted her lips as she cuddled into the covers, smelling her men. Curling up with her pillow, she opened her lips to that delicious musk – reveling in it as her Dragon roiled inside her with an orange-peel bourbon scent.

"She's awake." Layla heard Dusk's low voice from beyond the curtains.

"At last."

Adrian's smooth baritone was gentle, and Layla blinked as one cobalt curtain was drawn back. The light was horridly bright and she blinked. Dressed only in a pair of cinnamon silk sleep-pants as he slid to the bed, Adrian's hand was warm as he reached out, stroking back a lock of her curls, his aqua and gold eyes beautiful as the Mediterranean Sea. Leaning at her bedpost dressed in midnight-blue silk pajama pants, Dusk crossed his muscled arms, his eyes a deep sapphire like a high afternoon sky.

Layla watched them, her Royal Dragons. Feeling them, smelling their scents curling around her like relaxing in a hot spring on a snowy winter's day.

"How do you feel?" Adrian asked at last, his fingers stroking her face.

"Strange."

It was the first thing that came to Layla's mind. Before she could say more, her Dragon-energy suddenly rose, uncoiling like some massive thing of cruel spines, roped muscle, and wicked talons inside her. Heat rolled through her in a wave, spilling through her entire body like wind and water locked in a delicious dance.

Rising up through her core, it stretched out and Layla stretched with it, her body making an impossible arch as if she had bones and muscle where she'd never had them before. Her stretch was serpentine, sliding the sheets down from her nakedness as that movement roiled through to the tips of her fingers and toes – clawing them into the covers as if talons could have shot from her fingertips.

Layla's arms came up as she arched onto the crown of her head, that amazing sensation coming to completion within her. The scent of bourbon and orange peels simmered off her skin in a hot mirage as she felt her insides boil, her hands sliding through her curls as she writhed with power – sensual and dark and bright all at once.

Easing up from the sheets in the most erotic maneuver she had ever performed, Layla came to sitting. Tightening her shoulder-blades, she felt muscles flex where muscles had never been. Every pore of her body felt attentive with pleasure. Breathing in her own powerful scent mingling with the musk of her men made Layla shiver, her head falling back as she sat upon her knees, her long hair caressing her ass in the most delicious sensation she had ever felt.

Layla bared her throat, able to do nothing but breathe as she devoured the eroticism. This body wasn't the one she had known. Whatever had happened in that cavern had changed her as surely as her awakening in the art gallery had changed her before. When she could open her eyes at last, the day seemed brighter, sharper, every color more luminous. As if every gilded edge in her apartment had diamonds in the paint, making the world sparkle.

Her eyes open, her attention shifted to Adrian and Dusk. She saw both men staring, their lips fallen open, their bodies tense and faces wild with heat.

"Wow." Adrian breathed, staring at Layla with gold devouring his bright aqua gaze.

"You said it." Dusk gave a soft rumble, the thunder of his utterance vibrating the bed.

Rising, Layla watched them, her bound Royal Dragons. Their faces were eager at her nakedness and her power, and for the first time in her life she felt perfectly at ease being stared at. As she stood there watching them, she realized she could feel their lives breathing around her; wisps of thought, sensations of memory, pieces of dreams. Their emotions rolled through her, as if her Dragon called out to them and was answered.

Moving to the bedpost, she received her cobalt silk robe as Dusk held it out. His eyes were bright as he watched her but he said nothing, just nodded to the mirror by the bed. Donning her robe, Layla tied it loosely. New sensations rolled over her: the smoothness of the silk, the way it caught on her skin with tiny imperfections that rasped like a cat's tongue.

Moving to the mirror, Layla found a new face staring back at her. Everything was subtly different. Her dark eyelashes were thicker, her lips a bit more sultry, her cheeks flushed. Her skin seemed brighter like it was lit from within, her cheekbones higher. Layla had always been striking, but now her face had a regal fierceness as she turned her head this way; it was beautiful and terrifying as she turned that way.

Like she could become a dream or a nightmare – like she could cause love or fear or maybe both with the right set of her jaw or flash of her eyes.

It was her eyes that had changed most. Once a pale jade, they now shifted colors as waves of heat rolled through her, changing her irises to a vivid emerald, then a marine blue, then to Hunter's deep forest tones flecked with gold. The gold brightened, and by the time Layla's heat calmed, her eyes were a dark forest green in the center fading to jade in the middle, with a vivid ring of bourbon-gold around the outside.

Turning, she regarded Adrian and Dusk, both watching her with expressions of amazement – when her stomach suddenly growled, ravenous. Moving to the table, set with a brunch spread of bacon and eggs, blueberry pancakes, and fruit, Layla sat and began heaping a plate, thrice as much as she would have normally eaten. Still lingering by the bed, Dusk and Adrian glanced at each other, then looked at her with twin smiles of amusement.

"What?" Layla asked as she bit a piece of bacon. "Can't a girl eat breakfast?"

They laughed, both of them, bold and free. Layla brightened, chewing her bacon and feeling happiness rise all through her to hear them laugh together. Dusk's rolling laugh shuddered the floor, ending in a basso chuckle that just flat did it for Layla, while Adrian's perfectly elegant laugh of surprise was bright and winsome.

Layla grinned, munching with delight. Bacon, sunlight, and two ridiculously sexy men in her apartment, both shirtless.

Life doesn't get much better.

Dusk was still chuckling as he came to the table, hauling out a chair and taking a seat. Shaking his head, his eyes glowed with brilliance as he grinned at her, then began pouring coffee. "You, woman, can eat whatever you want, whenever you want it."

His innuendo was not lost on her and Layla grinned more, reaching for her coffee, which he'd of course mixed perfectly. Raising his eyebrows at Adrian, Dusk paused with the French press over another mug. With a far more easygoing smile than Layla had ever seen from him, Adrian waved a hand in acceptance and moved forward. Dusk poured and Adrian took the chair on Layla's other side, shaking his head with a grin as lovely as Dusk's.

"Eating bacon and making jokes." Adrian laughed softly. With a nod of thanks to Dusk as he received his coffee, Adrian reached out, smoothing his knuckles over Layla's cheek. "You have no idea how close to death's door you were. And now, power like I've never felt rises in you and you go straight for breakfast just like a normal day."

"Hey, I'm hungry." Layla spoke with her mouth full. "Don't interrupt a girl's bacon and coffee."

"I wouldn't ever presume so much." Adrian chuckled, giving her cheek one last stroke and then taking up his mug. Dusk was serving his and Adrian's plates now, and for a moment, everything seemed so ridiculously normal between the three of them that Layla laughed. They both looked at her, and she shook her head. But then Dusk and Adrian looked at each other, and smiles stole around the edges of their lips.

"I never thought a woman could bring us together, Adrian." Dusk spoke cheekily, sipping his coffee.

"Royal Dragon Binds have interesting powers, or so I hear." Adrian spoke back with a dark humor, sipping his coffee and lifting an eyebrow at Layla.

"Hey," Layla spoke around a bite of eggs. "As long as the two of you aren't tearing each other's throats out, I'm happy."

"So are we." Dusk murmured, setting his coffee down and gazing at Adrian.

Adrian gave him a nod, setting his coffee down also. Something important moved between the two brothers, something Layla didn't quite understand but could feel. It was Adrian who finally turned to look at her with a complicated emotion as he laced his long fingers and sat back with his elbows on his chair, watching her. "You've been opened to more of your power, Layla."

"You mean the change in my body and energy?" She asked, her mouth full of buttery croissant now. "And these sensations – like I can feel other people's emotions and thoughts in the air?"

Adrian and Dusk shared a look, Dusk with his eyebrows raised pointedly.

"What?" Layla glanced between them.

"We didn't know that would be one of your powers," Dusk turned to her, explaining. "It's called *current-reading*, the ability to read people's emotions and thoughts through the air. It's one of King Arini's abilities, actually."

"The powers of a Royal Dragon Bind are as unique as the person, Layla." Adrian was careful as he spoke. "It's impossible to predict what your magic will look like as it matures. Your powers are the ultimate wild card."

"Speaking of shit getting wild." Setting down her croissant, Layla eyeballed Adrian, heat rushing through her and making a scorched scent blossom in the air. She saw Adrian flinch as her wrathful heat roiled over him, unrestrained. She didn't rake it back. There was no place to stuff it away now that the hamsa-cuff was gone – and it felt good to be as angry with him as she wanted to be at last.

Though they were all being civil this morning after her near-death, Adrian still had his actions the night of the Samhain Masquerade to answer for.

"Are you going to be a jealous asshole over my Bind with Dusk, Adrian?" Layla growled low, letting her vicious heat simmer over him. "Or are you just going to try to rip our Bind apart again? 'Cause that was a ton of fun as I recall."

"I'm not going to try and rip our Bind apart again, Layla." Adrian's aqua gaze was penetrating, deep with apology. "And Dusk and I have talked, finally. He told me about Rachida's theory, that perhaps the Hamsa Bind cuff only enhanced your own desires."

"And?" Layla spoke, pinning Adrian with her eyes.

"And I can't change that." Adrian glanced to Dusk. "But if Dusk hadn't been bound to you six nights ago when we came storming into the Vault… you wouldn't be here, Layla. My magic wasn't enough to save you, not on my own."

Layla sat quietly, digesting that as her heat sighed away. Pushing her plate away, she took up her coffee, sitting back in her chair and cradling the mug as she watched both men. It was as close to an apology as she'd ever gotten from Adrian. She saw the truth in his eyes, even though she also saw it still hurt him that he wasn't her only bound lover. Though the two men shared a prickly moment as they sat at her table, Layla could feel an accord between them now, as if something important had happened while she was unconscious.

But Dusk suddenly frowned, turning to look at her. "Layla, do you ever remember having the same Bind experience with Adam as you had with Adrian and I?"

"No." Layla frowned, thinking about it. "Adam – *Hunter* as he called himself – was trying to convince me to join him in some god-awful crusade, but I don't remember having that explosive moment with him. Even though he took the cuff off me with his bare hands, we didn't Bind the way you and Adrian and I have. My Dragon rose and faced off with him. She was furious that he would think I could join him in murder. And so was I."

"Thank god." Adrian let out an exhalation, relief plain upon his handsome face. Leaning forward, he laced his hands on the tabletop with concern in his eyes. "Layla, did Hunter tell you how long he's been masquerading as Adam?"

Layla took a breath, knowing she had to tell him the truth. "Adam never survived the slaughter of his parents in Italy. The person you grew up with was Hunter all along."

"Fuck." Adrian sat back, the fingers of one hand lifting to his lips. He went positively ashen, sitting back in his chair with a deep and stunned stillness. Tears shone in Adrian's eyes as he opened his lips, then shut his mouth and shook his head. Adrian's tears didn't fall, but his gaze moved to Dusk. "Rachida."

Dusk was as sober as Adrian, and he only nodded as if he didn't trust himself to speak just yet. Rubbing his fingers over the tablecloth in a nervous tic Layla had never seen from him, Dusk's gaze flicked to her. "Layla, did Hunter say why he'd masqueraded as Adam for so long?"

"No, he only said it was convenient for his purposes." Layla spoke. "But he admitted to being both a Royal Dragon and a Royal Dragon Bind, and claims to be the oldest surviving member of my Lineage. His agenda has something to do with my Lineage being hunted through the ages because of our power. He kept making comparisons between *the Hunter and the Hunted* – asking which I was to be, which side I would take."

"So there are more Binds out there," Adrian's gaze was penetrating.

"So Hunter asserted, yes. In hiding." Layla nodded. "He also offered to teach me how to use my power. That was why he took my hamsa-cuff and destroyed it. Because he wants my powers unleashed for the world to reckon with."

"They are unleashed," Adrian spoke, his gaze intense. "The desert-funnel you raised in the Vault after Hunter took your talisman was unholy, Layla. It was partly your Bind to Dusk and I that fueled it, but partly not. When you went off alone after the party—" he glanced at Dusk and they shared a tense look, "we didn't know where you'd gone. I couldn't smell you anymore or see you in my mind. Your vibration went off the map Dusk feels inside his body. I knew the only place in the Hotel that could so thoroughly cut you off from us was the Vault, but when we got there—"

"When we got there, the sapphire door was broken – cracked." Dusk interrupted, holding Layla's gaze with a level intensity. "In all the Paris Hotel's history, the Vault has never been breached. It's a magical prison, Layla. Hunter had sealed it from the inside, as is possible when the Hotel is under attack. We shouldn't have been able to get in. But when Hunter removed your hamsa-cuff and you started cracking crystal pillars with your rage… you cracked a door that has incarcerated some of the strongest Dragons in Hotel history. You broke an unbreakable door. And you did it in human form, not Dragon."

Layla sat back. Heat rippled through her, as if sparked by the magnitude of what she'd done in her fury at Hunter. But it all seemed so impossible that she could have done as they asserted, and Layla blew out a breath. "How do you know it was me who broke the door?"

"Intense acts of magic leave a scent residue, and a vibrational one," Dusk spoke quietly. "The spiderwebbed cracks through the door smelled like you, and felt like you. When we ran down there and Adrian and I smelled that... we knew you were down there. And we knew that whatever was happening was bad."

"Hence why you stormed down with all guns blazing." Layla remembered their twin killing-strikes; how neither of them had been able to stop their unleashed power – even though at the last moment, they'd realized they'd thrown their lances at Layla. She had thought they might apologize, but neither of them did. What Layla got was a level intensity from both men.

"What we felt down in that hall was battle, Layla," Adrian spoke. "Dusk and I approached it in the manner warranted."

"The good news is that you survived," Dusk spoke darkly, though his face held a curious interest. "Two killing strikes from two Royal Dragons at once. Adrian and I believe it was three things that helped you survive: your own formidable power and your Bind to each of us. Once we started to revive you, your body leapt to our magics. It still took a long time to stabilize you, and longer still to heal the damage, but us both being there gave you what you needed."

"Leaving me different afterward," Layla spoke softly. "What about my talisman?"

"It's unrecoverable." Adrian spoke, his gaze dire. "Among its other properties, that cuff could protect Royal Dragon Binds from harmful events that would twist their powers dark. I'm sure Hunter knew that, and he made a point of getting rid of it."

"What do you mean?" Layla asked, frowning at Adrian now. "I thought you said the cuff's only abilities were amplifying my desires and Binding a Bind."

"Not just those things." Adrian spoke with a level intensity. "Your cuff was spoken of in ancient tales as being able to prevent a Royal Dragon Bind from turning evil. The stories of Binds… so many of them are awful tales, Layla. Tragedies of wrath and destruction, just like Hunter. There's a reason your Lineage has been hunted nearly to extinction – because Royal Dragon Binds often twist evil. It wasn't a fate I wanted for you. Neither Dusk nor I."

"So you both knew about the cuff's powers," Layla watched them, before her gaze pinned Dusk. "You *both* knew, and you didn't tell me."

"Adrian and I were of one mind in trying to protect you from the void-shadow, Layla, and from your powers twisting dark." Dusk spoke with apology in his eyes. "Though Adrian binding you through it wasn't part of the plan."

"Touching you that day in the art gallery was my own weakness," Adrian was wry but truthful as he leaned forward in his chair. "I saw you and I wanted you, even though I had told myself I wouldn't use the cuff to Bind you. But you overcame me that day, twisting our passions together. I didn't plan on touching your wrist when I put the talisman on you. But I couldn't help myself in that moment – I had to touch you. I needed to."

"So I'm just a seducer like Hunter, is that what you're trying to say?" Layla spoke, feeling something crumble deep within her. Deep inside, a black pit suddenly opened up, devouring her happiness.

Reaching out, Adrian lifted her chin, making her meet his eyes. "You are *nothing* like a monster that watches children get slaughtered

326

and impersonates them for over a hundred years, Layla. You have a chance. *We* have a chance to make sure your magic takes a better direction than his. Mimi was a shining light, even without a talisman to protect her. You are her daughter – and far more like her than you know."

Layla could see Adrian's ideals in her mind suddenly, and it smote her with hope. But when she recalled the way her eyes had settled into a dark forest green like Hunter's, with hot gold like a wrathful fire – her hope cracked like the pillars she'd broken in the Vault.

"But my rage sundered an unbreakable door." Layla spoke. "And now I don't have the Hamsa Bind to protect me from evil influences anymore. What's to stop me from turning cruel and crazy like Hunter?"

"I can think of two things you've got that Hunter doesn't." Dusk gave a pointed look between himself and Adrian.

"But the three of us—" Layla glanced between her two men, realizing how ridiculously complicated this all was. "How can our magic take a positive direction if the two of you can't even get along?"

They glanced at each other, Dusk's gaze level and Adrian's thoughtful as they shared a deep intensity. At last, Dusk looked to Layla. "When Adrian's family took me in I was raw, Layla. I was antagonistic in my grief and Adrian was a hothead with his own axe to grind because of his parents fighting. Sometimes we got along; sometimes we fought like banshees."

"Sometimes we helped each other," Adrian picked up the narrative. "And sometimes we just tried to kill each other out in the dunes where no one would see. We have a complicated past. Dusk and I... we cannot promise to always get along, but I can at least promise to try."

"I've already been *very* good." Dusk grinned, rakish and handsome as he sat back in his chair. "I haven't fucked you yet, and

327

that's an accomplishment for me. I was always more good-looking than Adrian though, so you'll probably come to my bed first."

And suddenly, Adrian laughed; that bright, free sound that somehow cleared the air. He was still chuckling as he reached for a glass of water, downed it, then set it back with a grin. "You might be good-looking, Dusk, but Layla bound me first."

"Only because you had the cuff," Dusk grinned, a challenge in his eyes.

"Only because I'm a better lover than you are."

Adrian's gaze flicked to Layla, something darkly possessive in his eyes as they flashed molten gold. That gaze made Layla's heart pound, her lips fallen open. Adrian's smile curled more, as if he could feel what she was experiencing. Dusk had stopped grinning, frowning between them now as Adrian sent a lick of wind curling up Layla's foot, pressing in at her ankle and hinting at the roaring passion he could give her – anytime, anywhere.

It made Layla shudder, her breath fast. With a murderous, sexy exhalation, Adrian sent his jasmine-spice breath pouring in through Layla's lips. His searing winds kissed over her tongue and dove down her throat – deep into her heart, drawing a sound of pleasure from her. Their eyes locked; Layla could feel Adrian moving inside her; deeper than any human lover could touch.

Just as deep as Dusk's thread of light had taken her before.

Smiling, Adrian broke their connection with a snap that made Layla shudder. "And that's not even a fraction of what I can do in bed. But you're going to have to wait to find out."

With a mean little chuckle, Adrian rose, then turned to address Dusk and Layla both. "If you'll excuse me, I have to speak with the Madame. A dangerous threat has come to the Hotel and whether we like it or not, we must answer. Take some rest, Layla. Dusk, if you leave her side even for a minute, I will personally murder you."

"Noted, I'm sure." But Dusk gave a subtle smile, his gaze still dark with competition as he rose from the table also. "You should know, Adrian, there's no charge I'd rather have for an afternoon. Or a night."

"If you fuck her while I'm gone, I swear I'll tear you apart." Adrian's gaze darkened; his power twisted through the room with a sting like desert sand, and Layla suddenly felt their accord straining. Dusk and Adrian were fiercely competitive, and too many women had come between them in the past. Two Royal Dragons, two big egos – and two big magics.

But Layla was the Bind between them. And she wasn't about to let their bullshit wreck this chance.

Layla rose, finding herself steady. Strong actually; as if she fed off the warring brothers' energies. Turning to face them, she put a hand to her hip, which would have been more sassy if she'd been wearing real clothing rather than a silk robe, but it was what it was.

"I don't believe what I do with my body is yours to dictate, Adrian. This is the first and last time I will tell either of you that I give my body to whomever I choose, whenever I choose. Fight about it, roar about it, and watch how fast I kick you both out of my life, magical Binds or no. Are we clear?"

"Crystal." Dusk grinned, his sapphire eyes lighting with amusement and a delicious passion.

"If you will it, so it shall be." Adrian spoke, watching her with his hot aqua eyes. "*Whatever lifts the corners of your mouth, trust that.*"

With his Rumi quote and a dark, sexy smile that told her just how up for this challenge he was, Adrian bowed. And with a smoldering gaze that sundered Layla to her core, he departed – throwing open her doors and leaving in a swirl of desert-spice winds.

CHAPTER 29 – DECISIONS

Adrian Rhakvir was commanding as he stood at the head of the long table in the vaulted meeting hall. Pinning the seated Hotel Department Heads with blistering aqua eyes, he simmered with power in the crimson sunlight setting beyond the vaulted windows. Dressed in a navy pinstriped vest and pants, Adrian's expensive ensemble caught the autumn light, his navy tie and platinum tie bar glowing. His dark hair was rakishly mussed, his shirtsleeves rolled to his elbows, showing the coiling red and gold dragon tattoo on his left forearm – which seemed to writhe with a life of its own tonight as he stared down the table at the gathered Department Heads, and Layla.

Every face was somber, every ear attentive. Wine and sundries occupied the table, largely untouched. Called together by Adrian, all were here to discuss the future of the Red Letter Hotel Paris – a future that was now uncertain.

"Friends," Adrian spoke in his commanding, silken baritone as he pinned them all with his gaze. "The Red Letter Hotel Paris has been compromised; our safety within these halls is no longer assured. Trust me when I say I am doing everything in my power to correct this, but in the meantime, we have problems to solve. You have all read the dossier Dusk prepared concerning our intruder, one *Hunter* masquerading as my own cousin Adam Rhakvir. You all know the extent of the problem he caused during his time here, and have read the testimony of the Phoenix King Falliro Arini. I have called you all together so we may thoroughly discuss this problem, to consider this issue from every angle. I will now hear your thoughts. Let us begin."

Layla watched people shift all along the high table, but Madame Etienne Voulouer spoke up at once, fanning herself with a zebra fan edged in silver lace that complimented her 1950's silver couture. "Have you spoken with the Board about this *Hunter*, Adrian? What do they have to say about our situation?"

"The Hotel Board of Owners have berated our security and browbeaten me on my lack of control over the situation." A wry smile took Adrian's face, more a grimace as he answered her query. "I have managed to convince them it was not the fault of our exemplary security team," Adrian nodded to Rikyava and Dusk, "but the problem of having a very ancient Royal Dragon Bind with unique abilities stalking our employees. As of now, we have no answers from them. But trust me when I say the safety of our family here is of my *highest* priority, and I am searching for answers independently."

Adrian's gaze settled upon Layla and she couldn't help but blush. She was not a Department Head, but since this discussion involved her, Adrian had suggested she be present. The cat was out of the bag that another Bind was stalking her. Adrian hadn't been able to hide it when she was abducted the night of the Samhain Masquerade – nor that the Vault was now out-of-order because of its cracked sapphire door and blasted columns.

The intensity of Adrian's gaze made heat surge through Layla. The Department Heads shifted, their looks ranging from discomfort to intrigue as they felt her magic – as she desperately tried to reign in her flare of passion and failed. Without her hamsa-cuff, her orange-bourbon scent washed through the room, making a number of people's lips fall open and others take deep drinks of wine.

Even Adrian shivered at the head of the table.

It had been hard to touch Adrian and Dusk since her recovery.

Every time she was near them, Layla's thoughts turned to lust and her magic with it. She'd not been able to share their beds since the morning she woke. Even the touch of their hands was enough to send her spinning, re-learning how to breathe. Layla could go about in public as long as they barely touched, but she wondered how far her passions would spread if she kissed one of them. As rash as Dusk and Adrian both were, neither had pushed their suits since she'd changed – and she wondered just how worried they were about her growing power.

Sitting beside her, Sylvania Eroganis gave a reassuring smile and settled a hand to Layla's thigh. It was soothing and Layla's magic eased, the Head Courtesan unperturbed by Layla's intensity.

Madame Voulouer cleared her throat as Layla's energy settled, then rose to stand at Adrian's side. "We cannot change the opinions of the Board, but we can address this inside our own Hotel, which Adrian and I have already begun to do. Our dearest Rikyava Andersen and our wonderful Dusk Arlohaim are leading our security systems through a vibrational catalogue of the entire staff, so we can identify any anomalies if this Hunter returns. From now on, every new hire will be introduced to the security imprinting, as will every guest. I have approved one hundred additional veteran Guard personnel to be released to us from various Hotel branches. Everyone will read and follow Dusk's new guidelines on security for their Departments. While the risk of infiltration by Hunter is high, we cannot assume any of us is safe. Rikyava, you will orient our new Guard personnel when they arrive in a week's time."

"Yes, Madame." Sitting across from Layla, Rikyava nodded tersely, dressed in her crimson Guard jerkin and weapons.

"In the meantime, we are operating on *business as usual*," Adrian continued, taking up the Madame's thread. "I want no disruption to our regular processes. Our guests must believe we have no troubles, and until we have answers, we will bolster this illusion with our usual wit and grace. Are we understood?"

Heads nodded around the table. A few people sipped wine, the tension needing some kind of reprieve as the sun set over the gardens. Layla's heat had finally lessened when the Madame fixed her tiger-eyes upon Layla, causing her to surge with embarrassment again.

"As many of you have guessed, we have a very unique problem due to this recent intrusion," the Madame continued. "Our young Concierge Ms. Layla Price is a Royal Dragon Bind, one of Hunter's Lineage. Recently abducted and relieved of her talisman by the intruder, she is now having difficulty controlling her increasing powers."

Heads turned to Layla; her energy cranked up a notch as the Madame smiled kindly. "Layla has been shining under the tutelage of our dearest Dusk Arlohaim. Yet her intense, uncontrolled powers are anathema to continuing her position in Concierge Services. I will now hear suggestions as to the best place to fit Layla at the Hotel, rather than working as a Concierge. We do not abandon our family, but we must address this issue promptly. The floor is open."

Layla sat stunned as the Madame resumed her seat, having had no idea her job was on the agenda today. Glancing at Dusk, she flared with anger like a torched orange grove. But though he was frowning deeply, he shook his head, indicating for her to say nothing just yet, settling a hand to her thigh and pouring a soothing vibration through her as silence fell around the table.

"I could take Layla on in the Guard." Rikyava cleared her throat, glancing to Layla with a tough but kind smile. "She's showing promise with battle-magics. Cracked an unbreakable door. Layla could be quite an asset once she establishes some control."

"Impractical." Head Courtier Reginald Durant spoke up, pinning

Layla with his ice-blue eyes from across the table. "Ms. Price would need years to train in blades, firearms, and all the basic ability the Guard have. Magic is not their only tool, and unconfined power like Ms. Price's is more of a liability in combat than an asset."

"Do you have a better idea?" Rikyava prickled, crossing her arms and glaring at Reginald.

"Any idiot can feel what Layla's becoming," Reginald spoke, cold like the North Sea as he glanced to Layla. "And if no one will say it, I shall – a Courtesan. Her powers breathe of passion and sex. We cannot have a surging eros-torrent occupying any casual department like Concierge, Catering, or the Guard. Some guests would love it when her power tastes them indiscriminately; others *will* call it a breach of privacy, and they would be right. It is my belief that Ms. Price's only option is to be instated as a Courtesan immediately, and assigned to a Partner for training."

"I am of a similar opinion to Reginald," Head Courtesan Sylvania Eroganis spoke up now, her silvery voice soothing as she turned luminous eyes to Layla. "Layla has great power, yet because her abilities are new, they are ranging as indiscriminately as her passions send them. She needs training in controlling her sensuality. And from what I've felt, I believe her powers are intimately suited to being a Courtesan. Perhaps even Head Courtesan someday."

Layla stiffened, *really* not liking the direction this conversation was going. She opened her mouth to speak but Dusk gripped her thigh hard. Layla glanced to him and he shook his head, though a deep apology was in his eyes. In that desperate glance, Layla saw that this conversation hadn't been his doing. But her placement at the Hotel also wasn't his decision. She had a flash of vision – an image of herself standing out on the curb of the Hotel with her bags packed. Clearly, the image had come from Dusk, and Layla understood what it meant.

Her job was on the line if they couldn't find an appropriate Department to place her in as her powers developed.

"Well! If Layla is suited to becoming a Courtesan, that leaves the issue of her Training Partner." The Madame glanced to Reginald. "Which Courtiers do you have that could lead Layla through a Courtesan's studies?"

"None." Reginald spoke in his ice-water voice – his gaze piercing upon Layla.

"But if she is to be a Courtesan in order to remain at our Hotel as her powers open, she must have a Partner." Madame Voulouer fretted with her fan. "Are none of your Courtiers accomplished enough to take Layla on for training, Aldo?"

"We have but one option for Layla's Partner – myself." Reginald's gaze drilled a hole right through Layla. "Only Sirens know how to wrangle such unbridled eros. If she will not have me as her Partner for training, Layla will not be taken on as a Courtesan at this establishment. As Head Courtier, my word on the matter is final. If she joins my department, she trains and beds with me – and me *alone*, until she learns to control what she is. If she will not acquiesce to becoming a Courtesan and suffer my training, then I move to have her dismissed from the Hotel altogether. We cannot tolerate her wild magic in any other department. She would be dismissed with an appropriate severance package, of course, but dismissed nonetheless."

Layla blinked, feeling her world spin. She stared at Reginald, her passions dying into a cavernous black hole at his ultimatum. She felt Dusk's low growl ripple around her and she saw Adrian set his jaw, his eyes blazing gold and furious.

Clearly, this wasn't what Adrian wanted, either – or what he had planned.

All around the table people shifted, feeling a coup in the air. For her part, Layla couldn't breathe. A Courtesan – a woman who sold her body for money. It was everything Layla had feared about the Hotel from her very first conversation with Adrian back in Seattle. Even worse, if she chose to stay and not leave Adrian and Dusk, she would have to take Head Courtier Reginald Durant, the cold-as-North-Seas Siren, to her bed.

Swallowing hard, Layla whispered, "No."

"What was that, darling?" Madame Voulouer gazed down the table. "Speak up, we didn't hear you?"

"No." Layla spoke up more robustly. "I won't become a Courtesan."

"Then you will leave this establishment." Reginald spoke from across the table, his face hard as stone.

"I didn't come here to be a Courtesan." Layla locked eyes with Reginald, feeling power seethe out from her and dig into the Siren like talons, though he didn't betray any discomfort.

"Yet that is what you are." Reginald didn't back down, holding her gaze with an icy intensity. "From the moment you stepped foot upon our grounds, I saw how Adrian watched you, and the way Dusk's eros leapt to you the moment you arrived. Men's eyes follow you wherever you go, and women's too. I've watched two of the most powerful drakes I've ever known start a battle *in public* because of you, and then you get abducted by one of the most dangerous creatures ever to walk our halls. Don't tell me all of that is pure coincidence. Because it's not. And if you try to lie to yourself, believe me, it will rebound upon you. Badly."

It was a scathing tirade, possibly the most Layla had ever heard the Head Courtier speak. As she sat there, flushing from rage, she felt her emotions whirl through the room. People shifted, and Layla suddenly realized that she could feel their desire in the air. She could feel all the Department Heads, most of them Royals in their own respective Lineages, responding to her magic.

Sex flooded the room, stirred up by Layla's power, all of it rushing her way even though she wasn't trying to project eros right now. Inside her body, Layla's Dragon roiled with pleasure to feel all that passion stirred up. It was like a drug to her. It was like when she'd been in the middle of the Samhain Masquerade, being spun from partner to partner.

A heady ecstasy; something her Dragon wanted more of.

As Layla had that thought, her Dragon roiled inside her eagerly, thinking about having as many partners as she liked. Casual partners, not true mates, but delicious all the same. An image of the *bacchanalia* rose in Layla's thoughts, and she felt how much it had arrested her on the day of her arrival at the Hotel. Her Dragon wanted to be in that public orgy. Feeling so many hands; tasting so many mouths. A simmering golden fire curled out from Layla's body as she felt her passion surge and she couldn't put it away. It didn't do harm as it rolled through the room, but it made people gasp and shudder with pleasure.

Reaching out again, Sylvania set a hand to Layla's thigh. But it was Reginald staring at her with his ice-cold intensity that solved the problem. Layla heard the rush of the ocean in her ears. A chill wave of power made her Dragon retreat with a strangled sensation. She shivered, not knowing how to fight it as goosebumps stood out upon her arms. As her mind was devoured by the sound of the sea, her eros quieted.

And in Reginald's eyes, she saw what he didn't say – that he had known he was the only person who could control her passion, right from the very beginning.

Her mouth dry, Layla at last found her voice. "How long would I have to train with you?"

"Until I am thoroughly satisfied that you are not a danger to our guests, and have learned at least the bare minimum of skills required as a Courtesan." Reginald's gaze was frigid upon her.

"Training as a Courtesan can last weeks to years, Layla." Sylvania supplied, her luminous eyes gentle as the glanced over. "It all depends on how fast you learn. But know that the position carries both power and choice. In the eyes of the Twilight Realm, a Courtesan of the Hotel carries immense social standing. Courtesans are not at anyone's beck and call – you only accept the Assignations that appeal to you. And often a Courtesan who couples rarely carries the highest value – if your skills and magic are worthy of the price. Which, from what we are all experiencing now, I'm certain will come to pass. If you desire it."

Her gaze locking with Adrian, her hand snaking out and finding Dusk's, Layla felt her world ripped apart just as it was finally being assembled. Sylvania's words were a comfort, but the decision was heinous. Layla didn't want to fuck for money, even though her Dragon was eager. She didn't care if the position carried higher standing than a Concierge, or if she could choose her partners. Layla had grown up believing that fucking for money was prostitution, no matter how elevated it seemed.

How could she reconcile that inside herself?

And how could she reconcile that with the two men she actually wanted?

Layla's gaze was still locked to Adrian's, and she saw a terrible knowledge in his eyes. He was silent as all eyes followed Layla's to look at him. With molten rage, he glanced to Reginald, but the Head Courtier held his ramrod-stiff seat, staring Adrian down in an intense standoff.

"I invoke a vote." Reginald spoke quietly, still staring at Adrian. "How many Department Heads here believe Ms. Price's magic is only suited to the Assignations department?"

Hands raised all around the table; nearly all of them. Only Dusk, Rikyava, and Rake kept their hands down, all three of them giving Reginald a chilly stare. Adrian didn't vote either, but Layla had a feeling he wasn't supposed to. As she looked around, she saw finally how the majority of Twilight Realm people saw her.

She finally saw that nearly all of them believed her magic was calling her to become a Courtesan.

"A vote has been cast, Hotel Head." Reginald spoke quietly, though his presence was intense. "Would you gainsay it?"

Layla watched Adrian bristle. She watched his energy roar, blistering and furious. Curls of aqua and crimson flame simmered in the air around him as a mirage was stirred up, his eyes blazing gold as they pinned Reginald.

"Adrian." The Madame spoke quietly. "Please. Place your personal feelings aside. For the good of our Hotel, I beg you to consider the wisdom of your Department Heads. All of us have the safety of this establishment in our hearts. Do you?"

Adrian simmered with wrath a moment longer. But then Layla saw the Madame's kind words sink in, and she watched him pull his scalding magic back. Closing his eyes, he took a deep inhalation. When he opened them, his magic had settled, the vibrant gold in his eyes no longer terrifying.

Though his gaze returned to Layla, devastated. "Layla. I leave this choice to you. A vote has been cast as to the proper department for you. And though I hate it to the depths of my being, I have to honor it. Furthermore, by Hotel law, I cannot override the Head Courtier's decision on a Training Partner for a new Courtesan. If you choose to remain in this Hotel rather than taking severance…then you would remain as a Courtesan, and abide by the Head Courtier's will."

"Choose, Layla," Reginald spoke, pinning Layla with his gaze. "Stay with the people who care about you and become what you truly are... or choose to be alone. Because as long as you deny what you are, then none of the people you love are safe around you. Believe me, I know."

In that moment, Layla saw something in Reginald's eyes – a flicker of memory shining through his power. He shut her out with a wave of white-crested water, but not before Layla had seen a pale woman with raven-dark hair, red lips, and beautiful lavender eyes embracing a far younger Reginald on a lonely northern beach.

With the vision, Layla had an impression of awfulness. As if whatever had happened to that woman had been Reginald's fault, maybe even a fault of his magic as a young man – and it haunted him still. Something about it gave Reginald an iota of humanity in all that austere ice and pale blue silk. And Layla suddenly realized that like Adrian and Dusk, Reginald was actually trying to protect her by giving her this horrible ultimatum – from something far worse that her magic might potentially cause.

It made her think of Luke. Of him twisting in spasms in the house back in Seattle, Layla's magic tearing him up inside. The image was so vivid and horrifying that Layla shuddered. Her heart twisted from what she'd done with her uncontrolled magic. She saw Reginald frown as he watched her, something deeply human moving through his pale eyes. They were suddenly not quite so ice-blue, not quite so cold as he watched her re-experience her trauma.

"If this is the best course of action for all of us here at the Hotel," Layla spoke at last, moving her gaze from Reginald to Adrian, "I hate it and I want that on the record – but I'll stay. My life is better with my friends alive and safe than without them."

Wretchedness swept Adrian's beautiful aqua eyes. But with a regal nod, he acquiesced to her decision.

"Well." The Madame rose, turning to face the assembly. "If anyone has more business?"

No one did. As Adrian dismissed the meeting with a hard sigh, Layla's blood suddenly ran cold. It was done. She had chosen to become a Courtesan and no one, not even Adrian, was opposing it. In a fluid motion, Reginald rose, stepping around the table to pass low words with Sylvania. Adrian moved down the table quickly as Dusk escorted Layla over to a fireplace roaring with a stiff blaze.

"Are you alright?" Adrian moved close, gazing down at Layla and setting his hands to her shoulders as Dusk stepped protectively to her back. Layla couldn't quite catch her breath, a sensation like drowning swamping her. Glancing at Reginald, who turned her way as if he could feel her regard, Layla could feel his magic in her body – and it wasn't anything she could stop, even though Reginald's control of her eros was a blessing.

Turning back, she gazed up at Adrian. His beautiful eyes were bleak, terrible like the Mediterranean Sea in a deadly mist. She could feel how much this decision was tearing him apart. Sharing her with Dusk was one thing; sharing her with Reginald and countless Assignation partners was going to kill him.

"Adrian…I'm so sorry." Layla reached up, cupping his face in her hands.

"It's not your fault," he murmured, his sad smile heartbreaking.

"Look at that bastard gloat!" Dusk's growl was furious as he glared at Reginald. "And he's already messing with her. Goddamn him, placing us in this position!"

But as Layla turned to look at Reginald, she saw he wasn't gloating at all. He wore a thoughtful expression as he watched their trio. His pale eyes pinned Layla again, and for a moment all she could hear was the ocean. All she could see was waves crashing against a rocky headland and the chill blue of Reginald's eyes, like icebergs in the barren north.

And the raven-haired woman. With a sluice of water over that vision, Reginald turned away.

Warm fingers found Layla's chin; Adrian lifted her face so she could meet his eyes. Twisting with gold, his gaze was tight with passion and pain. Stroking his fingertips over Layla's cheek, he produced a wash of shudders in her. Even just touching this much spun Layla up and her breath became fast.

Adrian noted it, agony in his gaze. "I can't even touch you without raising your Dragon."

"Reginald's right." Layla smiled sadly. "I can't control my power without the talisman. I need a teacher who can help me learn control. I detest everything about this new arrangement... but where are we without it?"

"Where are we with it?" Dusk sighed behind her. His arms cradled her as he set his chin to her shoulder. Layla felt his soothing rumble ease through her, but in his current state, his power was tinged with need and it spun Layla up further, flaring her magics through the hall and turning heads.

Adrian's smile was wry as he took his hand away. "Come on, let's go back to your rooms. Reginald won't call for you until tomorrow most likely—"

"I will call for Ms. Price now, actually," a sharp baritone interrupted them. Layla turned, seeing the Head Courtier, his hand extended in a courtly gesture as his pale blue eyes burned her down. "The three of you Royal Dragon fuckups have managed to cause obvious destabilization at our Hotel in a very short time, and such selfish actions will not be tolerated. I will see how much disaster in our fair establishment – and indeed, in Layla's life – can be averted by my training. As of now, she is under my care and your *services*, Hotel Head, Head Concierge, will not be necessary. Come, Courtesan. Your training begins. Say goodbye to your Royal Dragons. Your Partner, and our entire Hotel, require it."

Layla's heart shocked, encased in ice. Adrian gazed at her, bleak. But it was Dusk who leaned in behind Layla, speaking softly in her ear.

"Go with Reginald. He's a bastard, but he's not as much of a bastard as I am. We'll see you soon. And you better believe we'll be waiting."

Dusk's sweet words made Layla's heart clench. She turned to him, her lips so near his. But even that much closeness made her magic flare. A nudge from Dusk sent her toward Reginald's barren ice flow, though his gaze was terrible as he watched her go. As Layla stepped to Reginald she saw Adrian turn away, hands thrust deep in his pockets. She watched him break, turning his face aside. Layla could feel his tears as they fell, sighing across her skin with a woeful caress of desert wind. She could feel his heartbreak all around her – a sound of lonely winds swirling through midnight sand.

Layla took Reginald's hand as Dusk stepped to Adrian's side. Though they didn't touch, there was something brotherly about it. Adrian still had his face turned away and as Layla watched, he wiped his tears quickly with his thumb and forefinger, then strode from the room.

"Go after him," Layla spoke to Dusk. "I'll see you soon. I promise."

With a pained smile, the worst thing Layla had ever seen besides Adrian's tears, Dusk gave a deep bow. He strode after Adrian, the gallery thinning now as everyone went about their night. Reginald lifted Layla's hand and she turned, facing him. Though they touched, a chill wall stood between them – Layla's powers hiding deep inside her, Reginald's ice-blue gaze unreadable.

If hell had a sensation, it was this.

But then Layla heard the cry of a seagull. A soft wind blew through her mind, a scent of salt-spray easing out from the Head Courtier. Rather than chill, this wind felt like a summer's day on the water, with warm sunlight breaking through high-north clouds. An enlivening spray spritzed her, as if an ocean swell had broken on rocks.

Something inside Layla eased, feeling that sunshine. Her passions quieted under Reginald's soft vision of sea and sunlight. Watching her, the Head Courtier lifted her hand, setting his lips to her fingers. Layla felt nothing; no bloom in her powers, no flare of heat. Only an oceanic calm as Reginald kissed her fingers, the same way she'd felt when they'd danced in the ballroom.

"Courtesan." Reginald's voice was low and pleasant, something definitive in his pale blue eyes rather than wrathful now. "Are you ready to begin your training?"

Feeling that immense calm, Layla realized suddenly how tortured she was over Adrian and Dusk. How torn between them she felt, hoping she could have both but fearing losing it all. Staring at her, waiting, Reginald's ice blue eyes were tinged grey now like cool north seas, a sparkle of sunlight in them. As if he offered her a port in the storm, Layla felt her Dragon ease toward him – hoping. Hoping he could teach her to become clear. Hoping he could teach her how to manage her new life. Hoping he could teach her how to control this vast power inside her.

So she wouldn't become like Hunter – ever.

"I'm ready," she spoke, squaring her shoulders and lifting her chin.

"Then let your training begin."

With an elegant bow, Head Courtier Reginald Durant made obeisance before Layla. And then led her from the hall, the sound of the ocean in her ears.

The story continues in *Sea Dragon's Command: Royal Dragon Shifters of Morocco #3*,
A Red Letter Hotel Paranormal Romance

Loving this series?
Help Ava write more in the Royal Dragon Shifters of Morocco series by leaving a review at your favorite retailer!

COMING SOON!

Sea Dragon's Command: Royal Dragon Shifters of Morocco #3, the next book in the Red Letter Hotel Paranormal Romance series is coming soon.

Learn more at AvaWardRomance.com

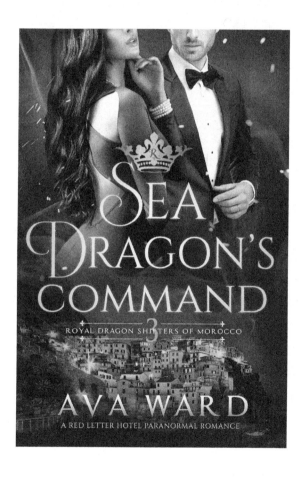

ABOUT AVA WARD

AVA WARD writes hot & sexy paranormal, fantasy, and sci-fi romance, and is the pen name for Amazon bestselling and award-winning fantasy author Jean Lowe Carlson. From dragon-shifters to otherworldly hotties, there's no limit to the heat! Discover the Red Letter Hotel romances, the decadent world of four bad-boy dragon shifter billionaires and the one woman who keeps them in line! **Discover more at AvaWardRomance.com**

Loving this series? Help Ava write more in the Royal Dragon Shifters of Morocco series by leaving a review at your favorite retailer!

Made in the USA
Las Vegas, NV
23 March 2021